TIME ECHOES

*To Josiah – Thank you for helping me
unlock another door to the beyond.*

OTHER BOOKS BY BRYAN DAVIS

The Time Echoes Trilogy

Time Echoes
Interfinity
Fatal Convergence

The Reapers Trilogy

Reapers
Beyond the Gateway
Reaper Reborn

Dragons in our Midst

Raising Dragons
The Candlestone
Circles of Seven
Tears of a Dragon

Oracles of Fire

Eye of the Oracle
Enoch's Ghost
Last of the Nephilim
The Bones of Makaidos

TIME ECHOES

BOOK 1 OF
THE TIME ECHOES TRILOGY

BY BRYAN DAVIS

Print ISBN: 978-1-946253-51-4

Epub ISBN: 978-1-946253-50-7

Mobi ISBN: 978-1-946253-49-1

First Printing – January 2017

Printed in the U.S.A.

Library of Congress Control Number: 2016918551

Cover Design by Rebekah Sather - selfpubbookcovers.com/ RLSather

Time Echoes is a rewrite of *Beyond the Reflection's Edge*, published in 2008.

CHAPTER ONE

A N ASSASSIN LURKED outside. At least Clara, my tutor, thought so. After surviving many harrowing escapes, I was used to being followed by shadowy figures. The latest, a guy who sat in a Mustang in the parking lot, was no big deal. Clara, on the other hand, imagined a blood-thirsty terrorist hiding around every corner.

Trying to ignore the potential danger, I sat on my motel-room bed tapping on my laptop computer, while Clara peered out the window. The Mustang driver had really spooked her. "Chill, Clara. He doesn't know which room we're in. That's why he's just sitting out there."

"I suppose you're right, but we'll have to deal with him when we leave." She closed the curtains, casting a blanket of darkness across the room. When she turned on a corner table lamp, its pale light seemed to deepen the wrinkles on her face and hands, though her dressy gown made her look younger than her sixty-something years. "How much more time do you need on that spreadsheet?"

"Just a couple of minutes." I winked. "Dad's abacus must be broken. It took almost an hour to balance his books."

"No excuses, Nathan. I saw you playing one of those shooting games a little while ago." Clara returned to her window vigil, a hand clutching the curtain. "He looks like one of the henchmen for that Colombian drug lord your father took down last year."

I pushed the laptop to the side, slid off the bed, and looked over Clara's shoulder. The black Mustang sat parked under a tree, the driver watching the motel's front door. An intermittent shower of leaves, blown around by Chicago's never-ending breezes, danced about on the convertible's ragtop. "He's not Colombian, Clara. He's Middle Eastern."

"Is that supposed to settle my nerves?" A pallor passed across her face. "My intuition says we should leave as soon as possible."

I shrugged. "Okay. I'll pack up."

"Make sure your father's mirror is protected."

"I'll double wrap it." I walked over both beds and bounced to the floor in front of a shallow closet. From the top of my open suitcase, I picked up the square, six-by-six-inch mirror, bordered by an ornate silver frame. Dad had called it a Quattro viewer when talking about his latest assignment — retrieving stolen data for a company that used reflective technology. I was supposed to keep the mirror safe while he was gone.

I gazed at my reflection, the familiar portrait I expected, but something bright pulsed in my eyes, like the flash of a camera. A second later, Clara's face appeared just above my dark cowlick.

I spun toward her. Strange. She was still near the window. When I turned back to the mirror, her image was gone.

As she walked up behind me, her face reappeared in the glass. I glanced back and forth between the mirror and Clara. The quick-changing images were just too weird.

The opening notes of Beethoven's Fifth chimed from my computer — an email alert. After wrapping the mirror in two shirts, I leaped back to my bed and pulled up the message, a note from Dad.

We enjoyed our anniversary getaway. I hope you and Clara had fun sightseeing. Your mother is rehearsing with Nikolai. After her first piece for the shareholders, she'll call you to the stage to play your duet. Nikolai repaired your violin. He says it's as good as new and ready to sizzle. Since it's the Vivaldi piece, you shouldn't have any problem, even with no practice the last three days. Just don't mention your performance to Dr. Simon. Trust me. It will all work out.

Clara flung a wadded pair of black socks. They bounced off my chin and landed next to my motorcycle helmet on the night table. "Put your tux on. I'll finish packing."

I trudged back to my suitcase and set the laptop inside. "We'll look amazing riding the Harleys through town, you in that fancy dress and me in a tux."

"Not through town. Just to our storage unit where we can park the bikes. Mike's picking us up there in the limo. No sense arriving at the concert looking like windblown scarecrows."

"Good enough. Maybe we can get Mike to take a picture of us so Mom and Dad can see how cool we look." I walked into the bathroom where my tux hung on the shower rod. After dressing in a rush, I reentered the main room while fastening the bowtie with barely a glance.

Attending way too many formal dinners had given me plenty of practice.

Two small suitcases and my backpack sat next to the door. Clara stood at the window, peering around the curtain once more. "He saw me, Nathan. He's getting out."

"Here we go again." I threw the backpack on and grabbed our suitcases. "We'll take the hallway exit."

She slid my helmet over my head and put hers on. "Let's go."

We rushed out of the room and jogged toward the exit at the end of the corridor. I looked back. The Mustang driver appeared from around a corner, a gun in hand.

He fired. A bullet zipped past and clanked into the exit's metal door.

I shoved it open, pulled Clara through, and slammed it as I shouted, "Run!"

While she took off in a trot, I set the suitcases down and waited a step or two in front of the door. Seconds later, it eased open a few inches. The moment the gun and a forearm appeared in the gap, I slammed the door. The arm crunched, the man yelped, and the gun dropped to the ground.

I threw the door open. The man staggered back into the hall and grasped his arm, his face twisting in pain. Using a head butt, I crashed my helmet against his nose. In a spray of blood, he toppled and collapsed.

After pocketing the gun and grabbing the suitcases, I ran to the motel's front parking lot. Clara had already straddled and started her Harley, her dress pulled up to her thighs.

While she revved the engine, I strapped the suitcases to the backs of the bikes and jumped onto my

Harley. I started the engine, swung the bike around, and scooted out of the lot, Clara close behind.

Once on the road, she accelerated to my side and called, "What happened?"

"I gave him a nose job. Tell you more later."

"You have blood on your helmet." She looked me over. "None on your tux, though. I assume the blood's all his."

"It is." I glanced back. No sign of the Mustang. Whoever that guy was, he meant business. He wanted us dead.

Inhaling deeply, I refocused forward. My hands trembled, the same hands that would soon have to flawlessly manipulate a bow and strings. Playing next to Mom was nerve-racking enough, but now with a murderer on my tail, I had to watch my back or my next appearance might be in a coffin.

CHAPTER TWO

THE SWEET TONES of Mom's divinely played violin faded, wafting through the air like a springtime aroma. A hush descended across the auditorium — stunned silence from gaping mouths in the audience. Then, applause erupted. Two hundred exquisitely dressed ladies and gentlemen leaped to their feet and volleyed a storm of cheers toward the stage.

Mom pushed back her raven-black hair, tucked her violin under her arm, and bowed gracefully. As the cheers rose to a climax, her ivory face reddened, the scarlet hue a stark contrast to her satiny black gown. Her smile broadening, she focused on Dad as he stood next to me. He clapped with vigor, making his old Nikon camera bounce against his chest where it dangled from a long strap.

With Mom's strings still singing in my ears, I clapped until my hands ached. As she bowed again, I cupped my hands around my mouth and shouted, "Brava!" to Francesca Shepherd, the greatest violinist in the world.

When the applause finally settled and everyone took their seats, Mom's expression darkened, and her cheeks paled. She glanced around the stage, two familiar worry lines etching her brow.

I looked at Dad. On his opposite side, Dr. Simon, short and bald with owl-like eyeglasses, stared at a text message on his cell phone. Dr. Simon angled the tiny screen toward Dad and said, "Solomon, Mictar is on his way." A hint of a British accent flavored his voice. "There is no time to lose."

Dad lifted a hand toward the stage and displayed four fingers. Mom nodded, then stepped forward to a microphone on a stand, her long dress sweeping the platform. She cleared her throat and spoke with a trembling voice. "Thank you, ladies and gentlemen. I'm overwhelmed by your response."

She pointed her violin bow toward my row about a dozen seats away. "I want to thank my music teacher, Nikolai Malenkov, for being here today. Without him I would not be playing violin, nor would I even be alive. When my mother died, he took me into his home, and he and his dear wife gave every bit of love a grieving ten-year-old could ever want."

The crowd clapped again. His face beaming, Dr. Malenkov set a hand over his heart and nodded, spilling his familiar unkempt gray hair over his signature large ears.

Mom turned toward me. "I hope you saved some warmth for our next performer, a young man who is on his way to stardom. I find no greater musical pleasure than to accompany him in our favorite duet."

Dad leaned close and whispered, "Play your heart out, and never forget how much your mother and I love you."

"Please welcome," Mom continued, "my son, Nathan Shepherd."

Applause erupted once more. Dad gripped my shoulder, and a strange tremor rattled his voice. "Remember what I've taught you, and everything will be fine. If you ever get into trouble, look in the Quattro mirror and focus on the point of danger. Nothing is more important."

"Okay. I'll remember." With no time to ask for more information, I rose and headed toward the aisle. As I squeezed past Clara's silk-covered knees, she patted my hand and whispered, "Go get 'em, Tiger."

Still pondering Dad's strange words, I felt as though I were floating outside my body, watching myself climb the four steps to Mom's level. Arched windows to my left cast filtered sunshine into my eyes as my shoes clicked on the hardwood stage.

When I drew near, Mom laid my violin and bow in the crook of my arm. "Just inhale deeply, my love, and follow my lead. Let your heart take over your hands, and your strings will sing with the angels." She kissed me on the cheek, then blew softly on my bow fingers, a ritual she began when I was only three. *To bless your playing*, she had said. The warmth of her breath always calmed me.

The audience quieted to a new hush. I raised the bow to the strings, my eyes on Mom and my calloused fingers pressed against the fingerboard.

I peeked toward Dad. Strange. He was gone. And so was Dr. Simon.

I shivered for a moment before refocusing on Mom as she laid her bow on her strings. With a long, lovely stroke, she began. Her violin sang a sweet aria that begged for another voice to join it.

As if playing unbidden, my hands flew into action, creating a river of musical ecstasy that flowed unhindered into the first stream of joy. The couplet of harmony joined to celebrate life — Vivaldi's dream of four perfectly balanced seasons.

Mom leaned as close as our vibrating bows would allow. Our strokes slowed, bending the music into a quiet refrain. She reached a rest in her part and whispered, "It is time for a long solo, my love. Perform it with all your heart."

I glanced at her, my hands playing on their own. A tear inched down her cheek as she continued. "I will join you again when the composer commands me." She backed away and lowered her bow.

I played on. Closing my eyes to block Mom's cryptic words, I reconstructed Vivaldi's theme, building measure upon measure until the composer called spring into birth. New melodies sprouted forth from earth's womb in all their majesty.

My heart sang along. I had never played this piece so well. Maybe an adrenaline rush boosted my level. Soon Mom would rejoin the duet. Good thing. The hormonal surge might peter out at any moment.

When the time came for her reentry measure, the first note failed to sound. I opened my eyes. My bow dragged across the strings and played a warped scratching noise.

Where was she? I stared into the audience and scanned the dumbfounded faces row by row. Dad's seat was still empty. Clara's was vacant as well. The auditorium seemed to swell in size, making me feel like a shrinking mouse, alone on stage with a toy violin and bow.

Whispers ran across the onlookers. Nikolai rose and pointed at a stage door to my left. "Your mother went that way, Nathan." He spoke in a kind, soothing tone. "Has she taken ill?"

"Not that I know of." My voice squeaked. I cleared my throat to force a normal tone. "She didn't mention anything."

I instinctively reached into my pocket to get my phone, but I had left it in the limo. Dad's rules — no phones at a performance. He and Mom and Clara wouldn't have theirs with them either.

A muffled pop sounded. I flinched. What could it have been? A blown circuit? But the lights were still on.

The side door opened. Dr. Simon entered and walked to center stage, heaving quick, shallow breaths. After lowering the microphone stand to his level, he wrung his hands at his waist. "Ladies and gentlemen, please pardon the interruption. Nathan's parents had to leave unexpectedly. We will have a short break and then hear from our guest pianist." He stepped back from the microphone and nodded toward me. "I will escort you home."

"Excuse me," Clara said from the open stage door. "I will take Nathan home."

Dr. Simon pushed his glasses higher on his nose, his eyes darting. "Well … I suppose that will be suitable." His gaze locked on the exit behind the last row of seats. Two men stood near the doorway, their arms crossed as they stared at the stage — one, a tall white-haired man dressed in an ivory suit, his face thin and pale, and the other, a man of average height wearing a navy blue blazer and khaki pants.

Dr. Simon tugged on his collar. "Clara, please meet me in the lobby in fifteen minutes. I have some important information to give you." His hands still wringing, he pattered off the stage and hurried toward the lobby.

I joined Clara at the door. "Did you see where Mom and Dad went?"

"Maybe. Come with me." Clara led the way off the stage and into a dim hall. We strode along the short corridor and down a steep staircase. Once we reached the halfway point, she stopped and whispered, "While you were going up on stage, your father and Dr. Simon took off toward the lobby, so I followed."

Holding my wrist, she descended the creaking steps while hurrying through her words. "When I got into the foyer, I caught a glimpse of your father and Simon ducking into this hall, and I managed to stay close enough to watch them go down these stairs. I tried to listen from up there, but I heard only your violin and a lot of whispering. Then a gunshot."

"A gunshot? Are you sure?"

"Positive. Then Dr. Simon ran back up, so I ducked out of sight and followed him to the stage."

When Clara and I reached the bottom of the stairs, we came upon two open doors, one in front that led into darkness and one to the left where a dim light shone from inside.

I whispered, "I wish I had kept that gun instead of giving it to the police."

"You had no choice." Clara nodded toward the door straight ahead. "Let's look around."

Carrying my violin by its neck, I peered into the darker room. A glow from a hidden source revealed a system of large air ducts hanging from a low ceiling as well as a narrow wooden catwalk a foot above the floor leading away into darkness, perhaps a maintenance area.

With Clara following, I turned to the doorway on the left and stepped inside. An old lamp sat atop an antique desk, its bare bulb illuminating the twelve-by-twelve-foot chamber and a hodgepodge of items — hard-shell suitcases, sports equipment, wicker baskets, ancient typewriters, and two unvarnished coffins, each sitting on a separate low table in front of a head-high, tri-fold mirror.

I blinked. What an odd collection. Were the coffins stage props? Maybe a group had recently performed a play with a graveyard scene.

As we closed in on the coffins, a body in each box came into view, barely visible in the lamp's weak glow. Even in the dimness, their identities were unmistakable — Solomon and Francesca Shepherd.

Clara gasped. My legs buckled. I lurched between the coffins and clutched the side of one to keep from falling. The bodies lay motionless — pale and quiet. A dark blotch covered Dad's breast pocket, and a hideous cut ripped Mom's throat open. Blood soaked her lovely gown, the same one she had so gracefully worn onstage only moments ago.

I dug my fingernails into the wood. "It ... it can't be."

"It is." Clara pointed at an ornate gold band on Mom's finger. "Look at her ring. There's not another one like it in the world."

A stair creaked somewhere above, followed by a familiar British voice. "Clara, I distinctly told you to meet me in the lobby. Coming down here was a big mistake."

She looked at me and whispered, "Dr. Simon?"

Nodding, I drilled a stare right through the wall in the direction of the voice. If that creep had anything to do with this, he would … The thought died in a swirl of confusion.

"I intended to explain what happened here without exposing Nathan to this carnage." Simon reached the landing and aimed a flashlight into the room. "It is most unfortunate that events have played out this way."

Clara pointed a shaking finger at a coffin. "What do you know about this?"

"Everything. I arranged it. You see — "

"You *what*?"

"If you will calm down, I will be glad to explain everything."

I pointed at Mom's body, my voice a blend of nervous laughter and trembling words. "They're fake, right? Mannequins. Wax copies."

Dr. Simon let out a sigh. "I'm afraid not. Their deaths are a most unfortunate — "

"You monster!" Clara slapped his face, knocking his glasses askew.

He calmly repositioned his glasses, then glanced at the doorway and whispered, "Now that my plan has gone awry, I need to make sure that your accidental discovery doesn't hinder our pursuits. I had planned for Nathan to join his parents, but if you continue shouting, we could all end up in coffins."

I pointed at myself. "You planned for *me* to join them?"

"In order to protect our secrets, Dr. Gordon and I decided — "

"Who cares about your secrets?" I lifted a tight fist. "Just back off. I'm walking out of here, and I'm taking my parents' bodies with me."

Clara picked up a baseball bat from the floor. "You'd better not try to stop us if you know what's good for you."

"I wouldn't dream of it," Dr. Simon said, "but you have far greater obstacles to overcome." With beads of sweat dotting his bare head, he nodded toward the tri-fold mirror standing behind the coffins. "We will soon have company, a man we must not rile. I insist that you remain silent and let me do all the talking."

I gritted my teeth. "Why should I do what you say?"

"Look." Dr. Simon pointed at the mirror. "You will see."

In the reflection, the three of us stood in the dim props room. Two other figures had joined us, the pair who earlier stood at the performance hall exit.

I swung my head toward the door we had entered. The other men weren't in the room.

Footsteps clopped along the hall above our heads. I wrapped my fingers around the neck of my violin and hissed, "Someone's coming."

Dr. Simon folded the mirror. As he slid it behind a bookshelf, a door creaked in the direction of the top of the stairs. He waved at Clara, whispering, "Hide your weapon."

She laid the bat at her feet. Heavy footfalls rumbled down the steps. When a man entered the props room, Dr. Simon's flashlight beam swung to him and illuminated an emblem on the newcomer's blazer — three infinity symbols in a vertical stack, close to each other so that their lines intermeshed.

"Dr. Gordon," Dr. Simon said, flashing a nervous grin. "You have come just in time. Where is Mictar?"

"He's nearby." Stroking his chin, Dr. Gordon scanned the room, first eyeing me, then Clara before calling out, "Mictar, it's safe."

More footsteps sounded from the stairs, slower and lighter this time. When Mictar entered, his thin, pallid face seemed to hover over Dr. Gordon's shoulder. His hair was slick, white, and pulled back into a collar-length ponytail.

As Mictar gazed across the room, a half smile turned one of his hollow cheeks upward. "What have we here, Dr. Simon?" His words echoed, though the air seemed to dampen everyone else's voice. "I hope you have not acted too hastily."

I shuddered. This guy seemed more like a ghost than a man, a walking corpse fresh from the graveyard. I tightened my grip on my violin. Now I had to get past three guys.

Dr. Simon laughed nervously. "I wanted to wait for you, but they were getting suspicious. I had to make sure they didn't run."

As if floating along the floor, Mictar padded up to the coffins and leaned his tall body over the lifeless forms one at a time, studying them from top to bottom. "A bullet in the heart and a slashed throat," he said, caressing Francesca's colorless cheek. "This is lovely work, Simon. Did you do the deed yourself?"

Folding his hands in back, Simon raised up on his toes. "Of course. No one else knows of your plan."

I boiled inside. I had to find a chance to attack, maybe when at least two of the creeps had their backs turned.

"Is that so?" Mictar licked the end of the finger that had touched Francesca's cheek. "Show me your palms."

Dr. Simon lifted his hands. Mictar drew close and latched on to each of Dr. Simon's wrists with his spindly fingers. After taking a long sniff of Simon's palms, Mictar furrowed his brow. "I smell the blood of your victims as well as the gun's residue, but the sweet aroma of residual fear is missing."

Simon cleared his throat. "The Shepherds displayed no fear at all."

Mictar nodded. "I see. But *your* fear is strong. I would wager that even the ungifted can detect its odor."

"Is that so unusual?" Dr. Simon jerked his hands away and wrung them more vigorously than ever. "Anyone who has seen your power would be frightened at your displeasure."

"That is true of my enemies. My loyal friends have no reason to fear me." Mictar reached into Mom's coffin and lifted her eyelid. "Her light is extinguished. They no longer have value."

"No value?" Dr. Simon said. "I don't understand."

Mictar stepped away from the coffin. "You disappoint me, Simon. I wanted Francesca's eyes while they still breathed the light, her eyes above any others. And I was hoping to keep at least one of the Solomons alive long enough to learn their secrets."

Simon squirmed. "I didn't know. I mean, if I had known, I would have — "

"You have no need to explain." Mictar turned to me and smiled. His pointed teeth revealed ravenous hunger. "I see you have brought an offspring to replace what has been lost. An excellent gift, indeed, for he will likely possess what I wanted from his mother."

"Of course I brought him," Simon replied. "Never let it be said that Flavius Simon leaves any task undone."

Mictar's rapacious smile widened. "You have spoken well, for your tasks are now complete. With the four adult Shepherds dead, I no longer have need of your services. The fewer people who know about my activities, the better."

Dr. Gordon grabbed Simon and twisted his arm behind his back. Mictar glided closer and raised splayed fingers. His cadaverous body seemed to become a shadow, darkening with each step.

I heaved deep breaths, trying to quell the shakes. What was this … this thing? I slid close to Clara and whispered, "Just stay cool. We'll get out of here somehow."

Dr. Simon thrashed to no avail. "Just give me another assignment," he cried. "I'll do anything you want."

"Anything I want?" Mictar covered Dr. Simon's eyes with his dark hand and spoke softly. "I want you to die."

Dr. Simon's body stiffened, and his mouth locked open in a voiceless scream. As sparks flew around Mictar's fingers, brightness crawled along his hands and toward his shoulders.

I spread out my arms, shielding Clara. There seemed to be no way to stop whatever was happening to Dr. Simon, at least not without risking harm to Clara.

After a few torturous seconds, Mictar pulled his hand back, revealing Dr. Simon's eye sockets, blackened by emptiness. Something had consumed his eyeballs and left behind nothing but gaping pits. With the sickening odor of charred flesh permeating the room, Dr. Simon collapsed.

CHAPTER THREE

MICTAR TOOK IN a deep breath and let it out slowly. "The combination of fear and death is an aroma surpassing all others." He turned to Dr. Gordon. "Collins and Mills stayed on guard in the hallway upstairs. Call them down. You will need help to dispose of five bodies."

Once again I readied my violin as a weapon. Five bodies? Not if I could help it.

Gordon pulled a phone from his pocket and pressed a button on the side. "Collins. You and Mills get down here."

I whispered to Clara. "It's now or never."

Clara slid off her high-heeled shoes and crouched toward her bat. "You get the tall one."

I lunged and swung at Mictar's head. The wood smashed against his thin cheek with a loud crack, and the tight strings sliced into his skin. The violin shattered into pieces, leaving only the fingerboard in my hands.

He fell against the wall and covered his mouth as dark blood poured between his fingers and dripped to the floor. Clara bashed Gordon in the groin. He collapsed to his knees and let out a loud groan, his eyes clenched shut.

We dashed out of the props room and looked up the stairs. Two men descended, a gray-bearded man in front holding a gun. We turned and ran through the other doorway into the dim air-duct room. Lowering our heads, we clattered along the narrow catwalk under a maze of interconnected duct work.

Dr. Gordon called from behind. "Don't worry about us. Get them."

When we reached the end of the room, a single bulb attached to the low ceiling cast light on a wooden door that rose no higher than my chest. I shoved the door with both hands. Although it bent a few inches, it snapped right back. I dropped to my bottom and thrust my feet against the latch. The wood cracked but stayed put.

Behind us, footsteps rattled the catwalk. I kicked again. The door splintered and banged open, revealing a four-foot drop to a hallway below. I sprang to my feet, ducked into the opening, and jumped to the tiled floor. When Clara followed, her white evening gown poofed out like a parachute as she dropped to my waiting arms.

I pointed at a fire-escape sign hanging above an open door. "That way."

We ran into a long alcove that ended at a tall window. I threw the sash up. Cool air blasted in. After stepping out onto a wobbly fire escape landing, I helped Clara through. Just as I pushed the window closed, the gray-bearded man appeared at the alcove entrance, his pistol drawn.

I gave Clara a push toward the stairs. "Go!"

While she clambered down, I looked back. The gunman fired. A bullet shattered the window pane and zinged past my ear. I leaped halfway down the first flight, shaking the entire framework. As my footfalls rang through the metal stairs, a shout came from above. "You follow. I'll get the car."

The moment Clara turned down the next flight, another gunshot cracked through the whistling wind. I hopped onto the railing, slid past Clara, and dropped feet first to the landing. "Come on," I said as Clara caught up. "He can't get a good shot through the steps."

When we reached a long, horizontal ladder near alley level, I leaped out, grabbed a rung, and rode the metal bridge to the ground. When the lower supports smacked against the concrete, Clara hopped on the rail, slid down, and joined me at the bottom.

As the rusty span sprang back up, Clara pointed down the alley. "The limo's that way." We broke into a hard run. I stayed one step behind, glancing back constantly. After a few seconds, the black Mustang we had seen at the motel careened around a corner three blocks away and roared toward us.

"They have wheels now," I said.

"So do we." Clara turned left down another alley where our stretch limo idled, its rear toward us. A stubby man in a chauffeur's cap leaned against the front fender, tipping back a bottle of Mountain Dew.

"Mike!" Clara waved her hands as she slowed. "I'll take the car."

Mike opened the driver-side door. "In trouble again?"

"More than usual." Puffing heavily, Clara slid behind the wheel. I leaped onto the hood and vaulted to the other side, then threw open the passenger's door and jumped in.

The Mustang, its convertible top folded down, skidded to a stop in front of us and blocked the alley's exit. Clara lowered the window and glanced between Mike and the Mustang, her eyes wide as she tried to catch her breath. "How do I get to the expressway?"

Mike pointed at the street in front of us. "That's Congress. Turn right, cross the bridge, and you're there."

"I saw Nathan's pack in the backseat. Are the suitcases still in the trunk?"

"Yes, Madam."

"Perfect. Now get out of sight." As the window hummed back to the top, Clara smacked the floor stick into gear. "Strap in."

I clicked my buckle and braced myself. "Ready."

She slammed down the accelerator. The limousine lurched forward, its tires squealing as she angled it toward a narrow gap between the Mustang and a lamppost.

As we closed in, the bearded man stood on the seat, propped a foot on the window frame, and aimed his gun.

Clara ducked behind the wheel. "Get down!"

I scrunched low but kept an eye on the action. A bullet clanked into our limo. Our fender clipped the Mustang, shoving it to the side.

Clara barged into traffic, raising a cacophony of honking horns, and accelerated. After weaving through a network of pickup trucks, various sedans, and yellow taxis, she settled in the left lane. "Tell me if you see them."

To the rear, the black Mustang roared into view, shifting back and forth as it darted past car after car. The bearded man set his fists on top of the windshield and aimed his gun at us again.

I shouted, "Step on it!"

Clara jerked the car through traffic, zigzagging from lane to lane. We bumped a Mercedes on one side, then a pickup truck on the other. Tires squealed. Horns blared. A bullet ripped through the rear window and into the dashboard, shattering the radio.

I ducked low and peered around the headrest. The Mustang continued giving chase about fifty feet away, the gunman now seated next to the driver. A pickup truck and two other cars merged into our lane and blocked its approach.

Clara slowed to a halt and pointed ahead. "They raised the drawbridge over the river."

About four car lengths in front, red-and-white crossbars had lowered. The pickup sat behind us, preventing escape in that direction. "Any ideas? We're sitting ducks."

"Not if I can help it." Clara jerked her thumb toward the rear. "Keep watching."

"What do you have up your sleeve this time?"

She clenched her fingers around the steering wheel. "Survival."

Behind us, the Mustang angled toward the left, inching back and forth to get enough room to escape the line of cars. "Looks like he might try to cross the median."

Clara scrunched down. "Tighten your strap, kiddo. We're taking off." She wheeled to the left and floored the pedal, sending the limo lurching across the median and into the oncoming lanes.

I grabbed my seatbelt and pulled it tighter. "You can't jump the gap. There's no way this tank can make it."

"And neither can that Mustang." With no crossbars in our lanes, we zoomed up the steep metal incline. The limo launched over the edge and into the air. It flew for a brief second before falling.

We splashed into the river. My head rammed against the ceiling, but my seatbelt pulled me back into place. When the bouncing stopped, the car settled into a slowly sinking drift.

Clara lowered the two front windows. "Shoes off. Get ready to swim." She squeezed through her open window and rolled out.

"Dad's mirror." I reached over the seat and grabbed my backpack, then slipped off my shoes and dove out my window and into the current. The icy water snatched my breath away. I paddled furiously with one arm, trying to keep my head above the wakes of passing sailboats.

A tiny splash erupted next to my shoulder, followed by a loud *Crack!* from above. At the drawbridge, the bearded man stood atop a supporting pylon, the pistol again in hand.

Clara spat a stream of water. "Dive!"

I submerged into the cloudy river. Saturated, my backpack felt like an anchor, but I couldn't let it go, not with Dad's mirror inside. The thought resurrected his words. *If you ever get into trouble, look in the Quattro mirror and focus on the point of danger.*

A bullet splashed above and glanced off my shoulder, slowed by the watery cushion. With cold stabbing every inch of our bodies, we couldn't stay down long. Barely able to see Clara in the murky water, I signaled for her to rise.

I popped back to the surface and shook the water from my hair. A second later, Clara appeared next to me. As the limo's roof sank below the rippling waves,

I unzipped the backpack, grabbed the wrapped mirror, and released the strap. Shivering so hard I could barely breathe, I threw off the shirts that wrapped the mirror.

Clara flailed in the water, sputtering, "What are you doing?"

"Dad told me to look at it if I get in trouble." I angled the glass until the bearded man on the pylon appeared in the reflection. With the bridge beginning to close, he lowered his gun and jogged onto the descending metal ramp.

From somewhere behind me, music played over a raspy PA system. I swiveled toward the sound. A tourist boat headed our way. A couple of passengers leaned close to the edge taking pictures with phone cameras, apparently oblivious to the danger.

Kicking to prop up my shivering body, I refocused on the mirror. In the reflection, the man aimed his gun once again. I cringed, expecting to get shot. Sirens blared in the distance. But would the police arrive in time to save us?

A bullet ripped through the frame, shattering it. I juggled the mirror until my hands clutched the bare glass's edges, rough but not sharp. Resisting the urge to glance at the bridge, I pulled the mirror closer and focused. In the reflected image, the police arrived and nabbed the gunman.

Another bullet zinged into the river inches away. "How can he still be shooting? The police caught the guy."

"No, they haven't." Clara grabbed my elbow and helped me stay afloat.

Spitting oily water as the waves slapped against my lips, I changed the mirror's angle slightly. The bridge had closed, and cars were crossing again.

Clara released me. "It's safe now."

I looked up at the bridge. Two policemen cuffed the gunman as the span lowered to a close. Hadn't that already happened?

A flotation ring splashed at my side. Another bumped Clara's shoulder. Lifelines ran from the rings to the tourist boat. While more passengers looked on, two men held the ropes and yelled something that the wind carried away.

I grabbed my ring and made sure Clara had a good hold on hers. Still clinging to the mirror, I rode the swift tugs toward the boat. Whatever this Quattro viewer was, it held a lot more mysteries than met the eye.

CHAPTER FOUR

I PULLED A BLANKET around myself and tucked it in at the sides. The woolen material felt good — snug, cozy, warm. Our rental Jeep's vent blew a jet of heated air across my face, adding to the pleasure. Wearing a pair of mid-top boots borrowed from the tour boat's captain, an oversized Chicago Bulls sweatshirt one of the tourists gave me, and jeans, gym socks, and underwear fished out of a police charity bin, comfort surrounded me. Considering the calamities that had crashed down just hours earlier, everything felt surreal and strange.

The ghastly image of my parents' lifeless forms pulsed in my brain. After our rescue, we learned that the police had found no bodies in the performance hall's props room, meaning that Mictar had them. Why would that creep want them anyway? What else could he do to my parents that Dr. Simon hadn't already done?

The painful thoughts sizzled like electric shockwaves. I had to concentrate on something else or I'd lose control. Leaning my head back, I cast a glance at Clara as she drove with a newly purchased mobile phone on her lap. Dressed in a purple jumper and matching shirt from the charity bin, she looked serene as she stared out the windshield, far more peaceful than most people would be after a near-death encounter. In spite of spending the night on a bench in the police station, she seemed wide awake.

Her outfit raised reminders of a Voodoo priestess I had once seen as I passed by an alley in Port-au-Prince. She fixed her dark eyes on me and chanted mysterious Creole verses into the midst of a boiling cauldron. Her brew suddenly spewed a plume of hot gasses and smoke. When it cleared, she was gone.

I shuddered. Too many mysterious things had happened in my life, and the mirror's strange behavior seemed to top them all.

After a few quiet moments, Clara spoke up. "Do you know what a safe house is?"

I gazed out the side window, but with dawn just beginning to break, it was too dark to see much, only the silhouette of the retreating Chicago skyline framed by a rising orange glow. "A place where someone hides, like in a witness-protection program."

"Right. I am taking you to a safe house your father prepared for you quite some time ago. I don't know what he learned about Mictar and Dr. Simon, but it's obvious it led to his and your mother's deaths, and you're the next target."

"But I don't know anything. Dad never told me much about his assignments."

"He kept them to himself to protect you, but the murderers don't seem to care about that." Clara pushed a button, turning off the Jeep's global positioning system. "I'll wipe the memory later. I don't want to leave any clues that might give away our destination."

Her last word throbbed. *Destination.* It sounded final, like perdition, a place to avoid at all costs. Yet, how bad could the safe house be? An old spinster's log cabin, squirreled away in a remote forest? Life could be worse than playing Scrabble all day while listening to her stories of years gone by. But not much worse.

"I'll have to leave you there," Clara continued, "so I can attend to some important issues."

"Can't I go with you? Nobody will be tailing you, will they?"

"No use taking any chances. Your father left me careful instructions in case something like this happened, and it's my duty to follow his directives to the letter. After we make one stop on the way, I'll get you settled at the house. But then I have to leave immediately to meet with your father's lawyer to receive your parents' estate on your behalf. After that, I'll return with some clothes for you and a replacement violin."

"So I'll be alone in the safe house?"

"No, no. Tony Clark, a man your father and I knew years ago, owns the house. He'll be there."

"Tony Clark?" I probed my memory for the name but found only vague echoes. "Dad might've mentioned him. I'm not sure."

"Well, your father must have talked with him recently to set up the safe house option. Everything will be fine."

"I hope you're right." As new warmth flowed into my cheeks, I pulled the blanket lower and dipped my chin close to my chest. Every moment brought new pain. Mom and Dad were dead, and now I had to hole up in a stranger's house. Not only that, my only real friend in the world was going to take off and leave me alone there. Could it possibly get any worse?

Clara reached over and rubbed my shoulder. "Going to the safe house is what your father wanted. You've always trusted him, haven't you?"

I raised my chin enough to nod. I had always trusted Dad, but he wasn't around anymore to make sure his promises were being kept.

She caressed the back of my head. "Nathan, I'm so sorry. There are a million things to do, and if I don't concentrate on my duties, I'll break down and cry."

A wave of sorrow swept in, sending a hot flash through my body. "I know what you mean."

"I'll get everything you need to make you comfortable in your new home. Anything to help you feel better."

I squeezed my eyelids shut and whispered, "I don't want to feel better." Tears begged to escape. A new shaking sensation crawled through my gut, more like a cathartic convulsion than a shiver. Thoughts of Mom — her gentle touch, her kind words, her matchless talent — flashed to mind. Then memories of Dad — his strong embraces and protective hands — seemed so real, almost as if he were touching my shoulder the way he always did when he wanted to share a philosophical thought.

I trembled. The pain was too much ... just too much. Finally, I wept. My head bobbed, and my nose began running. As Clara's fingers massaged my scalp, I swallowed hard. I couldn't let the pain boil over like that. Otherwise, I would soon be blubbering like a baby.

After a few seconds, I sniffed and looked at her through a blur of tears, trying to keep my voice steady. "I'll do whatever Dad said, but don't bother getting a violin. I'm quitting."

Clara's expression hardened for a moment, then softened again. "You shouldn't make promises you'll be sorry for later."

"I won't be sorry later."

"If you say so." She flipped on the Jeep's stereo. Violin music streamed through the speakers — Vivaldi. At other times the sounds would have made me feel better. Now? Not likely.

I sniffed again and wiped my eyes with the blanket. I didn't want to be comforted. I just wanted to go off and wander in the woods, feel sorry for myself for a while. I deserved it, didn't I? I had lost everything. It was time to mope and be miserable.

But Vivaldi had other ideas. As we drove on and on, the sweet violins bathed me in soothing majesty, stroking my aching heart with the very same four seasons of life I had recently celebrated with my own violin.

After a Beethoven sonata, a Mozart symphony, and dozens of miles of dazzling cornfields waving their autumn-browned stalks in the brightening sunlight, I slipped off my shoes and pulled my feet up under my body.

I gazed at Clara, blinking through diminishing tears. "Do you think there's any way their bodies were part of an elaborate hoax?"

Clara's lips wrinkled. "No, dear. You saw them yourself. That was no illusion. No trick. Feel free to deny it if it's part of your grieving process, but eventually you'll have to come to grips with reality."

I scowled. "Reality stinks."

"I can't argue with that. At least not right now."
Clara heaved a loud sigh. "Sleep, Nathan. You got what?
Two hours last night? Escape from reality for a while."

"Probably a good idea." I settled back and closed
my eyes. As the music played on, sleep arrived quickly, as
did dreams of the morbid scene back at the props room.
Mictar's ghostly specter lurked, a stalking shadow with
deadly hands ready to suck the life out of me. What kind
of creature was he? He seemed half human and half ...
something else.

Through a series of dream sequences, I battled
Mictar with a knife, an axe, and a chainsaw, always
losing my eyes to his killing hands and starting over. The
sequences felt like a morbid video game that allowed no
possible way to win.

After about the seventh round, Clara's voice swept
the phantoms away.

"Wake up, Nathan. We're here."

I rubbed my eyes and read the clock on the
dashboard — 11:20. Still morning.

Outside, rays of sunlight streaked through puffy
clouds, highlighting a tall Ferris wheel and at least a half-
dozen spires acting as center supports for striped tents of
various sizes and colors. I stretched my arms and spoke
through a wide yawn. "Where are we? Some kind of
carnival?"

"A county fair in central Iowa. This is the stop I told
you about." Clara parked in front of a chain-link gate near
a square sign that said, *Hand Stamp Required for Re-entry.*

I scanned the grounds. Only a few people strolled
along the flat grass, most lugging tools, ladders, or
buckets. One high-school-aged girl clad in denim overalls

and a gray T-shirt carried a claw hammer. As she passed close to the gate, she tossed us a glance and slowed her pace.

"Looks like it's closed," I said.

"All the better." Clara opened her door and stepped out. "Let's go."

When I joined her at the fair entrance, Clara flipped up the gate's latch and pushed it open. "Excuse me, young lady," she said to the girl. "Where may I find the house of mirrors?"

The dirty-faced blonde stopped and set the hammer against her hip, smacking her gum as she cocked her head. "We open at one."

Clara's voice altered to a formal, firm tone. "Had I asked for your hours of operation, my dear, that would have been an appropriate answer. Shall I repeat my question?"

"I heard you, Granny." The girl flicked her head back. "That way. Behind the merry-go-round. But the mirrors won't help you look any younger."

Clara gave her an icy glare. "Thank you." She stalked toward the tented attractions, muttering, "Impertinent, inconsiderate. If I were her mother, I'd …" Her words trailed off into grumbling.

I kept pace. That girl got off easy. One of Clara's tongue lashings could sting for hours.

As we passed the carousel, the operator turned on the motor, apparently testing the ride. The brightly painted horses sprang to life and rode up and down their poles as if dancing to the merry-go-round's lively tune, an accordion rendition of "Hello, Dolly!" that blared far and wide.

Just ahead, a sign on a blue-and-white striped tent said, *House of Mirrors*. Clara stopped in front of it, unfolded a sheet of paper, and handed it to me, raising her voice to compete with the music. "Here are your father's instructions. I already went over them."

I read the handwritten text silently.

Go alone to the center of the house of mirrors and find the only mirror that doesn't distort your image. Make sure the strobe lights are on, then stare at your reflection. Soon you will see a container. Guide your image so that it picks up the container. Look straight ahead and exit the hall. The container will be in your grasp.

"Strange." I refolded the note. "Sounds like some sort of magic trick."

"That's my guess. An illusion, I suppose." Clara nodded toward the tent. "No sense dawdling. I'll see you in a few minutes."

"What are you going to do?"

She glanced around at the various tents. "I saw a sign that says, 'Watch a teenager make his own bed.' That's something I just have to see."

I read the one sign in view — *See Dog Boy, the Only Living Canine Kid*. "It doesn't say anything about making a bed."

"Your sense of humor must be on life support." She nudged my ribs. "Better get going before Hammer Girl comes around with a security guard."

I pulled open a flap and ducked into the tent. Sunshine filtered through the canopy, giving me enough light to see. After passing through an unattended turnstile, I entered a wide hallway lined with mirrors on both sides and old-fashioned lanterns that colored the reflections with an eerie yellow glow. The first mirror widened my middle into a football shape. Another stretched me vertically into a wavy ribbon. A third shortened my body into the shape of a mushroom.

After checking the final mirror at the end of the hall, I entered a large, circular room. A pole at the center reached to the apex of the tent, supporting the canvas. At floor level, connected partitions encircled the chamber, hinged between each fabric-covered section. A mirror hung on each partition, some circular, some square, and some full-length vertical rectangles.

I walked around the room, glancing at the reflections, each one warped in some fashion. As I passed one of the full-length mirrors, a crouching girl appeared, dressed in red. The moment I stopped to get a closer look, she vanished. Now everything in the reflection seemed normal, the central pole behind me, the other mirrors all around, and my own image. This had to be the mirror Dad mentioned in his note, but where could that girl have come from, and where did she go?

Standing motionless, I concentrated on every input. The carousel's accordion theme drifted in along with the odor of burning oil. In the mirror, nothing else unusual appeared, but the dimness under the canopy made it hard to tell for sure. Now to find the strobe lights.

I spotted a switch near the entry corridor, hustled over, and flipped it up. A barrage of lights beamed down from a ring of high-powered bulbs at the midsection of the center pole. Flashing every fraction of a second, they transformed the chamber into a surreal digital video of the room with half the frames removed.

I walked back to the normal mirror. Everything seemed jerky, out-of-sync, hypnotic. The other mirrors took on a more dazzling aspect. The warped shapes looked like grotesque monsters, mutant images of myself on an alien planet. The effect was definitely cool.

As I stood several paces away from the undistorted mirror, I stared at the ground within the reflection's image. How could something show up that wasn't really there? That would be quite a masterful illusion.

The accordion music played on. The lights continued to flash, making me feel like I was blinking my eyes rapidly. A streak of scarlet zipped by in the mirror. Something appeared in front of my reflected image's feet but not in front of my real ones — a knee-high trunk, like a treasure chest from a pirate movie.

Keeping my focus on the mirror, I leaned over and guided my reflection's hands around each side of the trunk and pushed my fingers under it. As I straightened, my reflection lifted the trunk. With lights blinking at a mind-numbing rate, the scene felt like a nightmare — disjointed and unearthly.

Something weighed down my hands, but the flashing lights kept me from focusing on it. As soon as I walked into the entry hall, I blinked away a mass of pulsing spots. The trunk was in my grasp, weathered and brown with a fine wood grain that bore little if any varnish. It seemed too light to be holding anything inside. But if it was empty, why would Dad want me to get it?

I pushed the tent flap to the side and walked out, my vision still flashing.

"I see you got it," Clara said as she joined me from the side. "Let's get going. I ran into Hammer Girl again. She took off to call security."

I hustled behind her, trying to watch where I was going while checking out the trunk. It had no latches or lock, not even hinges or a lid. Never mind the impossible way I found the trunk; how was I going to get it open?

We hurried back to the Jeep and drove on. I told Clara about the strange mirror, the lights, and the girl dressed in red. Although we came up with several theories about how the illusion worked, we failed to figure out why Dad used such an odd way to deliver a trunk. For now, it would just have to stay a mystery, as would the scarlet-clothed girl.

CHAPTER FIVE

C LARA TURNED ONTO a narrow road and eased
the car between rows of browning cornstalks, short
enough to allow a view beyond them. About a hundred
yards away, a mansion sat in the midst of several majestic
shade trees surrounded by at least a thousand acres of
rolling cornfields.

"What town are we in?" I asked.

"No town, really. We're between Iowa City and Des
Moines, closer to Newton, Iowa, than anywhere else."

I glanced again at the farm-like surroundings. "I
guess Mictar won't track us here. We're in the middle of
nowhere."

"True. I even lost phone service a few miles back."

I pressed the window switch and lowered the
glass a few inches. The air still carried the morning's chill,
though it was now afternoon. "I hope Mr. Clark doesn't
mind me showing up out of the blue."

"Tony knows you're coming. I called just before we
left Chicago."

"Anyone else live here?"

"His wife — a lawyer, I think — and a daughter
named Kelly. Sixteen years old." Clara pulled into the
long concrete driveway and stopped under the boughs of

a mammoth cottonwood tree. An open garage revealed a pair of matching motorcycles but no car. "Tony said he's honored that you're coming. In fact, because your father's will so stipulates, he'll be your legal guardian, your new father, so to speak."

I grimaced. "Don't say that." I closed my eyes and shook my head. "Just … don't."

"Okay, okay. I understand." She opened the door and stepped out onto the driveway. "Just let me know when you're ready to go in."

After grabbing the Quattro mirror, now wrapped in a towel, I got out, walked to the front of the Jeep, and leaned against the hood, glaring at the house. Except for the satellite dish on the roof, the massive residence was a perfect setting for a movie about a rich land owner back in the days before combine harvesters. With its brick front and marble columns, the house seemed friendly enough, almost inviting, in spite of the would-be father who lived inside.

The cool autumn breeze swirled red and yellow leaves around my ankles, some of them funneling down from the cottonwood tree. Its deeply fissured bark and thick, serpentine limbs reached toward the ground like the long, gnarled arms of a giant.

I grabbed a triangular leaf out of the air and rubbed a finger along its coarsely toothed edge. The color of life had drained away, leaving only a pale yellow hue that reflected the sadness of its dying state. As dozens of other yellow leaves brushed by, I released the leaf into the wind, letting it join the parade of death.

I heaved a sigh and whispered, "I guess I'm ready."

"Then let's go." Clara marched toward the door, her purple sleeves flapping in the stiffening breeze. "Once you sound the call, you might as well be ready to charge."

I pushed away from the Jeep and followed, the wrapped mirror tucked under my arm. I hopped up one step to a tiled porch and bumped the edge of a welcome mat with my heavy boots. Red-twine letters woven into the bristly material spelled out, *If You Have to Duck to Enter, I'm Your Coach.*

Clara found a doorbell embedded in the brick wall and pressed it. A loud bong sounded from inside, a sweet bass, like the lowest note on a marimba.

A female voice sang through a speaker at the side of the door. "Who is it?"

Clara nodded at me. "Answer her, Nathan."

I leaned toward the intercom. "Uh ... It's Nathan. Nathan Shepherd. Clara and I are here to — "

"You're early!"

I cleared my throat. "I'm sorry. I didn't know what time we were supposed to — "

"But I'm not ready. I mean, we're not ready. Your room is — " A loud thump sounded from the speaker. "Ouch. Now look at what you made me do."

"*I* made you?"

"Ooooh. Just wait right there. Don't move a muscle."

I glanced at Clara. She gave me an I-have-no-idea expression and added a shrug. After a few seconds, loud, uneven footsteps stomped toward the door. It swung open, revealing a teenaged girl hopping on one bare foot. Her bouncing, shoulder-length blonde hair framed a pretty face with black smudges on each cheek.

She grabbed her toes and leaned against the jamb, scrunching thin eyebrows toward a button nose. Her cuffed jeans exposed her leg from midcalf downward. "That cabinet was heavy."

I focused on her pink toenails, the shade of pink on Barbie doll boxes and Pepto-Bismol bottles. "Think you broke a bone?"

She set her foot down and tested her weight on it while pulling her dirty white T-shirt to cover her midriff. "I don't think so. It's just — "

"You must be Kelly," Clara said, extending her hand. "I'm Clara Jackson, Nathan's tutor."

Kelly took Clara's hand and nodded. "Kelly Clark. Pleased to meet you." She reached her hand toward me. "Pleased to meet you, too, Nathan. Are you a Bulls fan?"

I shook her hand. "A Bulls fan?"

"Yeah." She pointed at my shirt. "You know. The basketball team. My dad loves them."

I glanced down at the logo. "Oh, that. It's borrowed. I'm not really a basketball fan."

"Oh." A faint gleam appeared in Kelly's eyes, and she flashed a hint of a smile. "Good."

"Are your parents home?" Clara asked.

"No. Dad's leading practice with the team today, and then he's going out to get stuff for tonight's dinner, so it'll be a while." Kelly pulled in her bottom lip and drummed her fingers on her thigh. "And Mom's … um … in Des Moines for … for personal reasons." As a pink flush tinted her face, she gestured with her head. "C'mon in. There're cold drinks in the fridge and— "

"I must leave immediately," Clara said. "Our lawyer is meeting me in Davenport so I can settle Nathan's affairs. I'll collect some necessary items for him while I'm there. We had a mishap of sorts last night and lost our luggage."

"Oh, that's too bad." She gave me a quick scan. "Nathan can't wear any of my father's clothes. They'd be too big."

Clara looked at her wristwatch. "It's still early, so I should be able to come back this evening with some things." She placed a hand on my shoulder and turned to Kelly. "Did your father tell you about Nathan's parents?"

Kelly's head drooped an inch. "Yes … he did."

"Then I'm sure you'll make him feel at home, won't you?"

A sympathetic smile spread across Kelly's face. "You can count on me, Ms. Jackson."

Clara kissed me on the forehead. "I think you're in good hands." As a tear coursed down her cheek, she whispered. "I'm sorry for leaving so abruptly, but I have a lot to do."

"It's okay. I understand." I gave her a one-armed hug.

"I'll see you tonight." Clara waved as she strode to the Jeep.

While she backed out and zoomed away, Kelly stepped to my side and watched with me. "So, you have a personal tutor? Must be fun."

"Yeah, it's pretty cool, I guess." The Jeep turned onto the main road. My last attachment to the life I once knew disappeared in a cloud of dust. My throat sore and tight, I forced out the only words that came to mind. "I don't have anything to compare it to."

She cupped her hand around my elbow and led me inside. "You tired?"

"Pretty tired." I stepped into the foyer, which opened up into a huge sitting room with a cream-colored leather sofa and loveseat on one side, a Steinway grand piano on the other, and a crystal chandelier suspended from the ceiling. The dangling crystals sprinkled tiny shivering rainbows on the walls where they tickled the faces on a half-dozen framed portraits, mostly of pleasant-looking elderly folks who seemed to grin at the sudden attention.

I resisted the urge to whistle at the rich décor. Kelly's mom had to be a successful lawyer to afford all this stuff.

The breeze from the open doorway nudged the chandelier, making the crystals sway. The prismatic colors converged on the wall and spun, and the sparkles tumbled in a kaleidoscopic merry-go-round. A moment later, the rainbows scattered into their former chaotic pattern.

Kelly closed the door and joined me in the piano room. "What are you staring at?"

"Everything." I took a deep breath. The aroma of polished wood blending with a hint of peanut butter carried a warm welcome message. "Your place looks great."

"Thanks. My mother really knew — I mean, really knows how to decorate."

I caressed the piano's glossy rosewood. "A Model B Victorian." I looked at Kelly. "What is it? Seven foot two?"

"Good eye." She nodded at the matching bench. "Go ahead. My father told me you play."

"Well, I'm a lot better at the violin, but maybe I can remember something." I slid into place in front of the piano and set the mirror at my side. After pushing up the keyboard cover, I draped my fingertips across the cool ivory keys. Then, with a gentle touch, I played the first measures of Beethoven's Moonlight Sonata. After starting out well, I fumbled through the piece, clumsily missing note after note. Heat surging through my cheeks, I stopped and stared at my trembling fingers. Apparently even my hands were grieving.

"Well, it's not *that* fancy." Kelly arched her brow. "When did you visit the Taj Mahal?"

"Taj Mahal?" I closed the keyboard cover. "Why did you bring that up?"

"You brought it up first."

I rose to my feet, sliding the bench back. "*I* brought it up? What are you talking about?"

"While you were playing the piano. You said you're glad you made it to the Taj Mahal. That's why I said our place isn't that fancy."

"No, I said I'm a lot better at the violin, but I'd try to play something."

Kelly closed one eye. "But after that, you said — "

"I didn't say anything after that."

As the chandelier's colorful sparkles passed across her face, she tapped her chin with a finger. "The stress must be getting to you. If you can't even remember saying something, you really need to get some rest."

"But I didn't say anything, I — "

"Your room's this way." Striding through the adjacent hall at a lively pace, she raised her voice. "Stay close. You'll get lost in this house if you don't keep up."

I grabbed the mirror and stepped in her direction, then halted. "Didn't you say your parents aren't here?"

She shouted from a distant room. "Right. Dad'll probably get back in about three hours after he gets stuff for your welcome dinner. I'm making a special dish tonight." She leaned out a doorway at the end of the corridor. "Why?"

"So that means we're alone."

"Oh, I get it." Kelly hurried back to the foyer, her feet slapping against the tile. "My father told me you'd have a lot of old-fashioned ideas," she said as she grabbed my hand.

"Old-fashioned?"

She pointed at herself, her blue eyes gleaming. "Don't think of me as a girl. Think of me as your sister."

"But I've never had a sister."

She guided me toward the bedroom. "And I've never had a brother. You could come in handy."

I pulled away from Kelly and followed as she turned through an open door on the right. I stopped under the lintel and looked in. A tri-domed hanging fixture and a lamp on a desk illuminated the enormous room. With high ceilings and soft beige carpet that seemed to run on endlessly, my new bedroom was even bigger than the piano room.

I blinked and looked again. No, the size was an illusion. A huge mirror covered the entire back wall and reflected the room's interior, exaggerating its spaciousness.

Kelly knelt and began collecting books from the floor. "Sorry about the mess. I was trying to adjust the cabinet shelves, and while I was talking to you on the intercom, the screwdriver slipped, and the whole thing fell over."

"No need to apologize." I set the Quattro mirror on the floor, lifted the cabinet, and pushed it upright, then scooped an armload of books and heaved them to the shelves.

As I bent to grab another load, I glanced at the room's mirror. In the image, looming shadows stretched across our heads and backs. The books, the cabinet, and the carpet disappeared, replaced by an endless layer of dead autumn leaves. Lightning flashed, and a breeze blew the leaves into a swirl, enveloping us and an unfamiliar dark-haired girl in a tornadic funnel.

I looked away from the reflection. There were no strange shadows in the room. No leaves. No storm. No unfamiliar girl. I spun toward the mirror again. Everything was back to normal.

Kelly grunted as she lifted an unabridged dictionary to the top shelf. "That's where Dad wants it. 'Got to keep Webster handy,' he always says. 'You never know when you'll need a paperweight.'"

I set a hefty world atlas next to the dictionary. "Or maybe two paperweights."

She snatched a dusty rag from a dresser, stuffed it into her jeans pocket, and spread out her hands. "So, what do you think? Pretty cool, huh?"

"Very cool. Thanks for all your work." I slid my hands into my pockets and nodded toward the desk. "I like having a desk. I read a lot."

"Really? I don't meet many guys who — " She squinted. "Are you okay? You're as white as a ghost."

I touched my cheek. "I think so."

"You'd better lie down." She stepped toward a queen-size poster bed and pulled back the comforter. "Seriously. You look like you could crash and burn at any second."

Letting out a sigh, I nodded. My hallucinating proved that she was right.

She fluffed the pillow and patted it. "I'll wake you up when dinner's ready."

I spoke through a yawn. "Get me up right away if Clara calls or comes back, okay?"

"I will." Kelly's eyes softened as she laid a hand on my shoulder. "Our home is your home. Just try to forget about everything and chill for a while. You'll feel better soon."

Her gentle touch felt warm and good. "Thanks. When Clara told me about your family, it was the first time I ever heard of you, so I was kind of nervous."

"Don't be. I'm harmless. Well, to my friends, anyway. And my dad's excited. He always wanted a son to play basketball with." She spread out her arms. "But all Mom and Dad could come up with was little old, five-foot-five me."

I laughed. Kelly's comical grin, combined with her grimy cheeks and sparkling eyes, chased away my sorrows, at least for the moment. Having her as a sister promised brighter days ahead.

After flicking off the desk lamp, Kelly turned a dial on the intercom speaker next to the door. Classical music flowed into the room, an unfamiliar piece by a string quartet. She turned off the overhead light, scooted out on tiptoes, and closed the door with a quiet click.

I stood alone. The draped window on the adjacent wall allowed the sun's afternoon rays to filter in and wash the room with muted light, creating a host of new shadows on the floor. A fresh blotter covered the center of the desk, bordered by a fancy pen and three pencils on one side and a pencil sharpener on the other. Propped on a back corner, an eight-by-ten frame held a computer-printed message, *Welcome, Nathan*, in bold blue letters. The message brought new warmth. Kelly was really trying to make me feel at home.

But it wasn't home. At least not yet.

I pulled my wallet from my back pocket, still slightly damp from its swim in the river, slid my fingers into a slot inside, and withdrew a photo — Mom and Dad, each with an elbow leaning against a snowman, a comical pose they had struck during a hike on Mount Shasta in California. Mom's vibrant smile stabbed my heart. Dad's silly grin deepened the strike. Tears welled. I pinched the bridge of my nose and laid the wallet and photo on the nearby night table.

After sliding into bed and settling under the comforter, I stared at the huge mirror through the space between the bedposts. In the deathly still air, the music seemed to grow in volume. A new piece began, Mozart's Requiem Mass in D Minor — lovely, yet haunting.

The window at my side hovered in the mirror's image as if suspended in thick liquid, gently swimming in a tight circle. As the room grew darker, my mind slumbered in a dreamlike haze. Mozart's Latin phrases streamed in. I translated the familiar lyrics, imagining the words and notes on a musical staff floating above my head.

Grant them eternal rest, Lord,
And may everlasting light shine on them.
You are praised, God, in Zion,
And prayer will be returned to you in Jerusalem.
Hear my speech,
To you all flesh will come.
Grant them eternal rest, Lord,
And let everlasting light shine on them.

Darkness pushed deeper into the room. Lightning flashed. A soft rumbling sound passed over the ceiling, while raindrops pecked at the window pane.

There will be great trembling
When the judge comes
To closely examine all!
The trumpet will send its wondrous sound
Throughout the region's tombs
He will gather all before the throne.

The hypnotic window, a soft light in the midst of deep grays and purples, stretched in all directions. As it filled the mirror, I tried to focus on the image. Was this a dream?

Death and nature will be astounded,
When all creation rises again,
To answer to the judgment.
A written book will be brought forth,
In which all will be contained,
By which the world will be judged.

The drapes covering the reflected window parted. Bright light seeped in, illuminating a hand as it emerged through a gap at the window's base. As the sash lifted, long, pointed fingernails bit into the varnish. The frame groaned, wood dragging on wood, and the gap expanded inch by inch. A face appeared, the thin, sallow face that had so recently burned an image in my mind with its hungry, greedy eyes.

Mictar was trying to enter.

King of tremendous majesty,
Who freely saves those worthy ones,
Save me, spring of mercy.
Remember, kind Jesus,
Because I am the cause of your suffering;
Lest you should forsake me on that day.

I fought against sleep. My mind screamed at my body to wake up. This was too real. That mirror had somehow pierced my dream, warning of an approaching murderer. I gritted my teeth and wagged my head on the pillow, but I couldn't seem to wake up.

Within the mirror, the specter climbed into the room, showing his thin frame in full profile, but his distinctive white ponytail was missing. He turned toward me. His face displayed no bruise, no sign that a violin had crashed across his cheek. He skulked into the reflection's foreground, his expression void.

My prayers are unworthy,
But, you, good Lord, are kind,
Lest I should burn in eternal fire.

His eyes glowing red, he pointed straight at me, as if he could see me from his side of the mirror. "Beware, son of Solomon, lest you use your gifts unwisely and thereby come to calamity. If you allow grief to sway your purpose, you will perish. If you pursue vengeance, your light will drain away. If you fear, you will fail, for the power of Quattro is not to be trifled with."

The scene near the back of the reflection transformed. The room's surroundings faded away, replaced by the two coffins that carried Mom's and Dad's bodies. Mictar reached into a coffin and withdrew a small sphere. As I focused on the object, its identity clarified. An eyeball.

Spare us by your mercy, God,
Gentle Lord Jesus,
Grant them eternal rest. Amen.

Mictar extended his arm, bringing the orb closer to me. "Learn the mystery of the light within. Only then will you vanquish the darkness and defeat your enemies."

I sucked in a breath, sat up in bed, and shouted, "Murderer!"

The coffins vanished. Mictar faded away. The mirror image warped, then straightened, showing my room and a dim image of myself sitting up in bed. Lightning flashed again, illuminating my tear-streaked face, gaunt and pale.

I shivered hard. I pulled my blanket close and flopped back in bed. It had to be a dream, the worst nightmare in history. As I turned to the side and tucked into a curl, cold fingers seemed to stroke my skin, sending new shivers across my body.

Closing my eyes, I clenched my teeth. The horrible images impaled my brain — Mictar, the coffins, the eyeball. Would the torture ever go away? Would Mom and Dad ever find peace?

Let eternal light shine on them, Lord,
With your saints in eternity,
Because you are merciful.
Grant them eternal rest, Lord,
And let everlasting light shine on them,
With your saints in eternity,
Because you are merciful.

The cold fingers lifted. My shivers settled. A sense of relief filtered in, and along with it, fresh tears seeped though my closed eyelids. Mom and Dad were gone. I would never see them again this side of heaven. As I let the tears flow, darkness overtook my mind, and I fell asleep.

CHAPTER SIX

RADIANCE POURED INTO the room. "Nathan. It's dinner time."

I sat up in bed and squinted at the hallway glow framing Kelly's dim silhouette.

She flipped on the overhead light. "Are you feeling better?"

"I think so." I slid out of bed, strode to the window, and tried to open it. Locked. The varnished sill carried no scratches. Windblown raindrops pelted the glass, painting tear streaks on my ghostly image.

"What's wrong?" Kelly asked from the door.

I whispered, "I'm not sure."

"A nightmare?" She walked in. Wearing clean blue jeans and a long-sleeved pink tunic, she set her hands on her hips and looked at the window. "Add a thunderstorm to all you've gone through and that'd give anyone nightmares."

"I could've sworn it was real." I stepped close to the mirror and stared at my reflection. Not only was my hair standing on end, my pupils had shrunk to the size of BBs, barely visible in the center of my blue irises. "There's something strange about this mirror."

"What do you mean?"

I touched a vertical line on the glassy surface, leaving a fingerprint over the image of my nose. "Is it divided into sections?"

"Three hundred and ninety-nine, to be exact." She wiped the print clean with the cuff of her sleeve. "Dad saw it for sale at a castle in Scotland and shipped it home. Some creepy museum curator convinced him that it could reflect what people were thinking." She pointed at the lower left corner. "One piece is missing. My dad said that your dad took it years ago for some sort of experiment. He never gave it back."

I picked up my mirror from the floor and slowly unwrapped it. "Maybe I have it." I knelt at the corner and slid my piece into the empty space. It fit perfectly.

A burst of radiance erupted from the spot and spread across the entire mirror. Seconds later, the light evaporated, like luminescent steam dispersing in the room.

Kelly laid a hand on her chest. "Wow! What was that?"

"Too weird." I pulled on the square, but it held fast. "It's stuck."

She stopped and touched the reflective mosaic's newest piece. "The glue on the wall couldn't be wet after all these years."

I pulled again, grunting. "Something's making it hang on."

A loud voice pounded my eardrums. "Welcome!" A burly hand grasped my arm and pulled me to my feet. "I'm Tony Clark."

I looked up. A bug-eyed man with a boot-camp crew cut stared down at me from what seemed like two feet above my head. I cleared my throat and squeaked, "Hi, Mr. Clark."

He spread out a huge palm and grabbed my hand. His long fingers wrapped around mine with a friendly, but painful grasp. "Call me Tony."

I squeezed him back with my violin-strengthened grip, more to relieve the pain than to show off.

"Now that's a manly handshake!" Tony said, glancing at Kelly.

She sighed and folded her hands behind her back.

Tony nodded toward the hall. "C'mon out to the dining room. Kelly really cooked up a storm."

She rolled her eyes and whispered to me, a look of embarrassment crossing her face. "A storm. Get it?"

As we walked down the hall, Tony laughed. "A storm. Get it? It's raining outside." His deep voice resonated through the corridor as his long legs swept past the grand piano. "Do you like Chinese?"

I quickened my pace to keep up. "Sure."

"Too bad," Kelly whispered, following close behind. "We're having Italian."

Tony stopped at the dining room and extended his arm toward the table. "Too bad. We're having Italian."

The aroma of garlic-soaked tomato sauce flooded my senses. A huge rectangular dish of lasagna graced one end of the table, and a salad marked each of four place settings, knives and forks aligned perfectly over folded napkins and a pristine white tablecloth. With five high-backed chairs on each side and one on each end, the table seemed more suited for a football team than for an only child and her parents.

Kelly touched my shoulder and whispered, "Daddy kind of rushed you in here. He's not exactly Mr. Sensitive. If you don't feel up to eating with us, I'll make an excuse for you."

"It's okay. I'll be all right." I nodded at the table. "Four plates?"

"Clara called while you were sleeping. She'll be here any minute. I know you said to wake you, but she said not to. She's kind of ... well ..."

"Forceful? Yeah. Don't worry about it."

Tony sat at the head of the table. "Sol and I called her Medusa back in Poly-Sci at Iowa. Her class was so hard we turned to stone. It'll be fun to see what she's like now."

I slid out a chair and motioned for Kelly to sit. She smiled, her gaze locked on her dad as she let me seat her. I walked around the end and seated myself on the opposite side.

Tony grabbed a knife, cut out a quarter of the lasagna, and heaped it onto his plate. "Dive on in," he said, handing the knife to me.

I glanced at Kelly. She gave me a quick nod, a sign that it was okay to serve myself before she could get hers. Just as I sliced into the lasagna, the doorbell chimed its low-pitched tone.

Kelly pushed her chair back. "That must be Clara."

Before she could get up, an authoritative voice sang from the piano room. "Tony, Tony, Tony. You left the door unlocked. I thought I taught you about home security in class." Clara appeared at the dining room entryway. "You never know when a strange old woman might barge in." She unbuttoned a rain-dampened overcoat. "And a wet one at that."

I hurried to her and helped with her coat. She seemed much bubblier than she had been earlier in the day. Maybe that meant good news.

"I'll hang it up," Tony said as he rose from his chair. He took the coat from me and walked toward the main entry.

While he was gone, I seated Clara next to Kelly. As I slid Clara's chair in behind her, the two exchanged glances enhanced by smirks, but whatever they were communicating, I had no clue.

When Tony returned, he reseated himself, grinning. "I locked the door. We already have enough strange old women in here."

"Always so clever, Tony." Clara nodded toward Kelly. "I met your daughter this morning. I was delighted to see what a beautiful young lady she is."

Tony frowned. "Of course she's beautiful. Is that a surprise?"

"Well, not to me, but didn't the other students vote you the most-likely-to-produce-a-troll award? At the time, I said it was ridiculous, and you have proven my opinion correct." She winked at me. "And I like being proven correct, don't I, Nathan?"

I returned the wink. "Rule number one: Clara is always right. Rule number two: If Clara is wrong — "

"See rule number one," Tony finished. "I heard that in her class more times than I can count." He gestured toward the lasagna. "Are you hungry?"

"Yes, indeed," Clara said, "but first things first. There's a trunk in the back of my Jeep. Would you or Nathan bring it in? It's not so heavy that an old lady like me couldn't carry it, but with the rain — "

"I'll get it." Tony waved a hand at me. "You three go ahead and eat." He disappeared into the piano room. Seconds later, the front door slammed.

Clara winced. "I hope I didn't upset him with the troll comment. He really isn't nearly as ugly as his classmates said. He's just … unusual."

Kelly clapped a hand over a widening grin and spoke through her fingers. "Don't worry. He'll be over it by the time he gets back."

I pushed the lasagna dish closer to Clara. "Any news?"

"Some. Our lawyer gave me an envelope from your father's safety deposit box. It contained money for your needs, so you won't be destitute."

"Here it is." Tony lumbered into the dining room and set the trunk on the floor, his face dripping.

Kelly rose and handed him a napkin. "Still raining hard, huh?"

"Very." He took it and mopped his brow. "It's raining pitchforks and — "

"Daddy!" Kelly hissed.

He gave her an innocent look. "I was going to say barn doors. Not the other one."

Trying not to guess "the other one," I rose, walked to the trunk, and laid my palm on its damp wooden top. "Clara, have you figured out how to open it yet?"

"Heaven's sakes, no," she said. "You and you alone should open it."

Kelly caressed the ancient wood with a finger. "I don't see any seam. It's like it doesn't even have a lid."

I grasped the top edge and lifted. Nothing moved.

Tony bumped me out of the way. "Let me try." He rubbed his hands together, then, squatting for leverage, he grabbed the top and jerked upward. The entire trunk lifted. Tony fell backwards, still hanging on and cradling the trunk against his chest.

Kelly stifled a laugh. "Are you hurt?"

"Just my pride." He scooted the trunk to the floor and vaulted to his feet, his eyes bugging out more than ever. "I've got an idea. Be right back." He marched out of the room.

I looked at Kelly. She just shrugged her shoulders.

A moment later, Tony strode back in, a cordless circular saw in hand. He pulled the trigger, making the motor whine and the jagged blade spin. "This'll cut through anything. If you're game, I'll give it a buzz."

I nodded. "Be careful."

"I'll just cut off the very top." Tony gunned the motor, set the blade next to an upper corner, and pushed it against the dark wood. The teeth squealed, but they couldn't seem to bite into the grain. Tony's face reddened. As he pushed harder, his muscles flexed, and sweat trickled down his cheeks. Finally, he pulled back and let the saw wind down as he wiped his face with his sleeve. "I don't know what that trunk's made of, but I've cut steel with this blade."

"So no one could open it to put anything inside," I said. "It's probably empty."

"It felt empty when I picked it up. Nothing rattled around."

Clara clapped her hands. "Well, we have quite a mystery to solve, don't we? I suggest that we all eat and rest. Then I'll go out and bring in another suitcase. Perhaps the rain will have let up."

After reseating Kelly, I sat again at the table. "Are you staying here tonight, Clara?"

"I'm afraid not. The suitcase I brought is filled with new clothes for you." Her eyebrows shot up. "Oh! I almost forgot your new violin. We should bring it in right away to get it out of the humidity. After supper you can test it out, and then I will be off to Davenport again where your trust fund is being set up. As executrix of your father's will, I must be present to sign the paperwork."

Tony sat in his chair and propped his elbows. "Do you know how much moolah he's getting?"

"Daddy!" Kelly said. "What are you thinking? His parents were just murdered!"

"Oh. Yeah." Tony's expression sagged. "Sorry."

"It's okay," I said, trying to smile. "Don't worry about it." Even as the words slipped out, I regretted them. It really wasn't okay. Tony's remark was crass. Kelly was right. He wasn't Mr. Sensitive.

Clara patted my hand. "We're all probably curious about the money situation, but I'm afraid it's another mystery. The financial instructions were sealed with a directive to open them two days after your father's passing, which is a Saturday, so we had to make special arrangements to ensure all parties were available. I'll call as soon as everything is settled, but even if your money is locked in a trust fund, you'll likely have a stipend for your living expenses."

After I retrieved the violin and toweled off, we all sat at the table and resumed the meal. Tony dominated the conversation, talking about basketball games in college with "Flash," my father, and how he wasn't given that nickname because of his speed, but because of his love of photography. That's what led him into photojournalism, then into investigative reporting, and finally into technology security. And, Tony lamented, what probably got him into trouble with whoever killed him and Mom.

"Flash was far too trusting," Tony said as he finished his story. "He refused to believe what I learned the hard way. You can't trust anyone. Everyone's in the game for themselves."

I bit my lip hard. This new *father* was worse than insensitive. He was Captain Clueless, an ape in human clothing. He needed to be set straight.

Just as I opened my mouth to object, I caught Kelly's gaze. Her sad eyes glistening, she mouthed, "I'm sorry."

Breathing a silent sigh, I gave her a nod, letting her know that I didn't mind so much. As her trembling lips turned upward, I smiled with her. She understood my nonverbal cue. My new sister was really pretty amazing. Ever since she answered the front door, she had shown me nothing but kindness. Obviously there was a lot more to her than a pretty face and pink toenails.

During the meal, I glanced at the trunk every couple of minutes. The lasagna, now barely warmer than room temperature, tasted good enough, but it was nothing more than a spicy stomach-filler. Wondering what might be in Dad's trunk consumed my thoughts. Since he made sure I retrieved it, it couldn't be empty. Maybe the inside was lined with instructions on how to defeat Mictar, or how to understand the technological secrets behind the strange mirror. Who could tell?

I caught Kelly's gaze again. Her eyes seemed melancholy, yet when she joined me in furtive glances at the trunk, her countenance carried a glimmer of hope that something new and exciting was about to happen. For years I had traveled with my parents all over the world, exploring strange, exotic lands and meeting hundreds of friendly people. Still, I always felt alone, no real friends, no one my age to talk to. But now I had a sister. What would it be like living with this sad, yet hopeful girl?

The mysteries of the evening sparkled in her eyes. We were definitely on the same wavelength. With two almost imperceptible nods, we silently agreed that we would figure everything out together, no matter what.

CHAPTER SEVEN

AFTER SETTING MY new violin and case on the desk, I pushed the trunk against the wall next to my bed and sat on its sturdy wooden top. Breathing a long sigh, I stared at my reflection in the mirror on the opposite side of the room.

The house lay quiet. Clara had rushed away, hoping to get to Davenport and catch a few hours of sleep before her meetings. With my help, Kelly had washed the dishes, then retired to her room, complaining of a headache, apparently brought on by allergies. Tony left the house with a basketball spinning on his fingers. "Got a pickup game with the boys," he had said.

I checked my new wristwatch, one of the many items Clara had brought in the suitcase. The analog face read 11:15, matching the digits on the radio clock on my desk. A Haydn quartet played from the radio's little speaker, soft enough to blend into the background.

I looked again at the mirror and raised my brow as if having a silent conversation with my reflection. Basketball, so late at night? Maybe one of those midnight leagues. Lots of guys go out and play basketball late on a Friday, right? My reflection shook its head, copying my own doubtful shake. Then again, maybe not.

Rising from the trunk and walking toward the mirror, I unbuttoned a new shirt I had tried on. With only a desk lamp to light the room, my frame cast a long, narrow shadow across the floor.

When I took off the shirt and tossed it behind me, something bright glinted. The light in the room dimmed, as if the power had sagged. I pivoted toward the lamp. Like a clumsy oaf, I had draped my shirt over the shade. I jerked it away and threw it onto the trunk, allowing the lamp to cast its light once more.

An odd darkness turned my attention to the mirror. In the reflection, my shadow grew, lengthening and widening until it shrouded my image in a dark gray cloud. Deeper within the mirror, the lamp's glow pierced the darkness and cast thin beams onto the trunk. My shirt had vanished.

I turned around. As before, my shirt lay on the real trunk. On this side of the mirror, the light and my shadow stayed normal.

Goose bumps crawling across my skin, I turned and faced the mirror once more. Still cloaked in a gray fog, the trunk, the lamp, the window, and my reflected self were the only visible objects.

Creeeak.

I locked my legs in place and slowly rotated my head toward the real window. The drapes hung motionless, covering the glass. I edged that way. One step. Another. With a wild swipe, I threw the drapes open and looked outside. Nothing. Just a dark, rainy night.

A peal of thunder rumbled, sending a new shiver up my spine. I released the drapes and walked back to the mirror. In the reflection, a hand emerged under the window's sash, pulling it up — no sharp nails this time, just a normal human hand.

I glanced back and forth, watching the action unfold in the mirror and keeping an eye on the real window, still in full light, still undisturbed. A man in a trench coat crawled through the reflected window, then a woman. The man raised a finger to his lips while helping the woman climb in.

My whole body shook. This couldn't be a dream. Was the mirror showing a reflection of my thoughts like the museum guy had told Kelly's father?

The man in the mirror, veiled in shadows, skulked to the trunk and opened it. I tried to peer inside, but I stood too far away to see anything. The woman, also in a trench coat, tiptoed straight toward me, her face becoming clear as she approached, beautiful and serene. My mother.

I gasped and glanced to each side. No one was with me. The woman in the mirror leaned over my reflection's shoulder and kissed his cheek. A hint of wetness brushed my skin. She grasped my reflection's hand and blew on his knuckles as her distinctive raven tresses spilled over his wrist.

I lowered my gaze to my real hand. Mom's were nowhere to be seen, yet somehow her breath caressed my skin, warm and gentle.

In the mirror, a sad smile crossed her face as she slowly turned away. When she joined the man in front of the trunk, their bodies blocked my view. They each pulled something from their trench coats, bent low, and placed the objects in the trunk. Then they turned toward me, allowing a beam from the lamp to illuminate the man's face.

I swallowed hard and whispered, "Dad."

He crawled back out the window and helped Mom through again. With a muffled thump, the window closed.

I locked my stare on the mirror. Only my own image, the lamp, and the trunk remained — the open trunk. I swung around. The trunk in the room was closed, my shirt still draping it. I pivoted toward the mirror and took a step in reverse. My reflection stepped backwards. I took another step. My reflection did the same. As I continued to edge back, the Nathan in the mirror closed in on the trunk behind him until his heels touched its base at the same time my own heels touched the real trunk.

Slowly bending my knees, I reached behind my body. My image lowered its hands into the open trunk. I could feel my own hands going inside, moving farther down than the top of the trunk should have allowed.

Were my hands really inside the trunk? I didn't dare turn to look. The trunk might slam shut and chop my hands off at the wrists.

I pushed down, feeling with my fingers. Each hand grasped an object — a stringed instrument on the left and a strap on the right. I coaxed the objects slowly upward.

Watching my reflection at a distance twice the length of the room, I pulled the objects out of the trunk and set them on the floor. I spun in place. The trunk was still closed with my shirt on top, but now a camera and a violin lay on the floor.

I dropped to my knees and snatched up the camera by its strap. Dad's Nikon! I set it down and picked up the violin. Mom's Guaneri!

As I caressed the polished wood, my throat caught. Tears welled. I scrambled for my new violin, snapped the case open, and grabbed the bow. After pushing Mom's

Guaneri under my chin, I rested the bow across the D string, then, with a gentle, reverent stroke, played a long, sweet note.

The sound penetrated my body and sent gentle vibrations along my skin. I played another note, then a melody, measures from the Vivaldi duet. Closing my eyes while gasping and crying, my soul drank in the beautiful music. My heart sang, and in my mind, Mom sang with me. I wept for her, for Dad, for myself, and for a life in ruins.

After finishing a crescendo, I let my arms droop and laid the violin gently on the floor. Still kneeling, I picked up the camera again and checked the counter — six pictures left untaken.

I focused the lens, then, with a flick of my finger, turned on the flash. Dad had never upgraded to a modern digital camera. He preferred the quality of film and the nuances of craftsmanship he could add by developing photos himself. I had spent many hours in dark rooms watching him bring negatives to life, even helping him at times and learning the basics of the art.

I caressed the Nikon's surface, marred by dozens of bumps and dings it had earned through its years. Now it was mine — more valuable than gold.

Aiming the lens at the violin, I pushed the shutter button. The camera flashed and clicked, and the auto-advance motor zipped the film ahead. I rose and looked at the mirror — back to normal, no open window, no weird shadows. The trunk in the reflection sat closed with my shirt on top.

I strode halfway across the room and raised the camera. What would a picture of my reflection look like?

I pressed the button. The flash bounced off the mirror and radiated back to the lens, sending an electric jolt through my hands. The camera flew from my grip, but I snagged the strap and swung it back up.

As I looked the camera over, I checked the indicators. The film had advanced, and the flash indicator showed a charge. Everything seemed fine. I draped the strap around my neck and let the camera dangle at my chest. Obviously taking a picture of the mirror wasn't a great idea.

Laughter filtered through the hall, male and female, then a shushing sound. After grabbing my shirt and throwing it on, I tiptoed to the bedroom door and paused while fastening the buttons under the swaying camera. A light knock sounded from the other side, then a whispered call. "Nathan?"

"Kelly?" I turned the knob and cracked the door open. "What's up?"

"Are you decent?"

"Yeah, I — "

"Good." She pushed the door and squeezed through. Dressed in a long bathrobe and fuzzy socks, she glanced around the room, her voice barely audible. "Who else is in here?"

I whispered in return, "No one else is in here."

"I was on my way to the bathroom. I heard voices."

I peeked out the door. "I heard a woman laughing. Could that be it?"

"No." She pushed the door closed with her back and held the knob. "That's my dad. He's ... uh ... playing cards, I think."

"Oh … cards." I furrowed my brow. "Is he playing solitaire?"

She lowered her head and shook it slowly. "He's not playing cards." After a few seconds, she lifted her head again. Her blue eyes glistened. "I guess your dad never did stuff like that, did he?"

"No." I crossed my arms over my chest. "He had a lot of old-fashioned ideas."

Kelly's lips curled downward. She spun to the side and bit one of her knuckles.

My heart sank. What a dumb thing to say. Her father was breaking her heart. I reached for her shoulder but pulled back. "I'm sorry. I didn't mean it that way."

Her voice cracked. "Yes, you did. And I deserved it."

I reached again. This time I let my hand settle on her shoulder. She flinched, but only for a second. "How long has your mother been gone?"

"Maybe three months, but they've been sleeping apart for years." She shrugged and forced a trembling smile. "She just found another guy and took off, like trading in an old car for a new model."

I pulled my hand away. "And you got left in the backseat?"

"Yeah. Something like that. She said I was more like a son than a daughter, so I'd be better off with Daddy."

I winced. "That had to hurt."

"Don't worry. I'm used to it." She shook her hair out of her eyes and turned toward me, wiping a tear. "Anyway, I heard other voices. They came from your room."

"Like I said, no one else is here." I gestured toward the mirror. "Just me and my reflection."

"I know what I heard, and it wasn't your voice. Someone said, 'Buckingham is as opulent as I imagined,' but I couldn't make out the rest."

"Buckingham? Like Buckingham Palace?"

"I guess so. I'm not the one who said it."

"Well, I didn't say anything about Buckingham Palace." I turned toward the mirror — still normal. "But lots of weird things have been going on."

She slid a finger behind the camera strap. "Like taking pictures of your room at midnight?"

"That's part of it." I held the camera up. "This is … I mean, was, my dad's camera. It was in the trunk."

Her eyes lit up. "The trunk? How'd you get it open?"

"Well … that's kind of hard to explain."

"Was anything else in there?"

"Yeah." I pointed at the violin on the floor. "That was my mom's."

Kelly scooted to the trunk and knelt, squinting at its weathered wood. "I still don't see any seam."

I crouched next to her and picked up the violin. My thumb brushed across a string and accidentally plucked it.

Kelly rose and sat on the trunk. "Did you say something?"

"No." I laid the violin down. "I was thinking pretty loud, though."

"About what?"

"Whether or not to tell you how I got into the trunk."

Two lines dug into her brow. "Why wouldn't you tell me?"

"Because it was so weird. You'll think I'm insane."

"Maybe I will." A wide grin crossed her face. "Maybe I already do. But either way, you have to tell me. I'm not leaving until you spill it."

I plopped onto the bed and looked at the mirror, hoping it would play some of its tricks so Kelly wouldn't be tempted to haul me away in a straightjacket. Yet, the longer I stared, the more normal the mirror seemed. Its images and shadows reflected the room with perfect precision.

A hand waved in front of my eyes. "Earth to Nathan. This is mission control. I'm waiting for transmission."

Blinking, I shook my head. "Sorry. I spaced out for a minute."

"No problem." She stretched her arms and yawned. "Just report your extra-terrestrial findings before I fall asleep."

"How about a multi-media presentation?" I lifted the camera to my eye and took Kelly's picture. "I'll include a photo of a female alien in my report."

CHAPTER EIGHT

A T THE WALMART checkout station, I paid for the photo package and stuffed it unopened into my jacket, keeping my promise to Kelly not to peek at the pictures until I got home. The jacket, a leather one borrowed from Tony, complete with a soft inner lining and a Newton High School "Cardinals" logo, felt good on this cool autumn morning, though the sleeves were too long.

Alternately walking and jogging as I carried Tony's helmet under an arm, I hurried to the parking lot where I had left Kelly's motorcycle. Finding the store hadn't been hard — near the Interstate, just as her hastily drawn map had indicated. Since her allergy-induced sneezes kept interrupting her verbal directions, she resorted to drawing the map, then took an antihistamine pill and went back to bed while I finished the roll of film outside.

I slid the helmet over my head, started the engine, and wheeled along the shopping center's perimeter road, a two-lane strip that ran parallel to the storefront on my right and the main road on my left.

When I reached an intersection, I had to stop for cars entering the shopping complex from my left. At the end of the line, a blue Mustang convertible turned onto the perimeter road and stopped parallel to my bike. The gray-bearded man who had tailed us in Chicago sat behind the wheel and looked straight at me.

I gulped. How did he get out of jail? And why would he come to Iowa? I couldn't bolt. That would give me away. And now that more cars were driving into the lot, I couldn't take off. I had to rely on the helmet to keep him from recognizing me.

The Mustang's window lowered. The driver pulled off a pair of sunglasses and raised his voice to compete with the bike's engine noise. "Hey, can you help me with something?"

I squeezed the bike's handlebars, ready to take off. "Maybe. What's up?"

"I'm looking for my nephew, a boy about your age, a runaway named Nathan. I'm helping my brother search around town."

"What's he look like?"

The man squinted, apparently trying to get a closer look at my face. "About five-foot-nine, short dark hair, square jaw. A lot like you."

His icy stare chilled my heart. He recognized me. I glanced around the parking lot. To the rear, a Walmart tractor-trailer approached, taking up most of the perimeter road.

The man extended a gun out the window and pointed it at me. "Take off the helmet."

I jerked the bike around and zoomed away in the direction I had come, hugging the right curb. The Mustang roared after me.

Just as I passed the truck's front cab, I glanced back. The Mustang closed in. The truck driver suddenly swerved, cutting off my pursuer. A horn squawked, followed by skidding tires. When I whirled around and idled my engine, a loud string of obscenities burned in the air.

With the truck nearly jackknifed between me and the gray-bearded man, the back of the truck driver's head was in view as he sat in his cab. Seconds later, the Mustang peeled out the main parking lot exit.

I rolled the bike up to the driver's window. A burly, fifty-something man wearing a Chicago Bears cap stepped out of the cab and crossed his tree-trunk arms over his chest. "Everything all right?"

"Yeah." I cut the engine and pulled off my helmet. "What did you do to spook him? He had a gun."

The driver nodded toward his truck. "I had a bigger one."

"Good thing." I took a deep breath and let it out slowly. "Thanks. I think you saved my life."

"Want me to call the cops?"

I shook my head. "I'd better just get home. I need to stay under the radar for a while."

He peeled off his cap and scratched through his graying hair. "Are you in a witness protection program or something?"

"I really shouldn't be talking about it." I extended my hand. "Thanks again, Mister ..."

"Stoneman." He shook my hand. "Glad to be of help."

"Yeah ... well ... I'd better get going."

He pressed his cap back on and raised his eyebrows. "You got far to go?"

"A few miles. Not real far, why?"

"Just wondering."

As Mr. Stoneman shuffled back toward his truck, I restarted the motorcycle, squeezed between the truck and the curb, and cruised to the exit, looking every direction for any sign of the Mustang. Prickles stung the back of my neck. Somehow not knowing where the gray-bearded man lurked was worse than staring down the barrel of his gun.

A loud diesel engine rumbled behind me. When I glanced back, Mr. Stoneman pulled up close and flashed a thumbs-up sign. I cruised toward home. With the comforting sound of the Walmart truck trailing me by a hundred feet or so, I savored the ride. Wind whistled through my helmet, and the musty aroma of damp earth filled my nostrils.

I pressed my hand against my pocket, feeling the photo packet inside. What might be on Dad's last roll of film? Maybe a keepsake photo of Mom I could frame and hang above the desk in my new bedroom. Or a clue to why Dr. Simon stole their lives. Or, better yet, some kind of message Dad had intentionally left behind, something that would help solve the mysteries.

As I closed in on the narrow road leading to the house, I peered over my shoulder. Cresting the hill behind me, the truck sent up a plume of black smoke from its vertical exhaust pipe, and its engine clattered. I waved and turned onto the road. A horn tooted in reply, and the big rig accelerated and sped past the intersection.

I skidded to a stop inside the garage and killed the engine. The helmet slid off easily, lubricated by sweat in spite of the cool day. After setting the helmet on a wall shelf, I walked up the step to the inner door and opened it. Although this was my home now, it still felt strange to enter without knocking.

Inside, I found Kelly sitting on a stool at the kitchen bar, a pen and an open notebook in front of her. I withdrew the photo pack, shed the jacket, and hung it over a stool. "Feeling better?"

"Loads." She tilted her head. "You look kind of sweaty. Already warming up out there?"

"It's still cool. I had a run-in with a guy who wanted to kill me."

Her voice spiked. "Kill you? Why?"

"It's like this ..." I gave her a quick blow-by-blow account and added my escape from the same guy back in Chicago.

When I finished, she looked me over as if reevaluating me. "What are you? Some kind of super spy?"

"No, I'm not a spy."

"Then what? A fugitive? A ninja?"

I laughed. "A ninja would be cool. I know some karate, just enough to defend myself and disappear. I guess that's like a ninja."

"Pretty impressive if you ask me." Kelly closed the notebook and patted a clear spot on the bar. "Let's have a look at the pictures."

I opened the envelope and laid out the photos, following the indexed thumbnail guide to make sure they were in chronological order.

"Okay," I said, pointing at the photo of Mom's violin, "here's the first one I took, so all these before the violin are my dad's, and all these after are mine." I picked up the one I had taken after the violin. Two shadows filled most of the image, and two red lights shone behind them.

I handed it to Kelly. "This should have been the mirror. What do you make of it?'

She held one corner and angled it toward the light. "Looks like two people in heavy fog. Like a pair of ghosts."

"What are those red things? Brake lights, maybe?"

Holding it with both hands, she shifted the angle a few more times. "I see a dark form around the lights, maybe a girl."

"Maybe it's the girl in red I saw at the carnival's hall of mirrors. Did I tell you about her?"

"Briefly." Kelly squinted at the photo. "It's too dark to tell the color of her clothes, but her eyes are reflecting red light, like a cat's eyes."

"I've never seen a cat with red eyes. An alligator, but not a cat." I pointed at the next photo. "And this one was supposed to be of you. The female alien."

She bent forward and studied the image, a girl sitting on the trunk. She appeared to be about ten years old. "Anyone you recognize?"

"She looks familiar, but I can't place her." I tapped the countertop next to the last three photos. "These are supposed to be the ones I took in front of the house this morning."

Kelly held the first of the final trio by its edges. "That's definitely our house. There's our cottonwood tree, but it's smaller, and the leaves are green like in summertime. And a girl is standing in front of it." She picked up the previous photo and held the two side by side. "It's this girl. And she's holding a violin."

"A violin?" I took the photo and studied the girl — the pretty face, the raven hair, the way she stood and held the violin and bow. Could she be Mom at a young age? "I figured out who she looks like."

"Who?"

"My mother." As I gave the photo back to her, my hands trembled. "I haven't seen many pictures of her when she was a kid, but this could definitely be her."

Kelly held the pair of photos together again. "You're scaring me, Nathan."

"Yeah. Me, too."

She laid both down and pointed at the last pair. "And these buildings aren't anything like my house. They're enormous." She looked at me. "Do you recognize them?"

"Yeah." Trying to keep my hand from shaking harder, I pointed at them in order. "That's the Taj Mahal, and that's Buckingham Palace."

CHAPTER NINE

HOLDING MOM'S VIOLIN in my lap, I sat on the trunk and stared at the bedroom mirror. Two faces stared back — my own, darkened by my somber countenance and evening's fading light, and Kelly's, wide-eyed and expectant.

After spending our Saturday taking pictures with Dad's camera and failing to notice anything unusual, I hoped for a repeat performance of the mirror's miracles, this time with a witness present.

Kelly, wearing loose-fitting jeans and a navy sweatshirt, fidgeted, first leaning on one hand, then on the other. "Are you sure everything's the same?"

I rose from the trunk and scanned the room. "The desk lamp's on, the curtains are closed, and my bed covers are pulled back."

"It might be a long wait. I'd better put the coffee on." She got up and peeked out the window. "Dad'll be back soon with the new pics, and Clara should be here any minute."

"Think we should let your father in on what's going on?"

Kelly turned to me and waved both hands. "No way. Only you, me, and Clara. If my dad gets wind of this crazy stuff, he'll go nuts."

"Nuts? What do you mean?"

She paced in front of the mirror, making it appear that twin Kellys were marching in stride. "He loves spooky things, so he'd set up a media circus. He's said a thousand times that he'd like to be on one of those reality TV shows."

"Think he'll look at the new batch of photos before he brings them home?"

She stopped and faced me. "Not likely. If anything, he'll be looking through the sports magazines he probably bought. He likes to do that while he drives. Scares me to death."

"I know what you mean. Like trying to jump over an open drawbridge in a limo."

Kelly narrowed her eyes. "You don't have to top my story, Nathan. I know you've been through scarier stuff than I have."

"I wasn't trying to top your story. I was just saying I know how you feel."

She gave me a skeptical stare that burned for a moment before softening. "Okay. I'll buy it. I should know by now that you're not anything like my dad."

"You mean he likes to top stories — "

"Never mind." She strode to the door and opened it just enough to squeeze through. "I'm gonna put the coffee on." The door closed with a louder-than-usual click.

I stared at the knob. Apparently Kelly had a few hot buttons to avoid, especially anything related to her father.

Signing, I shifted my gaze back to the mirror. The reflection wasn't going to perform on demand and prove that I'm not crazy. I had to stop dwelling on it. But what could I do while waiting for the new photos to arrive? Obviously there was no homework. I wouldn't start classes at Kelly's school until Monday.

I tucked Mom's violin under my chin. If only Dad were here, then I would have someone who would listen to my troubles. Or Mom. She'd play something soft while I talked, closing her eyes and nodding. She'd drink in every word, then, with her eyes open and her bow at her side, she'd whisper poetic wisdom, coating me with comfort whether I understood her counsel or not.

I raised the bow to the strings and began playing "Brahms' Lullaby," holding some of the high notes a bit, just as Mom used to do when her strings sang me to sleep years ago.

Tears welled again, spilling over my lids and trickling down my cheeks, but I didn't bother to brush them aside. I played on and on, closing my eyes and pretending to nestle in my own bed during those rare times between Mom's world concert tours and Dad's spy missions.

A vision of that bedroom came to mind. As the mental portrait of my younger self pretended to sleep, he peeked through a slit in his eyelids and watched Mom's flawless strokes, an angel from heaven sitting in a rocking chair, playing for the King of kings, and the little boy had a front row seat.

I played the final note, stretching it out and softening my touch to make it fade, but when I lifted the bow, the song began again, more vibrant, more beautiful than ever. I opened my eyes. In the mirror, Mom sat in the old rocker in my bedroom back home, playing the lullaby. A five-year-old version of myself lay in bed with the covers pulled up to his chin.

A knock sounded at the bedroom door, then Kelly's voice. "Nathan, what's going on? I hear voices again."

My throat tightened into a knot. I couldn't move or speak.

She pushed the door open, then closed it quickly. When she saw the mirror, she gasped. "Nathan! It's ..." She ran to me and grabbed my arm. "What is it?"

I laid the violin on my mattress. "That's my mom." My voice rattled. "And that's me in bed. This is exactly what I was thinking a minute ago, and it suddenly appeared."

Just as the sweet music eased to a quiet hum, the door swung open again. Clara barged into the room, her purse in one hand and a laptop computer case in the other. "Nathan, your practice is really paying off. You sound — " She stopped short, her mouth agape. "Oh, my heavens!"

In the mirror, Mom approached the foreground of the reflection, her eyes seeming to focus directly on me. She reached up and began pulling down a shade. "Good night, sweetheart," she said. "I'll see you in the morning." The shade slowly covered the entire image and faded it to black. Seconds later, the mirror returned to normal, reflecting our pale faces.

Tony's voice echoed in the hall. "Where is everybody?" He appeared at the door, his big eyes scanning the room. "Oh. Here you are."

As Kelly turned toward him, her voice shook. "Hi, Daddy."

"Got your prints." He tossed a photo package onto the bed and crossed his arms. "You all look like you've seen a headless ghost."

Kelly sprang to his side and pushed him out the door. "Nathan was playing a sad song on his violin. It made us all feel kind of blue, you know, with his parents dying and all." Her voice faded down the hall. "Coffee's ready. You want some?"

I scrambled for the package, tore it open, and dumped the photos, about twenty or so. As I arranged them on the bedspread, I glanced at Clara. "Take a look. Recognize anything in these pictures?"

She set the computer case down and walked to the bed, her voice trembling. "Nathan, what did I just see? Was that really your mother?"

"I'll explain later, or at least I'll try. Just look at these before Tony gets back."

"Very well." She withdrew a pair of glasses from her purse and peered at the first photo while I looked on. Within a dimly lit room, three laptop computers sat on a curved desk that abutted an equally curved wall. A Microsoft logo floated randomly across each screen. "No," she said, pulling back, "that place is unfamiliar to me."

I touched the second photo, even darker than the first. It showed a large room with a tall cylindrically shaped object at the center of the floor. "What do you make of this one?"

"Is that a telescope?"

"Maybe. It's sort of shaped like one."

Clara grasped my wrist. "Get me up to speed, Nathan. Where did these photos come from?"

"From Dad's camera."

While Clara sat on the bed, I gave her a rapid-fire update about recent events. I even played a few measures of Brahms Lullaby on Mom's violin to demonstrate.

When I finished, Kelly breezed back into the room. "I got him interested in a rebroadcast of an old Lakers game." She looked at the mirror. "Is it playing any more tricks?"

"No." I gestured toward the bed. "The pictures are, though. I told Clara what's going on."

"Including the voices?"

Clara blinked. "What voices?"

Again I took a minute to give her a quick summary and a few examples, including the Taj Mahal and Buckingham Palace comments.

"And I heard more voices just before I walked in here," Kelly said as she sat next to Clara. "I couldn't catch it all. A man said, 'The computers decode,' then a woman said something about a telescope, but it wasn't Clara."

"So there's a connection." Clara picked up the second photo and handed it to Kelly. "Does that look like a telescope to you?"

Kelly squinted at the image. "I'm not sure. Maybe."

"What else did the voices say?" Clara asked.

"I was out in the hall, so some of it came through the door kind of garbled." She laid the picture back on the bed. "The voices were pretty loud, Nathan. You must've heard them."

"I didn't hear anything but Brahms." I lifted the violin to my shoulder. "When it's next to my ear, I can't hear much else." I played several quick notes, ending with a high C.

Kelly's face turned ashen. Her lips parted as her jaw dropped open.

"Are you feeling sick?" Clara asked.

"No. I heard a voice again. Just now." She looked at us imploringly. "Didn't you hear it? It was a woman's voice, loud and clear."

I shook my head. "Not a word."

Clara locked her hand with Kelly's. "What did she say?"

Kelly's face fell slack. Her eyes opened wide, and she spoke in an eerie monotone as if trying to mimic a ghostly voice echoing in her mind. "Hurry, Nathan, before it's too late."

"Play some more," Clara said, pointing at the violin.

I laid the bow across the strings. "Brahms again?"

"Anything. Let's see what happens."

I restarted the lullaby, trying to play softly enough to hear the voices. Kelly closed her eyes. After a few seconds, she spoke softly. "I hear something. Quiet voices, like people whispering to each other."

"Can you make out what they're saying?" I asked.

She opened her eyes. "No. They're too quiet."

I switched to my part of the Vivaldi duet, increasing the volume slightly.

Kelly concentrated again, then shook her head. "Still just whispers."

After trying several different compositions and getting the same responses from Kelly, I lowered the violin with an exasperated sigh. "Are you sure you're hearing whispers?"

She set a fist on her hip. "As sure as you were when you saw that weird stuff in the mirror."

I pointed the bow at her. "Touché. I deserved that one."

Her lips thinned out. "Well, maybe we're even now."

I studied her countenance — combative with a hint of disappointment. I had no idea how to respond, so I held my tongue.

"How strange, Nathan," Clara said. "A voice spoke to you by name."

I spread out my hands. "But hurry and do what? What happens when it's too late?"

Kelly nodded toward the photos. "Let's look for more clues."

We picked up and set down several photos, most of them showing buildings and people I didn't recognize.

Clara snatched up the last photo. "Look, Nathan. Interfinity."

"Interfinity?" I peered over her shoulder at a picture of Dad standing next to a man wearing a white laboratory smock. "What does it mean?"

"It's a corporation that observes strange astronomical features. At first they were associated with alien hunters, looking for signs of life out in the great beyond, but later they moved into serious science, like figuring out all that stuff about dark matter and axions."

Kelly scrunched her eyebrows. "What are axions?"

"I don't know enough about them to explain." Clara wiggled her fingers as if typing on a keyboard. "I just typed Solomon's notes when he took a case for them. Someone had stolen Interfinity's technology, so he had to get it back, some kind of device that creates what they called an Interfinity corridor. I have no idea what that is, but I do remember that they used a special kind of mirror."

I pointed at her. "Another connection. A mirror."

"And that's probably why your father gave it to you for safekeeping." Clara walked over to the wall mirror and stared at her reflection, but the tall gray-haired lady on the other side just stared back with the same skeptical aspect. "Obviously there is much more here than meets the eye."

"So what do we do?" Kelly asked. "Go to Interfinity and see what's up?"

"That's one option, but I'm thinking we should go straight to the horse's mouth." As Clara stroked her chin, her glasses slid down her nose. "Nathan, you can access your father's webmail account, can't you? Perhaps we can find out more about his latest project."

"Yeah. I think I remember his password, but I'll need a computer." I pointed at the computer case Clara had brought. "Is that for me?"

"Since yours is at the bottom of the river, I bought you a new one." Clara retrieved the case from the floor and set it on my desk, her body blocking the lamp and casting a shadow across the carpet.

In the mirror, the light dimmed, and the walls darkened, but nothing strange appeared, though Clara's shadow seemed denser than most, almost like it had substance.

Kelly's eyes darted to the mirror and back. She had seen it, too, but when I opened my mouth to mention it, Tony's voice knifed into the room.

"Anyone hungry?" He swept in with a mobile phone in hand. As soon as he entered, the lamp in the mirror cast a reddish glow over his reflection. Hunching over and wearing nothing but an animal skin, his image looked like a caveman carrying a slingshot. "It's halftime, and my stomach's begging for a liver and anchovy pizza. I could order an extra large if anyone's got the munchies."

I edged away from the mirror, hoping Tony's eyes would follow me. "Liver and anchovies? You really put that on a pizza?"

"I guess your dad never fed you a real man's food." Tony flexed his bicep. "Stick with me, and you'll have guns like mine in no time." His reflected image grew long hair all over his body and looked like a chimpanzee showing off his muscles.

Kelly slid an arm around his and turned him toward the door. "Why don't you go to the Pizza Ranch and get an extra large with half liver and anchovies and the other half with ..." She raised her eyebrows at me.

"Uh ... pepperoni?" I offered.

Kelly nodded. "Yeah. Pepperoni."

"Pepperoni's cool. It has protein." Tony dug a set of keys out of his jeans pocket. "Anything else?"

Kelly patted him on the back. "Can you pick up some of those fruit drinks at Walmart? They're Nathan's favorite."

I lifted my brow at her, but she shot me a keep-your-mouth-shut glare. I complied. This was no time to protest.

"But that's the opposite direction from the Pizza Ranch," Tony said. "I don't have time to do both before the second half."

Kelly pushed him toward the door. "I'll record it for you, and we can all watch it together when you get back."

Setting his feet, he eyed the photos on the bed. "So what's up with the pictures? Any good shots?"

"They're old ones that belonged to Nathan's father." She pushed harder and guided him out the door and down the hall, her voice fading. "You'd better get going. I heard Nathan's stomach growling."

As soon as the door closed, Clara's shadow dimmed, and the reflection returned to normal.

I leaned a shoulder against the door. "That was close."

"I know." Clara laid a hand on her abdomen. "When I saw that chimpanzee, I strained so hard to keep from laughing, I think I reopened my hernia."

I stepped away from the door and swept a foot along the carpet. "I don't see any Clara guts anywhere."

"Good one." She patted me on the shoulder. "I'm glad you're getting your sense of humor back. Maybe spending time with Kelly is good for you."

"Yeah." Guilt squashed my momentary lightheartedness. How could I be happy so soon after my parents' deaths? "Maybe so."

Clara slid the photos together into a pile, careful to keep them in order. "By the way, I put a new phone in the laptop bag and a debit card for any immediate expenses, so make sure you find them and put them away."

"I will. Thanks."

She walked to the desk and turned the laptop on. "Better get started on your father's email as soon as possible. Your parents' funeral is on Tuesday."

"Tuesday? Did the police find them?"

"An anonymous person sent a photograph of their bodies and said he would reveal their location by Monday. If that tip pans out, I want to be ready, assuming the funeral home can prepare the bodies quickly enough."

I swallowed past a painful lump. "Do I have to go?"

She tapped on the keyboard. "Of course you have to go. You will be a pallbearer, and I was hoping you'd play something. Dr. Malenkov suggested that you and he should play the Vivaldi duet."

"No." I lowered my head, keeping her in view. "I couldn't handle that."

She gazed at me for a moment before nodding. "I understand. I'll arrange for different music."

"Thanks."

She took my hand. "Do you want to be a pallbearer?"

I kept my head low. "I guess I can do that."

Kelly barged in and leaned back on the door, slamming it shut. "That was close."

"Exactly what I said." I touched my stomach. "But I didn't know I liked Walmart fruit drinks."

Kelly flashed an injured expression. "I had to get him out of here, didn't I?"

"You didn't have to lie."

She set her hands on her hips. "Get real, Nathan. Don't tell me you never lie."

Clara forked her fingers at us. "Both of you hush. This is no time for a spitting match." She handed the stack of photos to Kelly. "If you two can't work together, we'll never figure this out."

Kelly lowered her hands. "If he keeps looking down on me, we can't work together."

Clara pointed a finger that almost touched Kelly's nose. "Listen, little lady, condescension isn't a one-way street. Maybe you need to come down off your high horse and trust him." Clara turned to me and shot a hot stare. "And that goes double for you, Mr. High and Mighty. You'd better learn to trust her." She stalked to the door, jerked it open, and stormed out of the room.

As soon as her heavy footsteps faded, Kelly spun toward the exit and took a hard step toward it.

I held up a hand. "Wait."

She halted and turned toward me, tears in her reddened eyes. "What?"

"I … uh …" I had no idea what to say, but I had to come up with something. Maybe I could follow what Dad always did when Mom got upset. Just ask questions. Get to the root of the anger. "Are you mad at me or your father?" I winced at my own words. It was a pretty dumb question.

"Both." She tapped her socked foot on the floor with a fast beat and turned toward the mirror. "He's a clueless buffoon. What's your excuse?"

I looked at the mirror over her shoulder. A tear spilled from one of her eyes.

Pulling her lips in, Kelly swung her head to the side, avoiding my stare. Her foot continued its frantic tapping. "Don't you have something to do besides stare at me? Like figuring out that password?"

"Not yet." A strange sensation poured over my body, a tingle that radiated across my skin. In my reflected image, an almost imperceptible light bathed my face, microscopic particles that attached to my skin.

Although I stayed motionless, my reflected head shifted, leaving the aura of light behind. Somehow the Nathan in the mirror had detached and moved on his own, first laying his hands on the shoulders of Kelly's reflection, then turning her around. "I didn't mean to hurt your feelings," my mirror image said. "You're my sister now, and I'll do anything to make sure you're my friend, too."

The real Kelly focused on the mirror. Her reflection wrapped her arms around my reflection and laid her head on his chest.

"I'm sorry for being such a jerk," her reflection said. "We just need to get to know each other better."

As the two reflections embraced, Kelly slowly turned and faced me. "Is ..." She swallowed hard. "Is that what you're thinking?"

I licked my lips. "Yeah. Pretty much."

She slid her arms around my waist and laid her head against my chest. "Then say it. Say it like you mean it."

Her trembling arms sent shivers up my back. I reached around and returned the embrace, keeping my touch gentle. I whispered into her ear. "You're my sister now, and I'll do anything to make sure you're my friend, too."

"And I'm sorry for being such a jerk." She looked up at me. "We really do need to get to know each other better."

I patted her lightly on the back. "Like Clara said, we need to trust each other."

"Do you trust me?" Her teary eyes sparkled.

I nodded. "Yes, I trust you."

She pulled away and lowered her head, silent for a few seconds before whispering, "I hope you'll keep trusting me, no matter what."

I glanced at the mirror. It had returned to normal, including Kelly's sad profile as she kept her eyes averted. I reached for her hand and interlocked our thumbs. "Trust is a two-way street. As long as we trust each other, we'll be fine."

Now looking at me, she tightened her grip on my hand, a hint of a smile brightening her face. "I can live with that."

I nodded at the mirror. "I don't think I like my thoughts being projected on a theater screen."

"Looks like my dad's wish came true. We have a reality show right here in our house." She let go of my hand and headed for the door. "I'll see you in a few minutes."

"Where are you going?"

"To record the game like I promised, but if anything happens on *The Nathan Show*, I want to hear all about it."

CHAPTER TEN

I AWOKE TO THE sound of chirping birds. With morning sun filtering through the drapes, the room carried an eerie dimness. The mirror reflected the gloom accurately, including my bare feet protruding from disheveled bedcovers, proof of the fitful night I had suffered, probably the result of my failed attempts to remember Dad's email password.

After two hours of trying, I had given up and collapsed into bed, only to face new troubles — dreams of walking through remnants of shattered violins, every fragment covered with blood, a trail that led to the twin coffins I had seen back in Chicago. In the dream, however, each coffin held only a human-sized black stone with strange symbols etched in white on its surface. They reminded me of —

"Rosetta!" I sat upright in bed. That was the key to the password. I threw off the bedspread, scrambled out from under the sheets, and plopped down in the desk chair. After punching the laptop's power button, I turned on the lamp and the digital clock's FM radio. As the classical station played a Tchaikovsky piano concerto, I squirmed while waiting for the boot-up process to finish.

A light tap sounded on the door. "Nathan?" Kelly called. "Are you up?"

I glanced down at my clothes. Gym shorts and T-shirt. That would do. "Yep. Come on in."

The door pushed open, and Kelly entered. Wearing a pink knee-length nightshirt that said, *Sanity Is Overrated*, and combing through tangled hair with her fingers, she shuffled her purple bunny slippers across the carpet and peered at the computer.

I grinned. "You look ... uh ... relaxed."

"I hardly slept a wink." She poked my forearm. "I'm your sister now, so you'd better get used to my frumpy fashions."

I scanned her from head to toe. Her bright smile and sparkling eyes outshone any frumpiness, and the tangled hair and casual attire made her seem down to earth ... real. "You look great."

She pushed my shoulder. "Sweet talker."

"No, really." I winked. "You're supposed to trust me, remember?"

"Well, then ..." She bowed her head. "Thank you for the compliment."

"No problem." I checked the digital clock on the desk. 8:15. Sunday morning. "What time is your church service?"

"Church? Um ... we haven't been ... I mean ..."

I waved a hand. "Don't worry about it." I opened the Internet browser and brought up Dad's email provider. "I remembered the password this morning." As I typed in "Rosetta Speaks," I recited each letter out loud.

Kelly looked on from behind me. "Rosetta? Like the Rosetta Stone?"

"Right." I scanned a long list of email folders, each with a number embedded — a count of the messages within. "Looks like I've got more than five hundred to go through."

She pointed. "Look at all those with Rosetta in the title. It must be important."

"Probably. I even had a dream about it. That's how I remembered the password." I pulled a tablet of paper from the desk drawer and scribbled a picture as I described the dream. "The stone was split in half, and the pieces were lying in two coffins, one piece in each coffin, and a trail of bloody violins led up to them."

"Bloody violins?" Kelly shuddered. "That's creepy."

I spelled out "Rosetta" in block letters on the pad. "I think the dream was sort of like a puzzle. Dad loves …" Like a bursting bubble, new sadness surged. I breathed a sigh. "I mean, Dad *used* to love puzzles."

Kelly rubbed my back. "You don't have to be careful with your words. I knew what you meant."

I nodded. "Thanks."

She gave me a playful rap on the head with her knuckles. "You know, I think the pizza put that dream in your head. That slice with liver and anchovies was inspirational."

I looked at her silly grin. She was trying to shake me out of my funk. "Actually, I kind of liked it." I thumped my chest. "I felt like a real man."

"Oh, no!" Clutching her throat, she stuck out her tongue and staggered with dramatic flair. "I ate an anchovy! I'm growing hair on my chest, and I left the toilet seat up! Don't ask me to stop for directions; I'm turning into a man!"

As I laughed, I caught a glimpse of Kelly's comical display in the mirror. The two Kellys seemed to be performing a weird tribal dance, completely out of sync with the classical music playing on the radio. The girl in the mirror turned fuzzy for a moment, then sharpened again, now dressed in loose-fitting khaki pants and a short-sleeved safari shirt. When the real Kelly turned toward the mirror, she released her throat and stared.

I shot up from the chair and joined her. I, too, was dressed in khakis in the mirror image. Our reflected surroundings morphed into a dim chamber with a faint glow seeping in through arched windows near a high ceiling. Shards of varnished wood littered the smooth floor, making a trail through a maze of music stands toward two coffins that sat on a long table in the gloomy distance.

I whispered, "This is my dream." I took two trembling steps closer. "That's the performance hall, the place where my parents were killed, but now the coffins are on stage."

Kelly sat on the bed, still staring. "The mirror's reflecting what you're thinking again. You put us both into your dream."

I pointed at my image as it crept side by side next to hers. "Where did I come up with the safari outfits? I never owned anything like that."

"I do. My dad wanted to take me hunting, so — " Her eyes widened. "That's exactly how those baggy old pants fit me. How could you know?"

In the image, a man in a navy blue blazer rose from behind the coffins. "How did you cross the barrier?" he asked.

I stepped closer to the mirror and whispered, "I can hear that guy."

"Me, too." Kelly got up and pressed close to my side. "Your imagination is going nuts."

"He's one of Mictar's men. His name's Dr. Gordon."

The Nathan in the mirror halted. "I crossed the same way as before. I had a dream, it showed up in the mirror, then music, a flash of light, and zap, I'm here. Why?"

"You're not carrying it," Dr. Gordon said. "How could you transport without it?"

The mirror Nathan crossed his arms. "I have my ways."

Dr. Gordon walked to the front of the coffins, a pronounced limp in his gait. "I asked you to bring it. I want to teach you how it works."

"It's too dangerous. I'm having it locked up forever."

"How will you return to Blue?"

"You seem to know how. I'll just follow you."

Dr. Gordon half closed an eye. "Very well. Come over here. I'll show you why I called you."

Glancing around, the Nathan in the mirror skulked forward, Kelly's reflection at his heels. He peered into one of the coffins and growled at Dr. Gordon. "How did they get here?"

"I suppose Mictar thought Earth Yellow would be a safe place to hide them."

His arm shaking, the mirror Nathan reached into the coffin and lifted a feminine hand. "How did you find them?"

A tall, dark figure in the mirror grabbed Nathan from behind and covered his eyes with a thin hand. As my reflected self struggled, I clenched my fist. "Mictar!"

The real Kelly yelled. "Don't just stand there, Kelly! Help him!"

In the mirror, Kelly leaped onto Mictar from behind and gouged his face with her fingernails. As my double slumped to the stage floor, Mictar reached around and tore Kelly from his back. With an aura of light surrounding him, he covered her eyes with his hand. Sparks flew from beneath his palm. She stiffened, and her mouth dropped open, but only a timid squeak came out. A few seconds later, she, too, collapsed.

Straightening his pulsating body, Mictar heaved in a deep breath and looked toward the ceiling. "Ah! The ecstasy of youthful vigor!"

Dr. Gordon hobbled forward and frisked mirror-Nathan's clothes. "He didn't bring it." He shifted over to Kelly and searched her body, running his hands along every curve.

The real Kelly shivered. "I think I'm going to be sick."

Gordon grabbed a shock of mirror-Nathan's hair and jerked his head high enough to speak to him face-to-face. As the wounded boy's features stretched out, his eyelids opened. Empty eye sockets encircled by black sooty scorch marks stared back at him.

A purplish vein on the side of Gordon's forehead pulsed. "I'll find it eventually. With you and your daddy dead, not many people are left who could be hiding it." He dropped mirror-Nathan, letting his face thump hard against the floor.

Gordon shifted over to Kelly and pushed open one of her eyelids, revealing a gaping hole. "A thorough excision, as usual."

"To get to the reservoirs," Mictar said, "one must open the spillways."

Leaving the bodies on the stage, Gordon and Mictar slowly descended the stairs to audience level, passing close to the front of the mirror. Every facial detail clarified. Mictar touched a deep scratch on his cheek. Within seconds, the wound vanished.

A fresh cut also marred Gordon's face, as if he had been in a fight. "We have to get to the girl's house," he said as he limped along. "The burglar is due to arrive in the morning. My leg should be fine by then." As the two men headed for the exit door, Dr. Gordon's voice faded. "That old fiddler didn't do too much damage."

The sound of a car motor shook my attention away from the mirror. I peeked through the window. The blue Mustang pulled into the driveway with the gray-bearded man behind the wheel. He stepped out, holding a gun at his side.

"We've got big trouble. That guy who's been chasing me is here. And he's got a gun."

The front door banged open.

"Daddy!" Kelly screamed. "Daddy! Help!"

The man burst into the room. As he aimed the gun at me, he pushed the door closed with his foot. "Easy enough to find you. The locals aren't exactly tight-lipped."

I stepped in front of Kelly. "Leave her alone. It's me you want."

"It's also easy enough to put a hole right through both of you." When he pulled the trigger, everything slowed to a crawl. Gunpowder flashed. Sparks flew in slow motion. The barrel expelled a brass-colored bullet that floated toward me, slowly closing the three-foot gap.

I gasped for breath, but my lungs froze. I tried to grab Kelly and duck, but my limbs and torso locked in place. Only my eyes and brain seemed able to function at all.

As the bullet continued its unyielding advance, I looked at the mirror. A young man clad in blue crouched next to the two bodies, a hand on each as tears trickled down his cheeks. Then the girl in red appeared within the reflection. She laid her palms on the glass from the inside.

The mirror darkened and expanded in every direction. The dead bodies pushed out from the glass, creating a hologram that blended with reality. The lifeless Nathan and Kelly floated inches off the bedroom floor as the two rooms merged into one.

I looked at the space between me and the gunman. The bullet moved within a foot of my chest, spinning slowly as it inched along. I mentally screamed at my body to jump, duck, collapse — anything to get out of the way.

Just as the bullet touched my clothes, darkness spilled over the room, like jet-black paint flowing down the walls. A falling sensation overtook my senses, a plunge into a dark void. At any second my body would crash against something below. Yet, the painful thud never came, just a new sensation — lying prone on a hard surface.

I pushed my hands forward, but they wouldn't budge. The surface at my fingertips felt hard and cool. Had I fallen? Had the bullet struck? If so, why didn't I feel it puncture my chest?

Another popping noise throttled my ears. I tried to look around, but my cheek stayed pressed against a wood floor. The room slowly brightened from blackness to a gray gloom. Someone lay next to me, a female form wearing the same safari outfit the Kelly in the mirror had worn. With her face pointed the other way, I couldn't be sure who she was.

I waited, trying not to breathe. Maybe the gunman would think I was dead and take off, if he was still nearby. After a few moments of silence, I whispered, "Kelly? Is that you?"

"Yes," she whispered in return. "Is he gone?"

"I think so." I pushed against the floor, sat up, and checked for pain. Everything seemed fine.

Kelly rose and knelt next to me. "Where are we?"

"I'm not sure." I climbed to my feet and helped her up. "I'm not hurt. Are you?"

"I don't think so." She wiped her hands on her shirt. "When did I put this hideous hunting outfit on?"

"You got me." I nudged a violin fragment with a laced boot and sniffed the air. The odor of fresh paint permeated the cool chamber. "This is just like my dream."

"I hope it's a dream. Either that or we're in the dark tunnel people talk about after a near-death experience." She closed her eyes and tilted her head upward. "Somebody please wake me up. I'll never shout at my alarm clock again if it will just wake me — "

Laughter interrupted her plea. We turned toward the sound. A rectangular image hovered nearby, a pond-like reflection that showed a skewed picture of my bedroom. In the image, Kelly and I, still dressed in our sleep attire, lay on the carpet, the gunman standing over us.

Kelly clutched a handful of my sleeve, whisper-shouting. "Are those our dead bodies back in your bedroom?"

I heaved shallow breaths. "I don't know. Everything's going crazy."

In the image, Tony burst through the doorway. He grabbed the intruder from behind in a headlock and wrestled him to the floor. The intruder freed an arm and smacked Tony's head with the butt of the gun. When Tony fell limp, the man squirmed out, struggled to his feet, and hobbled away.

As the image shrank and faded, the roar of the Mustang came through as well as the sound of gravel spinning from under its tires. The scene reshaped into a tri-fold, floor-standing mirror, reflecting our dumbstruck faces, khaki clothes, and gloomy surroundings.

Kelly clutched her stomach and dropped to her knees. "I think I'm gonna hurl."

While she vomited thin bile on the floor, I crouched and patted her back. "It's going to be okay," I said in a soothing tone, as much to settle myself as to calm her.

When she finished, I helped her to her feet. She pushed her hair back, her eyes flooded with tears. "We're dead!" Her cry echoed in the empty chamber as she called out, "We're dead," again and again.

"We're not dead. Somehow we transported into the mirror. This place is exactly what we saw from my bedroom."

She set her fists on her hips. "Oh, well, like *that's* a lot better! We're either dead or nothing but reflections in a mirror world."

"But we're still in physical bodies." I stooped and picked up a piece of a violin. With two curling strings still attached, the tawny wood carried a splattering of reddish stain. "And this place is too real to be just a reflection."

She turned toward the coffins and rubbed her upper arms. "So, if this is the same as your dream, do you think the Rosetta pieces are over there?"

"I don't think so. Did you see the lady's hand?" I strode toward the boxes, Kelly following. Our shoes crunched violin pieces as we weaved around the music stands. "Like I told you, this is the performance hall where my parents died. But it looks different, like it's been remodeled."

"In just a couple of days?"

"Fast workers, I guess." I stopped and pointed at the stage floor. "But the coffins were downstairs in a prop room."

Kelly crept closer to the coffins. Just as I took a step to follow, a siren wailed somewhere outside. The front entrance door burst open. Gordon limped in, reaching into his jacket. "Stay where you are!"

I grabbed Kelly's hand and pulled her through the stage's side doorway. We ran through the dark corridor and down the darker stairs, our heavy boots clomping on the creaking wood. Not bothering to look for a light, I dashed with her into the maintenance area and clattered along the catwalk.

After finding the low exit door, already repaired since my previous visit, I dropped down, pounded it open with my feet, and leaped to the hallway below. Kelly jumped down and joined me.

Again with Kelly at my heels, I dashed into the fire escape alcove and threw open the window. A cool rush of air breezed in. This time, in the middle of the night, the black stairwell seemed invisible against the dark background. It would be like stepping out into nothingness.

While watching the street below, I pushed myself through the window and felt for the metal grating with my feet. When it caught my weight, I straightened, helped Kelly out, and hustled down flight after flight, listening to Kelly's footsteps clanging to the rear.

As I ran, I glanced up at the dark window. No sign of Gordon. When I reached the horizontal ladder, I walked out onto it, grabbed a rung, and rode it down while Kelly waited at the landing. "Watch for him," I said. "There's an exit around the corner, so he might show up there and try to catch us from below."

When the ladder hit the pavement, we clambered down and leaped off. It then lifted slowly back into place with a grinding squeak.

Kelly pointed. "There he is."

From the corner of the building, Gordon jogged toward us, holding a gun close to his side.

I took Kelly's hand and spun in the opposite direction. We hustled into the alley where Clara and I had found the limo. I pulled Kelly against a brick wall and pinned my own body next to hers.

She panted as she whispered, "What are we going to do?"

"Fight." I raised a tight fist, held my breath, and listened. Heavy footsteps drew closer. When the pounding reached a climax, I leaped out and swung my fist, nailing Gordon square on the cheek and knocking him flat.

I crouched over his motionless body and looked for the gun, but darkness shrouded the area.

Kelly pulled my sleeve. "Let's just get out of here."

When I leaned to follow, Gordon latched on to my pant leg. "Without me, you'll never get home. You have no idea where you are."

"We'll take our chances." I jerked away and ran down the sidewalk with Kelly. The city of Chicago rose before us, towers ascending to dizzying heights. We turned right on Wabash and sprinted alongside the busy street. I listened for our pursuer, but the rumble of an approaching 'L' train on an overhead track overwhelmed every other sound.

I halted at the first intersection and pivoted. No one followed. We waited for the light to change and tried to blend in with the dozen or so pedestrians as we crossed the street.

A man in a lime green leisure suit and platform shoes approached from the other side. Something gold flashed on his chest, drawing my gaze to his open shirt where a gold chain suspended a silver-dollar-sized medallion in the midst of a dense nest of hair. A movie poster on a building across the street advertised the film *Animal House* opening July 28.

When Kelly and I reached the curb, I looked back again. Gordon jogged toward us, grimacing and favoring a leg.

The light changed. A bus rolled between us and Gordon and stopped to allow a late-arriving pedestrian on board. A Ford Pinto pulled up behind the bus and beeped its shrill horn. Although that model had been discontinued years ago, it looked brand new.

I searched for an escape and found a stairway leading to the train platform. "Follow me." We sprinted up the stairs. When we reached the turnstile, I skidded to a halt and eyed the uniformed attendant leaning against a column and staring off into space. "What do we need? A ticket? A token?"

Kelly leaped onto the turnstile's cross bar and vaulted over. The attendant jerked his head toward us and raised a hand. "Hey! You need a — "

"Sorry." I set my hand on the turnstile. "It's an emergency."

I jumped to the other side and dashed up another flight of stairs. After running out onto the passenger platform, I jogged along the line of cars, peering into each window. Where was Kelly? She couldn't have just disappeared.

A signal chimed. The train was about to leave. At the last car, Kelly pushed out from the inside and wedged her body between the closing doors. "Hurry!" she called, straining against the panels.

The doors popped open. Kelly lurched back and fell to her bottom inside. Just as the panels began to close, I leaped in and tumbled on top of her.

After untangling from each other, we rose together and grabbed a support pole. I sucked in a long breath. "I think we lost him."

"Maybe." Kelly brushed dust from her safari shirt. "I saw a couple of people get on while you were running this way, but I couldn't tell if he was one of them. It was too dark."

I scanned the nearly empty train. One old man sat in the seat closest to the front access door. As a light snore passed through his nostrils, his chin dropped to his chest and nestled in a coffee stain on his white button-down shirt. A sign above his head warned passengers not to pass between the cars.

"Good job back there," Kelly said as she punched the air. "Did it hurt?"

I raised my fist and looked at the knuckles, red but not bleeding. "It does now. I didn't feel a thing when I decked him."

As the car swayed from side to side, she braced herself against the back of a seat and peered out the window. "If he didn't get on this train, he's sure to follow on the next one."

"Let's get off pretty soon. He won't be able to guess where we stopped."

She slid into a window seat and fanned her face with a hand. "Give me a few minutes to catch my breath. I'm not an experienced spy like you."

I pushed a newspaper section off the seat and sat next to her. "I thought you did great."

"No, I didn't." She crossed her arms and shivered. "I was scared to death."

"So? You don't think I was scared?"

"You didn't act like it."

"Well, I was. I just did what I had to do. Survival instinct."

"Experience helps you survive. Rookies like me get killed." She hugged herself and shivered again. "But I do feel a little better knowing you were scared."

"Glad I could help." I looked at the newspaper on the floor at my feet. Bold type near the top spelled out "Nightmare Epidemic Continues." I squinted at the smaller print but couldn't read it.

Just as I reached for it, Kelly whispered, "Do you think your parents were in those coffins?"

I straightened, leaving the paper on the floor. "I don't know. That reflection of myself didn't mention it."

She looked straight at me. "Nathan, what's going on? Either this is the most vivid nightmare in history, or I'm going out of my mind."

"I'm in the same boat. Life's been a nightmare ever since I found my parents dead. One crazy event after another. And the girl in red showed up again."

Her brow lifted. "She did?"

"You didn't see her? It was when that guy shot at us."

Kelly shook her head. "I couldn't move a muscle. My eyes stayed locked on that bullet."

I spread out my arms the way the girl had. "It was like she controlled the mirror. Like she pulled us in here and pushed our dead reflections out into my bedroom."

A scratchy voice broke in. The driver announced the next stop, but it was too garbled to understand. As the train rounded a curve, the front half bent into sight, every car slowing as it approached a well-lit platform. A dark-suited man passed from car number two to three and limped toward the back of the train.

I grasped Kelly's wrist. "Time to get off."

"What? Why?"

I crouched and pulled her into the aisle. "Gordon found us."

CHAPTER ELEVEN

STAYING LOW, WE crept behind a partition next to the side exit door. As the train slowed to a crawl, I peeked past the rows of seats to the car directly in front of ours. No sign of Dr. Gordon yet.

"Ready to jump?" I asked.

Kelly took in a breath and rocked on her toes. "As ready as I'll ever be."

When the train halted, Gordon burst through the door between the two cars and limped toward us, aiming a handgun. "Don't move or you're dead!"

I froze. Kelly grabbed my arm. Her hot breaths puffed against my neck as the side door slid open.

Gordon pressed the gun barrel against Kelly's head. "Give it up, or I'll blow her brains out. Just come with me. Mictar wants to see you."

I thrust Gordon's weapon arm up and kneed him in the groin. When he doubled over, I kicked him in the chin. He snapped back and landed face up in the aisle.

After grabbing Kelly's hand, I leaped for the loading platform and hit the ground running. We scrambled down the stairway and sprinted along a sidewalk through a construction zone, leaping over broken concrete and dodging orange barricades as streetlights guided our way.

We stopped at a corner and waited for several cars to pass. I looked back toward the station. Gordon limped down the stairs while scanning the sidewalk in the other direction.

"I don't think he's seen us yet." When the final car passed, we bent low, crept across the street, and ducked into an alley. In front and on both sides, brick buildings stretched to four stories high. A fire escape rode up the wall to the left, similar to the metal stairs we had used earlier.

I looked at the horizontal bridge above. Hovering at least a dozen feet straight up, it might as well have been a mile in the air. I could never jump that high.

I scanned the alley and spotted a trash dumpster several feet away. "Think we can push the dumpster under the fire escape?"

Kelly looked at the suspended ladder. "If we do, he might use it to follow us."

"Maybe not. I think he's hurt." I set my hands on the side of the dumpster and gave it a hefty shove. It budged an inch or two.

Kelly leaned her shoulder against the worn-away lettering on the back. Looking at me, she said, "On three?"

Setting my feet, I gave her a nod. "Let's do it."

"One … two … three!"

While I shoved with my hands, Kelly pushed with her shoulder. As the dumpster slid, the metal bottom screeched against the pavement.

I pulled Kelly back. "With all that noise, we might as well send up a flare."

She looked at the ladder again. "Think we got it close enough?"

"Let's find out." I climbed the dumpster and perched on the edge closest to the fire escape, still a few feet away from directly underneath the ladder. I jumped and grabbed one of the rungs, but the rusted stairway stayed put.

Kelly scaled the dumpster, jumped from the top, and wrapped her arms around my waist. With a squeal, the ladder lurched a half inch but stopped. Swinging her legs back and forth, she forced our bodies to sway.

With every swing, my fingers slipped. As the hinges continued to whine, the stairway eased down in rhythmic pulses until we reached the ground. Once we set the supports in place, we dashed up to the first platform and waited while the bridge elevated, its hinges again squawking a rusty complaint.

Careful to keep our footfalls quiet on the metal steps, we hurried to the top of the building and ducked behind a parapet, a three-foot-high wall that bordered the roof.

I stretched out my numbed fingers and peeked down at the street. Dr. Gordon skulked into the alley, keeping a hand in his jacket pocket as he swung his head from side to side.

I jerked back and whispered, "He's down there."

Kelly leaned close. "Did he see us?"

"Hard to tell." Staying low, I walked to an access hatch at the center of the roof and tried the latch. Locked.

Kelly skulked across the roof and joined me. "If he thinks we're up here, he's bound to find us. He'll just come up the stairs on the inside."

"Not if we can get to the next roof." We walked to the far edge of the building and looked at the alley between us and the parapet on the other side. "What do you think? Maybe fifteen feet across?"

"At least." Kelly backed up several steps, puffed a few breaths, and sprinted toward the edge. She leaped onto our parapet, launched herself across the gap, and touched down on the other roof, but her foot slipped, sending her into a tumbling forward fall.

I backed up a few steps, ran ahead, and vaulted over the gap. When I landed on the gravelly roof, I stooped where Kelly lay curled on her side. "Kelly! Are you okay?"

She gave no answer.

I turned her body face up and cradled her in my arms. Blood streamed from a scalp wound, forking into three rivulets that traced across both cheeks and over her nose. I brushed gravel from her hair and used my sleeve to dab at the blood on her nose. "Kelly? Can you hear me?"

Her eyes fluttered open. "Where am I?"

"On a rooftop. You jumped from one building to another."

"Oh. Right. I remember now." With my help, she rose to her feet, wincing while letting out a groan. "My head feels like a hammer's pounding it."

"No wonder. You were out cold. I hope you don't have a concussion."

"It's not that bad. My vision's clear, so I think I'm okay." As she swept gravel from her pants, she turned to the other building. "I guess we'd better lay low for a while."

We sat side-by-side with our backs to the parapet, low enough to keep our heads out of sight. A pair of sirens wailed in the distance, one somewhere in front and another to the rear, farther away. Now that we were above the streetlights, only the glow of a half moon and a single exposed bulb next to the roof's access door illuminated our surroundings. Still, it was enough to shed light on Kelly's wounds. Blood oozed from her scalp into her ear and dripped from the lobe, falling into her hair and clotting.

"You've got a pretty bad cut on your head."

"I've had bad cuts before." She touched her scalp and winced again. "Dad makes me play basketball with the guys. To toughen me up, or so he says. One of his buddies plays like a gorilla with razor blades for elbows. He caught me square in the nose once. I bled like a stuck pig for almost an hour."

I grinned. "So that's why you jump like a kangaroo. All that basketball."

"Yeah. At least it's good for something." After staring straight ahead for a few seconds, she nudged me with an elbow. "Hey, you were awesome back at the train. Nice kick."

"Thanks." I squirmed, trying to get comfortable on the rough surface. "I thought you might be mad at me. It was a pretty risky move. He could've shot you."

"I *was* mad. For a second, I thought you were nuts. But you really came through."

"I'm just glad it worked out." I settled back and folded my hands on my stomach. "Okay, somehow we got transported to Chicago, but it looks different."

"Different? How?"

"Did you notice how people are dressed? One guy looked like a disco-hall reject. And the cars. I saw a shiny new Pinto. You can't even find them in junkyards anymore."

"I saw the disco guy and women with poofy hair. It's like we traveled in time or something."

"Or to some kind of parallel universe."

"You say that like it happens all the time." She altered her voice to a computer-like monotone. "Greetings, new arrivals from universe eighty-six. You are now in universe ninety-nine. Enjoy your visit. But before you leave, be sure to purchase souvenir hats and key chains at the Ninety-Nine Boutique."

I laughed and let my gaze linger on her. As blood trickled between her gleaming eyes, she seemed the picture of contrasts — humor and femininity packaged in toughened leather. "Well, I've been through a lot, but nothing this weird."

Kelly glanced around with narrowed eyes. "We need to get our bearings. Figure out what's going on. Maybe find a media source."

"A media source?" The article headline flashed to mind — *Nightmare Epidemic Continues.* What could it have meant? I looked at the night sky. With lights streaming from a hundred directions, the city's haze glowed, as if emanating a light of its own. It seemed heavy. Close. Too close.

Kelly nudged me again. "What are you thinking?"

"Just getting a feel for this place. It's stuffy. Kind of warm."

She nodded. "Too warm for October. More like June or July."

"Chicago in the summertime."

She raised a finger. "Which means the cottonwood tree at my house has green leaves now, just like in the photo."

"I see where you're going." I drew my knees up and draped my arms over them. "You're wondering if we got zapped to that universe."

"Or that time. I'm thinking we should go home and see if the girl in the picture is there. Maybe we can find some answers."

I interlocked my fingers. "The answers have to be linked to the coffins. We saw them here and in our world. It's the only connection we know about."

"Whoever the victims are, I'll bet they were murdered by Gordon and that Mictar guy. Remember what they said about the burglar and the girl?"

"Think it's the same girl? The one who looks like my mother?"

"Only one way to find out."

"Okay, so we head for Iowa." I reached for my back pocket and found nothing inside. "No wallet. We don't even have bus fare."

She set her arm in a hitchhiker's pose. "We have thumbs. We can bum a ride."

I twisted and looked over the side of the building. A tall bank clock showed 12:05. "Who's going to give us a ride at midnight, especially with you bleeding like that?"

She shrugged. "I guess we'll see who's brave enough."

When she started to rise, I pulled her back down. "Let's stay put a little while longer. At least until we're sure Gordon's gone."

For the next half hour, we chatted quietly. She prodded me for stories about my adventures, and after each tale, she asked for another. My final story involved an escape with Clara from a terrorist in Saudi Arabia. We zoomed on motorcycles down rough stone staircases and through filthy alleys teeming with rats until we vaulted over a deep channel our pursuer couldn't cross.

When I finished, Kelly's mouth hung open, then she swallowed and said, "Take me with you next time. I want to go for a ride like that."

I rose to my feet and dusted off the seat of my pants. "Trust me. It's not something to hope for." I walked to the roof access, a wooden door in a small dormer that rose about eight feet above the gravel. Although it was locked, a hard kick splintered the jamb and banged it open, revealing a steep flight of dimly lit stairs.

I tiptoed down. Kelly followed close behind. After the narrow first flight, the stairwell widened and brightened, finally coming to a dead end at a metal door. I pushed it open, revealing the seating area of a delicatessen, closed for the night and illuminated only by streetlamps outside.

Kelly looked at her bloodstained fingers. "Let's find the restrooms and get cleaned up before we hit the road."

"Good idea."

After washing, we met at the front door. "Easy enough to get out," I said as I turned the deadbolt, "but we can't lock it up again."

"So the manager loses a little pastrami from his fridge. He'll survive." When she pushed the door open, a horn blared in load pulses that vibrated the windows.

"A burglar alarm," I hissed. "Run!"

We rushed out to the sidewalk and headed for a crowd of people streaming from a corner pub about a block and a half away. Just before we reached the next street, I pulled Kelly to a halt. "Just play it cool. We didn't steal anything."

Slowing her breathing, she looked at me. "I'm not worried about the cops. I'm worried about Gordon. That alarm would wake the dead."

As we ambled toward the pub, a police siren whined in the distance. I pointed at the customers who were still filing out, most laughing, a few staggering. "Let's just blend in with them. No one will know."

"Except that we're underage, not acting drunk, and not smelling like booze." Kelly picked up a castaway beer bottle. "We could fake being drunk."

I pulled her into the doorway of a closed bail bond office and leaned against the brick building. "Not a great plan. We'll just attract more attention."

"Do you have a better one?"

I scanned the street. On the opposite side, a man in his early twenties wearing a muscle shirt was unloading a string-bound stack of newspapers from the back of a van marked *Stoneman Enterprises*.

"Let's ask him where he's delivering," I said, pointing. "Maybe we can get a lift." After looking both ways and seeing that Gordon was nowhere in sight, I strode to the delivery man, Kelly at my side. "You heading out west at all?" I asked.

"Yep." His collar-length brown hair falling into his eyes as he worked, he dropped the stack and cut the string with a flick of a pocketknife. "I take the early edition as far as Des Moines. I'm heading out as soon as I deliver these."

"Do you have room for a couple of hitchhikers hoping to go a little farther than Iowa City? We ... uh ... lost our transportation home."

"It'll take till morning to get there." He narrowed his eyes. "You look kind of young to be out drinking in this part of town so late at night."

Kelly held up the bottle. "Oh, you mean this stage prop. We're brother and sister. We were acting in a play at a theatre and lost our way on the 'L' train." She set the bottle down, pinched her pant leg with one hand, and touched her still-bleeding cut with the other. "See our costumes and the cool makeup job they did on my machete wound?"

The young man gave us a smirk that provided no clue whether he believed her or not. "With all my papers, there won't be any room in the back, but you can squeeze in up front."

I extended my hand. "I'm Nathan Shepherd, and this is Kelly."

The man wrapped my fingers in a powerful grip. "Gunther Stoneman."

"Pleasure to meet you." The name matched the sign on the van. Could he be related to the Stoneman who helped me at the Walmart? "Your name sounds familiar. Have we met?"

"Not that I can remember."

"Okay. Well, thanks for the ride."

"Sure thing. Go ahead and get in while I load this paper box. I'll be right back."

After Kelly boarded the van through the front passenger door, I slid in next to her, hip to hip. Kelly reached back, pulled a newspaper from a bundle, and spread it over our laps. The date on the front page stood out, as if pulsing — July 29, 1978.

CHAPTER TWELVE

KELLY WHISPERED, "Nineteen-seventy-eight?"
"Yeah. And it's summer, just like we thought."
I flipped the newspaper to a page of ads. "Look. Four
thousand bucks for a new car."

"That's fresh off the press," Gunther said through
the window on the driver's side. He opened the door and
climbed into his seat. "Maybe you could read out loud
while I drive. Pass the time. I noticed a hot-off-the-presses
bulletin on the front page. Might be interesting."

"Sure. No problem." As the van pulled away from
the curb, I fanned out the page and scanned the headlines.
A dark border squared off a short article at the top. "I
found the bulletin."

"Perfect." Gunther gave me a nod. "Let's hear it."

I began reading. "Police report that two musicians
were murdered backstage shortly after their quartet's
performance at Ganz Hall." I concealed a tight swallow.
That's where Kelly and I escaped Gordon just hours ago.
"Their bodies were found in twin coffins surrounded
by broken instruments. A woman who found the bodies
claimed that their eyes had been burned out. Although
police declined to comment about the victims' identities

and possible suspects, bystanders reported that two teenaged — " I stopped and cleared my throat.

"Tired, Nathan?" Kelly set her finger on the article. "Bystanders reported that two teenaged African-American girls left the scene, both wearing straw hats and purple miniskirts."

Gunther whistled into the fresh breeze blowing in through the windows. "African girls in straw hats? They should be easy to find."

Leaning close to Kelly, I whispered, "They didn't call black people that in nineteen-seventy-eight. Lying is going to get us in trouble."

She turned my way, also whispering. "Lying is keeping us in this van. If he thought we did it, he'd dump us at the police station for sure."

"If we told him the whole truth, maybe not."

"The *whole* truth? You gotta be kidding — "

"Is something wrong?" Gunther asked.

"No." Kelly straightened and focused ahead. "Nothing at all."

I folded the paper and set it on my lap. "Actually, Gunther, there is something wrong. We're the two teenagers the witnesses saw, but we're running from the murderer ourselves. We were going to be his next victims, but we escaped on the 'L' and got off at the station up the street. The police would never believe us, so we had to bolt. Now we're just trying to get home as soon as possible."

Gunther turned sharply onto a new road. "I already read the article, so I thought you might be the fugitives."

I tightened my grip on the newspaper. "Are you going to take us to the police?"

"I was, until you came clean. You two don't look like murderers to me. Your sister's a bad liar but not a murderer."

I sneaked a peek at Kelly. She clenched her fingers on her lap, her head low. "All right," she said, "now that I'm busted, do you have any Advil? My head's killing me."

"Advil?" Gunther asked. "What's that?"

"Ibuprofen. It's like aspirin … sort of."

"I have aspirin in the glove box. Help yourself." He pointed at a cup in a holder attached to the dashboard. "There's water, if you don't mind drinking after me."

"I don't mind." Kelly retrieved the bottle, took two aspirin, and washed them down. "Thank you."

"Not a problem. I can stop and get you a Band-Aid for that cut if you want."

"That's all right. I think the bleeding's slowing down."

"Suit yourself." After driving the van up a ramp and merging into traffic on a major highway, Gunther settled back in his seat. "Why don't you tell me your story while we head west?"

As the breeze stiffened and swirled through the van, rattling the newspapers in the back, I explained how I had found my parents dead in the props room at the same performance hall, and how tonight, Kelly and I were searching for clues, trying to figure out how they had died.

Although I left out the strange time shift and the visions in the mirror, every word I spoke was true. Finishing with enough details about our harrowing escape over the rooftops to make the story believable, I finished with a long sigh. "I guess that sounds pretty crazy, huh?"

"Not really. You know what they say. Truth is stranger than fiction." After offering a few sincere words of sympathy, Gunther took over the conversation, chattering on and on about his favorite books, his evening classes at college, his beloved Chicago Bears, and his life in general. Although his night job kept him up until dawn, he caught three short naps a day and subsisted on turkey-and-tomato sandwiches and Hawaiian Punch. And so the monologue continued as the van tunneled into the dark outskirts of the city.

Soon, Kelly's head listed. She leaned on my shoulder, and her breathing deepened to a rhythmic rumble. I tried to keep as motionless as possible. She had mentioned not getting any sleep the night before because of her allergies. Not only that, the crazy chase and her loss of blood gave her every reason to be exhausted. Even Gunther's frequent stops and door-slamming didn't faze her.

After a few hours, I caught myself dozing. The van door awakened me as Gunther battened down the hatches after another delivery. The sun's early-morning rays stretched across the horizon and painted the sky and clouds in a wash of orange and blue.

"We're just past Iowa City," Gunther announced as he slid behind the steering wheel. "I can take you straight to your house if you want."

"Sure." I nudged Kelly. "Can you give Gunther directions?"

"Directions?" She jerked her head up and glanced around, blinking rapidly. "Where are we?"

Gunther pointed at a wrinkled map attached by a rubber band to his sun visor. "Ten miles west of Iowa City."

Kelly yawned and rubbed her eyes. "Do you know where the Walmart is in Newton?"

"Walmart? There's no Walmart in Newton."

"Right." Kelly laughed nervously. "I must have been dreaming."

"I wouldn't mind having one there." Gunther shifted the van into gear. "That would be a great delivery job. I hear Walmart's a good company to work for."

As we pulled back onto the Interstate, Kelly leaned forward and squinted at the map. "Do you know where the exit for Highway fourteen is?"

"Sure do." Using his finger, he traced a line on Interstate 80 from Des Moines to Newton. "About seventy miles. I have a stop there."

"Good." She nodded toward the windshield. "I'll guide you from the exit."

Gunther narrowed his eyes at me. "Why couldn't you give directions?"

"Oh, he'd get us lost," Kelly said. "He knows he's terrible at — " She halted, squirmed for a second, and cleared her throat. "Nathan's not as familiar with the area as I am. He's been traveling overseas a lot, and you know how fast things change around here."

Gunther shrugged. "If you say so."

I focused on the road, not wanting to give Gunther a chance to read my eyes. He was suspicious enough already.

After about an hour of quiet travel, he turned off the main highway. Kelly seemed lost, frequently shifting forward and swinging her head back and forth. Finally, after several miles, she pointed at a street sign. "There it is. Turn right here."

Gunther pulled the van onto a narrow dirt road, narrower than the familiar road to our house. As we passed between cornfields, the van's draft brushed the stalks, shorter and greener than the ones we had seen not long ago.

Kelly extended her finger again. "There. There's our house."

Gunther rolled alongside the huge estate and whistled as he came to a stop. "Nice place. Looks brand new."

"We just moved here. That's why I had a hard time finding it." Kelly set a hand on my shoulder. "Let's get out."

I pushed the door open and jumped to the dirt road, then helped Kelly down. "Thanks," I said, nodding at Gunther. I held up the section of newspaper I had read earlier. "Mind if I keep this?"

"Not a problem." He smiled and winked. "Keep your sister out of trouble."

"I will." I tore off the front page, folded it, and put it in my back pocket. As Kelly and I walked toward the house, Gunther wheeled the van a few feet into the yard, made a U-turn, and drove away.

Kelly plucked a leaf from the cottonwood tree. "Green. And the tree's shorter."

I nodded. "Just like in the picture."

"It's spooky." She bent to the side and looked around the house's corner. "I wonder where the black-haired girl is."

"Let's check." I marched straight toward the door.

"Nathan, wait."

I spun toward her. "What?"

"We need a story." She caught up with me and touched the wound on her scalp. "No one's going to want to talk to a stranger who looks like this, especially so early in the morning."

"Another lie?"

She flashed an angry glare. "Get off your soapbox. It's getting old."

"Maybe, but the truth is always easier." I hopped up to the porch. "If we pretend not to notice our appearance, maybe whoever lives here will go along with it."

She joined me, raising her shoulder to wipe blood from her cheek to her shirt. "That's like pretending there's no elephant in the room when he's sitting on your lap."

"Scratch the elephant on the back and maybe he'll go to sleep." I knocked. "In case I haven't mentioned it, my mother's name is Francesca."

The door swung open, revealing a thirty-something redheaded woman wearing a blue smock. "May I help you?"

A graceful smile decorated her slender face, but her bloodshot eyes gave away an inner weariness, and the cane she leaned on revealed some kind of crippling handicap. Except for the red hair and hazel eyes, she looked a lot like Mom. The resemblance destroyed my confidence. "Uh … I …"

A raven-haired girl stepped into the foyer, clutching a three-quarter-size violin and bow. "Who is it? I heard someone mention an elephant." Wearing blue jeans, a black Iowa T-shirt, and white athletic shoes with purple trim, she stood shoulder height to her mother, maybe four-foot-eight, definitely the girl in the photo.

"I'm Nathan, and this is Kelly, I said, gesturing toward her. "We're kind of lost, so I was hoping I could use your phone."

The woman stifled a yawn. "Maybe when my neighbor gets off. We don't have a private line yet."

Kelly spoke to the girl in a friendly tone. "Are you Francesca?"

A suspicious expression tightened her features. "Yes."

"How old are you?"

"Ten." Her brow furrowed more deeply. "How did you know my name?"

Her mother's brow knitted in the same way. "Yes. How *did* you know?"

Kelly pushed my shoulder. "We found the right place after all." She looked at Francesca's mother. "I know it's kind of early, but we're here from the music school to interview your prodigy. We heard she has the potential to become one of the greatest."

A new smile emerged on her mother's face, proud, but still suspicious. "Well ... she *is* good. At least I think so." She gave us a curious squint. "How did you hear about her?"

"From her teacher, of course." Kelly glanced at me and began snapping her fingers. "What was the name again?"

"Nikolai. Nikolai Malenkov." I extended a hand. "And you must be Mrs. Romano."

She shook it with a firm grip. "Pleased to meet you." As soon as she released my hand, she again covered a yawn. "I'm sorry. I slept terribly. Bad dreams all night."

"It's okay. We're tired, too." I lowered my voice. "Were you worried about something?"

She copied my quieter tone. "Ever since my husband died, I worry about ..." She glanced at Francesca. "Well, about security, you know, being alone way out in the middle of nowhere, and since I have lupus, I can't defend myself. I'm thinking about getting a guard dog."

I gave her a nod. "Not a bad idea."

"What happened to you?" Francesca asked, pointing at Kelly's bloodstained sleeve.

Kelly quickly re-tucked her shirt's hem. "Sorry. It must have come loose on the way."

"I didn't mean that. I meant the blood."

"Where do you normally practice?" Kelly asked. "That would be the best place to do the interview and maybe get some pictures."

"In my room."

"Can you show me?"

"This way." As Francesca led Kelly toward the hall, Kelly looked back, gesturing for me to follow.

When I stepped in that direction, Mrs. Romano grabbed my arm. "Wait. I can't let you go in there without me."

"Sure. I understand."

She began a slow hobble toward the bedroom, her cane leading the way. "I'm not saying you're one of them, but with all the crazy people out there, I can't take any chances with my daughter."

"Of course. I'd be the same way." I placed a hand under her elbow and walked slowly next to her. Who could blame her for being suspicious? Two strangers with matching khakis showing up early in the morning claiming to be from a music school wasn't exactly normal, especially since one of them was bleeding.

With the thumping cane accentuating her words, she looked at me with teary eyes. "You remind me of my dear husband. Whenever my lupus acted up, he would walk at my side. Until leukemia took him away from me. He was such a gentleman." She stopped and patted my hand. "Thank you for raising that lovely memory."

I shook my head. "Don't thank me. Thank my father. He told me I should always treat mothers as treasures. Without them, where would we be?"

As a tear made its way to her cheek, she smiled. "You're a lucky boy to have such a wise father."

"Lucky?" I tried to keep my voice steady, but it wavered. "I *was* lucky, I guess. My father died recently. I'm still ..." A sob tried to break through. I bit my lip to quell it. "Well ... grieving, I suppose."

"Of course you are." Her hand trembled on her cane. After a few seconds of silence, she nodded down the hall. "Go on ahead to Francesca's room. Your friend is probably wondering what happened to you."

I drew back. "Are you sure?"

"I'm sure." She looked at me from head to toe. "Where's your camera?"

I tried to hide a nervous swallow. "Camera?"

"Aren't you going to take pictures?"

I patted my shirt. "I forgot to bring it."

"I have one you can borrow. I'll get it and meet you there. And I'll bring a couple of Band-Aids for Kelly. Poor girl looks like she's been in a knife fight."

As Mrs. Romano shuffled away in the other direction, I strode ahead and turned into my bedroom, at least what had been my bedroom, or would become my bedroom.

I scanned the inside. Instead of a huge mirror on the wall, a bright mural decorated the smooth plaster, a painting of a serpentine musical staff with happy-faced notes climbing on the lines like mischievous spider monkeys. I deciphered the notes — the first measures of "Brahms' Lullaby."

The artwork appeared to be designed for someone younger than Francesca. Maybe it had been there quite a while.

Against the wall opposite the mural, an open trunk sat on the floor, the same trunk that once held Dad's camera and Mom's violin. I stepped closer and looked inside. Sheets of handwritten music covered the bottom, maybe an inch or so thick.

"Where have you been?" Kelly asked.

"Just talking with Mrs. Romano. Sorry to keep you waiting."

"No problem. We've been chatting." Kelly looked at Francesca. "How long have you played violin?"

Francesca's expression was now softer, more relaxed. "Six years."

"Six years?" I repeated. "Do you remember why you started?"

"Why does anybody play?" She stared at me, her eyes filled with mystery. "Are you a musician?"

"Yes." I glanced at Kelly, then returned my gaze to Francesca. "Yes, I am."

Her serious aspect deepened. "Then you know why I play."

"You're right. I do." I looked into her beautiful brown eyes. "Because your spirit has to sing. Every musician's heart bears a song from the creator, and he spends his life trying to duplicate that song as an act of worship. His ultimate dream is to play it flawlessly for an audience of one at the great throne in heaven."

"That's exactly what my teacher says." Francesca raised a pair of fingers. "But there are two songs in your heart, one for God and one for the woman who will be your wife."

I resisted the urge to look at Kelly again. "My wife?"

"My teacher says if a musician marries another musician, they harmonize their songs into one, but when he marries a non-musician, he creates a new song for her and teaches it to her heart."

"I have heard that before from a very wise woman." I reached for her violin. "May I?"

She laid the violin and bow in my hands, her expression solemn. "Only if your spirit teaches me its song." As she released her instrument, she blew on my bow hand. Her breath tickled my skin, sending shivers up my arm. The sensation brought tears to my eyes. This ten-year-old girl, somehow, some way, was truly my mother.

She looked at me with sparkling irises. "My teacher always blows on my fingers. He says music is the breath of God."

My body flushed with warmth. As hot prickles covered my skin, I tried to shake off the emotional surge. I couldn't break down and cry. Not now.

I closed my eyes and raised the violin to my chin, reliving my childhood as I adjusted to the instrument's smaller size. Then, playing long, gentle strokes, I interpreted the mural on the wall and gave life to the lullaby. The violin sang like a nightingale, whispering a melody of comfort, security, even sadness, and my mind repainted the lovely portrait of Mom playing the same hymn as I lay in bed.

Barely opening one eye, I peered at Francesca. She played the part of the captivated child as she gave her own interpretation, swaying on her toes like an enchanted ballerina, every movement capturing the heart of my spirit's song.

"You're very good!"

Mrs. Romano's voice jerked me back to reality. I lowered the bow and nodded. "Thank you."

She leaned her cane against the wall and hobbled in. "I guess you really are music students. I tried to call Nikolai to check you two out, but his secretary said he never returned from his quartet's performance last night."

"Where did he perform?"

"At Ganz Hall in Chicago. Maybe he fell ill and stayed an extra day. He has been rather sickly lately."

I felt my back pocket for the newspaper. Should I tell her about the murders? Could Nikolai have been one of the victims? If only I'd had a chance to get a look at the bodies in the coffins.

She extended her arm. A camera dangled from her hand by a strap. "It's a Nikon F Two. Do you want me to show you how to use it?"

I recognized the camera immediately — Dad's. Could it have been a gift from Mom? I traded glances with Kelly, but her furrowed brow told me she had no more answers than I did.

"It's really not hard," Mrs. Romano continued, pointing at the camera body. "All you do is focus and press the button. The flash is electronic. You have to turn it on first, of course."

"Are you a photographer?" Kelly asked.

"Not really. It was my husband's hobby before he died." She gestured for us to gather together. "Squeeze in, and I'll take one of the three of you."

Keeping the violin and bow pinned under my arm, I stood next to Kelly and behind Francesca. When Mrs. Romano turned on the flash unit and raised the camera to her eye, the sound of wood on wood banged from the house's main entry.

I jerked my head toward the noise. "What was that?"

"The front door," Mrs. Romano said as her finger reached for the shutter button. "Happens a lot when it's windy. Must be a storm coming."

"I hear footsteps," Kelly whispered.

I clutched her hand. "We'd better — "

The camera flashed, bright and blinding, far brighter than any normal camera. Kelly squeezed my fingers. "What's that?"

A dark human-shaped shadow appeared at the bedroom doorway. A new flash exploded from its hand,

and a loud popping noise echoed all around. Mrs. Romano twisted and bent, her body warping like a reflection in a circus mirror. The entire room contorted into a kaleidoscope of colorful swirls.

Seconds later, the swirls spread out and repainted the room with new details — the wall mirror, my desk and poster bed, and the sprawled bodies of our dead twins. As each detail crystallized, the bands of color thinned out and swept over the two corpses. The bodies pixelated until the multihued dots blended into the flow. The swirls orbited the room twice and plunged into the mirror where they created a splash of color that spread across the surface and slowly faded.

When the movement settled, I rocked on my feet, dizzied by the chaos. Setting a hand on the wall to keep my balance, I felt a glassy surface — the mirror. I glanced down at my body, still clothed in khaki, and Francesca's violin still tucked under my arm.

Kelly clutched the front of her safari shirt. "We're back."

"What happened to my room?" Francesca asked. "It's so different."

Kelly set her hand at the side of her mouth and called, "Daddy!"

"Clara!" I shouted.

Francesca joined in. "Mom!"

Tony stormed into the room, his eyes bulging. "Kelly! Nathan! But you were — " He staggered backwards. "I mean, I saw you — "

Clara careened around the doorway. She stopped and stared. "You were dead! Your eyes were burned out!"

"Yeah, it looked pretty bad didn't it?" I spread out my arms. "But we're alive."

She rushed forward and embraced me. "Thank God!"

I returned her embrace, then pulled back and gestured toward Francesca. "This is Francesca Romano."

"Romano?" Tony said. "My father bought this house from the Romano estate when the old lady got plugged by a burglar back in — "

"Daddy!" Kelly barked. "Hush!"

Clara bowed her head toward Francesca. "I'm pleased to meet you, young lady."

"I'm pleased to meet you as well." Francesca's eyes misted. "But I need to find my mother. Do you know where she is?"

"No, I don't." Clara looked at me. "Do you?"

I let out a sigh. "I guess I'd better start from the beginning and tell you everything."

Kelly shuffled close to me and whispered, "Do you really want to tell my dad the truth?"

"I have to. He's already seen too much."

I pulled out the desk chair for Kelly and gestured toward the bed for the others. "Have a seat. This could take a while."

CHAPTER THIRTEEN

"SO," I CONCLUDED as I paced in front of the mirror, "we don't know what happened to Mrs. Romano. We don't know how we got into that alternate universe or how we got back. We don't know how several hours could pass there and only a few minutes here, and we don't know how we took over the clothes of the other Nathan and Kelly or where they went, but Francesca is proof that it all really happened."

I glanced at her as she sat on the bed next to Clara. Although she kept a stiff upper lip, as the saying goes, deep lines in her forehead gave evidence that she was worried about her mother.

Tony stared at me with his mouth partially open. He hadn't spoken a word since I began my story.

Seated in the desk chair, Kelly twisted a rubber band between her finger and thumb. "We don't even know the whole point of it all. Why did that stage appear in the mirror in the first place? And who could've been in the coffins? We think they were two musicians, but which ones? And who is the girl in red who keeps showing up?"

Clara drummed her fingers on the bed. "All this alternate universe talk makes me dizzy, but if you and

Kelly had dead bodies in this world, and you're still alive, maybe there's hope for your parents."

"You mean maybe they switched places like we did?" I shook my head. "It's too weird to hope for. And I wouldn't know how to begin looking for them."

Francesca slid off the bed. "Can you use the mirror again?" she asked as she walked toward her reflection.

"What do you mean?" I asked.

She touched the surface with her finger, creating the image of two Francescas making friendly contact. "Does it just show places in your mind, like in your dream, or does it come up with the places by itself?"

"I'm not sure. At first I thought everything came from my head, but I couldn't have dreamed about the broken violins without someone putting the thoughts in my mind."

She looked at me with Mom's familiar eyes. "Maybe just remember what you did before and try to do it again."

"Easier said than done, but I'll try." I imagined the coffins on the stage again and replayed the other Nathan's words. *I crossed the same way as before. I had a dream, it showed up in the mirror, then music, a flash of light, and zap, I'm here.* That had to be a clue, a big clue.

I scanned the four sets of eyes staring at me. "Hang on. I'm thinking."

"I know," Kelly said with a smirk. "I feel the heat rising."

I gave her a wink and returned my gaze to the mirror. Music and light were the keys. Whenever something weird happened in the reflection, music played and light flashed. But would it work every time? If so, how could I figure out where the next passage would lead?

I glanced at Francesca again. Still staring at herself in the mirror, she seemed mesmerized. Her eyes sparkled with light as she murmured, "Something's happening."

The image in the glass wrinkled, changing the surface to a jigsaw pattern. As it smoothed over again, the room in the reflection altered, and Francesca's reflection broke away. She withdrew a sheet of paper from the trunk and set it on a music stand, her back to us.

Lifting her violin and bow, she concentrated on the sheet and played. After a few strokes, she picked up a pencil from the stand and made a mark on the handwritten score. She then lifted her bow again and played on.

"That's me in the mirror," Francesca said, pointing. "I'm playing my birdsong piece."

"Birdsong piece?" I squinted at the music, but it was too far away to read. "Can you hear it?"

She nodded. "Can't you?"

"I can watch your fingers and imagine it, but I can't hear anything."

Tony rose to his feet. "So that crazy museum guy was right after all. This mirror shows your thoughts."

"Did you just think about your room, Francesca?" I asked.

"Yes." She picked up her own violin. "I was thinking about going home."

I glanced from one Francesca to the other. Was the mirror now reflecting her thoughts? Maybe there was a way to take her home and check on her mother's safety. "Can you play the same piece?"

"I don't have it memorized," she said as she raised her bow, "so I'll be a step behind." While watching her twin in the mirror, she played a series of short high notes, making her violin chirp like a songbird. The melody filled the room with the bright sounds of an early spring morning.

I walked to the lamp on my desk, ready to make the bulb flash, but the music stopped. I swung back to Francesca. "What happened?"

She touched the mirror with a finger. "I heard a door slam and a loud popping sound. Then I hid under my bed, like I was scared of something. But then it all disappeared."

I looked at the mirror. Once again it had reverted to a reflection of my room and everyone in it. In the reflection, Tony, seated on the bed, propped his foot against the trunk ... the open trunk. "Well, if you ask me, I think — "

"Freeze!" I raised a hand. "Don't move a muscle!"

"Why?" Tony asked. "What's going on?"

I stepped slowly backwards, keeping my stare fixed on the mirror. "Everyone just watch me in the reflection."

I backed to the trunk until my heels tapped the wood. Tony swung his head away from the mirror and toward the trunk. "Don't look," I ordered. "It might not stay open if you do."

"But it's not open," he said. "How can it stay open?"

Kelly growled, her gaze locked on the mirror. "Just do what he says, Daddy."

"Okay. Okay." Tony crossed his arms and stared at the reflection. "Satisfied?"

"Perfect." I reached back, bent my knees, and lowered my hands into the trunk. If the sheets of music were still there, they would be flat at the bottom. I would have to stretch farther to get them.

"Hey!" Tony pointed at the mirror. "It's open!"

Clara laid a palm on Tony's cheek. "Don't turn. Stay focused."

Nearly squatting, I sensed paper at my fingertips. I gathered the sheets and straightened. "Okay. It's safe to look."

When everyone turned toward me, Tony touched the top of the trunk, then swiveled back to the mirror. The trunk in the reflection was now closed. "How'd you do that?"

"I wish I knew." I leafed through the handwritten music compositions until I found a fairly complex piece several pages down. I mentally played the notes through the first few measures. "This is really cool, Francesca," I said as I turned the page toward her. "Did you write this?"

She pushed aside her dark locks, revealing flushed cheeks. "I wrote all of them, but I never showed them to anyone who knew how to read music."

"Let's see if your music changes the mirror." I handed the sheets to Francesca, walked to my closet, and retrieved Mom's violin.

"An impromptu concert?" Clara asked.

"Sort of." I set bow to string and smiled at Francesca. "Mind if I play one of your pieces?"

"Which one?"

"Choose your favorite."

She paged through her collection, pulled out a sheet, and held it where I could see it. "Can you read it? It's pretty messy."

I leaned closer to the page. "Not too messy." As I played, I glanced between the music and the mirror, watching for a change, but nothing obvious showed up. The melody, though simple at the beginning, grew in complexity, calling for difficult fingering.

Clara strolled toward the mirror and crossed her arms as she gazed at the room's reflection. "Everything's normal so far. The trunk's still closed."

I focused on the music. When I neared the end of the page, Francesca held up another, waiting for me to begin playing it before lowering the first sheet. "This is the end," she said. "I'm still working on it."

Following the scribbled notes, I increased the volume from *piano* to *forte* and shifted through a series of arpeggios. As I stroked the strings, I tried to concentrate on the notes and, at the same time, on thoughts of Mom and Dad. Were they still alive? If so, where were they?

The lamp in the mirror dimmed. The walls darkened. The music was doing its part. Now it was time to get a flash of light ready.

I used a foot to point at a desk drawer. Sight reading new, handwritten music was hard enough. Trying to talk at the same time was almost impossible. "Get the camera," I grunted.

Clara rushed to the desk, pulled out the camera, and draped the strap around her neck. "What should I take a picture of?"

"Wait." As the music reached a crescendo near the end of the page, the reflection undulated like ripples on a pond. The bedroom faded to black. New dark images formed deep within — ghostly shadows in a haze.

In the mirror, a ray of light from somewhere to the side cast a glow over the scene, bringing clarity to the dim room. A spacious chamber materialized. The outer walls curved around a circular floor. Two people skulked across polished tiles toward the source of light, a lamp on a desk in the far background.

They passed a shadowed object at the center of the circle, something that looked like a bulky cylinder on a pedestal aimed at an angle toward the ceiling.

I returned to the beginning of the page and replayed the measures, reaching for all the passion I could muster. It was working. The scene matched one of the photos from Dad's camera.

The two forms wore long trench coats with pulled-up collars as they walked away from the front of the mirror. The more curvaceous shape of the smaller person revealed her gender as she carried a violin case in hand. Near the top edge, copies of their hunched forms reflected their moves, but the copies walked upside-down, as if projected on the ceiling like an inverted movie.

When they reached the desk, they each took a seat in rolling swivel chairs. When they turned toward each other, their profiles came into view.

Clara raised a hand to her mouth. "Your parents."

I pulled the bow across the D string to play the final note and nodded at her. "Turn on the flash and take a shot of the mirror. Let's see if we can go there. But hang tight to the camera. The last time I did this, I got a jolt."

"Will do." After flipping the switch on the flash unit, Clara sidestepped to the center of the room and focused the camera. When the ready light came on, she pressed the shutter button. The camera flashed. The mirror reflected the light and shot back a radiant bolt that sizzled into the flash attachment, ripping the camera from Clara's hands. It fell to her chest and bounced at the end of the strap.

The mirror's image seemed to zoom in on Mom and Dad, sharply clarifying as it filled the glass with the upper half of their bodies. At the desk, Dad pecked at a laptop keyboard while Mom looked on.

I tucked the violin under my arm and set a hand on the mirror. It remained hard, impenetrable. As I caressed the surface near Mom's cheek, she turned toward me and sighed. "I'll try again, but it seems hopeless. I just don't have enough power."

Dad made a final tap on the keyboard and swiveled toward her. "We have to keep trying. No one else can stop Interfinity from coming."

"But if Nathan figures out how to use the Quattro camera and my violin, we might be able to do it together."

"It's too late for that. We have to push forward." Dad stood and reached for her hand. "The scope is in position. Give it all you've got. This could be our last chance."

As a frenzied mix of sounds began to play from somewhere in the background, she took his hand and rose from her chair, still clutching the violin case. Hand in hand they walked to the middle of the chamber. The mirror's eye followed them, panning back as if controlled by a cameraman.

When they stopped near the center of the circle, Mom withdrew the violin from its case and set it under her chin. As she placed the bow over the strings, she looked up. Her pupils danced with chaotic colors that intermeshed with her brown irises, and a gentle smile graced her lips as if a long-loved memory had found its way home.

Then, with a sudden burst of strokes, she played a series of high eighth notes that seemed void of melody, but, with her gaze still trained on something above, she soon brought the musical chaos into order, creating a glorious rendition of her birdsong piece, much fuller and more vibrant than her younger self had so recently played.

After several seconds, the colors in her eyes dispersed, and the black pigment in her pupils transformed into brilliant white. The whiteness expanded and flowed from her eyes, like twin lasers shooting into the twilight. As she played on, the lasers strengthened, becoming so bright they bathed her skin in a ghostly pallor.

Dad circled behind her. "Do you see it, Francesca?"

Nodding and breathing heavily, she increased to fortissimo, sending the loudest, most lovely notes yet into the upper reaches of the chamber. A bow hair broke away and flew wildly. Her fingers blurred, and her eyes blazed like the sun.

As a loud cracking sound blended into the musical flow, my fingers began to sink into the image. The glass felt like cool jelly, becoming thinner every second.

Dad's voice again rose above the din. "Keep it up, Francesca. You can do it."

I pushed through the mirror up to my shoulder. "I'm going in," I said, extending the violin toward Kelly. But just as she took it, Mom heaved a groan and crumpled to the floor. With a loud pop, her eyes flashed a ring of sizzling fire in all directions. The ring crashed against the mirror, sending me flying back into a pair of strong arms.

Tony lifted me upright. "You okay?"

"I'm fine." I shook the mental cobwebs away and leaped to the mirror. I laid a hand on the surface, now rigid again. "I was so close."

In the reflection, Dad sat on the floor cradling Mom. "What did you see?"

With her eyes still emanating a faint glow, she replied in a dreamlike whisper. "I stood at the edge of a chasm and gazed down into an endless void. A shimmering golden rope was fastened around a rocky projection at my feet. As taut as the strings on my violin, the rope seemed to span the celestial wound, but I couldn't be sure since it disappeared in the darkness."

"Anything else?"

She nodded. "I plucked the rope. It produced a perfect tone, an E, loud and lovely, and shook the ground, so much that I could no longer stand. As I lowered myself to sit, I noticed three other golden ropes. When the shaking ceased, I plucked the others and found that they were the A, D, and G strings. I tried to play the song by running as quickly as I could between the strings, but after only two measures, I became too weary to keep the timing." She blew out a long breath and shook her head. "I don't think I can try again, not without Nathan to help me."

Dad added his own sigh. "Then I guess there's no way we can do it."

She shifted in his arms and gazed at him hopefully. "He'll find the email —"

"It won't be enough. I thought he'd come with us, so I didn't put much information in it. It would be a miracle if he figured it out."

"There's still the girl, the interpreter." Mom turned her gaze back to the ceiling. "And there's always his supplicant. A Sancta can be mysterious and elusive, but she might be willing to help."

Dad tilted his head upward. "And Patar might show up."

"But would he help or hinder?" Mom asked.

"We'd be better off shoving that vision stalker and his brother back through the hole they came from and plugging it with a cosmic cork. Patar might help, but he's likely to scare Nathan away."

She took his chin in her hand and turned his head, setting his eyes directly in front of hers. "Our son will not be frightened. He will choose wisely. He has the same warrior spirit you have."

Dad's expression turned grim. "If Nathan starts punching through space-time walls, Mictar will get wind of it and follow the trail. Even a portal view might expose our whereabouts."

I pulled back from the mirror. A portal view?

Mom swiveled her head to the side and whispered, "I hear footsteps."

Dad lifted her to her feet. "Let's go." The scene darkened, then slowly illuminated again, growing brighter and brighter as the objects in the bedroom reappeared.

I slapped the mirror. "No! Don't go away!"

Kelly rose and extended the violin. "Can you try again?"

"I wouldn't if I were you," Clara said. "You heard Solomon. It sounds like all this hopping from world to world and poking around the cosmos and whatnot is putting them in danger."

Tony crossed his arms over his chest. "It sounds like he might already be in danger, like someone was coming."

"I heard." I backed away and flopped into the desk chair. What else could I do? Without another clue to go on, every option seemed like it ended at a brick wall. But at least now there was hope. At least Mom and Dad were alive, though the vision didn't explain the presence of their corpses.

I glanced at the digital clock on the desk. Still before noon. About twelve hours in that other world equaled less than an hour here. I looked at Kelly. "You got any ideas about what's going on?"

"Crazy ideas." She smoothed out her safari shirt. "With the whole clothes-swapping thing and clones of us getting murdered, maybe we really did travel through time."

I shook my head. "I don't think so. We made too many changes in the past without affecting the present. I mean, we have my ten-year-old mother in my bedroom. If she stays with us, then I couldn't have been born. Time travel doesn't make sense."

"Neither does jumping into another world with someone else's clothes on," Kelly said.

"I can't argue with that."

"What about their mention of a supplicant?" Clara asked. "And a Sancta?"

"I think they're the same person, and Mom said *she*, so I'm wondering if she's the girl in red."

"And this Patar fellow who might scare you?"

"No clue except that the name reminds me of Mictar." I got up, took the violin from Kelly, and put it away. "It looks like our only plan is to find the email Dad mentioned."

"But was that your father?" Kelly asked as she reseated herself at the desk. "There was more than one Nathan. Maybe that was the other Nathan's father. Maybe the other Nathan is the one they were talking about."

"There's a way to find out for sure. If the email my father talked about is here on Earth Red, then only Solomon Red could have put it there. If we find it, then the couple we just saw are my real parents."

"Not necessarily. Maybe both fathers did the same thing. Hid a message for their son in an email, I mean."

I nodded. "I suppose that's possible."

"Is there anything else we might have missed?" Clara asked. "A puzzle piece we might have overlooked?"

"Here's one piece." I pulled the newspaper from my back pocket and showed the article to Clara. "Do you know anything about this murder back in nineteen-seventy-eight?"

Clara's eyes darted as she read the page. "No. Nothing like this ever happened."

"How can you be sure?"

She touched the page. "I attended this concert. Your mother's teacher, Dr. Malenkov, and his wife were the violinists in one of the quartets, so I remember it well. Since my late husband was a percussionist, I was quite involved in the orchestra social circle. Eventually that's how I first met your mother, when she joined the CSO as its concertmaster at the age of twenty-one."

I creased the newspaper, laid it on the bed, and searched the article for more information. Since Dr. Malenkov never returned from the concert, maybe he really *was* one of the victims. Could he and his wife have been replacements for the pieces of Rosetta in my dream?

"Maybe." I shifted to the desk and touched Kelly's shoulder. "I have to search all the emails. Probably a job for Clara and me."

"Sure." Kelly rose from the chair. "It's lunch time. You and Clara can be the bloodhounds while the rest of us get some grub for everyone." She looked at her father. "Right, Daddy?"

"Right." Tony tore his stare away from the mirror. "We have a lot of tuna-banana salad left over and buffalo wings marinated in vinegar and mayonnaise."

Kelly reached for her father's hand and Francesca's. "C'mon. We're going on a safari hunt in the freezer."

As the trio walked down the hall, Tony's voice echoed, "I think we have some eels still frozen from the fishing trip. What do you think? Serve the eels with some of my special rattlesnake sauce?"

"No! Don't you dare!"

CHAPTER FOURTEEN

AFTER BRINGING IN a chair from another bedroom, I sat with Clara at the desk and scanned the contents of Dad's email inbox. A message from Dr. Malenkov focused on his visit to Chicago, expressing his concern about attending the shareholders' meeting given that he had no dealings with the company. Since he hadn't seen Francesca in so long, he just wanted to hear her play. Another email from him asked if her favorite flowers were still white roses. No hidden messages were obvious in Dad's responses.

Clara pointed at an icon on the screen. "It looks like there's something in the draft folder."

I clicked on it. "One message. It's addressed to Dr. Malenkov. Never sent."

We both leaned close and read it silently.

Nathan, in case you happen to find this, read carefully. I can't risk explaining everything. The mirrors lead to alternate worlds that are shifted from each other time-wise. Dr. Simon maintains a steady state for now, but danger of a rift is spiking. We must find a hole in the cosmic fabric and seal it, or Interfinity will result. We will need your help to produce the musical key. Tell no one that we have discovered how to heal the wounds.

-

My heart thumped. We had found the email, locked away in the draft folder where it couldn't be intercepted during transmission. The message didn't prove that my real parents were still alive, but it boosted my hopes.

"Very interesting," Clara said. "We have alternate realities that are out of phase with each other time-wise."

"So we didn't travel through time. We went to another world."

"Okay, but how do you explain the presence of your dead bodies here in our world?"

"Maybe everyone has an exact copy existing in the other world. Our copies died over there and somehow got transported over here." I looked at the mirror and sighed. "It's weird. I haven't even thought of them as real people. I only saw them in the mirror, like it was a movie or something."

"They were real," Clara said. "I felt for pulses in their lifeless wrists. I mopped their hair back from their ashen faces and stared at the scorched pits where their eyes used to be."

As I imagined my own eyes getting incinerated as well as Kelly's, nausea churned. I hung my head and whispered, "Yeah. This is all getting way too real."

"And how did this happen?" She tugged on the sleeve of my safari shirt. "These aren't your clothes. Or, then again, maybe they *are* yours. Maybe you're really the Nathan from the other world."

"That's impossible." I nodded toward my reflection. "I remember being here before I went over there. And I never saw this shirt before this morning."

"Fair enough. You're the Nathan I know. But there are still mysteries aplenty. First, and I think of this one because I am directly involved, there must be a copy of me in that other world."

"Most likely. What about it?"

"That Clara probably played the same role I did for you. She was the other Nathan's tutor."

"Okay. Where are you going with this?"

"Think about it. How could that other Nathan get together with the other Kelly unless ..." She gestured with her head as if waiting for me to fill in a blank.

I whispered, "Unless his parents were dead."

"Or he and the other Clara *thought* they were dead, just as we were thinking your parents are dead. It's the only reason that Clara would take that Nathan to the Iowa safe house."

"But who's right? About which parents are dead, I mean?"

Clara's expression turned grim. "Maybe both. The set of parents we saw might be from yet another world."

"That seems unlikely."

"Why unlikely? Has anything that's happened lately seemed *likely* to you? Think about what you saw. How did the light appear in your mother's eyes? Have you ever seen that happen to her in our world? And what was that dark chamber she was in? With all the reflections and colors, it looked almost like another house of mirrors. And that story about playing the violin strings? What was that all about?"

I heaved a sigh. "Thanks for killing my hopes."

"Your hopes aren't dead. They're just on life support. We have the email now. It's a good start."

"True." I picked up a pencil and tapped it on my knee. "Okay, let's get back to the clues. Dad wrote that

Dr. Simon maintains a steady state. Any idea what that means?"

"Maybe. Here's how I would piece the puzzle together." She set a finger on the screen. "The part about sealing the hole makes me think someone figured out a way to open passages between the worlds. Somehow this hole threatens to bring about some kind of catastrophic state called Interfinity, and Dr. Simon is keeping that from happening as long as he can."

"But he killed them. Why would Dad think Simon was on his side?"

"Your guess is as good as mine."

"And now Simon's dead, so Interfinity is probably on its way." I kept my eyes on the message, reading it again absentmindedly. "Didn't you say Dad had an assignment for a company called Interfinity?"

"Yes. And that reminds me. With all the excitement, I forgot to tell you that the police called this morning. They found your parents' bodies, so I have to go to Chicago early tomorrow morning to finalize the funeral arrangements. I'll pay Interfinity a visit after everything's settled."

As the image of their dead bodies blazed once more, I sank in my seat. My hopes plunged to new lows. The police in our world had a pair of bodies. Either they were my parents or they were from another world. The latter option seemed too ridiculous to be true.

I glanced at the suitcase on the floor of my closet, still not fully unpacked. "What time do we leave?"

"We?" She patted my knee. "You have to stay here."

"What? Why?"

She rose and stretched, speaking through an extended yawn. "You have to register for school on Monday."

"Can't school wait till we get back?"

"Not a chance. We set up your secret identity and filed your transcript, and I already informed them you'll be out on Tuesday for family matters. When you and Kelly come to Chicago for the funeral, we'll talk about what I find at Interfinity. Since your father says it's dangerous for you to be peeking through cosmic peepholes, you might as well stay here."

I let my shoulders droop. "Is Kelly's father coming to the funeral?"

"I asked him to, but he says he has to stay here. Kelly will have to drive."

"Why? I have my license."

"Because it's their car." She planted a finger on my chest. "And you'd better get used to the idea. Tony rides his motorcycle to his morning shift at a machine shop, then to the school for coaching in the afternoon. That means Kelly will be driving every day."

I sank another inch in the chair. "I guess I can deal with that."

"Of course you can. Kelly's a sweetheart. She even volunteered to help you through the registration process, and she'll probably want to introduce you to her friends."

I tightened my grip on the pencil but said nothing. Was the prospect of meeting Kelly's friends supposed to cheer me up? Still, if they were as cool as she was, meeting them might not be so bad.

The clatter of a metal pan rang from the hallway. "That reminds me," I said. "What are we going to do with Francesca?"

"What choice do we have? I should take her with me. She can't stay here by herself, and we can't very well send her home."

"Right. With Gordon and Mictar stalking her, it won't be safe for her here or there." I replayed our escape from Francesca's house. It looked like the burglar killed her mother in that world just like in my own world years ago. Apparently Gordon and Mictar had planned to kill this other-world Francesca and make sure the burglar got the blame. That meant I had at least done something right. Even though I had altered the events in Francesca's world, I had saved her life.

Clara clasped her hands. "So it's settled. I'll take Francesca with me to Chicago. She's not dressed for cool weather, but we can make a quick stop and buy something suitable."

I rose from the chair. "Thanks for taking good care of my mother."

"Oh, I'll take care of her. I'm going to warn her about the crazy son she might have some day." She gave me a sly wink and turned toward the bedroom door. "Let's go and see what Kelly came up with for lunch."

"Wait." I picked up a screwdriver from the top of the bookshelves and took it to the mirror. Kneeling at the bottom left corner, I inserted the blade behind the square I had placed in the matrix.

Clara walked closer. "What are you doing?"

"This is the piece Dad gave me. I put it here, and it wouldn't come loose. If I'm supposed to look in the mirror whenever I get into trouble, I want to take it to school with me."

"Good idea."

I pried the square from the wall and grabbed it. "Done."

A burst of light flashed from the mirror, making a hollow popping sound. Like a splash in a pond, ripples of radiance emanated from the center, fading as they approached the edges. After a few seconds, the light disappeared.

"Well," Clara said, setting her hands on her hips, "I think the big mirror's back to normal."

I balanced the extricated piece on my palm, eyeing it as I turned it slowly. "I feel like I'm holding another world in my hand, like billions of people are in there who have no idea that someone's got them all teetering in his grasp."

She shook her head. "That's too deep for me to think about, especially on an empty stomach."

"Then let's get some grub." Tucking the mirror under my arm, I climbed to my feet and headed for the hall. "But I hope eel pie isn't on the menu."

CHAPTER FIFTEEN

SITTING IN THE front passenger's seat of Kelly's
Toyota Camry, I stared at my watch. It was already five
minutes later than she said we needed to leave for school.
Being new was going to be hard enough. Getting there late
would make it worse.

I lowered the sun visor and looked at my eyes in
the mirror. Yep. Red streaks. Nightmares again last night.
This time about me driving Kelly's car in a crazy highway
chase. No wonder I was so sleepless, knowing Mom and
Dad were in trouble and I couldn't do a thing to help them.
And worse, I had to go to school when I should have gone
with Clara to Chicago to investigate Interfinity and learn
more about the strange mirror.

I unzipped a red backpack sitting on the floorboard
between my feet. Inside, the Quattro mirror lay wrapped
in a Gatorade towel and a sweater, safe and sound.
Without any books for padding, I'd have to be careful to
keep it from knocking against anything.

Although it was somewhat muggy this morning,
the radio had mentioned the possibility of a cold front
coming through, maybe before school let out in the
afternoon. Apparently the weather was going crazy. The
temperature was supposed to drop below freezing tonight.

I opened the backpack's external pocket and checked for my phone and debit card. Everything was exactly where it was supposed to be. Now if only we could get going.

The door slammed. With keys in hand, Kelly scooted toward the car. The legs of her loose-fitting beige slacks swiped together as she hustled. After opening the car door, she brushed her short-sleeved navy polo shirt, smoothing out a wrinkle where it overlapped her waistband.

She slid behind the wheel and pressed a button on the car's visor, triggering the automatic door opener. As the door rumbled upward, she thrust a key into the ignition and cranked the engine. "Good," she said, patting the dashboard. "Lando's behaving today."

"Lando?"

"A friend of mine gave the car that name, and it stuck." As she pressed the gas pedal, the engine revved, then idled at a slow, rattling hum. "Sorry I took so long. I couldn't decide what to wear."

I gave her another quick scan. Her hair, pinned back neatly with a pair of silvery barrettes, provided a full view of her face. "You look fine."

As she zoomed out of the garage and down the driveway, she smiled. "You think so?"

"Yeah. Kind of dressy. And modest." I bit my tongue and faced the front. "Sorry. That's crossing the line."

When the car straightened on the road, Kelly stepped on the gas. Her smile vanished. "Why? You don't think you can talk to me about modesty?"

As warmth flooded my cheeks, I fingered my backpack zipper and slid closer to the door. "No. I mean, yes I can talk about it. I just thought it might be ... I don't know. Sensitive?"

She turned onto the main highway and accelerated again, her lips thin and taut. After a few seconds of silence, she spoke barely above a whisper. "You're right. It's sensitive."

I pulled the zipper back and forth along its track. "Are your friends going to notice a change?"

"Most likely." She glanced at me for a half second before refocusing on the road. "No offense, Nathan, but I'm not looking forward to this at all."

"Are you worried about what I'll think of your friends?"

She breathed a nervous chuckle. "Not exactly."

I checked my own clothes. I didn't have many options, only what Clara had bought after our luggage went for a swim in the river, but no one would think jeans and a black polo shirt were too geeky, would they? "This isn't going to be easy for me, either."

She kept her stare on the road. "Why is that?"

"I've never been to a real school before. I'm sure to do something that'll make me look like an idiot."

"You'll be fine." Kelly withdrew a phone from her pocket and glanced back and forth between the road and the screen as she manipulated it with her thumb. "Just relax and be yourself."

She slid the phone back to her pocket and flipped on the radio. The wail of an electric guitar screamed from the speakers, scratching out note after note in a cacophonous frenzy. She changed the station and scanned through the frequencies. "You like classical, right?"

"Sure. Classical, baroque, romantic. It's all good."

"The classical station isn't one of my presets, but I'll find it."

"No worries. I like almost anything with a melody."

"Okay." She punched a button. "Country music usually has a melody."

"That'll do." I closed my eyes, leaned against the window, and lost myself in the wash of warbling steel guitar riffs and lamenting lyrics about a cheating wife. Every few seconds, I partially opened one eye and sneaked a look at Kelly. With her stare trained on the road and both hands firmly gripping the wheel, she displayed the perfect portrait of a careful driver. Yet, with her knuckles turning white, something more had to be going on. I let my gaze wander up to her face where a tear began to trickle toward her cheek.

She punched the radio power button and swiped at the tear. "Did you hear something strange?"

"You mean besides the singing?"

"It's kind of a moaning sound. Sort of muffled. It didn't come from the speakers."

"Nope. Nothing like that." I reached into the backseat and pulled my violin case into my lap. "Could this be talking again?"

She angled her head. "I don't hear it now."

I flipped up the case's latch but left the lid closed as I caressed the cool black surface.

"Whose violin is that?" Kelly asked. "Yours, Francesca's, or your mother's?"

"Francesca took hers to Chicago. I wanted to make a good impression with the orchestra, so I brought my mother's."

"The way you play?" She rolled her eyes. "I don't think you have anything to worry about. They'll think you're the second coming of Mozart."

"I didn't want to take any chances."

She pointed forward. "School's right around this corner."

As she turned onto an oak-lined road, the building came into view, a modern, two-story brick structure, L-shaped with a tall flagpole just outside the crook of the elbow. In front of the pole, a long white banner extended from one yard stake to another, red block letters spelling out *Cardinals*.

I leaned forward. "It's bigger than I thought."

"Not huge. About a thousand kids." With the parking lot nearly full, she rolled into a space in the back row. "Let's get moving. First period's in five minutes, and we have to get you registered."

Pulling along my backpack and violin, I ducked out of the car. Kelly had already charged ahead. I balanced my load and followed her, trying not to look like a doting puppy trotting in her wake.

As I passed between two parked cars, a driver flung open his door. With a deft twist, I lifted my load high and squeezed through the narrow gap, then accelerated again while glancing back. The driver, wearing a dark blazer, got out of his Lincoln Town Car and crossed his arms, watching me run. Although I had swept past the man in a hurry, I saw enough of his face to give me the feeling that we had met before.

Now jogging more slowly, Kelly made a wide circle around a clique of girls and breezed past the flagpole before waiting at the main entrance's double doors. With a brisk wind kicking up, the pole's ropes snapped against the metal, tapping out a rhythmic jangle.

I raced across the expanse and joined her as she held one of the doors open. I brushed past, pulled open the closest of a second set of doors, and propped it with a knee while Kelly entered.

After striding to the middle of a circular lobby, she paused and pointed at a hole in the ceiling where a circle opened to the second floor. "We call this area the rotunda." From the floor above, two girls leaned against a railing and looked down at us with blank stares.

"Let's go." She led me toward the adjacent office.

A girl wearing jeans and a red T-shirt emblazoned with a logo that was probably fashionable bustled through the office doorway. "Hey, Kelly girl," she said. "You're looking …" Her gaze drifted up and down Kelly's body for a moment. Then, flashing a nervous smile, she continued. "Prim today."

"Thanks." Kelly pinched the girl's cheek. "And you look positively conformist."

As the girl walked away, she looked back and aimed a finger at Kelly. "I'll get you for that, my pretty." With a wide grin, she added, "And your little dog, too."

I pointed at myself. "Am I supposed to be your little dog?"

"Oh, don't mind Daryl," Kelly said with a wave of her hand. "That's a *Wizard of Oz* quote. She's a computer genius and a movie geek."

As Daryl jogged down the hall, her long red hair flapped against her back. Her height, build, and facial structure matched Kelly's. If not for her hair and freckles, she could be Kelly's clone.

"Is she your friend?" I asked.

"My best friend. Why?"

"Just wondering. You said her name's Daryl, right?"

Kelly nodded. "Daryl Lin Markey. I've known her since third grade."

"Third grade," I whispered as I closed the door to the hallway. It was kind of cool to see best friends poking fun at each other like that.

Inside the office anteroom, two women stood behind a counter looking at a clipboard together. When we drew near, one of them stepped up to the counter. "May I help you?"

Kelly smiled. "Good morning, Mrs. Washington. I brought the new student my dad told you about."

The silver-haired lady pushed her half-lens glasses down her nose and peered over them. "Kyle Simmons. Correct?"

"Uh-huh. He's staying with us for a while."

I set my pack and case down and extended a hand over the counter. "I'm pleased to meet you, Mrs. Washington."

After shaking hands, Mrs. Washington searched through a stack of file folders on her workspace. "Daryl had your paperwork out on Friday. I'll have to find it."

A new voice breezed in from the side. "He's good looking and polite, Kelly. Nice catch." A tall, shapely girl sashayed along the office's inner hallway. She propped three books against her waist, her fingers interlaced underneath. "Or should I say, *nice rebound?*"

Kelly spoke in a condescending tone. "Better stick to makeup and hairspray, Brittany. Basketball terms are a bit out of your league."

I looked at the two girls. Obviously this wasn't playful banter, and Brittany was about as genuine as press-on nails. But what could I do? This was their territory, not mine.

Apparently unfazed, Brittany strutted closer in her low-neck ribbed tunic. "Kelly and Kyle has a nice ring to it." She winked. "I guess living together gives you … well … opportunities."

Kelly arched her brow at the taller girl and spoke in an innocent tone. "I'm sure I have no idea what you're talking about."

Brittany let out a mock gasp. "You don't? That's not what Steven told me."

Speaking through clenched teeth, Kelly sharpened her voice. "No. I don't."

Brittany touched a bejeweled heart pendant dangling from a necklace. "Well, I must say that I'm surprised. From what I understand, your mother took a few *opportunities* while your father was at away games. You could have learned a lot from her."

Her cheeks ablaze, Kelly raised a tight fist. "Listen, Brittany, you might be taller than me, but I swear, if you start — "

"Swear?" Brittany covered her mouth. "Nuns don't swear, do they?"

Kelly drew her head back. "Nuns? What are you talking about?"

"I heard from Daryl that you changed." Brittany's eyes moved up and down, scanning Kelly's clothes. "But I didn't know you went Catholic school on us."

"Miss Tyler," Mrs. Washington said, glaring at Brittany. "You may leave. You've already caused enough trouble for one morning."

A book slid from Brittany's pile. She chirped a girlish "Oops" and kicked it toward me. As I squatted to pick it up, she bent way over to receive it, obviously flashing as much skin as she could.

Averting my eyes, I handed her the book. "Here you go."

"Thank you, Kyle." When she rose, she blew me a kiss and continued her strut toward the door. "I'll have to tell Steven about your change, Kelly. He might want a new picture of you to add to the one taped inside his locker. You know which picture I'm talking about."

When she closed the door, Kelly balled both fists. "Acid-tongued ... witch."

Mrs. Washington slid a sheet of paper toward me and nodded at Kelly. "Say whatever you want. My lips are sealed."

Kelly loosened her fingers. "If I said what I was thinking, the paint would peel."

"Well, someone needs to put that girl in her place." Mrs. Washington tapped on the sheet. "You and Kyle are in every class together except last period. Kyle has orchestra during your PE class." She laid two pink memo slips on the counter. "Here are your tardy passes."

Kelly snatched her pass. "Let's go. Chemistry's already started."

I picked up my schedule and pink slip and grabbed my pack and case. "Thank you, Mrs. Washington."

We quick-stepped through the empty halls, passing vertical banks of blue lockers on each side. Kelly halted at a locker and spun the combination dial. "No time to dump your stuff at your locker. We'll find it after chemistry." She opened the door and grabbed a textbook, then drew back, her eyes growing wider. "Are you sure you don't hear anything?"

I glanced around. "Just the fluorescent lights humming."

"That's not it." Her voice softened to a ghostly whisper. "A man groaning. Like he's in pain."

I lifted my violin case. "Check it carefully this time."

She bent over and set her ear close to the case. After a few seconds, she shook her head. "It's not coming from there."

"Look," I said as I lowered the case, "I'm not doubting you, but if I can't hear it, I can't help you find it."

"I know." She closed the locker door. "Let's get going."

After marching halfway down another hall, we stopped at a classroom where a nameplate read *Marshall Scott*.

Kelly reached for the doorknob and looked back at me, her face reddening. "I should have told you this earlier. Brittany mentioned Steven. He's my old boyfriend from last school year, and he wants me back. He might not be too happy when he sees us together."

"Maybe he already knows." I shrugged. "Wouldn't Brittany have told him about me by now?"

Kelly shook her head. "Brittany's in math for morons this period. She couldn't pass chemistry if her life depended on it."

After taking a deep breath, she opened the door. As we walked inside, I scanned the classroom from the teacher's space on the left to the three rows of two-person worktables on the right. Every student looked at me. A couple of girls smiled, while everyone else turned their gazes back to their desks.

Kelly extended her pink slip to a bespectacled, gray-haired man up front. "Mr. Scott," she said, gesturing toward me, "this is Kyle. I've been assigned to show him the ropes around here."

I handed him my tardy slip and schedule. Using long, bony fingers, Mr. Scott opened a class roll book and scribbled down the information. "Welcome, Mr. Simmons." His voice was nasally but not unfriendly. "I hope your previous school has introduced you to stoichiometry. Otherwise, you will find it difficult to catch up."

I took back the schedule and smiled. "Thanks. I think I'll be okay."

"Very well." Mr. Scott pointed his pencil at a boy at the front table near a window on the far end of the room. "Steven, please be kind enough to move to the empty spot next to Daryl so Kyle can sit with Kelly. They'll have to share her textbook until I locate another one."

"Sure thing." A shaggy-haired boy with a dark goatee rose to a staggering height, glaring at me as he shuffled past. "Cute violin case," he mumbled.

After I pushed my backpack and case under Steven's old space on the left side of the table, I sat in a red metal chair. Kelly opened the chemistry book and slid it to the middle of our workspace. "I still hear it," she whispered. She then cleared her throat to mask her comment.

Mr. Scott poised a marker over a transparency sheet on an overhead projector. After rambling for several minutes about the importance of laboratory safety, he stopped and scanned the classroom. "Who can tell me the chemical formula for silver nitrate?"

I glanced at Kelly, but she was busily writing something on a notepad and covering it with her hand.

"Come now," Mr. Scott continued. "This is review. We just did this equation on Friday."

I looked around the room. One boy yawned, a girl filed her nails, and most of the others just stared straight ahead. Finally, I raised my hand.

"Yes, Kyle."

"Um … A G N O three."

"Excellent." He wrote the symbols on the overhead. "Leave it to the student who wasn't even here on Friday to know the answer."

I firmed my chin. The sarcastic tone in Mr. Scott's voice was more than a little irritating. Besides, it wasn't fair to level that charge against the whole class, especially Kelly. I lifted my hand again. "Excuse me, Mr. Scott, but Kelly wasn't here either. She was helping me settle in at her house."

A deep voice piped up from behind us. "Yeah. I'll *bet* she was."

As muffled snickers erupted around the room, Kelly ducked her head and covered her flaming ears.

"Quiet!" Mr. Scott shot a menacing glare. When the murmuring subsided, he pointed his marker at Steven.

"See me after class." He then shifted the marker toward me. "Kyle, I realize you're new here, but I must ask you to abide by my rules. You will not speak unless called upon."

I straightened in my seat. "Yessir."

"In any case, there is no need to defend Kelly. Her test scores will speak for themselves."

A few more snickers flittered about but faded quickly. Obviously I had already acted like an idiot, and it was only first period. This might prove to be a long day.

Kelly raised her hand. Her entire face had turned red as a beet.

Mr. Scott looked at her. "Yes, Kelly?"

"I'm feeling sick." She laid a hand on her stomach. "I have to go to the restroom."

He nodded toward the door. "Go ahead."

Keeping her gaze averted from me, Kelly tapped her notepad as she passed in front of our desk.

I angled my head and read it. *It's coming from your backpack. Make an excuse to go to the restroom. Lie if you have to!*

While everyone watched Kelly shuffle toward the door, I silently tore the top page from the pad and folded it in half. I then slid out the backpack and unzipped it in one motion.

When the classroom door clapped shut, I withdrew the mirror, unwrapped it, and looked into its reflective side. My father hung suspended by chains against a stone wall, while another man, veiled in shadows, held a knife to a woman's throat. Seated on the floor, the woman faced the wall, preventing me from seeing her clearly, but the dark locks streaming down her back gave away her identity — Mom.

"Now," Mr. Scott continued, "when we combined the silver with the nitric acid we created a reaction that produced a gas called what?"

My hands shaking, I pulled the mirror closer and studied the hanging man, turning the surface away from the window to avoid the glare. Although Dad's face was dirty and he appeared older than usual, there was no doubt about who he was.

"Anyone?" Mr. Scott prodded.

The image faded away, leaving only my worried face along with the wide eyes of a girl staring over my shoulder — Daryl.

The mirror changed again. Although Mr. Scott had not moved from the projector, he appeared in the reflection, stumbling and falling hard to the floor between the front desk and mine. He lay motionless, blood oozing from his nose.

Mr. Scott walked toward me. "Kyle, what are you doing?"

I laid the mirror on the desk and lunged in front of Mr. Scott just as he tripped over a power cord. He fell on top of me, softening his landing.

Someone slid a hand behind my head. "Are you all right?" she asked.

In a daze, it took me a second or two to recognize her. "Yeah, Daryl. I'm fine."

While Mr. Scott got up and brushed off his pants, Daryl helped me to my feet and pointed at the mirror. "I saw you fall in the mirror before it happened."

"Nonsense, Daryl," Mr. Scott said as he put his glasses back on. "Kyle obviously saw that the tape on the cord was loose and couldn't warn me in time." He patted me on the back. "I'm grateful for your quick action."

I stuffed the mirror into my pack and pulled the violin case out from under the desk. "I … I need to go to the restroom." I slung the pack over my shoulder and backed toward the door. "That is, if you don't mind."

Mr. Scott nodded. "Go ahead. And put that mirror in your locker. It's too much of a distraction."

"Sure. No problem." When I reached the door, I set a hand on the knob. "Which way to the restrooms?"

"I'll show him." Daryl ran to the door. "Back in a minute."

She led the way down the hall, chattering rapid-fire. "That mirror thing is so cool. What is it, anyway? Sort of like a scenario predictor? The microprocessors must be super fast to analyze all the probabilities and display the most likely outcome in such high resolution. It was perfect video quality. I'll bet the military would love to get their hands on it, or maybe stockbrokers and gamblers. Yeah, that's it. Sports bookies would kill for a device like that."

She took a breath and turned a corner. "I want to learn virtual reality programming and apply it to holographic imaging. The video gaming industry would go nuts over it. Can you imagine physically walking through a shooter game where you can see your targets all around you without having to wear a bulky helmet? It would be *Battlestar Galactica* come to life."

"Wait." I halted.

"What?"

I pointed at a recessed area in the wall. "The restrooms, right?"

"Oh, yeah. Right." Daryl blushed. "I got carried away." She nodded toward the left side. "Men's room that way."

"Yeah. I saw the sign." I stepped into the alcove and paused in front of a two-tiered set of water fountains. "Thanks."

She crossed her arms and leaned back against a locker at the opposite side of the hall.

"Daryl … I can make it from here."

"Oh. Right again." She spun and hurried along the tiled floor, looking back once before turning into the adjacent hallway.

Taking two long, quiet steps, I shifted over to the ladies' side of the alcove and paused. There was no door to knock on. I gave the tiles at the side of the doorway a light rap with my knuckles, but it hardly made any sound at all. I leaned in and whispered, "Kelly?"

No answer.

I breathed a deep sigh. Maybe I had taken too long to leave the classroom. Maybe she had gone to the car. I spun to the men's room and breezed inside. Might as well take care of business before searching for her.

As I approached a urinal, a loud "Pssst" made me halt.

"Nathan. Over here."

I leaned toward the bank of toilet stalls. "Kelly?"

"Yes. Last stall."

I hustled to the back of the restroom and faced the closed door of the handicapped-access stall. "What are you doing here?"

Her reply came in a sharp whisper. "Waiting for you."

"In the men's room?"

"Good guess, Mr. Obvious." She pushed open the stall door. With her athletic shoes on the toilet seat, she squatted low. "I knew you wouldn't set foot in the ladies' room, and we need to talk privately."

I glanced at the entry door. "What if someone walks in?"

She grabbed my sleeve, pulled me into the spacious stall, and closed the door. "If someone comes in, the only shoes they'll see will be yours."

I set the violin case down and pulled the mirror from the backpack. "I saw who was moaning."

"Your father. I heard someone say his name, like he was being taunted."

"I guess right after my mother heard footsteps, someone captured them." I extended the mirror to her. "I'll try to activate a viewer. Can't worry about cosmic holes."

She grasped the mirror with both hands. "Go for it."

I opened the case and set the violin under my chin. "I feel kind of strange playing in a bathroom stall."

"Definitely strange, but the echo effect will be awesome."

I raised the bow to the strings. "I think *pianissimo* is called for here."

"The softer the better."

I lifted my brow. "You knew what I meant?"

"Five years of piano. My mother taught me."

"Nice. I'd like to hear you sometime."

While I played the first measures of "Brahms' Lullaby," we stared at the mirror. Within seconds the background darkened, framing our reflected faces with blackness. Soon, our images disappeared, and the darkness faded, giving rise to a dim stone wall, the same wall Dad had been hanging from, but now only four loose chains dangled from their attachment points.

"He's gone," I whispered.

"I think I hear voices. Try playing louder."

I increased the volume to *mezzo piano*, loud enough to create an echo in the porcelain-coated room.

Mr. Scott's voice blended in with the violin's tones. "Kyle? Are you in here?"

I stopped playing. "Yes."

Kelly scooted back on the toilet while I slid my feet into position in front of it and sat down.

"The fall bloodied my nose," Mr. Scott said, "so I thought I'd clean up and check on you at the same time. Now I see why you're delayed."

I cleared my throat. "Thanks. I'll be done soon."

"You must really be enamored with your violin to be practicing even in there. I usually read a magazine, but to each his own, I suppose."

"I guess so. Violin music really moves me." I grimaced. What a stupid thing to say.

Mr. Scott laughed. "That's a good one."

Water splashed from a sink. "Kelly never came back to class," he continued. "I called into the ladies' room, but no one answered."

Sitting on the toes of Kelly's shoes, I squirmed to get more comfortable. "I did, too. I don't think she's in there."

"I'll send Daryl to look for her." The towel machine whirred, and the sound of tearing followed. "I'll see you back in class." A few seconds later, all was quiet.

Kelly pushed me out of the way. "We have to get home," she whispered. "Now."

"What did you hear?" I asked as I repacked the violin.

With the mirror still in her grip, she stepped off the toilet lid. "I'll tell you when we get out. The less talking we do, the better."

I nudged the stall door with an elbow, slid through the opening, and skulked to the entryway. After peering around the corner and finding no one around, I motioned for Kelly. "All clear."

"Wait." She pushed the mirror into my backpack. "Okay. Let's go."

We stepped out just as Daryl came into view in the hallway. Kelly ducked her head to take a drink from the water fountain.

Daryl stopped. Her eyes darted back and forth between Kelly and me. "Well," she said, a deep furrow in her brow, "this puts me in an awkward position. I could simply tell Mr. Scott that I found Kelly coming out of the restroom, which would be truthful, but it wouldn't be a complete report. And this story would be the most delicious lunchtime gossip since Brittany and the band director."

Kelly rose from the fountain and hooked her arm around Daryl's. "Listen, brainiac. Here's your complete report. We have a mirror that sees into alternate worlds, and it gets activated by music. Nathan was playing the violin in the toilet stall while we watched for another world to appear. When he plays, I hear voices that tell me what's going on. We experimented in there so we could do it in private and not scare the entire school." She released

Daryl's arm and looked her in the eye. "Tell that to your gossip girls at lunchtime."

Daryl's mouth dropped open. She took in a deep breath and let it out, stuttering, "I … I believe you."

"Good." Kelly stalked down the hall, pulling me along.

Daryl called out, "Aren't you coming back to class?"

Kelly turned and walked backwards. "We have to travel to another world to rescue his father."

"That is so Narnia!" Daryl folded her hands in a begging posture. "Can I come? I've never been on any kind of adventure!"

I halted. "You have no idea how dangerous this is."

"But I can help. I've studied stuff like this all my life!"

"How could you study cross-world travel?"

Daryl bit her lip. "I … well …"

A deep voice entered the hallway. "Tell them, Daryl." A tall man wearing a dark blazer stood at the corner, his eyes trained on us. "They already know about Interfinity." As he drew closer, his piercing eyes and a pulsing vein on his forehead clarified. *Dr. Gordon.*

CHAPTER SIXTEEN

D ARYL PUSHED PAST me and extended her hand.
"Dr. Gordon. Why are you here?"

He shook Daryl's hand. "Because the new student fits the profile."

I looked at Dr. Gordon's cheek. His skin was smooth, no sign of the cut he had suffered only a day earlier. "What profile?" I asked.

"I know who you are, Nathan. Daryl alerted me to your presence on Friday when someone registered you under a false name."

Kelly glared at Daryl, her fists tight.

Dr. Gordon waved a hand at Kelly. "No need to pour wrath on your friend. I am the head of research and development at Interfinity Labs. We handpick the brightest students in the country to come to my seminars. When Nathan's father was murdered, I knew Nathan would go into hiding, so I asked my seminar graduates to be on the lookout for a new arrival in their schools. I told them that finding Nathan was a life-or-death emergency, so Daryl's actions were not treacherous in the least."

Kelly bent toward Daryl. While the two girls whispered, I looked at the breast pocket on Dr. Gordon's blazer. It carried an emblem embroidered in gold, three infinity symbols, just like the one he wore when he was with Mictar. "You're right about life and death," I said, glancing around for escape routes. "One of the people looking for me tried to kill me."

Dr. Gordon sighed. "Yes, my competition is quite aggressive."

"Why is it that one member of your *competition* looks very familiar?"

"I know why you're guarding your words. All I can say is that I am not who you think I am. We can discuss the particulars at my Chicago office, but it's important that we go there immediately. There is much to be done and very little time to do it."

I shook my head. "I can't go with you. My parents' funeral is tomorrow."

"Yes, I know. I will arrange for overnight accommodations, and I will make sure you get to the service on time."

"Well …" I had to dodge him somehow, long enough to throw him off my trail. "I have to go home and pack some stuff."

"That's not a problem. I will give you a ride."

Kelly set her hands on her hips. "Wait just a minute. I'm not letting a stranger come to my house. You talk a good talk, and you have an official-looking emblem on your bellhop blazer, but that doesn't mean you're anyone we can trust."

Standing straight, Daryl cleared her throat. "I'll go home with them and make sure they come back here."

Dr. Gordon shook his head. "That won't be good enough. I'm afraid I'll have to insist — "

Kelly jabbed a finger at Daryl. "You just want to get your hooks into my new boyfriend."

Daryl shoved Kelly, making her backpedal into my arms. "You don't have the brains to compete with me, you dumb jock."

I helped Kelly regain her balance. Their little act was too transparent to be believable. "Let's just go and — "

A bell sounded. A second later, students poured out of classrooms. Kelly jerked away from me and shouted at Daryl. "Don't call me a jock, you cyberspace geek. I'll — "

"Cat fight!" a lanky boy yelled. Within seconds, students surrounded the combative females as they stood glaring at each other with their fists clenched.

A muscular male adult pushed through the crowd, shouting, "What's going on here?"

Kelly thrust her finger toward Dr. Gordon. "Mr. Ryan, this pervert tried to kidnap me."

As excited chatter buzzed through the corridor, Kelly continued, her voice meek and trembling. "When I came out of the bathroom, he was standing at the water fountain. He said I had to go with him."

Mr. Ryan grabbed Dr. Gordon's arm. "Let's take a walk to the office."

Dr. Gordon tried to shake free. "This is absurd. I assure you — "

"Just shut up and come with me." As he pushed Dr. Gordon along, the crowd of students funneled behind them. "Kelly," Mr. Ryan called, looking back. "Meet us in the office. We'll need your statement."

Kelly grabbed Daryl's wrist and pulled her close to me. We stood against the lockers and waited for the students to disperse. Daryl folded her hands and renewed her begging stance. "Now you're taking me with you to the other world, right? I mean, I did what you wanted. Don't leave me here to face Dr. Gordon when they let him go."

"A promise is a promise." Kelly tugged my sleeve. "We'd better hustle before they figure out what really happened."

"What really happened, Kelly?" Steven emerged from the restroom alcove. "I know when you're putting on a show, and that was one of your better performances."

"Buzz off, Steven." She turned toward the exit. "We're in a hurry."

Steven grabbed Kelly's arm and jerked her toward him. "Not so fast. I want to know what's going on."

I pulled Kelly free and stepped between her and Steven. "You heard the lady. She said to buzz off."

He wrapped long fingers around my throat and pushed me against the lockers. "A lady?" He laughed. "She's got you fooled."

"Steven!" Kelly pushed him, but he didn't budge. "Just stop it."

I squeezed out a choked, "Get in the car. I'll meet you outside."

"But — "

"Kelly." I curled my hand into a fist. "Just do it."

Daryl picked up my violin, and Kelly grabbed my backpack. As they ran down the hall, Kelly called, "Don't hurt him too badly."

Steven loosened his grip. "Don't worry. I won't."

"She wasn't talking to you," I said, tilting my head up to look him in the eye.

"Okay, smart guy." He shoved me against the lockers and thrust a fist. I ducked out of the way. When his fist slammed into a locker, I grabbed his wrist, twisted his arm behind him, and bent back his thumb, applying pressure. He let out a yelp. "Let me go!"

I spun him around face to face, still holding his thumb in a torture lock. I whispered, "Kelly asked me not to hurt you." I pushed him back, releasing the hold. "Don't make me disappoint her."

He massaged his thumb. "You'd better watch your back." He then turned and hurried around a corner.

I jogged toward the main entrance. Since the student drop-off site was the only place I knew to go, I would have to pass by the office ... and Dr. Gordon.

As I approached a throng of students gathered in the rotunda, I bent low and tried to sneak through the crowd. Just as I passed the office door and quick-stepped toward the exit, Dr. Gordon shouted, "There he is! That's Nathan Shepherd!"

I burst outside and sprinted past the flagpole. When I stopped at the curb, Kelly's Toyota peeled out of its parking space and zoomed toward me. I looked back at the school. Mr. Ryan opened the door and ran toward me, yelling, "Hold it right there!"

Kelly skidded to a stop in front of me. Daryl threw the passenger door open, and I dove headlong across the front seats. My chest landed on the center console, my legs curled across Daryl's, and my head flopped face down in Kelly's lap.

I twisted face up, my knees near Daryl's nose. As heat scorched my ears, I said, "Sorry about that."

Kelly pinned my chest with an elbow. "Just stay cool. You're fine."

Mr. Ryan grabbed the door handle. "Don't move."

"Sorry. Gotta run." Kelly stomped the gas pedal. The car shot away, ripping the handle from Mr. Ryan's grip. Daryl pulled the door closed and laughed, shaking me as her spasms pulsed.

Kelly covered her mouth. As she held her breath, suppressed laughing spasms jiggled my head.

"What's so funny?" I asked, looking at her between her arms.

A wide grin spread across her face. "Oh … nothing."

"You are!" Daryl's cheeks turned redder than her hair. "You're so embarrassed!"

Heat spread to my own cheeks. "Well, I'm not used to being in such awkward positions."

"That's perfect!" Daryl reached around my legs and clapped her hands. "That's so perfect!"

I rose and slid over the console toward the backseat, trying to keep my balance as the car swept around a curve. "What's so perfect?"

"You are." Daryl turned in her seat and smiled. "I didn't think such old-fashioned guys existed anymore."

"Old-fashioned?" I seated myself between my backpack and violin case but kept a foot on the console's glove box. "I've been called that before."

"Daryl, you had it right the first time." Kelly tugged on one of my shoelaces. "Perfect is the best word. He's a perfect gentleman."

"Thanks." The warmth in my cheeks spiked. "I guess."

"No problem." She looked at me in the rearview mirror. "How did you get away from Steven? Did you have to hurt him?"

"Let's just say I'm not at the top of his friends list." I looked out the windshield, trying to recognize the surroundings, but everything zipped by too fast. "Where are we heading?"

"My house real quick, then I thought Chicago would be best. Catch up with Clara and see what's going on at Interfinity. Dr. Gordon probably already knows where I live, but maybe we can grab some stuff and hit the road before he shows up."

"What about Daryl? Won't she need some clothes?"

"I'll pack extra for her. She's borrowed my clothes before."

Daryl touched Kelly's shoulder. "You got a fresh toothbrush I can borrow? I'll share jeans, underwear, and soda straws, but I gotta have my own toothbrush."

"Not a problem."

I pulled my foot down to the floorboard. "Kelly, what did you hear when we were in the stall?"

"I'll tell you later." Her eyes locked with mine in the mirror. "It's kind of … personal. It can wait."

I reached into the front pocket of my backpack and withdrew my phone. "I'll call Clara and get her up to speed."

"Be sure to tell her about Dr. Gordon. He'll probably head back to Interfinity."

I punched in Clara's number and waited through the trill. After the third ring, her familiar voice buzzed through the earpiece. "Yes, Nathan?"

"Where are you? At Interfinity?"

Her voice dropped to a whisper. "We are. Francesca and I blended into a school group's guided tour. I'm looking for a chance to sneak away, maybe get into the offices when they close."

"Make sure you look for the office of Dr. Gordon, the head of research and development. He showed up at the high school looking for me, so he can't possibly get back there in time to walk in on you. I'll tell you more later, but we need to stay away from him no matter what."

"Why was he looking for you?"

"Not just looking. He was going to make me come back with him to his office, but Kelly and I got away." As the car rounded a sharp curve, I clutched Daryl's seat. "We'll be heading toward Chicago soon. We have to come to the funeral anyway."

"I'll figure out a place to meet. I assume you have your debit card, so you have plenty of money. Be sure to take care of all the travel expenses."

"Gotcha."

"Don't call again," Clara said. "I'll estimate the time of your arrival and call you."

"Sounds good. We'll see you in a few hours." I terminated the call.

As the Camry roared down the country highway, Kelly explained our story to Daryl, cutting out enough details to keep it short.

I added what happened when I first saw my parents in the coffins and the pursuit by the gunman in the Mustang, then finished with my suspicions about Dr. Gordon. "The guy who chased us in that other world looked exactly like him, but when he showed up at school he didn't have a cut on his cheek. Until I know otherwise, he's a murderer in my book."

Daryl interlaced her fingers behind her head. "Well, it's a good thing I'm coming along. Let me tell you what I know."

"Cool your jets." Kelly pressed the brakes and skidded into a turn down our cornfield-bordered road. "Let's get our stuff. You can tell us the rest on the way to Chicago."

Kelly pushed the garage opener and zoomed inside. After screeching to a halt, she closed the door, jumped out, and ran into the house with Daryl hot on her heels. I slid my backpack on and followed them through the laundry area, across the kitchen, and into the formal living room.

Kelly pointed down the hall. "Daryl, you first in the bathroom. We won't have time for a lot of stops."

The moment Daryl scooted away, Kelly pulled me close. "When you played in the stall, I heard your mother and father talking." She breathed a gentle sigh. "Nathan, I've never heard anything like it. They love each other so much."

I dipped my head. "Yeah. I know."

"Anyway, your father said he was being tortured to draw you to them. They think someone named Simon is behind it, but they're not sure."

I refocused on her. "But Dr. Simon is dead. How could that be?"

"Your parents are dead, too, but they still seem to be talking."

The sound of a toilet flushing came from down the hall, followed by a closing door. Kelly glanced that way and sped through her words. "They're worried about you. Something's gone wrong with their plan, and if you follow the clues they've left behind, you could be in big trouble. They said Simon might have set a trap, thinking you'll respond to your father's suffering and come to help him."

Daryl peeked around the corner. "That sounds like *The Empire Strikes Back*. Darth Vader tortured Han Solo to get Luke to show up. That was a trap, too."

I nodded. "And Luke went anyway. Just like I have to go now."

Daryl flashed a thumbs up. "That's what heroes do." Angling her thumb toward the hall, she grinned. "Speaking of having to go, who's next in the bathroom?"

Kelly pushed my backpack. "You go. I already went."

"In the guys' bathroom at school?"

"Why not?" She pushed me again. "Hurry. Then pack your stuff while I get mine. "

I rushed through my bathroom break and picked up my toothbrush on the way out. When I arrived at my bedroom, I flipped on the desk lamp and laptop computer, threw my suitcase on the bed, and hurriedly packed it. I glanced at the mirror on the wall. Everything seemed normal. The trunk was closed. The lights stayed constant.

I pulled open a desk drawer and lifted Dad's camera by its strap. No sense in leaving it behind for Gordon to steal. I laid it among my clothes, and, after zipping the suitcase, I slid into the desk chair and accessed the Internet. A quick search located Interfinity's headquarters and a map to the location. Just as I clicked the print button, Kelly bustled into the room, a duffle bag strap over her shoulder and a pillow tucked under her arm.

"You ready?" she asked.

I nodded at the suitcase on the bed. "Yeah. I just sent a map to the printer."

She set her bag and pillow down. "I'll get it."

I packed the laptop and grabbed my suitcase, then paused to get one more look at the mirror — still normal, a perfect reflection. This might be my last chance to see the big mirror for quite a while. Maybe I could try to get a final clue before leaving.

Moving quickly, I slid off the backpack, fished out the mirror, and reapplied it in the blank corner section. It stuck in place and sent a shimmer of light across the glass. I pulled my new violin from under the bed and took it out of its case. Then, with a few quick strokes, I played part of a Sibelius piece that had been running through my head — Finlandia.

As I watched the mirror, my eyes glowed the same way Mom's had, though not as brightly. Soon, the glass surface flickered and transformed into a close-up of Dr. Simon's profile. He clutched a steering wheel and bounced as if driving over a bumpy road. Beyond him, farmland whisked by. Several black-and-white cows grazed in fenced, grassy fields, and, in another lot, a big-wheeled tractor dragged a plow through rich black earth.

Simon's lips moved. After a few seconds, his voice became audible, a slow, careful speech seemingly designed for recording.

"Nathan Shepherd, if you can hear me, you have learned that music is the key to opening a video and audio portal between worlds. You might have also learned that flashes of light allow you to move between the worlds once the portal is open."

Kelly walked into the room and stared at the mirror. "What the — "

"It's Dr. Simon. Shhh."

I played on as he continued in monotone. "You can use a flashlight, a flickering lamp, almost anything that surpasses a certain lumens minimum, but that is far too technical for this message. I need you to come here to help me stop a madman who is trying to manipulate these cross-world boundaries for his own purposes. I know you have lost your mother and father, but there is still hope. Come to this place so that we can prevent Interfinity from happening. The entire cosmos is at stake."

Simon took a deep breath and restarted the message.

I lowered the bow and packed the violin. Within seconds, Dr. Simon's image faded, and the mirror returned to normal. After sliding the violin case under the bed, I grabbed the screwdriver from the shelf and pried the mirror section loose again.

Kelly shivered. "I don't like how he said that."

"I didn't like anything he said." I stuffed the mirror into the backpack. "What part bothered you?"

She mimicked his deadpan tone. "The entire cosmos is at stake."

"He's baiting me." I slid the backpack on and picked up my suitcase. "Listen, I saw Dr. Simon's eyes get burned out. He's dead, at least the guy I knew. So this one has to be a copy."

"From the world where the copies of us died?"

"Maybe, but whoever he is, he's probably luring me, just like my parents said."

"So what are you going to do?"

I picked up Kelly's bag and slung the strap over my shoulder. "Be a hero."

"Don't overload yourself, hero." She grabbed her pillow and my laptop from the floor. "I'll get these."

We hurried out to the Camry. As the garage door rumbled open, Daryl lifted a bag into the trunk and tossed the keys toward Kelly. She caught them, hopped into the car, and started it. I shoved the other bags on top of Daryl's and closed the trunk. When I opened the back door to get in, Daryl was already sitting there clutching Kelly's pillow in her lap.

"Ride up front," she said, reaching for my backpack. "When I get done with my story, I'm gonna lie down and snooze."

I gave her the pack, climbed into the front seat, and closed the door. Kelly zoomed out of the driveway and onto the main road. When she accelerated to a safe cruising speed, she looked at the rearview mirror. "Okay, Daryl. Time to spill it. Tell us everything you know about Interfinity and Dr. Gordon."

Daryl closed her eyes and leaned back in her seat, a proud smile spreading across her face. "Interfinity used to be called StarCast. They got a lot of press about their project to send radio signals into space, you know, hoping to contact intelligent life out there." She opened her eyes. "Remember the movie ET? This was bigger, like souped-up, extraterrestrial phone tag. Crazy, right? But, guess what? They got an answer."

Kelly's brow lifted. "From an alien?"

"No. That's the weirdest part of all. They got an answer from themselves."

"From themselves?"

"Yeah. And a whole lot quicker than they thought possible."

"Did the signal bounce off something?" I asked. "Maybe it went in a circle."

"Nope." Daryl gave me a mischievous smirk. "You of all people should be able to figure it out. Keep guessing."

"Keep guessing? That could take hours." I leaned my head back and looked out the window. The countryside zipped by, dressed in its autumn attire — red maples, withered corn stalks, and a flock of birds migrating southward, making Vivaldi's "Autumn" play in my mind.

The soft violins eased my tensions. I closed my eyes and imagined the notes' arrangement on the staff, each one appearing in its proper position as it played. When the pages filled, a breeze picked them up and carried them into the sky, page after page joining in a musical chain reaching toward heaven. When the last page drifted away, I opened my eyes. "They didn't send words into space. They sent music."

Daryl pushed on my seat. "Smart boy."

"What made them decide on music?" Kelly asked.

Daryl restarted her rapid-fire chatter. "They tried everything, but when they sent music, they finally got an answer, and it was the same music they sent out. So they started experimenting with different varieties. They recorded about a hundred songs, mostly classical, but some rock and country, even some polka, and they started broadcasting them in order. But do you know what happened? They received song number five on the list while they were still sending song number three."

"So it couldn't have been bouncing back at them," I said.

"Brilliant deduction, Holmes." Daryl pushed my elbow with her foot. "So after all their experiments, they came up with a wild theory. When Dr. Gordon presented his paper about it during a seminar at a fancy scientists' convention, he got laughed out of the building, and he lost his grant from the National Science Foundation."

"I'll bet that ticked him off," Kelly said.

"Definitely. He went out and got what you might call" — Daryl drew quotation marks in the air — "alternative funding from some kind of fringe group."

"How do you know they're fringe?"

"Are you kidding me? Anyone who would throw money at this crazy project has got to be fringe."

Kelly looked at her again in the rearview mirror. "But you don't think it's crazy, right?"

"Normal people think it is, but, as you know" — Daryl pressed her thumb against her chest — "I'm far from normal."

"No argument from the sanity section." Kelly rolled her eyes. "Go on."

"Anyway, Dr. Gordon sponsored this seminar for students who were interested in learning about radio telescopes and broadcasting into space, which sounded reasonable enough to a lot of teachers, so about a hundred kids showed up. But as he got to know the group, he pulled some of us aside into a special workshop and explained his newest theories."

She lowered her voice to a dramatic whisper. "He believes there are multiple worlds exactly like ours, you know, mutlidimensional stuff, only they're slightly off time-wise." She set her palms close together. "While something happens here …" She wiggled the fingers on one hand. "It happens a little while later in one of the other worlds." She wiggled her other fingers to match. "But it might have already happened in yet another world."

"So that's why they got the music before they sent it," I said. "Copies of scientists at StarCast were sending it from another world, but the copies were ahead on the timeline."

"Exactly." Daryl leaned back and sighed. "It's fun talking to smart people. I don't have to spell everything out."

"How many worlds are there?" Kelly asked.

"Dr. Gordon identified three, but there might be more. We tried to pry more information out of him, but he went all Gandalf on us. You know …" Daryl leaned between the front seats and glanced at Kelly and me in turn. "Keep it secret. Keep it safe."

Kelly pushed her back with an elbow. "You and your movies."

"Dr. Gordon seemed to be a good guy," Daryl continued, "so when he emailed me about Nathan's parents and said he could help find the killer, I decided to keep a lookout and tell him if Nathan showed up at our school. I heard he sent the same message to a lot of kids at other schools." She winked at me. "I guess I got lucky."

Kelly frowned. "You're lucky I don't kick your butt for keeping me out of the loop." Watching her side mirror, she merged onto the Interstate. "Let's just settle back and chill. We have about five hours to go."

I closed my eyes. "What about your dad? You gonna call him?"

"Later. I'll tell him we're out on a date. He'll love that."

I opened one eye. "Really?"

"Well ..." Kelly let a smile break through. "He likes you."

"Yeah," Daryl piped up. "And after Kelly decided to give up guys because of her mom's running around — "

"Daryl," Kelly growled as she tightened her grip on the wheel. "You're asking for it."

"What's the big deal? Everyone knows about your parents. Anyway, Steven decided with parents like that Kelly would be an easy target, so one night she had to put him in his place."

Kelly's cheeks turned bright red. "Daryl, cut it out!"

"Why? I'm complimenting you. He deserved that kick in the — "

"Daryl! If you don't stop it, I'll — "

"So Kelly said she'd never date anyone again unless the perfect gentleman came along, and that worried her dad. I guess he thought she'd turn butch or something, but since she just called you a perfect gentleman — Alakazam! Everyone's happy."

Kelly raised a fist. "You won't be happy when I kick you and your motor mouth out of the car and make you walk home."

"You wouldn't dare. I know all your secrets." Daryl fluffed the pillow, lay on the seat, and closed her eyes.

"Wake me when we get to Illinois. I like to blow kisses at state welcome signs."

Kelly gripped the wheel with stiffened fingers, her arms tight and her stare locked straight ahead.

I pulled my lips in. No way was I going to breathe a word. If Kelly got any hotter, steam would spew out her ears.

After a few minutes, a light snore sounded from the backseat. Kelly let out a long sigh and relaxed her grip. A tear glistening in her eye, she whispered, "I guess I don't have much left to hide, do I?"

I gave her a slight shrug. "I didn't hear anything bad."

"Daryl made it sound a lot better than it was." As she turned toward me, the tear meandered down her cheek. "I'm not the kind of girl you'd be interested in."

"Don't you mean …" Leaning toward her, I lowered my voice. "… you *weren't* that kind of girl?"

She wiped the tear, but a new one streamed from her other eye. "Does it make any difference? What's done is done."

"Yeah. It makes a difference." I rubbed a finger along the seatbelt strap, swallowing to keep my voice steady. "It makes a big difference, at least to me."

Her lips formed a trembling smile. "Why?"

"Like you said. What's done is done." I lifted my shoulders in another casual shrug. "I love you for who you are now."

Kelly's eyes narrowed, and a hint of anger spiced her voice. "Don't use that word on me."

I drew back. "What word?"

"I've heard it too many times. My mom used it. My dad used it. Steven used it. And none of them ever meant it. They just *used* it."

"You mean *love*?"

She brushed a fresh tear from each eye. "You can't possibly love me yet. Don't say it unless you really mean it."

Not knowing how to respond, I folded my arms over my chest and slid away. Who would've thought I could get into trouble by using *that* word? I *did* love my new sister, so didn't it make sense to let her know?

I gazed at her, trying to figure out the demons that stalked her mind — unfaithfulness, betrayal, abandonment. As more tears streamed, she kept her eyes focused ahead.

I let out a quiet sigh. Kelly didn't need to hear the word; she needed to see it acted out.

Reaching under the dash, I touched the glove box. "You got any tissues in here?"

"Should be some."

I opened the box, withdrew a pack of tissues, and handed her one. "Want me to drive for a while?"

She dabbed her eyes and nodded. "We need gas anyway."

I yanked on the cuff of Daryl's jeans. "Wake up, O Keeper of Dimensional Secrets. It's time to dock the Millennium Falcon."

Daryl yawned. "You know, you shouldn't talk about movies so much. It gets kind of annoying."

After stopping at a convenience store, filling up with gas, and grabbing some snacks, I set a bottle of Dr

Pepper in the cup holder and started the car. "Everyone ready?"

"I am," Daryl called from the backseat. She pulled a Hershey's Kiss from a bag and unwrapped the foil. "Anyone want a kiss?"

"Not from you," Kelly said. Now sitting in front on the passenger side, she leaned against the pillow squished between her head and the window, closed her eyes, and pushed my leg with her sock-covered toe. "Ask Nathan. He looks like he could use a kiss."

I reached back. "Sure. I'll have one."

Daryl laid a kiss in my hand. "As you wish."

"Thanks." After peeling off the foil wrapper and popping the candy into my mouth, I scanned the radio dial and found a classical station. I kept the volume low, hoping the music wouldn't activate the mirror in the back. During a soothing Chopin sonata, Daryl fell asleep, and Kelly eased into a restless doze. Her eyelids twitched from time to time, and her brow furrowed. Once, she let out a low groan and whispered something imperceptible.

I squeezed the steering wheel. Bad dreams. But it would be a shame to wake her up. With her lips pursed, her eyes closed, and her hands spread softly on her lap, she looked more like a child than a young woman. Still, she had probably experienced far more pain than any child should have to suffer.

I mentally replayed her recent *love* tirade. It was tragic. She couldn't even stand hearing the word. Maybe she hadn't experienced enough real love.

Leaning toward her, I slid my hand under hers and held it, barely touching her skin. Her fingers twitched and returned the light grasp. I caressed her knuckles with my thumb. Maybe my touch would chase the phantoms away.

Kelly gasped. Her eyes flashed open. She jerked her hand away and laid it on her chest. "I had the worst dream!"

Daryl's heavy breathing ended with a snort. "What's going on?"

"Kelly had a bad dream." I looked at her. "Want to tell us about it?"

She gestured with her hands. "We were driving behind a big truck, some kind of tanker, and then we —"

A phone rang. I scanned the console and the seats. "Where did I put it?"

As the ringing continued, Kelly searched the floorboard. "Here." She picked up my phone and gave it to me. "I'll tell you the rest later."

I touched the Answer icon and raised the phone to my ear. "Hello?"

"Nathan, are you almost here?"

"Hi, Clara. We still have about three hours to go. Why?"

"Tell Kelly to floor it. I need you to — "

Silence followed.

"Clara?" I looked at the phone's screen. The call had dropped.

Kelly slid closer. "What's wrong?"

"Just a second." I called Clara's phone and waited through several trills. When her voice mail picked up, I disconnected and set the phone on the console. "I think Clara's in trouble."

CHAPTER SEVENTEEN

I PRESSED THE GAS pedal. As the speedometer pushed past eighty, I checked the rearview mirror. A dark car followed pretty far back, but it kept pace.

Kelly set a hand on the dashboard. "If a state trooper catches you, it'll take a lot longer than three hours to get to Clara."

"True." I lifted my foot and checked the mirror again. The car had closed in enough to identify the model, a Lincoln Town Car. "We're being followed. He took off when I did, and now he's slowing down."

Kelly looked out the back window. "Could it be Dr. Gordon?"

"He drove a Lincoln like that one. I saw it at the school."

She swiveled forward and tightened her seatbelt. "Then floor it. Now we *want* a cop to catch us."

As I accelerated again, Daryl flopped back in her seat. "All right! It's adventure time!"

I shook my head. "High-speed adventure is overrated."

"Don't be a stick in the mud, Marty. Set the time circuits. When we hit eighty-eight miles per hour, we're going back to the future."

I checked the speedometer, already at ninety.
"Daryl, can you find my mirror? It's in my backpack."

"Sure." After pulling it out, she held it on her lap.
"What now?"

"Just look at it. Use it like a rearview mirror and tell me what you see."

She held the mirror in front of her face. "Ew! I'm a mess!"

As the speedometer passed one hundred, the engine whined and rattled. I turned up the radio and looked at her through the rearview mirror. "Watch the road. Not your face."

"I can do both." Daryl pushed her hair back and primped her curly red bangs. "Nothing yet."

I weaved around cars, alternately braking and accelerating again as I changed lanes. After a minute or so, Daryl called out, "What am I supposed to be looking for?"

Kelly reached back, grabbed the mirror, and propped it on the dashboard. "We'll all watch it together."

I glanced from the road ahead, to the rearview mirror, to Dad's mirror, while continuing the mad dash, banking left, then right, then left again. The Lincoln drew closer, following in our wake like a skier behind a boat and matching us swerve for swerve.

"Kick it, Nathan!" Daryl shouted. "You have the smaller car. Take it somewhere he can't follow."

Ahead, a conversion van and a gasoline tanker drove side by side, blocking the way. I pressed the brake and, after easing onto the shoulder, I floored the pedal again and began passing the tanker. The Camry's two right tires rumbled on the grass, shaking us.

"Nathan, this is my dream," Kelly said. "If it stays the same — " She thrust a finger. "A bridge!"

I jerked to the left, missing the bridge abutment but clipping the tanker's front fender with the Camry's rear. The driver slammed on his brakes. His trailer fishtailed and slapped the conversion van into the median. The Lincoln zoomed between the trailer and the side of the bridge, but when the trailer swung back, it spanked the Lincoln in the rear, sending it lurching ahead.

The tanker tipped over and skidded. As the tank's side scraped the bridge's metal floor, showers of sparks flew everywhere.

Daryl squealed, "It's gonna blow!"

"Did it explode in your dream?" I asked Kelly.

"I don't know." Keeping a hand on Dad's mirror, she hunkered down. "I woke up before this part."

I floored the pedal again. In the car's mirror a tanker lay on its side at a safe distance away while the Lincoln continued giving chase. "It didn't explode, but Gordon's still on our tail."

Kelly straightened and pointed at Dad's mirror. "Look!"

In the reflection, a deserted country road wound through a tree-spotted meadow. "That might be our escape route, but I need a light. What do we have?"

Daryl searched around her seat. "Where's your camera?"

"In the trunk."

Kelly pointed at the keys in the ignition. "There's a little flashlight on the ring, but it's not very bright."

"You got anything brighter?"

"My father sometimes keeps a ..." She reached under her seat and withdrew a foot-long camper's flashlight. "Here it is."

"I'll hold the mirror," I said, grabbing its edge. "Get ready to turn it on."

"Here he comes." Daryl bounced on her knees as she looked out the back window. "Think he'll push us off the road?"

"Or worse. He might have a gun. I'd keep my head down if I were you."

"Gotcha." Daryl ducked low. "Avoid lead poisoning."

Kelly held the flashlight close to the reflection. "Let me know when you're ready."

I checked the image again — still just a country road. "Ready. Turn it on."

She aimed the flashlight at the mirror and pressed the button. As soon as it blinked on, the light surrounding the car dimmed.

Daryl rose from her crouch. "That's weird. I don't see him anymore."

Outside, rolling pastures whisked by, some dotted with trees. I slowed the car to a normal speed. The engine's whine quieted, but the rattle continued. "Perfect. Exactly what I hoped for."

Kelly put the flashlight away, took the mirror, and set it on her lap. "Were you thinking about this road?"

"No. I meant I hoped for the escape. It's like the mirror chose the place."

Daryl leaned forward between the front seats. "You gotta love it. We cause a highway pileup, vanish in a puff of smoke, and reappear in the middle of nowhere."

"This isn't a movie," Kelly said. "Those people might have been hurt."

Daryl crossed her arms. "Don't guilt trip me. I had nothing to do with it. I'm just along for the ride."

"Daryl's right about one thing," I said. "We're in the middle of nowhere."

"Look." Kelly pointed ahead. "That intersection has a sign. It might be a highway marker."

When we reached the intersection, I stopped and read the number. "Route two-fifty-one."

Kelly whispered, "It's *Illinois* two-fifty-one."

Daryl pushed into the front to get a look. "You mean I missed the welcome sign?"

"We all did," I said. "We made some kind of quantum leap over the border."

Kelly looked at the sky. "Do you see what I see?"

Tiny snowflakes floated down and landed on the windshield.

I let out a sigh. "Now we have weather worries."

Daryl squinted at the crystals. "Did you guys see *The Day after Tomorrow*? It was so cool! Weather disasters all over the world."

"Thanks for the calamity forecast." I resisted the urge to say more. No use scaring anyone. But could the approach of Interfinity have anything to do with the weather? And how did Kelly's prophetic nightmare fit in?

Kelly pulled her phone from her pocket and tapped on the screen. "We really must be in the middle of nowhere. I'm not getting a signal."

"So, no maps. The one I printed doesn't show this road."

She slid the phone away. "With the cloud cover, I can't even tell which way north is."

"Speaking of north," Daryl said as she wrapped her arms around herself, "it's getting as cold as Hoth in here."

I turned on the heater. "We'll find a gas station and buy a map. If they don't have one, I'll ask for directions."

"You're a guy," Daryl said. "Isn't it against one of the rules of manliness to stop and ask directions?"

I smiled. "It's not manly to stay lost when fair maidens need to find their way home."

Daryl reached forward and compressed my bicep. "Oooh, Kelly. Strong and sensible in the same package. Can we clone him? One for you and one for me?"

Kelly pushed Daryl's arm away. "As long as I get the original model."

"I won't quibble. His clone would be better than the clowns I've been out with."

I groaned. "How many more hours of this do I have to put up with?"

"That depends, Mr. Knight in Shining Armor." Daryl patted my shoulder. "You get us to our castle, and we'll stop acting like hopelessly romantic schoolgirls."

"That's a good motivation." I drove on. After a few minutes, we found a Shell gas station. I pulled in and glanced around. With a stack of bald tires in front of an empty mechanic's garage, a dirty window advertising several brands of beer, and no protective canopy over two older-style pumps in front, it didn't hold much promise of carrying an up-to-date map. Still, it was worth a try.

"Better pull out our sweatshirts," I said as I opened the door. "I'll see what they've got."

Daryl held out her hand. "Fork over the magic money card, and I'll fill the tank."

"Those pumps don't look like they'll take cards. Just start pumping. I'll use cash. Stop it at twenty dollars if it goes that high."

When I walked in, a bell jangled over my head. In the background of the dim store, a radio played a news broadcast that blended with a static buzz. I spotted the source, a little portable sitting on a snack display in a corner.

A stout bald man with a three-day beard sat on a stool behind the counter. A shelf filled with cigarette packs and snuff stood on each side, a tall jar holding red licorice sticks sat on the counter in front, and a rack of hunting magazines hung on a wall behind him.

"Help you find something?" the man asked.

Keeping an ear tuned to the radio, I gave him a nod. "Do you have a roadmap?" From the news report, the word *nightmares* caught my attention.

"Sure."

As the man waddled to the back of the store, the radio announcer broke through the static. "One expert claimed that media hype rather than paranormal sources has incited most of the outbreak, but he admits his theory doesn't explain how the first of these dreams began in Chicago before the phenomena became well-known."

After a brief pause, the announcer continued. "The unusual winterlike storm continues to spread throughout the Midwest, bringing heavy snow to — "

"Buck twenty-five, tax included," the man said as he returned to the counter. He plopped the map down and slid it toward me.

I reached into my pocket. "Is that all? I thought it'd
be more." I laid a crumpled dollar bill and a quarter on the
counter. "I guess there's not much demand for maps now
that they're available on the Internet."

"The Internet?" The man slid the money into his
register. "What are you talking about?"

I stared at him for a moment. He seemed sincere.
Not a hint of a wink or a smile.

I pulled a twenty from my wallet and laid it on the
counter. "If we don't pump that much, I'll come back for
the change."

"What are you filling? A Sherman tank?"

"No. A Toyota." I pushed the door open and
walked out while looking at the map. The price read $2.95.
Could it have been on sale?

Now wearing a black sweatshirt, Daryl twisted the
lid on the gas tank. "I topped it off at fifteen even."

"Good. I gave him a twenty." I read the price-per-
gallon on the pump. A little higher than normal, but not
much. Daryl tossed me my sweatshirt. I caught it and
pulled it over my head, still clutching the map as I pushed
my arms through the sleeves.

"Are you going back for the change?" she asked.

"I'm not sure. He seemed confused, like he was
from another time period. He didn't even know about
the Internet." As the snowfall thickened, I strode to the
driver's door and got in. I laid the map on Kelly's thigh
and shoved the key in the ignition. "Let's just leave."

Kelly unfolded the map and compared it to the one
I printed earlier. "Believe it or not, we're only about a mile
off the main highway that we would have been on anyway,
and we're about a hundred miles ahead of pace."

"I'm ready to believe anything." I turned the key. The engine churned but wouldn't fire.

Kelly groaned. "Not now, Lando!"

I pumped the accelerator, but the Camry just kept grinding. "How do you get Lando to start when he's being stubborn?"

"Dad cleans the spark plugs and lubricates the cylinders, but it might be the cold weather. I'm not sure if anything will do any good."

I withdrew the key. "Do you know how to do all that?"

"Sure. I just need some carburetor cleaner and WD-forty."

I read the window ads, searching for automotive supplies. Nothing but food, drinks, and tobacco. "It doesn't look promising."

"I'll check." Daryl reached out her hand. "Grease my palm, moneybags."

I pulled another twenty from my wallet. She snatched it, jumped out of the car, and jogged into the station's mini-market, her red hair bouncing in the snowy breeze.

Kelly pulled her feet up onto the seat and set her chin on a knee, gazing at me. As cold air seeped into the car, I settled back and focused on her searching eyes. "What's up?"

"Just trying to figure out how to say I'm sorry."

"Sorry for what?"

"I'm not sure." She shrugged. "Everything, I guess. You're so different. I can't figure you out. Neither can Daryl. But she just acts natural around you, so I guess I should, too."

"I'll try to do the same, but ever since my parents died …" My throat narrowed. As my gut threatened to push out a sob, I bit my lip to force it back down. I couldn't possibly say another word without losing it completely.

She laid a gentle hand on my shoulder. "Just take your time."

"Thanks." A tear trickled down my cheek. "Sorry I'm not as easygoing as your friends."

"Daryl and I will help you. And besides …" She leaned over the console, wiped the tear away, and kissed my cheek. "I'd rather be with a kindhearted mourner than a celebrating fool."

Daryl flung open the rear door. "Leave you two alone for one minute and look what happens."

Kelly fell back to her place. "Just a kiss of comfort, Miss Bigmouth."

"I only report what I see." Daryl bounced into her seat and closed the door. "A big yes-sir-ee on the cleaner and the WD-forty." She held up a blue and yellow can. "This was the last one. And the man said, 'No charge.' He owed you five bucks." She slid my twenty into the center console.

"Good. Now we can fix the car and get back on the road."

"But there's a problem. The store guy says the snow's backing up the highway. No one was prepared, so it's a mess. Lots of delays."

I slapped the steering wheel. "But Clara's in trouble. And Francesca."

"Nathan …" Kelly smiled as she sang my name. "When you can't change the weather, you have to learn to chill."

210 | <small>Time Echoes</small>

I heaved a sigh. She was right. No use banging my head against a wall. "At least let's get the car started. We'll see how far we can get."

"The store guy said we could borrow his tools," Daryl said. "Do you need them?"

Kelly nodded. "If the problem's something other than the spark plugs, I'm not sure what I'll need."

"Back in a flash!" Daryl opened her door, scurried to the market, and returned seconds later with a toolbox and a clean white rag. "Open the hood and let the grease monkey do her thing."

As I searched for the lever, Kelly got out and circled to the front of the car. When I popped the hood, she raised it and set the prop rod.

Daryl and I got out to see if we could help, but we became no more than shivering observers while Kelly expertly removed, cleaned, and reinstalled the spark plugs. When she finished, she wiped her hands on the cloth and nodded toward the driver's seat. "Give it a try."

I hopped in and turned the key. The Camry roared to life and purred, sounding better than when we had started.

Kelly slammed the hood. "Gotta wash up," she called as she walked with the toolbox through the curtain of snowflakes.

When she disappeared into the store, Daryl climbed into the backseat and shut the door. "Now that we're alone, it's my turn to give you a kiss."

I kept my gaze locked forward. "That's okay. You don't — "

A foil-wrapped piece of candy dropped into my lap.

Daryl giggled. "Sorry. Couldn't resist."

I snatched up the candy and turned toward her. She smiled and blew me a kiss. "I'll get you to chill out eventually."

I let my own smile break through. "Thanks. I appreciate it."

"Listen, Nathan." Her expression turned serious. "You're a super guy. Maybe the best I've ever met. But I gotta tell you. Kelly's hurting. A lot. Sometimes the pain makes her lash out. So don't let that get you down. Put on a bulletproof vest or asbestos underwear or whatever super guys do to protect themselves. And just be patient. She's worth it."

I nodded. "Thanks again. And I agree. She's worth it."

Kelly ran back and jumped into the car, the can of WD-40 still in her grip. "All set. Let's make tracks."

"Not long, skidding ones, I hope," I said as I backed out.

With the map on her lap, she peered through the steady snowfall and guided me through a series of turns that led to the main highway. As forecasted, cars lined up bumper-to-bumper on the four-lane road.

I glanced at the map. "Any other routes?"

"Sure. But it'll take forever."

"It'll take longer than forever if we use the Interstate."

Following Kelly's new instructions, I turned around and traveled narrow, snow-covered roads, slipping and sliding on occasion. Traffic proved to be much lighter, but the slow going ate away at our time. Radio reports were no help. Weather forecasts seemed to change by the minute, as did road and traffic conditions. No one knew what was going on.

After a couple of hours, the clouds raced to the east, giving way to sunshine that quickly cleared the roads of snow and ice. I rolled down my window and let the warm breeze circulate through the car. As my hair flapped in the wind, I looked at Kelly. "This is getting out of control."

She pulled off her sweatshirt and tossed it into Daryl's lap. "It's either the most realistic nightmare I've ever had, or I'm ready for the loony bin. Take your pick."

I stopped at an intersection and stripped off my own sweatshirt. "We need a third option."

For the next hour, we rode quietly, always watchful for new oddities or anyone who might be following us. When we neared our destination, we began looking for signs of the observatory.

Soon, we passed a driveway that led to an expansive building. One section stood three stories high and another topped out at two. At the far end, a cylindrical building was capped by a white dome with a narrow telescope opening from the apex to the base — the observatory, probably the home of Interfinity's telescope.

I stopped well away from the building. "We'd better hide the car and go on foot. Gordon might've called ahead and told them what we're driving."

After glancing around for any onlookers, I drove the Toyota over the curb and into a wooded area. I parked under an evergreen tree and gestured for Kelly and Daryl to lean close. "Listen. I've done this kind of thing before, so just follow me and don't be shouting stuff like 'Nathan, be careful' because careful isn't going to get the job done."

I pointed at the mirror. "Daryl, I'm going to trust you with that. Guard it with your life."

She saluted. "Aye-aye, sir."

"Kelly, you take the violin. Leave everything else here. We need to travel as light as possible."

She retrieved the case from the rear floorboard. "Got it."

With me leading the way, we skulked through the woods toward the observatory. When we drew close, we found a narrow stone path that led to a back door in the two-story section of the complex.

I grabbed the door's metal handle and pulled. "Locked," I whispered.

Kelly pointed at a numeric pad on the wall. "Want to make a guess?"

"Waste of time." I looked through a square, head-high window embedded in the door. Inside, a short, empty hallway ended at another hallway perpendicular to it. Standing at the intersection, a tall man in a short-sleeved, blue security-guard uniform yawned and looked at his watch. The logo on his sleeve matched the one Dr. Gordon wore on his blazer — the triple infinity sign.

I backed away and scanned the gray cinderblock walls. "Look for an open window."

Daryl pointed up. "I see one on the second floor."

I strode to the wall and pushed my fingers into a gap between two blocks. "There's a narrow ledge above the first floor. If I can get there, I might be able to stand on it and reach the sill."

Daryl shook her head. "That's a big if, Spider-Man. And the ledge isn't any wider than half a foot."

"There's got to be a way to get up there." I stepped back and scanned the lush grassy field surrounding the building. "The lawn's well kept, isn't it?"

Kelly followed my gaze. "Yeah. So?"

"If they keep the landscaping equipment on site, maybe there's an outbuilding we can search. It might have a ladder."

Daryl pointed. "A path."

A thin trail of pulverized leaves led away from the building. Their mower bag probably had a leak.

Ducking low, we followed the path across the lawn and stopped behind a thick clump of trees. A small metal storage shed stood between two saplings, its door open, exposing a lawn tractor parked within.

I walked inside and looked around. A stepladder leaned against one wall, and a coiled rope with an attached towing hook lay on the ground. Perfect.

While I hauled the ladder and Daryl carried the rope and hook, Kelly, still holding the violin, hurried ahead to scout for onlookers. When we returned to the observatory, I grasped the rope near the hook and began swinging it back and forth.

"Wait." Kelly set the violin case down. "Let me."

"Just like shooting hoops?" I asked as I passed the rope to her.

She let the hook dangle under her hand. "Not quite. But I have a good feel for throwing things." She swung the hook back and heaved it upward. It flew into the open window and landed with a dull clank inside.

We rushed to the wall and flattened ourselves against it, gawking at the window to see if anyone would look out. I shifted my gaze to my violin case, sitting in the open where Kelly had left it. Anyone peeking out the window would see it for sure. Five seconds passed. Ten seconds. No one appeared at the window.

I pushed away from the wall, grasped the rope, and pulled until it caught something and held fast. "Now for the stepladder."

After we set it up, the girls steadied the legs while I scrambled to the top. Taking hold of the rope again, I scaled the wall, pulling fist over fist and pushing my shoes against the concrete until I could stand on the ledge between the floors. From there, I leaped and grabbed the windowsill with both hands.

Twin gasps rose from below. I could almost feel their anxiety as I muscled up to the window, pulling with my arms and scrambling with my knees and feet. Finally, I managed to get my chest up to the sill, allowing me to slide the rest of the way in.

I stood and looked around. A long oval conference table surrounded by leather swivel chairs sat in the center of the dim room. A folder had been placed in front of each chair along with a pen and a glass of water. A meeting was about to start.

I dislodged the hook from the window's interior apron and leaned out the opening. Reeling the line through my hands, I lowered the hook toward the ground and whisper-shouted to the girls. "I'll try to open another window somewhere lower."

When the hook touched down, I released the rope. As soon as the end snaked its way to the bottom, the back door on ground level creaked open. The girls swung their heads toward it.

The security guard stepped out. Holding the door open, he nodded at Kelly and Daryl. "May I help you ladies?"

Kelly picked up the violin and walked to him, so close she had to tilt her head up to look him in the eye. "Could you tell us where the tour group is?" She twirled her hair around a finger, giving him a sweet, innocent smile as she swung the violin case back and forth.

"Sure. The tour's almost over, though." He glanced at Daryl. Holding the mirror against her side, she copied Kelly's hair-twirling act, but she looked more clumsy than innocent. "How did you two get back here?"

Kelly pointed toward the side of the building. "We walked from that way."

The guard squinted at the ladder. "What's that doing there?"

I pulled my head back and continued listening.

"Some guy was using it a minute ago," Kelly replied, "but he's gone."

Sounds of another conversation drifted in. Opposite the window, a closed door stood near each end of the room, probably the entrances from a hallway. People would be coming in through one or both of them at any second.

I spotted a table near the door on the right. A coffee pot sat next to a tray of donuts stacked like a pyramid. The door on that side would be the entry point. Holding my breath, I quick stepped toward the other door, picking up one of the folders as I passed. Just as the entry door swung in, I quietly opened the other door and slid out.

Not bothering to look back, I strode confidently down the carpeted hall. As I imagined a dozen eyes staring at me, tingles spread across my neck, but no one called for me to stop. To the left a door led to a stairway. I pushed it open, stepped inside, and leaned against a wall. Now all I had to do was find the tour group without being noticed.

I crept down the stairs. When I reached the lower level, I opened the door leading to the hall and looked both ways. The guard was gone, probably helping the girls find the tour group. I padded along the carpeted corridor toward the observation building and found a door at the end as well as another corridor to the right. A sign on the door's window said, *Security Level A Required*. A keypad hung on the wall next to the door. I tried the knob. Locked. No surprise.

Conversation buzzed from the end of the right-hand corridor, moving closer. I retreated and spotted a set of restrooms. As I hustled toward the men's room, I kicked a crumpled foil wrapper lying on the carpet just outside the ladies' room door. I snatched it up. A Hershey's Kiss. And another wrapper had been wedged at the corner of the Ladies nameplate. I laid a palm on the door. Should I knock or just barge in?

Chattering noises grew. No time to decide. I jerked the door open and tiptoed into the small room, listening for the slightest sound, but it seemed to be unoccupied. I walked to the farther of two stalls and pushed the door open. Inside, my violin lay on the floor, bracing the mirror as it leaned against the wall.

Just as I stepped inside to pick them up, the restroom door swung open. I closed the stall and sat on the toilet seat.

A gruff voice called from the hallway. "Hurry up!"

Soft footsteps padded my way. In the adjacent stall, two athletic shoes came into view, white with purple trim.

I tightened my throat, trying to sound like a woman. "Francesca?"

A gasp echoed. "Who's there?"

I shifted to my normal tone. "It's Nathan."

"What are you doing in the ladies' room?"

"Looking for you and Clara." I leaned closer to the partition. "Do you know where she is?"

"In the observatory building. Some guys locked us in a room. One of them said they're looking for you. He's waiting for me in the hall."

"We can't let him find me."

"What do you want me to do?"

"When he takes you back to Clara, make sure he pays attention to you. I'll be following, so you can't let him look back."

"Okay, but I have to go now."

"Don't worry. I'll be right behind you."

"No. I mean I have to *go*."

Francesca's guard rapped on the door. "I said hurry up!"

"Go ahead."

While trickling sounds emanated from her stall, I opened the violin case, revealing a scrap of paper wedged in the strings. I folded the conference room report into a pocket inside the case's lid, removed the scrap from the strings, and read the scribbled note. *Nathan, we'll try to get into the telescope room. Meet us near the door.*

I stuffed the paper back into the case and latched it. Now to find the telescope room.

Francesca whispered, "I'm ready."

I set a hand on the partition. "I'll give you a head start. Remember to keep him busy."

"Got it." Her shoes shuffled out of the stall. After a quick splash sounded from the sink, she disappeared from sight.

I picked up the violin and mirror, hurried to the restroom exit, and pushed the door open an inch. A heavyset man walked alongside Francesca, the only two people in the hall.

Francesca suddenly crouched, holding her hands over her stomach and moaning. The guard squatted next to her. "What's wrong? Are you sick?"

She moaned even louder. The guard scooped her into his arms and carried her toward the high-security door at the end of the hall.

I bolted from the restroom and marched with fast, quiet steps. When the guard reached the end of the hall, he set Francesca down, but when she let out another loud groan, he picked her up again.

I stopped within ten feet of the door and pressed myself against the wall.

The man set a thick finger over the numeric pad and punched in four digits. When the door buzzed, he pulled it open and carried Francesca inside.

I leaped for the door and jammed my foot in the gap to keep it from closing. Still using my foot, I opened the door a few inches and peeked in. The guard carried Francesca down a curved hallway and, seconds later, walked out of sight.

After squeezing in, I let the door close silently and followed. As the walls bent gradually to the right, I used Dad's mirror to watch the area to the rear, glancing between it and the corridor ahead.

The click of a door latch sounded from somewhere in front. I turned around and walked backwards, watching the mirror again to guide my steps. When the guard appeared in the reflection, I stopped and glanced back — nothing but walls and carpet. Yet, the mirror still showed the guard as he closed a door and walked toward me.

If the mirror told the truth, he would see me in seconds.

CHAPTER EIGHTEEN

I SET THE VIOLIN case down and focused on the guard in the mirror. As he drew closer, his thick biceps and thicker neck clarified. Although he wasn't that close in reality, my hands began to shake. He would be tough to beat in a fight.

He suddenly spun an about-face and walked in the opposite direction. After a few seconds, he disappeared. The door latch sounded again, not from the mirror — for real. Clumping footsteps drew closer, but the mirror showed only empty carpet.

"Arnie! C'mere."

The voice came from somewhere beyond the guard. The footsteps halted for a moment, then resumed and diminished.

Something red flashed in the mirror, like a scarlet garment whipping across the reflection and vanishing. I looked down the hall. Nothing. Had that mysterious girl in red come again?

I picked up my violin and resumed walking backwards. As I approached the door the guard had closed, nothing appeared in the reflection. I tucked the mirror under my arm and wiggled the knob gently.

Locked, of course. I tapped lightly with my knuckles. "Clara? Francesca?"

"Nathan?" Clara's breathless voice drew near. "Is that you?"

"Yes. How long have you been in there?"

"Too long."

I wiggled the knob again. "I don't think I can overpower the guard, so — "

"Hush and listen. Do you see a keypad by the door?"

I looked at the wall. A digital keypad hung a few inches from the jamb. "Yeah. But I didn't see him punch in a code."

"Francesca says he covered it with his hand, so she couldn't watch, but she heard the tones."

I studied the telephone-style buttons. "Each number has a different tone? That's not very secure."

"The difference is minuscule, but Francesca can detect it."

I poised my finger over the pad. "Okay. What do I push?"

"Punch zero through nine slowly. Francesca is listening."

My heart pounding as I watched for the guard, I pressed the numbers, pausing between each one. A few seconds after I finished, Francesca called out, "Eight, four, seven, one."

I entered the numbers. When the lock clicked, the door opened, pushed from the inside by Clara.

"Where's Kelly?" she whispered as she and Francesca walked into the hall.

"We got separated."

"Follow me. It's not safe to stand around here."
Clara bustled down the hall in the direction the guard had
gone and ducked into an elevator alcove. When Francesca
and I caught up, Clara pressed a series of numbers into
the keypad by the door. "I found this code in Dr. Gordon's
office — six, six, five, three. Memorize it."

The door opened. All three of us squeezed into the
one-man elevator car, making it bounce slightly. In order to
fit, I had to keep the mirror at my side and hold the violin
case in front. Francesca, wearing thick leggings and a long-
sleeved, knee-length tunic, squeezed between Clara and
me.

The door closed again, leaving us with only a dim
glow from a low-wattage bulb in one corner of the ceiling.
"Push the button for the third floor," Clara said. "I can't
reach it."

Unable to see any numbers on the darkened
buttons, I squirmed and felt with my pinky for the third
button from the bottom. As soon as I pushed it, the car
jerked. Then, as the motor whined softly, we glided
upward.

Clara whispered into my ear. "From the
conversation I overheard, they should all be gone."

"Who are *they*?"

"Mictar and his scientists." When the car halted,
she said, "Turn around."

The three of us twisted in place, rubbing shoulders
and elbows as a door on the opposite side slid open.
We stepped into an enormous, dome-covered chamber.
Above, shining pinpoints dotted a purplish curved ceiling,
creating an evening-sky canopy that enfolded the room in

twilight. A few desk lamps at workstations near the outer walls provided an adequate amount of light for exploring.

I turned back to the elevator door. Since we were on the top floor, the shaft ended at our level inside a tall closet-like room that protruded from the wall. Just above the door frame, a red numeral three shone from a matchbook-sized LED screen. "So Mictar was here? Is he part of Interfinity?"

"He's not on their organizational chart, but from what I heard, he acts like he runs the place." She walked toward the lighted desks where three laptop computers lay open and turned on. "I'll tell you more in a minute. I have to figure out how the controls work before they get back."

"And we have to find Kelly and a friend of hers named Daryl." I walked to the center of the floor. Standing on an octagonal wooden platform, a cylindrical metal pedestal supported a huge telescope. Its wide lens pointed toward a breach in the dome — a narrow, rectangular hatch that opened to the evening sky. "I found a note from Kelly that said she would try to be near the telescope room door."

I set the violin case down and felt the pedestal's smooth surface. "This place reminds me of where my parents were in the mirror."

"I noticed that as soon as I saw this room with the tour group." Clara pointed at an area near a wooden door that had been cordoned off by a series of thick ropes that sagged between metal support poles. "We were allowed to get that close, and after one of the scientists gave a talk, they cleared us out. When Francesca and I sneaked back in, and I started snooping on one of the laptops, they caught us and threw us in the room where you found us. If Kelly's hanging around out there, it won't be safe for her."

"I'll be right back." I hurried toward to the tourists' area. After I stepped over one of the ropes, something shiny on the floor caught my eye. I bent low and touched two crumpled foil wrappers only inches from the door. "More Kisses?"

"Kisses?" Clara walked closer with Francesca close behind.

I picked up the foil balls and showed them to her. "Hershey Kisses wrappers."

"So?"

I turned the door's deadbolt. The door jerked open, and Kelly and Daryl burst through. Kelly spun back, grabbed the knob, and closed the door gently. "Whew!" she said in a hoarse whisper. "That was close!"

"How long have you two been waiting there?"

"Just a minute or so, this go 'round." She pointed at a watch on Daryl's wrist. "We timed the guard's circuit. When he came by to check this door, we ducked into a janitor's closet. Then when he left, we knelt here and stuffed a couple of candy wrappers under the door."

"How'd you know I'd find them and figure out it was you?"

Daryl patted my cheek. "Because you're Super Guy. And we noticed you collected your stuff at the restroom, so we knew you were clued in to our clues."

"No more time for chitchat," Clara said as she strode toward the computer desks.

I followed, gesturing for Kelly, Daryl and Francesca to come along. "Clara, this is Daryl, a friend of ours. She's a computer genius, so she should be able to help."

"Glad you're here, Daryl." After sliding into a desk chair, Clara scanned the laptop. "Let's see if we can figure this thing out."

Daryl pointed at a control icon on the screen. "That one says, *Dome Mirror Magnitude*. Sounds harmless."

"Let's try it." Clara clicked a mouse pad button and slid her finger down the surface. The pinpoints of light on the ceiling faded away. Seconds later, an aerial image appeared, a reflection of all five of us looking up at the dome.

"It's a huge, curved mirror," Kelly said, tilting her head upward. "That explains why Nathan's parents were upside down on the ceiling."

Daryl sat in front of one of the other laptops. "I'll see what this station can do."

I set my mirror on the desk and leaned close to Clara's computer. A three-dimensional rendering of the room's telescope filled most of the display area. "Which control did you use to switch to mirror mode?"

Clara pointed at the slider bar widget on the screen. "I dragged it all the way down to the bottom."

"Let's turn it back on for a minute." I moved the slider to the top. The ceiling faded to purple, a darker purple than before, and the pinpoints reappeared. I set my fingers on the keyboard. "I'll bet we can adjust the telescope's position by changing the coordinates in those three text boxes."

I changed each number by a single unit. The telescope in the middle of the room hummed and shifted slightly as did the entire dome above, moving the opening in the ceiling to match the telescope's new direction.

Clara aimed her gaze at the ceiling again. "I'll wager that the mirror's showing what the telescope sees. It's the evening sky."

A tapping noise drew our attention to Daryl as she clicked her fingernail on the other computer's desk. "Check this out."

I scooted over and studied the screen, but I couldn't make any sense out of the boxes, numbers, and words. "What am I supposed to be seeing?"

Daryl set her finger over a screen icon. "Look. Three windows labeled Earth Red, Earth Blue, and Earth Yellow. Earth Red is highlighted, so I'm guessing the mirror is showing the stars in the Earth Red world."

She glided the mouse pointer across the screen. A line connected Earth Red and Earth Blue. When Daryl let the mouse hover over the line, a message popped up saying, "Network Active."

I let out a low whistle. "A multi-world computer network."

Captions under the three windows showed the date and time for each world. I glanced at my watch. Earth Red's time matched mine, so that settled which world was ours. Earth Yellow showed December 1978, and Earth Blue showed October of this year; five days in the future.

Kelly crossed her arms as she studied the screen. "How can the computer know the date and time in the other worlds?"

"Sun, moon, and star positions." Daryl looked at the ceiling. "If they can precisely monitor the heavens in each world, they can know exactly what time it is there."

I bent closer. "Watch how the seconds change on Earth Blue. Sometimes they go slow, and sometimes they go fast. And on Earth Yellow, they're going a lot faster. What's up with that?"

"Like I told you before," Daryl said, "the worlds are in parallel, but they aren't anchored to each other in time. It's sort of like three boats on a river that catch different currents. Sometimes one will go faster than the other, then it might slow down again."

Kelly leaned in. "So it's like Earth Yellow is trying to catch up with the others."

"But that could change." Daryl set her finger on the mouse pad. "Let's switch it and see what happens. I want to get a look at the future." She clicked on the Earth Blue icon. The mirror flickered, and the stars shifted slightly.

"That didn't do much." I backed away from the desk and looked up. "But I guess we shouldn't expect it to. It's only five days, and it's about the same time of night."

Daryl squinted at the screen. "Here's a selector in the corner that's set to Optical Telescope. The other option is Radio Telescope."

Clara flicked her thumb behind her. "Interfinity has a hookup to a radio telescope about ten miles away. That selector probably allows them to control it from here."

"Let's see what happens." Daryl clicked on the radio telescope option. The mirror on the ceiling flashed, and the starry canopy changed to a frenzied jumble of tiny multicolored shapes — polygons, ribbons, ovals, and indistinct globules — each morphing from one shape to another. "Well, that looks interesting … whatever it is."

I stared at the chaotic display. It was mesmerizing, almost hypnotic.

Daryl leaned back in her chair and looked up. "It's probably a computer rendering of the radio noise from space. Some programmer translated it into a visual array."

Clara shook her head. "But what good is it? It looks like a chimpanzee's finger painting."

"Maybe it's loaded with information," I said. "It just has to be decoded."

Staring wide-eyed at the ceiling, Francesca breathed a quiet, "Aren't the sounds amazing?"

"What sounds are you talking about?" I asked.

"Can't you hear them? It's like every shape up there is singing a note, but they aren't in harmony."

I looked at Daryl. "Is there a volume control?"

"Maybe this is it." As Daryl adjusted a slider bar, thousands of dissonant musical notes poured from speakers embedded somewhere in the walls.

I covered my ears. "It's like the worst orchestra in the world. Every musician's on a different page, and Clara's chimp is conducting."

"I hear a melody," Francesca said. "It's mixed up inside the noise, but I hear it."

"Do you recognize it?"

Francesca shook her head. "But I think I could play it." Her pupils reflected the cacophony of colors above, just as Mom's eyes had done.

I hustled to the case, flipped it open, and handed Francesca the violin. As she settled it under her chin and curled her fingers around the neck, her brow furrowed. "Yours is bigger than mine. I'll have to adjust."

She poised the bow above the strings, her eyes closed as she concentrated. Then, setting the bow hairs lightly on the A string, she played a long, quiet note, moving her fingers along the string to adjust the sound. She then shifted to the E string and did the same.

She stopped and sighed. "This is hard. The melody is fast and mixed in with the noise."

"You can do it." I patted her on the back. "Just keep trying."

Francesca resumed playing notes, sometimes several in succession that kept to a melodic scheme. As the minutes ticked by, her connected phrases lengthened, and the notes blended together into a design that became more and more familiar.

I stared at the colors on the ceiling and whispered, "It's Dvořák, from the New World Symphony."

The shapes broke apart and seemed to bleed their pigments into each other, creating new forms, indistinct and miscolored — humanoids with knobby blue hands and spaghetti-thin green torsos.

As they blended, Francesca's eyes brightened with the same white light that shone from the eyes of her adult namesake, yet not quite as brilliant and without the expanding beams.

I touched Francesca's shoulder. "Can you play it louder?"

Without a word, she stepped away and, dipping her head and arms, began stroking her instrument with passion. Her fingers danced along the neck, while her bow flew back and forth in a hypnotic sway.

Heavenly music filled the room. Her eyes began to blaze. The colors sharpened, as if called to order by the musician's bow. The shapes molded into real human forms, two men standing in a dimly lit room.

I tried to keep an eye on the scene above while at the same time watching my mother, in the guise of a youthful prodigy, play her part of this strange New World performance. She had become a generator of musical energy, a dynamo who could somehow feed on the cosmic sounds and pour out their vitality in a visible spectrum. Yet, her arms sagged a bit. Playing like this would soon drain her.

Above, the men in the mirror image sharpened to photo-realistic quality, moving about their scene in apparent real time.

Daryl pointed. "Dr. Gordon's there."

As if drawn by the music, Clara walked with a swaying rhythm to the center of the room. I joined her, mesmerized by the scene above, an exact copy of this chamber, yet populated by a different set of characters, including Dr. Gordon who stood next to the telescope in the middle of the room. He and Mictar, looking as pale as ever, seemed to be conversing in the Earth Blue world.

A bandage covered part of Dr. Gordon's cheek. So there had to be two Dr. Gordons, one on Earth Blue who tried to kill Kelly and me, and one on Earth Red who showed up at the high school.

As the scene continued brightening, Mom came into view in the background. She sat in one of the rolling swivel chairs, her head erect and her chin firm, though her hands were bound behind her back.

Mictar's thin, pale lips moved, but no voice emerged. Leaning toward Mom, he wrapped his spindly fingers around her throat, and his voice broke through the chaotic noise. "If you don't tell me the secret of Quattro, I will feed on your eyes."

She glared at him, saying nothing.

He shoved her backwards. She tipped in her chair and, unable to brace herself because of her bonds, toppled over. As she looked up at him, her expression still defiant, he pointed toward a wall. "Take her to her room."

Mictar stalked away. Dr. Gordon untied Mom, helped her rise, and led her somewhere out of sight. The room in the reflection lay vacant.

I growled, "We have to get there."

"A flash of light?" Kelly asked.

I waved a hand toward the wall. "Everyone look for light switches. Quick. Before Francesca gets too tired."

Clara hurried toward one side of the room. Daryl ran to the other. I rushed to the desk and grabbed my mirror while Kelly stood in front of Francesca and spoke a mile a minute. "You're amazing. Better than any rock star. I wish I had talent like yours. Just hang in there."

Francesca grimaced but played on, her intonation staying true. I rejoined her and helped with the encouragement. "Just a few more notes. You can do it."

"I found the switches," Daryl called.

Lights blinked on from around the base of the perimeter. Trumpet-shaped track lights shot white beams toward the ceiling that gathered at the top of the dome. Each beam split into a hundred thin shafts of light that rebounded toward the floor, some piercing Kelly, Francesca, and me, while other shafts surrounded us in a laser-beam cage.

Francesca stopped playing. The ceiling reflection descended toward us, sliding down the laser pathways and along the perimeter wall. Within seconds, the scene from the other world spread over the trumpet-like fixtures and blocked their glow. Clara and Daryl faded along with the failing lights.

Soon, our surroundings took·shape. We remained inside the observatory dome, but the telescope aimed in a different direction, only two laptop computers rested on the workstation table, and the tour group door stood wide open. The mirror above displayed the starry sky, darker purple than before, with more yellowish-white pinpoints.

I looked toward the light switches. Clara and Daryl were nowhere in sight. A motor hummed from the elevator. Above its door, the red numeral switched from a 2 to a 1. "Dr. Gordon must be taking Mom to a room downstairs. We have to follow him."

Kelly stepped near the elevator call button. "Think it's safe to go this way?"

"Can't risk calling it. They might notice the signal."

She nodded toward the tour door. "We could go that way, but if this world is the same as ours, we'd need a code to get into the secure area."

"I don't know that code. I just caught the door before it closed."

Francesca raised her violin bow. "I know the numbers. The guard couldn't cover the pad because he was carrying me."

"The code might not be the same in this world," I said, "but it's worth a try."

The elevator motor kicked in with a low thud and began humming. The number above the door changed back to a 2.

"Let's go." I gave Kelly the mirror and repacked the violin and bow. Kelly leading the way, we raced through the open door and along the carpeted hall. After turning

234 | TIME ECHOES

into another corridor and hustling to the end, she jerked
open a door leading to a stairwell. Once we filed inside
and the door swung closed, I pulled Kelly and Francesca
into a huddle near the top step. "Let's think for a minute."

Kelly laid a hand on her chest. "Speaking of
thinking, I think my heart's kicking my lungs."

I set the violin case down, leaned over the metal
rail, and looked at the gap between the flights of stairs.
"This place is familiar."

"It should be." Kelly took a deep breath and let it
out slowly. "If you go down to the second floor, you'll be
next to the room where you climbed in the building."

"So on the first floor it'll come out near the secure
area." I turned to Francesca. "What's the code?"

She closed her eyes and recited. "Nine, three, eight,
zero."

I whispered the numbers. Strange. The code on the
door where they kept her and Clara was eight, four, seven,
one. The two codes followed a pattern. "When we get to
the first floor, I'll sneak out by myself and try the numbers,
while you watch from the stairwell. If they work, you two
follow."

After picking up the violin and descending the
stairs with the mirror tucked at my side, I opened the
hallway door a crack and peeked out. No one was around.
I slipped into the hall and headed for the door to the secure
area. When I passed the adjacent hallway that led to the
rear of the observatory, a light flickered in that direction.

I looked back toward the stairs. Kelly's eyes
appeared through a tiny sliver in the doorway. Raising a
finger, I mouthed, "Just a minute" and set the violin case
down.

Running on the balls of my feet, I hurried to the exit door and looked out its square window. Well to the right, a light shone from a fixture hanging on the curved wall of the domed building. Since night had taken over the skies, not much else was visible.

Just as I was about to turn back, lights flashed outside. A small car drove into view, scuffing the sandy driveway as it skidded to a stop.

The driver jumped out — a tall, muscular guy wearing a tight gray sweatshirt. With his oversized hood pulled up, shadows covered his face, and billows of white puffed from within. Obviously it was a cold evening on Earth Blue. Maybe the freakish weather had invaded this world as well.

As the driver shuffled to the back of the car, the trunk popped open. He withdrew a square white box about the size of a small toaster oven, then leaned over and peered into the car's window as if looking for something on the backseat.

He jerked his head around. Another set of lights flashed in his face. He raised a forearm to shield his eyes, then, ducking his head low, rushed toward the observatory.

A black Mustang convertible screeched into view and smacked into the side of the smaller car. The Mustang driver leaped out, carrying a shotgun at his hip.

CHAPTER NINETEEN

I CROUCHED IN THE corner next to the hinges. Since the hall was barely wider than the entryway, there was nowhere else to go.

The security pad beeped four times. When the lock disengaged, a barrage of shotgun blasts ripped into the metallic entrance, sounding like a thousand pebbles thrashing an aluminum garbage can. Something thudded against the door and pushed it open. The sweatshirt-clad man fell into the hallway, still holding the white box at his side.

Lying facedown across the threshold, his buckshot-riddled body propped the door. Blood spread across the back of his sweatshirt, connecting dozens of holes in a wash of muted scarlet.

I leaped up and looked outside. The attacker was reloading, his attention on the shotgun. I grabbed the victim's wrists and pulled, but something caught. He wouldn't budge.

Groaning, the man turned his head and looked up at me with bulging eyes. "Nathan?"

I dropped to my knees. "Mr. Clark? Tony Clark?"

Tony slid the box into my hands. "Clara sent this for your father. She said it might be his only hope."

The gunman engaged a new shell with a loud snap and stalked toward us. Tony pushed against the floor, and, with my help, rose to his feet. Staggering in place, he shoved me. "Get the box to your father. I'll hold him off." He took a long stride out the door and slammed it shut.

Tony's distinctive voice penetrated the metal barrier. "Back off, Jack!"

Like booming thunder, the shotgun replied with two volleys. More pellets rained on the door, followed by a thud and the scraping sound of Tony's body sliding down the outer side.

I clutched my stomach but kept silent, not daring to breathe. I eased toward the door's window and peeked through the glass. Tony lay motionless in front of the door, his chest a ragged mess of bloody, shredded cotton. Showing no hint of movement, he had to be dead. But I couldn't leave him without checking.

The Mustang driver, his shotgun again at his hip, stalked toward the door. Although he also wore a hooded sweatshirt, light passed across his bearded face. He was the same driver from Earth Red who broke into the Clarks' house. Or was he the Earth Blue copy?

I ducked into the corner and fixed my gaze on the bloodstained box in my hands. The doorknob rattled. I scrunched lower and looked up. The man pressed his face against the window, making his nose look pink and bulbous. With a grunt, he thrust his shoulder against the door, but it held firm.

Inching forward in a painful crouch, I held the box in one hand and kept the mirror in front with the other, allowing a view of the window while I crouched as low as possible.

The butt of a shotgun smashed through the glass, sending shards over me. The man extended his arm through the hole and stretched for the doorknob, but it was out of his reach.

When he withdrew his arm, I waited and listened. The mirror continued reflecting reality, nothing that would help me decide what to do. A cold draft descended from the shattered window, carrying with it the man's low voice, grumbles peppered with obscenities. Seconds later, the shotgun's clacking noise cut into the sounds.

I cringed. Would he try to shoot his way in? As I eyed the box, Tony's words echoed. *Clara sent this for your father. She said it might be his only hope.* Taking a deep breath, I nodded. I couldn't save Tony, but I could try to save Dad. It was now or never.

Tucking the mirror and holding the box, I lunged and ran down the hall.

"Hey!" the man shouted. "Wait!"

I shuddered. Would a shotgun blast follow the killer's call? Just as I turned the corner toward the stairs and looked back, a swarm of pellets smashed into the wall. The gun's echoing boom immediately followed.

Kelly and Francesca rushed from the stairwell. "Who's doing all that shooting?" Kelly asked.

I showed the box to her. "Someone shot the guy who delivered this." I couldn't bear to tell her the victim's identity. "We have to get out of here."

Kelly picked up the violin case. "Let's haul."

Gesturing for the girls to stay close, I edged toward the exit corridor. "My guess is he'll shoot the lock to try to break in. When I give the word, we'll run to the secure area. Since he doesn't know the codes, we should be safe in there."

"Until he shoots through that door, too. And what if the code's different in this world?"

"Then get ready for some unexpected ventilation."

The shotgun boomed. I shouted, "Now!" We rushed across the exit hall and scrambled down the additional twenty feet to the door leading to the secure area.

"I'll watch the mirror," I said, holding it up. "You punch in the code."

Kelly gave Francesca the violin case and raised a hand to the keypad. "What were the numbers again?"

"Nine, three, eight, zero." I braced the mirror in one hand and pressed the box against my opposite side. In the reflection, the area behind me was clear except for debris from the shotgun blast.

As she punched in the numbers, the pad beeped, but no disengaging sound followed. She pulled the door handle. "Still locked."

Two people appeared in the mirror. A quick glance to the rear proved that they weren't really there yet. "Try another code with the same pattern. Maybe seven, five, six, two."

She entered the digits, then balled her fist. "I messed up."

"Try again."

"I hear footsteps," Francesca said. "Like someone running."

I checked the mirror. Two men carrying scoped rifles dashed toward us from the far end of the hall, though they weren't visible yet in reality. "Guards are coming. They must have heard the gunshots."

Francesca pointed. "There they are."

At the end of the hall, a pair of guards careened around a corner and stormed our way. One shouted, "Put your hands up!"

"What do we do?" Kelly asked.

In the mirror, the guards crouched in fear. A distraction was coming. Probably the shotgun guy. I whispered to Kelly, "Just stay calm and be ready to press the buttons."

Another gun blast sounded from the exit hallway. The guards halted just before the intersection and dropped to their haunches.

I yelled, "There's a guy with a shotgun out there! We've been trying to get away from him!"

One of the guards touched the other on the shoulder. "Cover me, Dave." Lowering his head, he charged toward the exit. The other guard stood and fired round after round toward the door, aiming high enough to miss his partner.

The shotgun sounded again, followed by the clanking racket of a door banging open. The second guard rushed toward the exit.

I hissed, "Now!"

Two more weapons fired, a rifle and a shotgun. Someone cried out, "Dave! Dave!"

Kelly spoke the numbers while punching them in. "Seven ... five ..."

The Mustang driver appeared in the mirror and turned toward us, but I dared not tell Kelly.

Another shotgun blast thundered. A man groaned. A single set of footsteps approached, slow and labored.

"Six ... two." The lock buzzed. She flung the door open.

We hustled through and closed the door. I took the violin case from Francesca. "Everyone low."

While the girls sat with their legs crossed and their backs to the door, I leaned the mirror and violin against the wall and set the box to hold them in place. I sat to Kelly's left and whispered, "Don't make a sound. If he thinks we're in here, he might blast through."

The thuds of stomping feet drew nearer, out-of-rhythm footfalls that slowed as they approached. Kelly trembled. Francesca gritted her teeth. Both stayed completely silent.

Something slapped against the door. Beeps sounded from the security keypad, but the latch stayed quiet. A deep groan filtered through the wall, then muttered curses followed by more uneven footfalls that faded to silence.

I exhaled. The girls did the same. I rose and peeked out the door's window. A bloody handprint smeared the glass, but no one was in sight, though a red trail marked the gunman's path.

I reached a hand to each of the girls. "Looks safe. At least for now."

When they pulled to their feet, I collected the violin and box while Kelly picked up the mirror.

She touched the box's blood-spattered top. "What's in it?"

"I don't know." I looked it over. Like the trunk, there was no obvious way to open it. "We'll figure it out later. First we have to check the room where they kept Clara and Francesca."

We hurried along the curving hallway. When we reached the door, I paused, looked both ways, and rapped lightly. I held my breath and listened. No answer.

I looked at the keypad and punched eight, four, seven, one. The lock clicked. I pulled the door open, revealing a dark room.

Kelly reached in and swiped her fingers across the wall. Lights on the ceiling flickered to life, though they were dim.

I peered inside. The room, about twelve-by-twelve feet, held a short wooden stool, a green beanbag chair, and scattered sheets of paper. On one of the stone walls, four chains dangled from rings embedded at points spaced roughly where hands and feet could be locked in place.

This was where Dad must have hung. The torture had provoked moans that punched through cosmic boundaries and entered Kelly's ears not long ago.

While I propped the door with my foot, Kelly walked in and touched one of the dull chains. "So the cries of pain brought us here. Now what?"

I picked up one of the sheets and read the script, definitely Mom's handwriting. Maybe the words held a clue to where they had taken her. "Let's gather these and get out of here."

As I held the door and kept watch down the hallway, Kelly and Francesca collected the sheets.

"I found a stub of a pencil," Kelly said, holding it in her fingertips.

"Knowing my parents," I said as I took the papers, "this is all in code. Let's find a safe place to decipher it."

I leaned again into the hallway. No one was in sight. "Let's stay in the secure area. With that murderer stomping around out there, this might be the only safe place."

Kelly winked. "Is there a ladies room in this hall?"

"Good idea."

After locating a ladies' restroom, we entered and settled on the floor. Sitting next to Francesca, I held the white box in my lap with my back against the cool, tiled wall. At a sink, Kelly ran water over a handful of paper towels, handed them to Francesca, and pulled another towel from a wall dispenser. "Want to wash your face, Nathan?"

"In a minute." I gave the box a light shake, but it made no noise. "Maybe I should look at it in the mirror like I did with the trunk."

Kelly sat on my other side with the violin case between us and mopped her forehead with a moistened towel. "I guess it won't hurt to try."

A low boom thundered from somewhere in the distance. Kelly flinched. "It seems like we're just waiting for him to find us."

"At least the noise lets us know how far away he is."

"Now *that's* a comforting thought." She wadded her towel and tossed it at the wastebasket across the room. It sailed in and thudded at the bottom. "I wonder if Clara and Daryl got away in our world."

"We can hope." I nodded toward the restroom exit. "We could try to go back, but I can't leave without finding my parents."

Kelly laid a hand on my arm. "Not to be a cloud of doom, but remember that they might not be your real parents."

"I remember." I let my head droop. Did it matter which world they were from? What would Kelly think if she knew her Earth Blue father got blasted by a shotgun? Would it make a difference to her? Probably not. No matter how much she hated what he did, she'd be devastated. It wasn't a good time to tell her. Not yet.

Francesca threw her wadded towel toward the wastebasket, but it hit the side and fell to the floor. She let out a sigh and looked at me. "When are you going to tell me what's going on?"

I shifted toward her. "Tell me what you know, and I'll try to fill in the gaps."

She lifted three fingers. "There are three worlds. You and Kelly are from one, I'm from another, and this is the third one."

"Right. Keep going."

She lowered her hand. "Then it gets really crazy. You're looking for your mother." She pointed at herself. "But you think *I'm* your mother."

"You're going to be the mother of a copy of me in your world, which happens to be behind my world in the flow of time. This world we're in is ahead of mine by five days. Or at least it was when we left my world."

"But if there are only three worlds, and we're in the one that's ahead of yours in time, how do you see stuff in your mirror before it happens? Doesn't that mean there's a fourth world?"

"Good deduction." I turned toward Kelly. "I wonder if Gordon and Mictar believe there's a fourth world."

"They already know about three," she said. "Since *cuatro* means four in Spanish, they probably believe it."

"My father spelled Quattro with a Q, so maybe it doesn't translate to four like it does in Spanish. Since he probably knows a lot more about it than they do, they're trying to turn the screws on him." I looked at the mirror in my hands. It had come through for us at every dangerous turn. No wonder Dad wanted me to look at it in times of trouble. It really worked.

"Wouldn't my mirror also be in this world?" I asked Kelly. "If Gordon and Mictar knew about it, wouldn't they do anything to get it? And if they already killed us in this world, they should have been able to take it from me."

"Unless you didn't have it with you when you died. Remember what Gordon said when he searched our bodies … I mean, the other Nathan and Kelly bodies? He was upset that the other Nathan didn't bring something with him. The other Nathan said it was locked up forever." She picked up the box. "Want to bet it's in here?"

"Could be." I stared at the bloodstained surface, imagining the square of polished glass sitting inside. If Tony wanted Dad to have the mirror, how did he expect Dad to open the box? Wouldn't he need a Quattro mirror to get to the mirror inside?

Kelly pulled a barrette from her hair. "I think I see something. If I can just get rid of a little of this blood." With her locks dangling over an eye, she scraped the barrette against the box's surface. "I got it." She held the box close to the wall's light fixture and squinted. "It says, 'To Flash, from Medusa.'" She looked at me. "To your father, from Clara."

"Right." I brushed the dried blood away. "But how could she know where to send it?"

Another shotgun blast boomed in the distance, louder than before.

Kelly rubbed her goose-bump-covered arms. "Let's just try to get it open."

I rose to my knees, turned toward the wall, and leaned the mirror against it, then slid the box into the mirror's view. I stared at it for several seconds, but nothing happened.

"I guess I'll look at the coded pages while we're waiting." I picked up the stack of paper and reseated myself. Since the pages were numbered, I rifled through the sheets until I found page one, then gave the rest to Kelly. "Can you sort these while I work on this one?"

"Sure." She divided the stack and handed half to Francesca. "Want to help?"

Francesca grinned. "Anything for my son."

I returned the grin. "Thanks, Mom." Settling back against the wall, I dug the pencil stub out of my pocket and underlined every three-syllable word on the page. Dad and I had often used this algorithm for handwritten notes. The last letter in the first underlined word would be the first letter in the decrypted note. The second to last letter in the next word would follow, and so on. When I reached the beginning letter of a word, I would start again with the last letter of the next three-syllable word.

I pointed at the first word — *Royalty* — and jotted *Y* in the margin. The next word was *pollution*, so the second letter was *O*. Next came *interrupt*, so the letter was *U*.

I continued the tedious process, penciling the letters neatly around the margin and adding hyphens where I thought one word ended and the next began. When Kelly handed me the second page, I copied the decoded letter string over to it.

From time to time, I glanced at the mirror, but the box stayed closed. As I grew tired, I paused after every deciphered word, leaned my head back, and closed my eyes for a few seconds.

Two more shotgun blasts brought new chills, but I stayed calm and worked methodically. I couldn't afford to make a mistake. One missed three-syllable word or a miscounted letter would ruin the entire decryption. I resisted the urge to read the message. Not knowing what it said forced me to work faster.

Kelly's yawns grew frequent, and Francesca fell asleep on the floor, but I had to keep going. Finally, I took a deep breath and set down the last page. "Okay, let's see what we've got."

Kelly scooted close and looked on.

I whispered the words. "Your goal, stop Mictar from making Interfinity, collision of worlds. Trust Gordon Red. Not Gordon Blue. Trust Simon Red. Unsure of Simon Blue. We are your parents from other world, not your real ones. Help us escape to stop Mictar, but get to the funeral on Earth Red."

I let the page slip from my fingers. My throat tightened. I tried to speak, but nothing came out. Mom and Dad really were dead. Although the mystery of how the instructions appeared in an Earth Red email account remained, it seemed impossible to deny this new revelation. Nathan Blue was dead, so they couldn't have been writing the message to him.

Kelly rubbed my shoulder. "Oh, Nathan. I'm so sorry."

I leaned my head against the tiles and squeezed my eyelids closed. As tears seeped through, I took a quick breath and choked out, "I really thought ... I could find them ... I still hoped they were alive."

She slid her hand into mine and interlocked our thumbs. "But we can still save the other Nathan's parents."

"I know." I blinked through my tears. "But Nathan Blue is dead. I'm an orphan, and his parents are childless."

She brushed her fingers across my knuckles. "I guess, if you want, you could trade places. You could be their son, and you'd have new parents."

"You know it wouldn't be the same."

"Maybe I don't." She released my hand and folded hers in her lap. "I'd take your parents from the other world any day."

I gazed into her sad blue eyes. "I guess I can't blame you for that. You have it pretty rough."

As a flush of red colored her cheeks, her tone sharpened. "You don't know the half of it. My father makes me play basketball with guys more than a foot taller than me, and when I get punched in the face, he laughs and makes fun of me if I cry. Last year, when he wanted Steven on the team, he made me go out with him, and he even picked out a low-cut dress for me to wear." Her gaze drifted to her chest. "I guess he notices I'm a girl only when it's convenient."

I gave her a sympathetic nod. "That's really tough. I can't imagine what it's like."

She sighed. "And you already know he brings women home, even though he and Mom aren't divorced yet."

"Yeah." I lowered my head. "I'm sorry."

She touched my knee. "Don't be. It's his fault, not yours."

I looked at her fingers, still smudged from cleaning the spark plugs. Again, this strange blend of femininity and toughness seemed enchanting. "I guess I always hope people can change, you know, decide to reform. Maybe your father has a spark of … chivalry, I guess. We just have to find it and help it grow."

"My dad?" Kelly rolled her eyes. "Get real. He's so stubborn, he makes mules look compliant. To him, chivalry means not whistling at scantily clad women."

I closed my eyes. The earlier comment about her dress latched on to my brain and wouldn't let go. I had to ask about it. After a few seconds, I looked at her again. "Can I ask you one question?"

"As long as I'm spilling my guts, you might as well."

I spoke softly, trying to convey a tone of sympathy. "That dress … the low-cut one. Did you wear it?"

Kelly tightened her clasped hands. Her cheeks flushed again as she whispered, "I wore it."

"Because your dad made you wear it?"

Focusing on her lap, she shook her head. "To be honest, I liked it. I knew it was wrong to be recruiting bait, but I liked how I felt when I wore it. I liked the way Steven looked at me. But that changed in a hurry."

"How?"

A tear slid toward her cheek. "During the summer, my father was playing an away game in his league, so I went out with some girlfriends to the mall in Des Moines, and I saw my mother in a restaurant with a guy I didn't recognize."

The tear dripped to her jeans, and her voice pitched higher. "She was wearing my dress, and the guy was staring at her. I wanted to scream, 'Mother! What are you doing? Are you some kind of hooker?'"

She pointed at herself. "But then I realized that I was the hooker. I was the one trying to hook a guy into doing something by giving him a look at my ..." She glanced at Francesca, who had begun to stir. "My body."

"So what did you do?"

"When my mother got home and went to bed, I sneaked into her room and got my dress. I burned it the next morning."

I drew my head back. "You burned it?"

"It was kind of ceremonial. I went to the backyard and laid it over some dried cornstalks along with this skimpy tank top I had and set it all on fire. Then I buried the ashes and stomped on their grave." She let a thin smile turn her lips. "I swore out loud that I wasn't going to be like my mother, so I started replacing my wardrobe bit by bit. And when I met you, it made me more determined than ever."

I set a finger on my chest. "I made you determined? How?"

"Nathan, don't make me get all sensitive and sappy. I've bared my soul enough for one day."

"No problem. You don't have to say another word." I took her hand, raised it to my lips, and gave her a soft peck on her knuckles. "But you gave me a great compliment. Thank you."

When I let go of her hand, her cheeks turned redder than ever, but she just stared at me and said nothing.

I peeked at Francesca as she snoozed on. "So people *can* change. Even your father."

Kelly shook her head. "You don't know him like I do."

"How can you be so sure? He might — "

"Nathan." Kelly pointed. "Look at the mirror."

I spun toward it. In the reflection, the box was open.

CHAPTER TWENTY

KELLY EXTENDED A hand toward the box. In the mirror, her fingers passed through the flipped-up lid and stopped at the top of the opening. At the real box, she pushed down on the lid, unable to penetrate. "That's creepy."

I slid close to the mirror and straddled the box with my knees on the floor. "Okay. Just like with the trunk, don't look at the real box while I do this."

"Gotcha."

While staring at the reflection, I leaned forward and moved the real box out of my field of vision. I then guided my mirror hands over the bloodstained top, which opened away from my body, blocking a view of what was inside. I reached in and felt something flat, smooth, and glassy, just like the mirror, but as I slid my fingers farther down, they came across something more tactile and bulky.

I grasped the bulky object and, lifting carefully, placed it on the floor. Then, I picked up the box and turned it over, hoping to dump out anything left inside, but it seemed empty.

After closing my eyes for a brief moment, I set the box down and looked at it on the floor rather than in the mirror. As expected, the box was closed.

I pushed it out of the way. A mirror identical to the other one leaned against my thigh. My father's camera was attached to the back, secured by layers of duct tape. I picked up the package and showed it to Kelly.

As she touched the silvery tape, her lips twitched. "Who would attach a camera to a mirror with duct tape?"

"Kind of strange, isn't it?" I began peeling the tape back and rubbing glue residue from the mirror. Since I had the benefit of knowing what happened to her Earth Blue father, shouldn't she have the same benefit? It would be tough, but she could handle it.

"The shotgun guy's been quiet. He might be dead or passed out." I motioned toward the hall with my thumb. "It's probably safe to show you something you need to see."

Kelly laid the camera strap around her neck. "Lead the way."

After I gathered the violin case and both mirrors, and Kelly coaxed Francesca out of slumber, we left the restroom and exited the secure area.

We padded through the hallways and stepped over the two dead guards. At the rear entrance, a breeze poured through a basketball-sized hole that perforated the jamb and door where the lock used to be. The door swung open an inch or so, making the hinges squeak, then thudded shut again. As it repeated the opening and closing cycle, the hallway appeared to be breathing.

I set my load down and pulled the door open. Bloodstains smeared the threshold and the concrete pad on the outside, but Tony's body and car were gone.

Headlight beams swept across the lawn and aimed our way. I hustled the girls back inside and guided them into the same corner where I had hidden. As I eased the door closed, I kept watch through the shattered window. I whispered, "The car looks familiar."

Kelly rose from the corner and peered out. "That's our Camry."

As the car turned into the light, the driver's face came into view. "It's Clara." I swung the door open and ran outside, followed by Kelly and Francesca.

The car stopped in a skid. Clara jumped out and embraced me. "Oh, Nathan! It's really you!" She laid her hand behind my head and pulled me close as her entire body shook. "My dear boy, I thought I'd never see you again."

The passenger door opened. Daryl emerged, shivering in a gray hoodie. When she saw Kelly, her eyes shot open. "You're here!"

Kelly spread out her arms. "In the flesh."

Daryl ran around the car and hugged Kelly. "I can't believe you're both alive."

I allowed Clara to enjoy the embrace, not wanting to reveal that I wasn't the Nathan she remembered. Still, there was too much to do. I pulled back and looked into Clara's glistening eyes. Dried tear tracks stained her cheeks. "Are you all right?" I asked.

She brushed away a new tear. "Many terrible events have taken place, but as soon as I gather my wits, I will explain."

"Right. We all have to get our bearings." I nodded toward Kelly and Francesca. "We're from another world, and you're — "

"Residents of Earth Blue," Daryl said, "and you're from Earth Red. Daryl Red explained everything to me."

I narrowed my eyes. "Daryl Red contacted you? How?"

"Apparently Interfinity has a rudimentary network connection between the worlds. It's not like they can browse the web from across the cosmic wires, but Daryl Red figured out how to send me an email." She grinned. "I'm so proud of her."

"We knew you aren't from Earth Blue," Clara said. "But I couldn't stop my emotions from gushing. We already miss Nathan and Kelly so much."

Kelly's stare riveted on the Camry. Her voice took on a slight tremble. "Did Daryl Red tell you to bring the mirror and camera to us?"

Daryl Blue nodded. "We were trying to get those things to Nathan's parents … or the other Nathan's parents, I guess." She shook her head, making her red hair fly in the breeze. "It's all so confusing, but Daryl Red gave me the code for that door, so we thought we could get it done."

Looking at the blood on the doorstep, Kelly cleared her throat. Punctuated by suppressed sobs, her words broke into shattered pieces. "Who … who brought … the box … to the door?"

Daryl Blue embraced Kelly again. "Kelly, I have something awful to tell you."

Clara grabbed my arm and led me to the Camry, whispering, "We put him in the backseat. I wanted to show you first."

I peered through the window. Tony's body lay face up on the blood-soaked fabric, his sweatshirt ripped and still dripping red. Even though I had already seen his corpse, a gut-wrenching pain stabbed my heart.

Kelly tore away from Daryl Blue's arms, rushed to the car, and pressed a palm against the window. She squeaked, "Daddy?"

Clara laid her hands on Kelly's shoulders. "He's not — "

Kelly banged her fist on the glass and cried out, "Daddy!"

"Quiet!" Clara slapped her palm over Kelly's mouth and pulled her away from the window, whispering, "He's not your father. He *is* Tony Clark, but he's the Tony Clark in this world, not your world."

As Kelly stared at Clara, her eyes widened.

"Do you understand?" Clara asked.

With her mouth still covered, Kelly nodded.

Clara slowly lifted her fingers and motioned for everyone to move into a shadow close to the building. As the five of us huddled, she whispered, her eyes constantly darting. "Here is what we know, or at least, think we know. In this world, Nathan and Kelly are dead, and now Tony is, too, so it's clear that whoever wanted that box will murder anyone who stands in his way.

"From what we gathered from Daryl Red and Clara Red, Nathan Red's parents are also dead, but their counterparts are alive in this world, probably prisoners somewhere in the observatory. We knew enough about the Quattro mirror to realize that if Solomon had it, he could use it to escape. The idea was to get the box to Nathan Red so he could open it with his mirror, and he'd get the box to Solomon somehow.

"Nathan Blue had hidden the mirror and camera in a bus-depot locker in Chicago, so, since we were already in town for Nathan's funeral, we brought the items to the observatory. Tony Blue insisted on going to the door alone while Daryl Blue and I hunkered down in the car, but, as you know, he didn't make it.

"When the murderer went into the building, we dragged Tony's body to the car and parked under the trees where no one could see us, but where we could still see the back door. We caught a glimpse of you taking the box, so we decided to wait and see if you would return. When you did, we came out of hiding."

"Why do you think my parents are the ones who died?" I asked. "Since you took Nathan Blue to Kelly Blue's house, you must have thought his parents were dead."

"We did think so. When I took my Nathan to the stockholders' meeting to play a duet with his mother, Dr. Simon met us at the performance hall and told us Nathan's parents were dead and to flee right away, that I should get Nathan to a safe place."

"So you never saw the bodies?"

Clara shook her head. "Which is why I am suspicious about Dr. Simon's word. Maybe he whisked them away to some bizarre mission or experiment."

"In other words, we still don't know which parents are dead or alive."

"I'm afraid not, Nathan. I'm sorry."

The lack of a conclusive answer made me want to scream. I had to change the subject. "Okay, switching gears. Why did Nathan Blue hide the mirror and camera in the box? And how did he get them in there?"

"He decided the risk of the camera and mirror falling into the wrong hands was too great, so he put them in a metal box, and Tony welded the lid shut. Earlier,

Nathan Blue tested the mirror to see if it could open the box when it was empty, and it worked. Since we assumed you know how to perform the opening magic, and Solomon knows how to use the camera and the mirror, we hoped you could get them to him so he could escape or transport himself and Francesca out of there."

"Okay," I said. "We're up to speed. We'd better get going." I slid my hand around Kelly's arm and gave her a light pull, but she stayed put, her gaze again locked on the car. "Are you all right?" I asked.

Kelly whispered, "I just realized something."

"What?"

She turned to me. "He's a hero, isn't he?"

"Definitely. He gave his life trying to help us."

"Do you think all people in this world are exactly the same as in ours?"

I slid my hand from Kelly's arm down to her fingers and interlaced them with my own. "Clara and Daryl are just like they are at home, and it sounds like the other Nathan and Kelly were just like us."

Her fingers tightened. "So maybe my father ..." Her voice faded away.

"Really is a hero?" I gazed into her shadowed eyes. "I know your father would have done exactly the same thing."

She tightened her grip on my hand once more before pulling away. "Thanks. I know you really mean that."

"Come on. We have to search the building without being seen by the nut job with the shotgun."

Daryl ran ahead to the door and pushed it open. "What are we waiting for? I want to see the cool telescope room my newly discovered twin told me about."

"But it might not be safe," I said.

"It's safe." She held up a mobile phone. "Portable email. Daryl Red's keeping me up-to-date. She and Clara Red figured out how to monitor our world's telescope room from their world, and it looks clear of bad guys. We're good to go."

Kelly picked up the violin case while I tucked both mirrors under my arm. Keeping a careful watch for the shotgun man, we entered, skulked into the secure area, and stopped to check the prisoner room again. After finding it empty, we continued to the elevator.

"We'll have to go in shifts." I punched six, six, five, three into the security pad and pushed the call button. Fortunately, the Earth Red code worked for the elevator here. "Kelly and I will go first, then Clara, Daryl, and Francesca."

When the door opened, Kelly and I stepped inside. Once in the elevator car, I pushed the button for the third floor. A red light within the button flashed on. When the door began to slide shut, Daryl raised her cell phone and looked at the screen, but the door closed before she could tell us what it said.

As the car glided upward, a muffled call sounded from below. "The guy with the shotgun is up there!"

Kelly punched the second-floor button, but it stayed dark. "It's too late!"

"And no place to hide." I pressed the mirrors together as one and angled them toward the door. In the image, the door opened, revealing the murderer with the shotgun aimed directly into the elevator car. My reflected self leaped at him with a high leg kick, deflecting the gun just at it fired. The force of my blow knocked the man to the floor.

Kelly set the violin case down and reached for the mirrors. "You can't do that if you're holding those."

I pushed the mirrors into her grasp. "Point them toward the door."

She angled the mirrors that way, her hands trembling. "Ready ... I think."

"We can do this." When the car slowed to a halt, I set my feet. "Here we go."

The door slid open. Just as the man aimed the shotgun, I leaped into a flying kick that knocked the barrel to the side. A blast of orange erupted from the end, and a deafening crack sounded. The force of the kick threw the man onto his back.

I lunged, grabbed the gun, and trained it on him. Kelly hurried to my side, carrying the violin case and mirrors. Behind her, the elevator closed, and the motor restarted its quiet hum.

As dim moonlight from the ceiling mirror cast a glow over the man's bloodied face, he coughed and wheezed. Kelly set the violin down but kept her grip on the mirrors. "So he's the one who killed my Earth Blue father?"

"Yeah." I lowered the gun to my hip. "He's half dead."

The man coughed again, his breaths gurgling as blood oozed from his nose and mouth. "Just ... just shoot me ... and get it over with."

"Maybe I should." I raised the shotgun to my shoulder and set my finger on the trigger. "You went to Earth Yellow with Mictar and Gordon to kill my mother. You took the burglar's place so you could find Francesca and murder her. And you killed Mrs. Romano."

His grin revealed a set of blood-covered teeth. "Smart boy."

"Why? They couldn't possibly hurt you."

The man's eyes began to roll upward. "Kidnap one to … to learn the secret … of Quattro … then …" He let out a long breath and closed his eyes. His body fell limp, and his jaw slackened.

I prodded him with the gun. No sign of breathing. "He's dead."

"I can't say I feel sorry for him." Kelly crossed her arms. "He's a monster."

The elevator motor stopped, and the door slid open. The moment Clara Blue, Daryl Blue, and Francesca Yellow squeezed through, Daryl hustled toward the computers on the worktables.

I stood in front of the dead attacker. "Francesca, if you're squeamish, don't look."

"Thanks for the warning." She turned her head and walked with Clara toward Daryl, who was already busily tapping on a keyboard.

Pressing the mirrors against her side with one hand and carrying the violin case in the other, Kelly followed them, the camera still dangling at her chest. "I guess you must still be in contact with Earth Red," she said to Daryl.

"Hot line to the great beyond." Daryl pulled her phone from her pocket and slid it onto the desk, making it spin. "My twin told us about Nathan kicking that guy's butt. Now I need to sync her up on our mirror so we can talk face-to-face."

I propped the gun on my shoulder and joined them. "Does Francesca have to play the music again?"

"No." Daryl stared at the laptop screen. "Daryl Red found a music generator that deciphers and plays the radio telescope's connecting feed. She's showing me how — " She pointed at an icon in the lower left corner. "Yep. Here it is on my screen."

As she adjusted the control, the mirror above changed from a starry sky to the mesmerizing array of colorful shapes we had seen before. Each shape vibrated and danced to a cacophonous stream of musical notes played from speakers in the walls.

Daryl's fingers flew across the keyboard. Seconds later, the notes blended into a perfect harmony of violins playing a ghostly tremolo and a French horn adding a subtle, restful flavor.

"It's Strauss's Blue Danube," I said as I set the shotgun on the floor.

The shapes in the mirror broke apart and bled into each other, painting an aerial view of the telescope room floor. In the reflection, Clara Red seemed to be speaking, but no sound came through.

Daryl Blue waved at her likeness in the mirror above. "She's got good taste in clothes. I love that top."

Kelly smirked. "Maybe she'll let you borrow it."

Craning my neck, I strained to listen. "Can anyone hear what they're saying?"

"I hear something," Francesca said. "Something about the funeral."

Daryl Blue leaned close to the laptop screen. "Apparently Daryl Red hasn't figured out how to turn the voice volume up while the music's playing, so she's typing Clara Red's words." Daryl Blue pointed at the advancing letters on the screen and read them aloud. "You have to get back to Earth Red in time for the funeral. It's morning here. The service is only a few hours away."

I touched Francesca's shoulder. "Since Earth Yellow is catching up so fast in time, we have to get Francesca back, or her whole life will be messed up. She might never meet my father, and I'll never be born there."

Kelly set the mirrors on the desk. "Can we risk it? Your Earth Blue father said you had to be at the funeral on Earth Red. What if we get trapped or delayed on Earth Yellow?"

Clara Blue looked at the ceiling. "Maybe you should risk going to Earth Yellow. You can probably ruin one of Mictar's goals."

"What goal is that?" I asked.

"If you time it right, you can get the third Quattro mirror before Mictar does. He's sure to go after it."

"Good thought." I looked at Kelly. "What year did your father buy the mirror from the guy in Scotland?"

"About fifteen years ago. Not long after I was born, I think."

I stepped close to Daryl Blue's workstation. "At the rate Earth Yellow is catching up, when will it get to fifteen years ago?"

She squinted at the screen. "Impossible to tell. Sometimes it zips along, and sometimes it's just a little bit faster, but it still has about fourteen years to go. It's nineteen seventy-nine there now."

"That raises an interesting question," Clara Blue said. "I don't think Francesca is aging here at her Earth Yellow rate, or else her body cycles would be crazy. Will she suddenly age if she goes home, or will she be younger than she's supposed to be?"

I looked at Francesca as she stared at the ceiling, apparently pretending to be oblivious to our conversation though she likely heard every word. "Both choices stink. Either alter Francesca's life drastically or miss the funeral. And I have to stop looking for my Earth Blue parents no matter what."

Kelly raised her hand. "I vote for going to Earth Yellow. Since time is passing faster there than here, Earth Red will kind of slow down while we get Francesca home. We'll have more time to get the job done and maybe get back for the funeral."

I pointed at her. "Brilliant. Let's do it."

"I'll adjust the settings," Daryl said. "Earth Yellow coming right up."

Kelly gazed at the ceiling. "Where will we go on Earth Yellow? Did this observatory even exist thirty years ago?"

"Great question." I stood next to her and watched the mirror. The chaotic rainbow of colors returned along with a new blend of dissonant noises. Soon, a harmony of notes emerged, and the scene above coalesced — a daytime view of a spring forest with windblown leaves plummeting to the ground, clouds racing overhead, and a squirrel scampering up a tree like a furry bullet.

I let out a low whistle. "That squirrel's had too much coffee."

"Time's passing faster," Daryl said. "I suppose it'll slow down in your perspective when you get there."

I searched the landscape but found no sign of civilization. "Do you think we'll come out where the observatory is going to be?"

"Most likely, but who knows?" Daryl continued tapping on the keyboard. "Let's get the show on the road. You and Kelly stand with Francesca in the middle of the room."

"I'd better get the body out of the way." I hustled to the dead gunman, grabbed his wrists, and dragged him to the wall.

"Check his pockets," Clara called. "Maybe we can find a clue of some kind."

I searched the man's pants pockets and found four shotgun shells and a wallet. In the wallet, I found a plastic card embedded with an odd set of letters and numbers.

After laying the wallet on his chest, I returned to Clara and set the items on the desk. "If you have to leave, hide the shotgun and shells in the ladies' room downstairs so we'll know where to find them when we get back."

Clara grabbed a rolling shotgun shell and stood it upright. "If we have to leave, you might have a hard time getting back."

"Maybe not," Daryl said. "Daryl Red might be able to get you home."

"And what if she has to hide, too?" I asked.

"Stop being a worrywart. I found the security codes for all the doors. In fact, I can change them from here if I want to. Daryl Red can change the codes there, too, so we can frustrate the bad guys for quite a while."

"Are you taking the mirrors?" Clara Blue asked.

"Just one of them." I picked it up and tucked it under my arm. "Better odds to keep one of them safe." I led Kelly and Francesca to the center of the room. "Ready with the lights?"

Clara Blue walked to the wall and flipped the switch. "Here we go."

The trumpet fixtures on the perimeter wall flashed on, sending white beams toward the ceiling. When they bounced from the apex, they forked into dozens of semitranslucent shafts that reshaped into brilliant vertical bars around us and melted our surroundings.

The forest scene materialized at all sides. Racing clouds seemed to put on the brakes and slow to a normal speed. Instead of plummeting, leaves floated to the ground in meandering spirals, blown off their erratic paths by gusts of wind.

In the distance, a bank of dark clouds spread a blanket across the sun and cast a deep shadow over us. Lightning flashed. The cloud-to-ground strike sent a rumbling boom across the forest and tremors through the ground. Large raindrops pelted the leafy floor, making a crackling sound. A fresh breeze blew through my hair, cool and invigorating as it kicked up a swirl of dead leaves at my feet. They flew in a cyclonic waltz, blocking the surrounding freshness in a dreary blanket of decay.

I peered through the flurry. I had seen this place before, the mirror's very first apparition back in my bedroom.

A sudden gust blew the leafy whirlwind away, clearing our view. Nearby, a tri-fold mirror, twice my height and three times as wide as my arm span, stood upright, supported by four-by-four wooden posts embedded in the ground.

I pointed at the mirror. "Let's check it out."

We shuffled through dead leaves, the previous autumn's carpet that spring had not yet swept away, and stared at the seemingly impossible, but now familiar, reflection, an aerial view of the telescope room. Clara and Daryl Blue waved at us from the computer desk.

I returned the wave. "Interfinity must have erected this here as their transportation dock for Earth Yellow."

"Amazing." Kelly touched one of the panels. "I guess they thought of everything."

I held out a palm to catch the spattering rain. "But we didn't think to bring an umbrella."

Francesca pointed toward the horizon. "Look!"

As the leaves kicked up again, I bent to follow her line of sight. A dark funnel spun down from the approaching cloud bank. "A tornado!"

CHAPTER TWENTY-ONE

"IT'S COMING TOWARD us!" Kelly swiveled her head from side to side, the violin case still in hand. "Which way to the road?"

I spotted a narrow strip of ground with fewer leaves than the surrounding area, maybe a trail. "Both of you follow me." Holding the Quattro mirror, I dashed along the path.

As wind whistled through the trees, leaves and twigs rained along with nickel-sized water droplets. "Are you with me?" I called back to Kelly and Francesca.

"Right behind you!" Kelly shouted.

Francesca called, "And I'm right behind her!"

I leaped over protruding roots and fallen trees. "We have to find a low area, a ditch or a rainwater trench."

"I'm looking." Kelly's hoarse voice battled the chaotic noise. "But it's all flat."

I caught sight of the tornado again, an enormous black funnel of spinning fury. It churned through the forest like a wild monster, uprooting trees and spewing them into the sky. The deafening rumble drowned out nearly every other sound.

I stopped and spun. Kelly and Francesca caught up and stopped with me, both breathless.

"Give me the violin," I said.

Kelly extended the case. Without a word, I gave her the mirror, took the case, and popped the latches. She held the mirror where I could see the swirling demon behind us. As the tornado screamed closer, I jerked the violin to my chin and sawed the bow across the strings, playing a wild rendition of Be Still My Soul.

The monstrous funnel drew closer. In the mirror, its black twisting wall slung dirt and debris everywhere. The wind blew a vicious slap that knocked Francesca and Kelly to the ground. Kelly struggled to her knees and held the mirror in place, clutched in both hands.

With my back to the cyclone, dozens of rocks and sharp wood fragments slammed into me, my body a shield for the two girls. Then, the reflection changed to a dim forest road with a van parked near a tree. "I need a flash of light!"

In the mirror, the girl in red appeared, like a ghost floating near the van. She folded her hands and looked skyward, her lips moving. Then she vanished.

As if in response, lightning blasted from the sky, knifing into a nearby tree and slicing off a huge limb over our heads. The tornado lurched forward. Kelly clenched her eyes shut. I bent over, waiting to be crushed or swept away.

Then everything fell quiet.

I straightened and scanned the area. My violin case lay open on a paved road. A commercial van sat near the shoulder, void of a driver. Lettering emblazoned the side panel, but dizziness made the words unreadable. The girl in red was nowhere around.

My arms and legs shaking, I set the violin in the case and looked at Kelly. Still holding the mirror, she looked back at me with her mouth hanging open. "Are you all right?" I asked.

"Just scared half to death." She pushed a hand under Francesca's arm and lifted her to her feet.

"Thanks." Francesca brushed off her clothes. "That was a close one."

My vision settling, I shut the violin case and latched it. "I saw the girl in red again, but she — "

A new voice interrupted. "Okay, now I've seen everything."

I pivoted. "What?"

A young man leaned against the van, watching us with his arms folded over his long-sleeved T-shirt. "Like I said. Now I've seen everything." He pushed away from the van revealing the lettering on the side — *Stoneman Enterprises*.

I blinked. "Gunther?"

"In the flesh. I stayed out of sight until I recognized you." Carrying a tire iron, Gunther frowned as he walked toward us, a set of keys jangling from a ring on his jeans belt loop. Although his hair was shorter, his face hadn't changed.

"Well, it's great to see you — "

"Yeah, I'll bet it is." His voice sharpened to a menacing tone. "For a couple of kidnappers, you sure have a lot of divine help ... or is it demonic help?"

"Kidnappers?" I backed away, spreading my arms in front of Kelly and Francesca. "What are you talking about?"

"You still have her." Gunther stopped and pointed the tire iron at Francesca. "Now I can finally clear my name."

"Clear your name?"

"I didn't want to believe you kidnapped Francesca. I thought maybe someone else took all three of you."

"We didn't kidnap her. We're trying to get her home."

Gunther gave me a sarcastic smirk. "It's taken you almost a year to decide to do that? A little slow, aren't you?"

"Cool it a second," I said, holding up my hands. "Just tell us what's happened since we've been gone, and I'll explain everything."

"All right … if it'll humor you." Gunther kept a firm grip on his tire iron, but his tone softened. "That day I dropped you off, I noticed a guy drive in as I was leaving, so I went back to check it out. When I saw him sneaking toward the house with a gun, I took this tire iron and chased him. I got there just as he shot the lady of the house, Mrs. Romano."

Francesca winced but said nothing.

"I clobbered him," Gunther continued, "but he was a tough nut to crack. He fought back and got away, but I didn't chase him, 'cause I wanted to stay and help. You two were gone, kind of vanished into thin air. I called the police, and when they showed up, they asked me where Francesca was. I had no idea a girl even lived there, so I just told them everything I knew.

"They didn't believe me at first, and when they couldn't find her, they put me in jail for two days. When they developed the film in the camera Mrs. Romano had with her, they saw the three of you. But here's the really weird part. In one picture, there was a big mirror behind you, and it showed the guy with the gun behind Mrs. Romano, but there wasn't any mirror in the room.

"Anyway, they decided to keep me locked up for a while, because it also showed me getting ready to bash the guy's head, proving I was there with you. Since they didn't have any evidence that I actually kidnapped her, and since I obviously didn't have time to dispose of three bodies, they finally let me go. No charges, but rumors kept me out of the job market."

He inhaled, as if ready to finish. "Fingerprints at the scene didn't match anything on file, and they showed the photo to thousands of people and put it on TV, but they came up empty."

I nodded toward Kelly and Francesca. "That's because we went to another world, kind of like an alternate universe. We were gone only a little while, and time moves faster here than it does there."

Gunther dropped the tire iron. "Another world?"

"Look," I said, spreading out my arms, "I know it sounds crazy, but I told you the truth before, and you believed me, and I'm telling the truth now. Didn't we just appear out of nowhere? Where do you think we came from?"

"You got me there." He picked up the tire iron again and leaned closer to Francesca. "Tell me, did these two kidnap you? You can tell the truth. I'll protect you."

"Kidnapped me?" She huffed a short laugh. "Of course not. They rescued me."

"You mean their whole crazy story is true?"

She nodded. "Every word."

"All right, then." Gunther exhaled heavily, shaking his head. "I guess I'll have to believe the impossible again." He extended a hand toward me. "Welcome back."

I shook his hand. "Thanks for showing up. We need a ride."

"Where are we?" Kelly asked. "And why are you here?"

"We're near the Iowa and Illinois border. I had just finished a class at school, and this professor-looking type came up to me in the hall. He showed me a photo of Francesca and asked if I knew her or the two of you. I wasn't sure I could trust him, so I said something like, 'What's it to you?'

"He told me your names. He also knew about me being in the house when it all went down, and he wanted me to help him find the three of you, something about saving your lives. He said he needed someone Nathan could trust, but this guy was sure you wouldn't trust him. So he couldn't do it himself."

"What did he look like?" I asked.

Gunther made circles with his hands and set them over his eyes. "He wore owl glasses, and he's short with kind of a round head."

I looked at Kelly. "Sounds like Dr. Simon. Must be his counterpart in this world."

"He didn't tell me his name," Gunther continued. "He said that if I wanted to be of service, I should drive to a safe place and wait for you there."

"What safe place?"

"I asked the same question. He said it didn't matter where I went as long as I was there within a certain time frame that he wrote down."

I lifted my brow. "So he knew when the three of us would arrive?"

"Well, not exactly. It was a two-hour window."

"How long did you have to wait?"

Gunther glanced at his wristwatch. "Only twenty minutes. I brought my textbooks to study, so it wasn't a problem. When I went to jail, I got fired from my delivery job, so I decided to concentrate on school. Figured it was about time I graduated."

"What about the tornado?" Kelly asked. "Didn't it affect you?"

"The radio said it was a hundred miles to the northeast. Just caught a little thunderstorm on my way over here."

"We were right in its path," I said. "It nearly blew us to kingdom come." I looked at Kelly. With her hair frizzed out and her clothes ruffled, I realized that I probably looked just as mangled. I brushed through my hair, knocking out a shower of leaves, twigs, and dirt. Kelly and Francesca took my cue and finger-brushed their hair.

One question lingered. How could we possibly show up in a place that Gunther just pulled out of a hat and at exactly the time we were about to get blown away by a tornado? If we could find Simon, whatever color he was, he'd have a lot of questions to answer.

Gunther looked around as if worried about someone watching. "This other-world stuff is too deep for me. I'm just your driver, so if you want a ride somewhere, let's get going."

We piled into the van, Kelly and Francesca in the front seat and me in the rear cargo area. I leaned forward, bracing myself on Kelly's headrest. "Think we should check out your house?"

Kelly shook her head. "Too risky. That's the first place they'd look for us. And, besides, we don't know how much time's left before we have to get back for the funeral."

"True." I glanced at my wristwatch, but, of course, it couldn't possibly keep track of time on Earth Red. "I wish we had a cosmic clock." I pulled my phone from my pocket and looked at the screen. No signal, of course. "Gunther, can you take us to a telephone? I want to make a call."

"Sure thing. There's a Texaco station and a McDonald's a few miles up the road. You hungry?"

"Famished." I withdrew my wallet and showed Gunther a twenty-dollar bill. "They probably won't take these new-style twenties, will they?"

Gunther took the bill and narrowed his eyes. "Are you into counterfeiting now?"

"Never mind." I retrieved the bill and pushed my wallet back into place. "I have some older fives and ones. The cashier probably won't look at the dates."

After eating lunch and using the restroom, Gunther, Kelly, and Francesca returned to the van while I used a pay phone at the gas station to call Nikolai. When I hung up, I motioned for Kelly.

She hopped out. While she jogged toward me, I adjusted my watch to match the time on the station's outdoor clock.

"What's the news?" she asked as she came to a stop.

"I talked to Francesca's violin teacher. On our world, he and his wife raised her after her mother died. I asked him if he would take Francesca in. He got super excited. He even started crying. Of course he'll take her."

"That's great news." Kelly looked back at the van. "By the way, Francesca's been crying ever since you went to the phone booth. Her mother's death finally sank in. It hit her like a ton of bricks."

I stuffed my hands into my pockets. "Just let her cry as long as she wants. I know how she feels."

"How long did you cry when your parents died?"

"I don't know." As a slight tremble crossed my lips, I firmed my chin to quell it. "I'm not sure I've stopped yet."

"Sorry." She averted her eyes. "Stupid question."

"No, it wasn't. I've been holding it all in." I took a deep breath. I had to change the subject. "Anyway, Nikolai lives in Iowa City, but he insisted on meeting us at a place in Davenport in an hour to save time. We'd better get going."

As we walked to the van, she nodded toward the highway. "Davenport is right across the river. Gunther said we're near the border, so it shouldn't be far at all."

"That'll help." When I opened the van door, Gunther was sitting alone in the front, reaching over the seat and caressing Francesca's head as she lay on a mat in the back. Curled in a fetal position and heaving an occasional spasm, she clutched a stuffed rabbit in her arms.

"The rabbit is Mr. Bunn," Gunther said. "My little sister left him with me months ago. Francesca climbed back there and laid down with him, saying something about not being too old for cuddling with a bunny."

As my own tears threatened to flow, I clenched my eyes shut. "Thanks, Gunther."

Kelly slid in first, and I followed. "I found a place for Francesca to live," I said.

"You did?" Gunther's brow arched up, but his tone seemed less than joyful. "Where?"

"Her violin teacher in Iowa City. He and his wife are childless, so they're looking forward to doing whatever they can to help. He said he'd meet us in Davenport in the Galvin Fine Arts Center at St. Ambrose University."

"I know where that is." Gunther started the van and shifted the gear. "Fifteen minutes. Twenty, tops."

"Better take it easy, though. If anything happens and we're caught with a supposedly kidnapped girl, we'll never see the light of day, especially you. If you want, we could drop you off somewhere, then take her to Nikolai, and pick you up later."

"Don't worry about me." He pressed the accelerator. "Francesca lost her mother. I'd do anything for her."

While traveling just under the speed limit on Interstate 88 westbound, I told Gunther the entire story as quickly as possible, relating every detail I could remember.

I finished with the disarming of the shotgun-wielding murderer and our transport to the future location of Interfinity Labs, which happened to lie right in the path of the tornado. "So, now we have to try to get Francesca's life back in order. She has to eventually meet Solomon Shepherd and marry him on the twentieth of December in nineteen eighty-six."

Gunther glanced at his rearview mirror. "So do we tell all this stuff to her violin teacher? What was his name? Nikolai?"

"Nikolai Malenkov. I guess we'll have to. He needs to know that someone's out to kill Francesca. He can't protect her otherwise."

"True, but I could keep an eye on her, help her find Solomon, kind of guide their steps until they meet each other."

"You want to be her guardian angel?" I asked.

"Sure. Why not?"

"Wouldn't watching her take too much time?" Kelly asked. "I mean, you have your own life to live."

Gunther chuckled. "You probably noticed that I'm not exactly a normal guy. I mean, I'm a truck driver who believes this crazy story you're telling me. I might not be the best student around, but it doesn't take a genius to see that there's a higher power behind all this multi-world weirdness. Maybe this is exactly what I was meant to do." He shrugged. "I have one semester to go. I'll find a job near Iowa City and be her invisible guardian."

Kelly gave him a peck on the cheek. "You're a special man, Gunther."

"Yeah," I said. "We'll never forget you for this."

Gunther's face flushed. "Just stay away from twisters for a while. I can't be waiting for you out on wilderness roads every time you pick a fight with one."

When we arrived at the university, Gunther parked in the Galvin Center's nearly empty lot. Only an MG roadster, an old red pickup truck, and a motorcycle occupied any of the fifty or so spaces.

I jumped out and searched the area for Nikolai, hoping I could identify a younger version of Mom's gentle music teacher. As I crossed the parking lot, Kelly hurried to join me. "Any sign of him?"

"Not yet. He said he's driving a Volvo. I told him what the van looks like, so maybe he'll find us."

"Has it been an hour?"

I checked my watch. "Just about. He should be here soon."

Seconds later, a light blue Volvo turned into the parking lot and pulled in next to the van. The driver, a thin-faced man with a full head of salt-and-pepper hair, lowered his window and glanced around nervously before speaking. "Are you Nathan Shepherd?"

"Yes." I bent to address him at eye level. "Nikolai?"

"Yes, yes." He stuck his head out the window and lowered his voice. "Where is Francesca?"

I pointed at the van. "In there. I thought you said you were bringing your wife."

"I was, to be sure, but I received a call immediately after yours warning me not to retrieve Francesca. It was a man, a friendly man, actually, who said I would be endangering her life." He checked his rearview mirror and glanced at the fine arts center before continuing. "I couldn't leave you waiting for me, so I sent my wife to a safe place and came alone."

"Did you notice if anyone was following you?"

He nodded. "When I left my house, a green pickup truck was parked at the curb two blocks away. I am sure I saw the same vehicle later on the highway, but it passed me quite some time ago. The driver paid no attention to me as he went by."

"That's not good." I straightened and scanned the area. Behind a tree near a house across the street, a man spied on us with binoculars. I quickly averted my eyes. "Don't look around, but we're being watched."

Nikolai stiffened, and his voice grew jittery. "Do you have a suggested course of action?"

"We have to lose him, maybe do something he won't expect." I looked at the entrance to the center — three double doors bordered by brick columns that rose to the roof. We could hide in there and formulate a plan. "How well do you know this place?"

"Quite well. I have performed here three times. I chose this meeting place because of my familiarity with it."

"Can you lead us to the stage?"

"Of course." Nikolai opened his door and got out.

I collected my mirror and violin from the van, while Gunther woke Francesca. Although tear tracks stained her cheeks, she had stopped crying. When I explained the option of her going to live with her violin teacher, she offered a whispered *okay* and said nothing more as we walked to the building.

When we passed through the front door, the lovely sounds of Dvořák's magnificent cello concerto greeted our ears. Somewhere, a cellist had just begun an early measure of the solo portion and hit every note with vigor and ringing clarity.

"The stage is in there," Nikolai said, nodding toward an open door at the end of a hallway.

Something flashed near my hand. I lifted the mirror. The reflection slowly altered, changing from my tired pale face to a dim room. As the image sharpened, a small stuffed rabbit came into view. I whispered, "Mr. Bunn?"

Nikolai gave me a curious glance. "Who?"

"A stuffed rabbit named Mr. Bunn," Kelly said as she looked over my shoulder. "What does it mean?"

"Let me think." Since the rabbit lay back in the van, the reflection was far out of place. Why would the mirror show it to me? And why was I thinking of the mirror as an object that had a will and a purpose? Because the girl in red kept appearing in it? If she acted as the mind behind the mirror, what was she trying to tell me?

I looked closer. Around the rabbit lay wads of black fabric. Where did that come from? It wasn't in the van, at least not yet. Did that mean I would have to look for the material while we searched for a way to dodge the guy with the binoculars?

"I'm working on an idea." I strode through the door and hurried down the stairs at the side of the seating area, then climbed up to the stage. As I passed the cellist sitting at the middle of the raised platform, I gave him a nod. "Nice touch."

The cellist, a young man with long arms and a bright smile, lifted his bow. "Thanks."

"Would it interrupt your practice if I have a look around?" I asked.

"No. Go ahead."

"Thanks." I continued into the backstage area. As the others caught up, I scanned the paneled gray floor. "Look for a lot of fabric — maybe sheets, robes, cloaks, something like that."

"Curtains?" Kelly lifted a wad of black material, revealing a second, similar wad underneath.

After setting the violin and mirror down, I picked up the corner of the second heap of fabric — a theater curtain. These could be used as a disguise, or maybe a ruse to throw our stalker off track. "I have an idea. Francesca, do you mind if Gunther carries you?"

She tilted her head in a dubious manner. "I guess it's okay."

"Good." I nodded at Gunther. "Go ahead. Like a cradle."

"As long as she doesn't mind." He picked her up and held her aloft. "Comfy?"

"Sure," she said, one arm around his neck. "No problem."

"Now the next step." I draped the curtain over Francesca and tucked it around Gunther's arms. "Can you breathe all right under there?"

Her muffled voice penetrated the fabric. "It's smelly, but I'll be fine."

"This shouldn't take long." I held out my arms, fashioning a second cradle. "Okay, Kelly, up you go."

She pointed at herself. "You're going to carry me?"

"Sure. All bundled up, no one will know the difference between you and Francesca."

"All right, but no jokes about me being short."

With one arm on Kelly's back and another behind her knees, I hoisted her into my arms. "Gunther will take Francesca to the van while you and I go with Nikolai in his car. That way, the stalker will probably think I have her."

She laid her arm around my neck. "We could add to the deception."

"How?"

Kelly nodded toward Francesca. "She took her shoes off."

I glanced at her. As Kelly had said, Francesca's bare feet protruded from under the curtain.

"So," Kelly continued, "if we put my shoes on her and leave my bare feet uncovered, the stalker will be more likely to think I'm her."

"Great idea." I turned to Nikolai. "Will you make the transfer?"

"Of course." Nikolai pulled Kelly's shoes and socks off and carried them to Francesca.

Kelly wiggled her toes. "I have cherry-red polish on my nails."

"Then pull your feet in," I said. "We'll have to count on the shoes to convince him." I turned toward Nikolai. "Would you please cover Kelly with the other curtain?"

"Gladly." After Nikolai tied the second shoe on Francesca, he draped the other curtain over Kelly, covering her toes. "I will get your violin and mirror."

"Curl up," I said to Kelly. "Try to make yourself smaller."

She shifted around under the curtain and nestled her head against my chest. "How's this?" she asked, her voice muffled.

"That'll do." I pushed out a quick breath. "Good thing you're a lightweight."

Her voice sharpened. "I weigh one twenty!"

"Feels like one nineteen. All muscle, I'm sure." With Gunther and Nikolai at my side, I walked toward the stage's stairway. As I passed the cellist again, I gave him another nod. "Keep up the good work."

He stared at me with his mouth open. "Uh …
thanks."

When we reached the door, I whispered to Gunther,
"Don't look at the stalker. Let's just load them up and get
out of here. I'll head north. You head south. Once we're
sure no one's following, we'll meet where you picked us
up."

Gunther shifted Francesca a bit higher. "Sure
thing."

Nikolai jogged ahead and opened the back doors
to the van and his Volvo. I laid Kelly on the backseat of the
Volvo while Gunther put Francesca in the van's rear cargo
area.

After closing the car door, I extended a hand
toward Nikolai. "Mind if I drive? If someone's trying to
kill Francesca, it could get dangerous."

"An excellent suggestion." Nikolai gave me the
keys. "I am a rather squeamish driver."

While I started the car, Nikolai hurried around to
the passenger's side and set the violin and mirror on the
floor in front of him. At the same time, Gunther boarded
his van and fired it up.

After giving Gunther a nod, I eased out of the
parking lot and headed for the main highway. "I'll take a
direct route to see if he's following us."

Kelly spoke up from the backseat. "Do I have to
stay hidden and miss all the action?"

"Probably better. If anything happens, I'll give you
a blow-by-blow."

When we reached the Interstate, I turned east and
punched the accelerator. The rearview mirror revealed no
green pickup and no obvious followers.

After a minute or two of silence, I asked Nikolai, "Can you help me solve a mystery?"

"I will try."

"Remember that night at Ganz Hall in Chicago when a double murder took place?"

"Yes, of course. My wife and I played in the quartet. It was a frightening night indeed."

"What happened? Do you know who the victims were?"

"I will tell you what I know, which isn't much. Helen and I stayed after the performance, because a young violinist who played before we did wished to speak to us about Vivaldi, his favorite composer. The three of us sat on stage for a long time. Eventually, someone turned the lights off without realizing we were still there. We thought it amusing at first and simply went on with our conversation. Soon, however, someone entered the side door and set up a floor-standing mirror.

"We guessed that he had not seen or heard us, so we stayed quiet to see what his intentions were. He went out, and moments later, he and another man brought in two coffins and arranged them on tables on the opposite side of the stage.

"Since we could see bodies in the coffins, we became quite nervous and tried to remain perfectly quiet, but one of the men, a tall, pale-looking fellow, saw us. The two men became violently aggressive toward us, so we defended ourselves. Unfortunately, the only weapons we had were our instruments, which did not survive the battle. After quite a skirmish, they captured us and locked us in a storage closet. It took some time, but we were able to break out. I sustained several serious cuts, as did the young musician, but my wife was unharmed."

"The police reported that two musicians from a quartet were killed and found in the coffins," I said. "Is that true?"

Nikolai sighed. "It is true that two members of my quartet were murdered, but they were not the bodies in the coffins, at least not the ones we saw before we were captured. I suspect that someone switched them."

I echoed his sigh. "At least you and your wife got away."

"A blessing for us, but we are still grieving the loss of our friends. They were a fine couple. Brilliant musicians."

After a moment of silence, Kelly piped up from the backseat. "Now we know why you didn't make it home on time."

"Yes, we stayed overnight in the hospital and answered the authorities' questions the next morning."

Something green in the rearview mirror caught my attention. The pickup truck shifted from one lane to another, then out of sight behind a bigger truck. "I see the pickup. It's a couple of hundred feet back."

Nikolai turned and looked. "Does he appear to be following us?"

"Let's find out." I pressed the accelerator. "If you don't mind, would you play something on the violin? And I'll need the mirror."

He laid the mirror in my hand and pulled the violin from its case. "This is a strange concert venue, but I will do as you say."

"Just watch." I set the mirror at my side. "Explaining would take too long."

"What shall I play?"

"Anything."

Nikolai raised the violin and began a Beethoven sonata. As we zoomed along in the right-hand lane, the pickup kept pace but stayed back, apparently satisfied to keep us in sight.

After a few miles, we passed a police car hiding in a gap in the bushes at the side of the highway. As soon as the pickup zipped by, the car flashed its lights, roared onto the pavement, and gave chase.

The pickup accelerated and rapidly closed the gap between it and our Volvo. Trouble was now only seconds away.

I held the mirror on the dashboard and looked at the reflection — nothing but light blue. "That's weird. All I see is blue, like the mirror's pointing at the sky."

Kelly sat upright. "Since our cover's blown, I guess it's okay to be seen."

"Should be." Ahead, the bridge over the Mississippi River loomed. "Pinch point coming up. No way to escape while we're on the bridge."

A heavy jolt shook our car, shoving us close to the right shoulder. I wrenched the wheel back to the left while keeping a grip on the mirror. "The truck rammed us!"

Kelly looked over the backseat. "Slow down. The cop's closing in. Maybe he'll help."

"We can't count on anyone to help." I pressed the pedal. "We'll take our chances in Illinois."

As I sped across the long span, the truck bumped us again, this time pushing from the left rear corner. I tried to correct, but the Volvo slid toward the low concrete barrier that served as the bridge's protective railing, slowing both vehicles to a crawl. "Kelly. Help me hold the mirror."

She thrust herself forward and lay prostrate over the seat while bracing the mirror. "Got it."

I grabbed the wheel with both hands and fought back, jerking to the left and banging the truck. Nikolai kept playing, though his bow strokes jiggled badly.

"I still see the sky," Kelly shouted. "What does it mean?"

"No idea." The steering wheel froze. As the passenger's side panel squealed against the concrete, the truck turned toward the Volvo at a ninety-degree angle and locked us in place. Its engine roared as it shoved again and again.

Kelly rocked back and forth, grabbing the wheel to keep from rolling. "He'll push us over the edge!"

Nikolai called out, "The police are running toward us, but I think they won't make it in time."

Kelly latched on to my arm. "What'll we do?"

"Pray like you've never prayed before!"

Nikolai switched from Beethoven to Handel's Messiah. "If I die," he shouted, his bow swaying wildly, "I will die in the arms of Christ!"

In the mirror, the blue sky melted away, replaced by the stuffed rabbit. "The mirror changed," I called as I fought with the wheel and pumped the accelerator. "I see Mr. Bunn again."

With a deafening rumble from its engine, the truck gave a final shove. Our car rolled over the barrier and dove headfirst toward the river.

Still clutching the mirror, Kelly screamed. As the plunge's G forces pressed me against the seat, I laid an arm over her back and gritted my teeth. "Just ... hang ... on!"

Nikolai hugged the violin and case, closing his eyes as he prayed out loud. "Our Father, who art in heaven ..."

As the water raced toward us, the car began a slow spin. I reached for the door, pulled its handle, and kicked it open. The interior light flashed on. A splash erupted, and a fierce jolt rattled my bones. Then, darkness engulfed everything.

CHAPTER TWENTY-TWO

A PAINFUL THUMP ON my backside snapped my eyes open. My vision pulsed with photonegative blackness. I whispered, "Kelly? Nikolai? Where are you?"

An excited voice shot into my ears. "Nathan? Where did you come from?"

"Gunther?"

"Yes. Can't you see me?"

I rubbed my eyes, clearing my vision. I sat cross-legged on the back cargo floor of the delivery van with a stuffed rabbit in my hand. Gunther sat in the driver's seat next to Francesca, driving through light fog on a rural highway as he glanced at me in the rearview mirror.

"Now I can." I looked around the dim van. Kelly lay facedown next to me, moaning. Beside her, Nikolai sat with the violin and case in his lap, leaning against the side panel. His eyes were open, but he seemed to be in a daze.

"How'd we get here?" I asked.

"I was going to ask you that," Gunther said. "I heard a loud bump, and you just showed up. But I'm getting used to you doing impossible things."

"I guess we got transported again." I turned Kelly over. As her arms tightened, clamping the mirror against her chest, she winced, accentuating a bloody gash across her forehead just below her scalp. Using my thumb, I wiped away a trickle of blood oozing toward her ear. "It was just in time, too. That pickup pushed our car over the side of the bridge, and the last thing I remember was splashing into the Mississippi."

Gunther flashed a thumbs up. "That's exactly what we need. It's perfect."

"Perfect? We're pretty beat up, especially Kelly."

"I don't mean that." Gunther draped an arm over his seat and looked back at us. "Does anyone need to go to a hospital?"

"I don't think so." I scanned the cargo area. "Do you have a first-aid kit?"

"You bet. Ever since that day Kelly needed an aspirin, I started packing one." Gunther pointed toward Francesca's feet. "Can you look under your seat for a white metal box?"

While she searched, Gunther slowed the van and pulled onto a strip of grass at the side of the road. "What I meant was, they'll think Francesca's dead, so they won't try to find her anymore."

"Maybe, but the pickup driver might have seen Kelly. Nikolai and Francesca should hide out somewhere. They can't just show up back at home and start violin lessons again."

Francesca handed Gunther the first-aid kit. "Found it."

"Thank you." Gunther passed it back to me.

I flipped up the box's lid, ripped open a sterile pad, and dabbed Kelly's three-inch-long wound. Her socks and shoes lay nearby, apparently put there by Francesca once she had retrieved her own. After cleaning the wound, I looked at Nikolai. "Are you okay, Dr. Malenkov?"

"I think so." He set the violin and case down with shaky hands, his eyes wide and fixed straight ahead. "It was ..." He swallowed and licked his lips. "It was very much like a nightmare I have had the last several nights. I fall toward the water, and when I near the surface I feel a great wind and see a bright light. Then, I wake up."

"I think nightmares are epidemic here." I gently pried the mirror from Kelly's tightened fingers. Blood stained the top edge. "Looks like she smacked herself with the mirror, but I can't tell if she hurt anything else."

Kelly whispered, "I'm just sore all over. Nothing real bad."

"The cut on your head's pretty bad."

Her eyes opened. "Where are we? I heard Gunther."

"We're in his van." From the kit, I withdrew three adhesive bandages and tore the first one open. "And we're still on Earth Yellow. The Quattro mirror transported us from the river just in time."

She sat up and turned toward the front. At the sight of Francesca, she smiled, though tightness in her lips revealed her pain. "So our plan worked perfectly."

"Except for an unscheduled tumble off a bridge. Yeah, it was great." I picked up her socks and shoes and set them close to her. "Here you go."

"Thanks." Kelly began putting them on as she looked at Dr. Malenkov. "What about your car?"

He waved a hand. "It is nothing. A big piece of metal. We used it to save lives. I am content."

"Where are we going?" Kelly asked.

"No place in particular." Gunther touched the map, still attached to the sun visor. "Now that you're all here, we can plot a course."

I leaned forward and tried to read the map, but it was too far away. "We have to get back to the transport site where the tornado struck. It's in the middle of nowhere in this world, but the Interfinity observatory is going to be there someday."

"If we find the path of the tornado," Kelly said as she tied her laces, "all we have to do is follow the damage."

Gunther set his finger near a dark line on the map. "The news said the twister first touched down out in the boonies just west of Rockford. I'll start heading that way."

"Dr. Malenkov," Kelly said, turning toward him. "Why don't you ride up front with Francesca? You'll be more comfortable."

"Very well." After setting the violin in its case and snapping the lid closed, Nikolai extended his hand. "May I have the rabbit, please?"

I gave it to him. "For Francesca?"

"No. For me." Nikolai held the rabbit close to his chest. "I think Mr. Bunn is the only occupant of this vehicle who understands what is going on less than I do, so he will be my partner in ignorance."

I laughed. "I'll explain as much as I can on the way, but we'd better get going."

After Nikolai settled into the front seat with Francesca, and Kelly and I arranged ourselves comfortably on the floor in the cargo area, we cruised down the road, still cutting through light fog. I explained everything I could remember, and Kelly filled in the gaps.

When I finished, Nikolai clasped his hands together. "Nathan, I am very curious about how music seems to open a passage between the worlds. Have you noticed any pattern? Are some pieces more effective than others?"

"I think classical works best. The Interfinity radio telescope picked up a lot of noise from space, and Francesca was able to hear classical music inside all that racket."

"It is no surprise," Nikolai said, "that melodies and harmonies are inherent in the created order. The cosmos comprises a multitude of symphonies, each one playing hymns in praise of its creator's magnificence."

I gazed into the maestro's deep gray eyes. "But wouldn't that mean Vivaldi or Beethoven or Mozart didn't actually write their music? I mean, if they just heard it in creation and pulled it out of the air, they aren't the geniuses we think they are. They're just great listeners."

"Oh, no," Nikolai said, waving his hand. "Such a conclusion is not necessary at all. If man creates a masterpiece out of nothing, he celebrates God, the one who did the same when he fashioned the world."

"How could music open a door between worlds?" I asked.

"I have no idea, but here is something that might help, something my teacher taught me when I was Francesca's age back in my mother country. When a musician composes, he is a translator of the divine voice. He sets the majesty of creation into a combination of notes that has never been heard before, yet it tells a story that has been spoken by God ever since the beginning of time."

I looked at my knuckles, wishing a breathy kiss would brush by. "My mother used to say something like that."

We drove on in relative silence, though Gunther spoke up from time to time to provide location updates. When we found the tornado's touchdown point, we followed the path, navigating back roads strewn with debris. After several minutes, Gunther stopped in front of a large sign with red block letters that said, *Future Home of Interfinity Labs — 1986.*

"How convenient," Kelly said. "It's still going to be seven years until it's built."

I nodded. "Let's get a closer look."

While Gunther, Nikolai, and Francesca stretched their legs, Kelly and I walked to the sign, a four-by-four foot square that stood a few inches higher than my head.

I kicked a clump of dirt where one of the posts entered the ground. "Freshly dug."

She pushed on the sign, tilting it back an inch or two. "Not sturdy at all. It couldn't have survived the tornado."

I stuffed my hands into my pockets and gazed at the surrounding landscape. Uprooted oaks and snapped pines littered the field. Hardly a tree stood upright as far as the eye could see, a stark portrait of devastating fury. I shuddered. That same fury had come within seconds of making kindling out of us.

The sound of heavy footsteps approached — Gunther trudging our way. "Figure out anything?"

"Just that we're as confused as ever," I said.

Kelly picked up a three-foot-long branch stripped of leaves and, squinting in the glare of the midday sun, pointed at the sign's letters. "Daryl said the company used to be called StarCast. Shouldn't the sign say that instead of Interfinity?"

"You're right." I touched the red paint at the bottom of the *I* in Interfinity — still tacky, not more than a few hours old. Someone worked quickly to help us find this spot, someone who thought Interfinity was the only name we knew. "Could Dr. Simon be setting up a meeting?"

"Or maybe an ambush," Kelly said.

"Now that Francesca has a home, I guess we'll just follow the breadcrumbs and try to get back to Earth Red." I shielded my eyes and looked again into what was left of the forest — skinny trunks broken like matchsticks, their upper halves either lying on the ground or hanging on by tufts of exposed wood fibers. With all this devastation, figuring out exactly where we had appeared in this world seemed impossible.

I crouched and pointed between two clusters of shrubs. "If this road is in the same place as the one in our world, the temporary mirror should be about a hundred yards straight back, that is, if it's still standing."

Kelly crouched with me, then stood again. "I can't see it from here. I hope it didn't break."

"Let's check it out."

"I'd better stay with Francesca and Nikolai," Gunther said, "in case we get some unexpected company. If you're not back in half an hour, I'll assume you jumped to another world again."

"We'll get our stuff and say good-bye." The three of us walked back to the van. Francesca stood next to the passenger door, Nikolai at her side.

After retrieving the violin, I extended my hand toward Francesca. "It's been great getting to know you."

"Same to you." She walked past my hand and hugged me. "Thank you for everything."

I returned the hug with my free hand. "It was a pleasure."

Kelly joined us in a three-way embrace. After a few moments, Francesca pulled back. Her chin quivered, shaking loose gathering tears and casting them to the ground. "I can't ever really go home, can I?"

Firming her lips, Kelly shook her head. "I'm sorry."

Francesca gave her a resigned nod. "Thank you for all you've done."

Blinking away my own tears, I smiled at Francesca. "When your son's born, don't listen to his complaints about practicing his violin. Okay?"

She patted my cheek, pain obvious in her eyes. "Don't worry. I'll chain him to his music stand."

"Thanks, Mom." I gave her a wink and backed away. Barely able to speak through my tightening throat, I nodded at Kelly. "Let's go."

As we circled to the driver's side, Francesca crawled to the middle of the front bench, while Nikolai sat by the door. Gunther had already slid behind the wheel. "Don't forget this," he said, reaching the mirror through the open window.

I set the violin down, took the mirror, and grasped his shoulder. "If we do make a leap out of this world, you watch over them, okay?"

"Like you said, I'll be a guardian angel. Keep in touch if you can."

"We will." I picked up the violin and handed the mirror to Kelly. Together we walked toward the Interfinity sign and the ravaged field. Puffy white clouds streamed from the horizon and drifted across the sun, providing relief from the glare as we passed the sign and entered the devastated forest.

"Do you think we'll ever come back to Earth Yellow?" Kelly asked.

"Eventually. Simon Blue's probably hanging around on Earth Yellow, so we'll have to contact him to figure out what's going on."

I picked up the pace, stepping high over broken branches. It took only a few minutes to locate the tri-fold mirror, flat on the ground and covered with green leaves, some still clinging to fallen branches.

"The mirror side's down," I said as I lifted the edge. "Maybe it survived after all."

Kelly dropped to her knees and peeked underneath. "It's dirty, but I don't see any cracks. The support boards broke at ground level, so we'll have to see if it'll stand without them."

After clearing the debris, we pulled the mirror upright and angled the three panels, balancing it until it stood on its own. The smudged glass reflected an aerial view of the telescope room.

"Daryl Blue still has us tuned in," I said, "but I don't see anyone."

"Maybe they're staying out of sight in case trouble shows up." Kelly bent forward, narrowing her eyes as she studied the image. "I see a fly."

I leaned closer. Near the edge, a dark bug flew in slow motion. "It's barely moving at all, like it's hovering."

"So time's still a lot slower there than here. That's a good sign."

"Maybe. But that's Earth Blue. We need it to be slower on Earth Red." I stepped to the mirror, lifted my shirt, and began wiping the center panel with it. "If I have everything straight, we'll go back to Earth Blue first, and then we'll have to jump on another world-hopping roller coaster to get back to Earth Red."

"So do we flash a light, or do they?"

I backed away from the glass. "I think we do."

"It looks like they don't know we're ready to come back. We'll probably have to make some music, too."

"Do you still have the key ring light?"

She pulled the keys from her pocket. "Right here."

"I hope it's enough. The lights in the telescope room really put on a show, and that thing's kind of puny."

"It's worth a try." Kelly flicked the flashlight on and set the pale beam at the center, barely visible in broad daylight.

"Not bright enough," I said. "What else can we use?"

She pulled on the strap around her neck. "The camera?"

I shook my head. "The last time I took a picture of one of the mirrors, it gave me a pretty wild jolt. The same thing happened to Clara. We don't want to cook the lens. Last resort, maybe."

Kelly looked toward the road. "Headlights from the van?"

"No way. Gunther would never make it through all the broken trees."

She looked up. "We could try the sun. It's hiding behind some clouds, but when it comes out, it'll be like a flash."

"That might work." I set the violin down and strode to the back of the mirror. Using both hands, I began shifting the frames to catch the sun's veiled rays.

Kelly set the smaller mirror beside the violin and helped me. "I guess before the tornado hit, the trees blocked the sun. What'll keep it from transporting something accidentally after we leave?"

"If we turn off the music from the Earth Blue side, I think this would become a regular mirror again. Someone would have to open it with music from this side to go anywhere."

"Okay," Kelly said. "Let's give it a try."

Something moved behind one of the broken maple trees. I kept my gaze on Kelly though I watched the tree from the corner of my eye. "I saw something."

"What?"

"I don't know. Something behind you." I walked casually to the front of the mirror. "We're not alone."

Kelly hugged herself and rubbed her upper arms. "Don't do this to me, Nathan. It's not funny."

"I'm not kidding." I picked up my mirror and angled it toward the maple. In the image a wavy-haired, bespectacled man peered at me from behind the tree. "You might as well show yourself, whoever you are. I already see you."

"An interesting paradox, indeed."

I swung around. Exactly as the mirror had predicted, a man stuck his head out and looked at me through dense, circular glasses. Although his thick head of hair contrasted sharply with that of the man I knew on Earth Red, his soft voice and hint of a British accent were unmistakable. "Dr. Simon?"

"Yes." He walked into the open. Wearing a leather jacket and blue jeans, he didn't fit the professorial stereotype the Earth Red image always tried to maintain. And he seemed much younger, definitely young enough to be Simon's Earth Yellow version.

"As I was saying," he continued, "this Quattro phenomenon is quite interesting. You saw me peek out at you in the reflection, yet I could have decided not to do so. The only reason I did was because you saw me. The logic seems circular."

I stealthily set my feet, ready to fight if necessary. "You could've stayed where you were to see what would happen."

"Theoretically." Simon wrung his hands. "But my need to talk to you was far greater than my curiosity."

I scanned him for a weapon, but he seemed unarmed. "What do you want?"

Simon sped through his words. "In order for us to continue our tests, we want to try to avert a certain disaster here on Earth Yellow. Of course, this is exactly what we have always wanted to do — use this technology for the good of mankind, and now you have given us a chance to succeed in our endeavors."

"Who is *us*?" Kelly asked. "Do you work for Mictar?"

He waved a hand. "Not at all. There are two competing forces. Dr. Gordon from Earth Blue and Mictar make up one side, while my counterpart on Earth Blue and I, as well as Dr. Gordon from Earth Red, make up the other side. It has taken until quite recently to decide how to apply our abilities, and you have given us a timely opportunity. With Quattro assisting us, our prospects are greatly enhanced."

I set a finger on my chest. "So is that why you need me?"

"Since you are the only one available who knows how to use it ..." Simon folded his hands at his waist. "Yes, that is why we need you."

"I'm the only one available? Does that mean you don't know where my father is? He knows how to use it."

"Mictar is holding your parents hostage." Simon took a breath and puffed out his chest in a comical manner, though he was probably trying to look brave. "If I could free them, I would."

"Why don't we concentrate on rescuing my father? Since he knows more about Quattro than I do, he's a better option than I am."

"We already have that goal in mind. My Earth Blue counterpart has set a plan in motion that we hope will rescue the prisoners, but it must wait until the Earth Red funeral."

I crossed my arms. "What's the plan?"

Simon's hand wringing intensified. "If I told you, I would lose some leverage in persuading you to avert the disaster."

"But if I try to stop it, I might not make it to the funeral on time."

"My counterpart assures me that we should make it. Time passage here in comparison to the other dimensions has been increasing of late."

I flopped my arms at my sides. "All right. What do I have to do?"

"In both Earth Red and Earth Blue, an airliner crashed at O'Hare airport in Chicago on this date." Simon withdrew a folded sheet of paper from his jacket pocket and handed it to me. "This describes how the aircraft failed. The engine on its left wing fell off due to an improper replacement procedure, and it stripped the hydraulic system and retracted the slats, keeping the pilot from knowing what to do to properly correct its tilt. Our task is simply to prevent the crash on Earth Yellow by using Quattro. This way, we can study how we might harness its power in the future."

I scanned the article. "Why don't you call the airline? Just say something like you got a tip that a terrorist messed up that engine, and they should check it out."

"That might work quite well, but it also might not. I am not willing to put two-hundred-seventy-one lives at risk." Simon withdrew a pair of tickets from his back pocket. "I need agents on board who will make sure the passengers survive."

I stared at the tickets. One bore my name, and the other, Kelly's. It was as though Dr. Simon held a pair of execution orders in his stubby fingers, and Kelly and I were the condemned prisoners.

CHAPTER TWENTY-THREE

I TOOK THE TICKETS. "So you want us to fly in a doomed jet."

Simon shook his head. "Not at all. The airliner won't be doomed if you prevent the disaster."

"I get that, but let's just warn the airline." I pushed the tickets toward him. "It would be crazy to fly with them."

"Keep the tickets." Simon folded his hands. "If warning the authorities is a sufficient rescue plan, then they will either repair the engine problem or conduct the passengers to another plane. If you are confident in this course of action, and you care for the lives of your fellow human beings, why should you fear taking the flight?"

"Because ... well ..." I heaved a sigh. "Okay. You got me."

Kelly patted my shoulder. "He wants to skip the flight, because he has to get back in time for the funeral."

I shook my head. "I could use that excuse, but it wouldn't be true. I just have cold feet."

"As I said," Simon continued, "you should have no fear. If you do your job wisely, you will be able to complete your mission, whether by the power of persuasion or the power of Quattro." He turned and gestured for us to follow. "We have dawdled too long. Now we must hurry."

As we followed his lead, Kelly swiveled her head. "I don't see a car anywhere."

From a pocket, Simon withdrew a small key ring and tossed it to me. "I have been told that you are capable of riding a motorcycle."

I caught the pair of silver keys. "Yeah. Pretty well."

"My counterpart from Earth Blue dropped me off with two Hondas that I hid under some fallen branches." He passed a line of broken trunks and stopped at a pile of debris that rose twice as high as his head. "Can Miss Clark ride as well?"

"Like a pro," Kelly said. "I have my own bike at home."

I laid a hand on her shoulder. "Look, Kelly. You don't have to risk this. I can probably get it done by myself."

Narrowing her eyes, she planted a hand on her hip. "What're you going to do? Leave me out in the woods?" She pressed a finger against my chest. "And whose life is it, anyway? If you're going to risk yours, I'm with you to the bitter end."

I gazed into her determined eyes. Her courage was amazing. And her loyalty? Breathtaking. I gave Simon a nod. "Sounds like we're in this together. We'll both need a bike."

Simon pulled one of the large branches off the pile of debris. "I expected you to stay together, but you might have misunderstood my question. When I asked if the young lady can ride, I was wondering if she would be able to ride with you, not on a motorcycle of her own. I don't have another mode of transportation for myself."

"All right if I drive?" Kelly asked me. "I know you're Mr. Super Spy, but it'll give me a chance to prove my skills."

I waved a hand. "Maybe you'd better not. I'm sure you're good, but if things get ugly, I've got more experience in getaways."

She flashed a hurt expression. "We're not going to run into trouble between here and the airport."

Simon pulled two more branches from the pile. "I don't care who controls the motorcycle, but we must leave immediately. You will ride together on the blue motorcycle in whichever manner you decide."

"Look, Kelly," I said, spreading out my hands, "I've ridden in — "

"Never mind." Kelly began helping Simon clear branches, her tone defeated. "You don't have to explain. I'll ride in the back."

I pulled a limb off the pile and set it to the side. Her disappointment was obvious, but I had to stay firm. I really did have a lot more experience.

After clearing off the bikes, I loaded the violin and mirror in the blue motorcycle's saddlebag, hopped on, and adjusted one of the rearview mirrors. "Looks like it has plenty of horsepower."

"For our needs, yes." Dr. Simon climbed aboard a similar red model and pushed a helmet over his head. "Helmets on, please."

While Kelly pulled an elastic band from her pocket and tied her hair back, I grabbed a shiny blue helmet from a handlebar and put it on. Without a word, Kelly took a sparkle-coated maroon helmet from the other handlebar and slid it on. She then climbed onto the back of the saddle and grasped the sides of the seat.

Dr. Simon started his engine and revved it a couple of times before easing his way through the mangled forest.

I started our bike and followed. As we headed away from the road Gunther had used to find the area, we zigzagged to avoid branches and splintered stumps while bumping over hidden dips and swells in the otherwise flat land. Kelly let out a few oomphs but kept her grip on the seat.

Within a few minutes, we reached a hardened dirt road. Simon gave us a thumbs-up signal and sped away on the smoother surface. Leaning forward, I gave chase and quickly closed the gap before slowing to stay a few bike lengths behind.

When we merged onto a paved highway, Kelly wrapped her arms around my waist. "I'm sorry," she shouted over the engine noise.

As the stiff headwind whistled, I twisted my neck and shouted back. "Sorry for what?"

"For wanting to be the driver even though I knew you're more experienced."

I laid a hand over hers, interlocked under my ribcage. "Don't be sorry for that. I like assertiveness. I hope you'll always tell me what you want."

"I won't if you don't give me a chance. Let me prove myself. If you shoot me down, I'll stop being assertive."

I pondered her words but not for very long. She was right, without a doubt. I slowed to a stop, set a foot on the pavement, and looked back at her. "Show me your stuff. Catch up with Dr. Simon."

She grinned. "Now you're talking."

We got off and switched places. When she set her hands on the handlebars and I held to her hips, she called out, "Hang on, Mr. Spy!" We took off like a shot and accelerated to breakneck speed. As she closed the gap between us and Simon, she swerved from side to side, apparently getting a feel for the bike. She really was quite good.

Once we came within a few bike lengths of Simon, we turned onto an interstate highway and settled to a steady cruise for about two hours. When we arrived at Chicago's O'Hare International and pulled into Terminal Three's passenger drop-off zone, we rolled up beside Simon and stopped. I checked my watch — 2:17.

I took off my helmet and tucked it under my arm. "What time does the flight leave?"

Simon slid off his helmet, mussing his hair into a frazzled mop. "The actual runway time in your world was a minute after three." He handed me the keys to the red motorcycle. "Leave the helmets. It will lighten your load."

After Kelly and I dismounted, I set my helmet on the seat and stuffed the keys into my pocket. "We'd better hurry. Getting through security might take a while."

"I have heard about your nine-eleven terrorist attack," Simon said, "but it hasn't happened here. Security is not as tight."

Kelly gave Simon a suspicious glare. "What are you going to do while we're risking our necks?"

"My counterpart will arrive soon to pick me up, but we will stay long enough to ensure that the motorcycles are not taken away. Assuming that you will successfully prevent the disaster, you may then use the bikes to go back to the observatory site. From there, you will return to Earth Blue before you resume your journey home to Earth Red."

I raised a finger. "Just one more question. Do I have to play music to get through the mirror or does it have to come from the Earth Blue side?"

"You may control the mirror's functions by playing a certain melody on your violin." He withdrew a slim iPod from his shirt pocket along with attached ear buds. "We have recorded on this device from your world all the known compositions that open the cosmic passages. If you look at the display screen you will see a note that explains where the compositions work and to which destinations they will take you."

"Cool. That'll help a lot."

I reached for the iPod, but Simon pulled it back. "The music device isn't yours to keep." He dialed up a selection and handed me the ear buds. "Do you recognize this?"

When I plugged the buds in, a familiar piece filtered into my ears. After I listened a few more seconds to be sure, I nodded. "It's Waxman's Carmen Fantasy."

Simon arched his brow. "Can you play it?"

"Mom loved that piece, so she played it a lot." I took out the buds and gave them back to Simon. "She tried to teach me, but I never could get it right. I have some of it in my head, but I don't know how much."

Simon wrapped the wires around the iPod. "Let's hope you don't have to test your memory. If Interfinity's mirror is tuned to Earth Blue and the music is playing from that side, you shouldn't have a problem. Just use the sun for a light source, as I heard you planning."

"The way things have gone," Kelly said as she hung her helmet on the handle of Simon's motorcycle, "something will go wrong."

I detached the saddle pack from the motorcycle and held it at my side. "Let's move. The more time we have to convince them to cancel the flight, the better."

After passing through the terminal's sliding doors with Kelly, I checked the flight number on my ticket and searched the listings on a monitor. "There it is. Flight one-ninety-one." We picked up our boarding passes at the ticket counter and hurried to the security checkpoint. As my saddle pack passed through the X-ray machine, I leaned close to Kelly. "This is nothing compared to how it is in our world."

"Good thing. Even a mirror might be considered a weapon."

"Or a violin."

When we arrived at the gate, the passengers had lined up at the jetway door and were slowly filing in. I marched straight to the check-in desk where a tall, slender young man stood typing at a computer terminal. He looked up and gave me a mechanical smile. "May I help you?"

I tapped a finger firmly on the counter. "Listen, this might sound really stupid, but what if someone had a bad feeling about this flight, like a premonition about an engine falling off the wing, would you check it out?"

Dropping his gaze back to his desk, the clerk scratched a note with a pencil, apparently unmoved. "Sir, that happens all the time. Many people fear flying, so they have nightmares about their flights, and with the recent epidemic, more than half the passengers on any flight have had nightmares about their plane crashing."

The mention of the nightmare epidemic raised a bunch of new questions, but I didn't have time to ask more than one. "Aren't some of the nightmares coming true?"

"Some, yes, but we can't possibly check out every bad dream." The clerk looked up, again wearing the mechanical smile. "In any case, air travel safety hasn't changed at all, so passengers are flying at the usual rate."

"I guess that makes sense." Backing away, I gave him a friendly nod. "Thank you."

I bumped into Kelly and spun toward her. "I could make a ruckus and claim the engine is messed up, but they might not believe me, and then they'd probably haul me off for interrogation. I'd never make it to the funeral in time."

"Call in a bomb threat. No one would know you did it."

"You mean use a pay phone?"

"Or a customer service phone."

I scanned the area and found a yellow phone on the wall near the gate. "Those might be traceable. As soon as they answer, they'll know exactly where I am."

"Then I guess the pay phone is the only way."

I reached into my jeans pocket. "I have some change. I hope I can find the number for the airport."

"Just dial the operator or nine-one-one."

"Did they have nine-one-one thirty years ago?"

"I guess you'll find out soon enough."

I looked down the long corridor and spied a bank of six phones about a hundred paces away. Three men and

312 | Time Echoes

one woman stood chatting at the ends of the short, silver cords.

With Kelly following, I hustled toward them, but as soon as I closed in, a forty-something woman in a business suit took one of the two open phones, and a teenager wearing a Northwestern T-shirt took the other.

I pivoted and whispered to Kelly. "We can't afford to wait. Let's get on the plane and speak to the pilot. They sometimes have the cockpit door open when passengers are boarding."

"What time is it?"

I checked my watch — 2:36. I looked at a monitor to verify. A digital clock in one corner displayed the same time. "Two thirty-six. It's going to crash in about twenty-five minutes."

We quick-stepped back to the gate and stood at the end of the line, now dwindled to about ten passengers. A gray-haired man in front of us turned around, nervously tapping his cane on the floor. "Another procrastinator. I know how you feel."

"Really?" I said. "How do I feel?"

Although the man's bare forearm rippled with muscles, animating the tattoo of a fierce-looking dragon, his fingers trembled around the cane's hooked end. "If you're like me, you're scared as a cat in a rocking chair showroom. I had a bad dream about this flight, and I was going to skip it, but my wife said I was being silly. She said everyone's having nightmares, and the trip was too important to cancel because of a dream."

"Why are you going to Los Angeles?" Kelly asked.

"Booksellers' convention. I'm an author, and my first book's coming out. I'm a retired cop. Lots of stories to tell, you know."

When we arrived at the jet's entry door, I peered toward the cockpit. The door was already closed — no chance to talk to the pilot.

Hot prickles spread across my neck, followed by a stream of sweat. What now?

As I turned into the closer of two aisles, a sea of faces across the cabin seemed to rotate toward me — a young woman with a pixie haircut settling a newborn in her lap, a uniformed Hispanic man pushing a military duffle bag into an overhead bin, and a little girl bouncing in her window seat, shaking her red Shirley Temple curls as she clutched her daddy's hand — precious lives, souls who had no idea that only a few minutes separated them from a meeting with the Almighty.

While I waited for the soldier to finish loading his duffle, Kelly grabbed my hand from behind. "It can't be more than fifteen minutes away," she said, her whisper turning hoarse. A muffled clump sounded from the front of the cabin. "And they closed the door."

"I know. I know." I had to get the pilot to come out, but how? Noise? Maybe music? But it would have to be a piece that would cause a ruckus, something to scare the passengers. Danse Macabre ought to do it.

I nodded toward my saddle pack. "Can you get my violin?"

She unzipped the bag, withdrew the violin case, and flipped open the clasps. "What are you going to play?"

"I have something special in mind." With every head turned toward us, I set the violin under my chin, raised the bow, and let out a nervous laugh. "A bon voyage piece, if you don't mind."

The redheaded girl clapped and shouted, "Play Turkey in the Straw!"

The girl's father reached for his wallet. "Do you take requests?"

I gave them a smile. "Sure, but let me play this one first."

As soon as the violin sounded the first note, a female voice interrupted. "What are you doing?"

I twisted toward her. A flight attendant stood behind me, an angular-faced brunette with a confused look on her face. I restarted and played while speaking loudly enough for everyone to hear. "One of the passengers told me he's scared the plane is going to crash, so I thought I'd calm him down. This piece is called Dance of Death by Saint-Saëns."

"Dance of Death?" The attendant cleared her throat sharply. "Sir, I must ask you to stop and take your seat. You'll frighten the other passengers."

"But it's such a lively piece." While I continued playing, another flight attendant picked up a telephone and pressed a button.

The first attendant pulled my arm. "Sir, I must insist that you stop."

I lowered the violin and nodded toward the front of the plane. "May I speak to the captain?"

Just as the attendant turned, the cockpit door opened. The captain, dressed in a navy blue jacket and white shirt, thumped toward us and halted about three rows away. He crossed his arms in front. "What seems to be the problem?"

The attendant pointed at me. "This gentleman — "

"Sir," I said. "May I have a word with you in private?"

Narrowing his eyes, the captain glanced at the attendant briefly, then nodded. "Come to the front."

After handing the violin to Kelly, I followed him to the boarding area. The pilot spun sharply and spoke in a harsh whisper, barely moving his lips. "The comfort of my passengers will not be compromised. I cannot tolerate any action, even the playing of a violin, that might upset their confidence in the safety of this craft." As he leaned closer, his eyes seemed to pulse with rage. "Do you understand?"

I took a step back. "Yessir, but I had a ... a premonition, I guess you'd call it. So did another passenger." I angled my head toward the wing. "Your left engine has a problem. Something bad's going to happen to it."

The captain extended a rigid finger toward the wing. "That engine is fine. Every part of this jet is checked according to a strict schedule. I'm not about to let mass hysteria over nightmares, Bigfoots, or Loch Ness monsters endanger this flight." He leaned so close his hot breath blew across my cheek. "Do I make myself clear?"

I steeled myself, forcing my voice to stay calm. "Yessir. But — "

"No buts, or your butt will be off this aircraft." The captain spun an about-face and stormed back into the cockpit, closing the door with a loud clap.

I winced. That guy meant business. But who could blame him? He'd probably heard a thousand nightmare stories. At least he had enough patience not to kick me off the plane right away.

I checked the seat number on my boarding pass and headed down the aisle. When I met Kelly, I whispered, "Let's just find our seats," and continued striding toward the back.

As I walked through and glanced at the row numbers, passengers stabbed me with icy glares, but I ignored them. When I found our number, I stopped and looked out the window. Our seats were next to the wing. "Wouldn't you know it? We have the emergency row."

When we slid into place, I folded the empty saddle pack and shoved it under the seat in front of me, while Kelly laid the violin case under the seat in front of her. As she handed me the Quattro mirror, she leaned close. Her whispered voice spiked with alarm. "Are we really going to take off?"

"I have to save these people somehow," I whispered back. "If you want to leave, it should be easy to get kicked off. Just make a scene, and I'm sure the pilot will oblige."

"I can't leave without you." She locked her arm around mine. "But how do you plan to stop the crash?"

"Maybe the mirror can transport us all out of here." I glanced at my watch. 2:55. But the second hand had stopped. Maybe it had quit working.

When I tried to get a look at the wristwatch of a man in the seat across the aisle, he extended his arm and turned the watch toward me. "It is two fifty-five, Nathan, son of Solomon. Will the brief delay you caused be sufficient to bring about your desired end?"

Gaunt and white haired, the man was the image of Mictar, though he had no ponytail, and his eyes carried none of the murderer's malice. Yet, they seemed just as unearthly — dark, fiery, and piercing.

Every sound in the cabin dampened to silence, and every movement ceased, including the air jetting from the vents. Even Kelly's rapid breathing stopped as though she had frozen in place.

My reply came out in a stutter. "Who … who are you?"

His lips seemed to move in slow motion. "I am Patar, the one who sets free."

"How do you know my name?"

"I have been watching you," Patar replied, his voice wafting through the eerie silence. "Your defiance of my brother, Mictar, and his schemes is courageous and good, but you are wandering in dangerous lands. There are other ways to prevent the ultimate conflict." He pointed a slender white finger toward the front. "You still have time to escape."

I let my gaze move across the colorful array of faces, some smiling, others anxious, each one a reflection of an inner array of hopes and fears. "But what about all these people? Shouldn't I try to rescue them?"

His pale lips bent downward. "That is a question of moral duty. I cannot answer it for you."

"*Can* I rescue them? I mean, is the crash predetermined?"

"Predetermined?" He raised a single eyebrow. "That word is far more complex than you realize. In order to explain, I will refer to a parallel you have come to rely upon — the mirror you call Quattro. Do you think it provides glimpses of the future?"

I looked at the mirror, now on my lap. It showed only my face, pale and worried. "I think so. Everything in the reflection always came true."

"Then do you think the images are predetermined?"

"I ... I really don't know. Why don't you just tell me?"

"Very well. What you see in the mirror merely reflects the ruminations of your mind — what you expect, what you long for, what you fear. The mirror is not a window to the future; it is a view port into what might be. Its power to make these images come true is quickened by your faith in what you see and how you respond to it. You might call it a reflection of your supplications as well as predictions based on what your supplicant knows."

"My supplicant? I've heard that word before. What does it mean?"

"I cannot hold this suspension for long, so I lack time to explain. We should focus on the mortal consequences of your decision to board this aircraft. You will learn about your supplicant later."

"All right. Suppose the mirror shows a way to escape. If I act according to what it shows me, then we have a chance."

"Correct."

"What if it doesn't show me anything?"

"Then I assume the plane will crash. You and your loyal friend will die along with everyone on board."

"Okay ... I guess that's true." A lump swelled in my throat. "I have another question. Suppose we survive. What do I do about this ultimate conflict you mentioned? And how do I fight Mictar?"

Patar stood, stepped across the aisle, and laid a hand over my eyes. I clenched my eyes shut and tried to get away, but my arms and legs froze in place.

The hand clamped down, but not tightly. "Fear not, son of Solomon, and open your eyes. I am bestowing a gift that will, if your heart is prepared, protect you from my brother. When the time comes to use it, the depth of your courage will ignite this power."

As light flashed, I relaxed and opened my lids. Soothing warmth bathed my eyes, like bathwater swirling around aching muscles.

After a few seconds, Patar lifted his hand and backed away. "Choose whatever path you must, but beware." His voice lowered to a snakelike whisper. "If these souls are cheated out of death, their escape might create more darkness than light. Take care not to stir darkened pools when you know neither the depth of the water nor the creatures that lurk beneath the surface." He then morphed into a human-shaped cloud of thin mist and disappeared.

The passengers jerked back into motion. The vents emitted cool air once again, and Kelly lurched toward the aisle. Catching her breath, she leaned toward me and whispered, "What just happened?"

"I'll tell you later." I sank in my seat, a queasy feeling churning my stomach. What should I do now? Patar seemed to think I should let all these people die. How could a force of good possibly want that? Still, if Patar was Mictar's enemy, shouldn't I trust him? And he seemed to know all about Quattro, but would a Mictar lookalike really be on the right side, or was he in this battle with his brother for his own benefit?

As I closed my eyes, the gaunt phantom's face hovered in my mind. So this was the person Dad mentioned, the one who might scare me away. Yet, Dad also said Patar would tell me the right thing to do. Did that mean I should get up and leave? Patar didn't exactly say to do that.

I opened my eyes. My heart thumped like a jackhammer. I looked again at my reflection in the mirror, still on my lap. My chin quivered, and my tense lips had turned nearly white.

Kelly looked on. With her eyebrows bent low, she glanced from the mirror to me and back to the mirror again. Her voice carried softly to my ear, a slight tremble giving away her fear. "What are you going to do?"

"I don't know. I just don't know." I watched myself lick my pale lips, hoping the mirror would give me some sign that it would do its magic, but nothing changed. Even without the mirror's help, I might be able to save everyone, maybe scream that I saw someone tamper with the engine until the passengers demanded a maintenance check. Then the airline would probably check it and find the problem, and the police would arrest me for causing it. But at least I would save everyone on board.

Maybe if the mirror showed the engine falling off before it happened, the passengers would see it and shout for action, but would the captain believe them? I could also play something on my violin that might bring an image to the mirror and transport us to a safe place. But would Kelly and I go alone? Would everyone on the airplane go with us? Or would it not work at all, abandoning Kelly and me to suffer in the devastating carnage?

The girl in red appeared in the mirror, this time looking straight at me. She waved as if entreating me to follow, then ran into the mirror's dark background and disappeared.

I glanced at Kelly. For the moment, she had turned toward the aisle. She hadn't seen the girl. Maybe I should just do what she asked, follow her, trust her to control the mirror once more.

"Kelly," I whispered. "Let's see what the mirror will do now." While she watched, I lifted the mirror toward the window and adjusted the angle until the wing appeared in the reflection. Everything seemed normal, just a copy of the long metal appendage and a gleam of sunlight near the tip. After a few seconds, the pavement in the reflection lurched, then moved forward. In the mirror, the jet was backing up. Soon, the same would happen in reality. "It looks like we're going to take off."

She replied with a quiet whimper. "Do you have a plan?"

"Just ..." I tightened every muscle, trying to keep my body from shaking. "Just that I have to let the plane take off."

"But we can still escape first, right?" She reached for her buckle. "We can get up and demand that they let us leave."

I grabbed her wrist and pulled her hand away from her belt. "Just trust me. It's going to be all right."

"But how can you be so sure?"

"I saw the girl in red. I think she's going to help us." I nodded toward the seat in front of hers. "As soon as the flight attendant checks everyone, get my violin out."

She sat up straight and pulled away from me. "Here she comes."

I slid the mirror behind me. As the brunette attendant strode down the aisle glancing at buckles, I settled back and smiled. When she reached our row, she halted. Wearing a chilling frown, she pointed at Kelly. "Stow the camera, please."

Kelly drew the strap over her head and laid the camera under the seat in front of her.

After checking our area, the attendant continued her march toward the rear of the plane. When she reversed course and returned to the front, Kelly grabbed the camera and draped the strap over her head again. Then, using her foot, she guided the violin case toward me along the carpet. I caught the case with my own foot and lifted it to my lap.

Just as the mirror had predicted, the plane lurched and began a slow backwards roll. Kelly clutched the arms of her seat, her knuckles white.

I opened the case as quietly as possible. After removing the violin and bow, I laid the case on the floor and pushed it back in place with my foot. Then, I retrieved the mirror and braced it on my knees.

Kelly reached for the mirror and held it with one hand. "Got it."

"Thanks." I adjusted the mirror to show the wing. "Keep it right there."

The plane stopped. With a high-pitched purr, the engines came to life and propelled us forward. As the wheels rumbled toward the runway, I closed my eyes. A crash was inevitable. Only Quattro could save us now. But whom would it save?

I opened my eyes again. Although in reality we were still heading for the runway, the mirror showed the tarmac lines speeding past the window. Then, in the midst of a huge billow of smoke, the engine flew up from the front of the wing, tumbled over the top, and hurtled back toward the tail area.

I jerked my head away. It was really going to happen. The plane was doomed.

In reality, the jet turned onto the runway's black-streaked pavement and accelerated. With each tiny jolt over the runway's grooves, Kelly flinched, shaking the mirror.

I set the bow on the strings. My timing had to be perfect. If I played too soon, a frightened passenger or an angry flight attendant might snatch the violin away. If I played too late, the world-transport window might not open in time, if it would open at all.

With long, easy strokes, I began the first measure of "Amazing Grace." Years ago, Mom had taught me the song, one of my first pieces when I was barely more than a toddler holding an eighth-size violin in my chubby hands. And as I played, she played along and sang, her voice matching the composer's passion.

The plane jerked. Just as the nose tipped upward and the landing gear lifted off the ground, the engine flew up in front of the wing and zoomed past the window. A chorus of gasps spread across the field of seats like a gust of wind. Screams erupted. Hands latched onto armrests. A rumbling roar from the good engine on the right pounded through the cabin. The jet rattled, a bone-jarring shake that chattered teeth and jiggled loose skin on white-knuckled passengers.

Kelly cried out, "Nathan! I don't want to die! I'm not ready to die!"

I stopped playing and grabbed her hand. "Don't give up. Hang on. It's the only way we can survive."

Strangling my fingers, she breathed rapid, heavy breaths. "Get a grip, Kelly. Get control of yourself." Her breaths eased, long and quiet, but her hand stayed latched to mine.

I pulled free and played on, adding more passion. As we continued our upward lift, Kelly jumped, again shaking the mirror, but she bit her lip and hung on. The camera dangled in front of her, thumping her chest with every jolt. The plane banked slowly to the left, much more steeply than it would for a turn. Screams again broke out as passengers tipped to the side, reaching, grabbing, clawing to stay upright.

Kelly squeezed her eyes closed. Her face quaked as she stretched out a long, plaintive cry. "Nathan! Help me!"

Leaning against the window, I swept the bow through the end of a measure. What could I do to help? What could anyone do? The mirror displayed a sea of twisted, burning wreckage and dozens of bloody, charred, and dismembered bodies scattered across the tarmac. At any second, Kelly and I would join them.

CHAPTER TWENTY-FOUR

A S THE JET shook harder, more screams filled
the cabin —calls to Jesus, cries for mercy, and
unintelligible wails. An overhead bin popped open,
spilling a duffle bag and a canvas overnighter on top
of two men across the aisle. The smell of burnt fuel and
rubber filled the air.

Kelly braced herself on the seat in front and sang
the first phrase of my tune, her voice feeble and quiet.
"Amazing grace, how sweet the sound, that saved a wretch
like me." Every word rattled through her chattering teeth
as she hung on to the mirror. During the second phrase, a
woman joined in from behind as did a man somewhere to
the side.

The jet angled to ninety degrees and flew sideways.
The cabin lights flickered off, leaving only shafts of
sunlight knifing through the windows. More bins flew
open. Suitcases and garment bags rained throughout the
cabin. Smoke billowed from somewhere out of sight and
spread toward us.

The mirror blazed with fire and falling ash. Still
playing the violin, I glanced out the window. The tip of
the wing sank, just thirty feet from a fatal brush with the
ground.

As Kelly and the others sang on, I stopped playing and reached the end of my bow toward the reading light in the overhead console. Would it work? Or was the plane too crippled to deliver power to the bulbs? I caught a glimpse of the camera, swinging back and forth from the strap around Kelly's neck. I hissed, "Take a picture of the mirror."

Her body quaking, she grabbed the camera, pointed it, and pressed the shutter button. It clicked, but the flash unit stayed dark. "I have to turn it on."

"No time." I strained to push the console button, fighting the horrible quaking of the wounded jet. Giving the bow a desperate shove, I hit the switch. The light flashed on.

The mirror reflected the weak beam, splitting it into multiple shafts. Two beams pierced Kelly and me, while others zipped past us. The light felt like a hot laser that sizzled through my skin and burned deep in my chest.

Kelly released the mirror, but it stayed upright on my lap and expanded in every direction, even in depth as it seemed to absorb my legs and reach toward Kelly's.

My body slid into the mirror's grip. I looked to the side, still able to see through the plane's window. The wingtip struck the ground, sending the jet into a wild tumble. The jolt threw Kelly into me and shoved us fully into the mirror.

Holding out my violin to keep it safe, I rolled to a stop in an open field. The jet cartwheeled only a few feet above my head, and the nose section knifed into the ground about fifty yards away, digging a rut before breaking loose from the fuselage. The rest of the body slammed down and smashed a hangar in a thunderous explosion of horrible thuds, cracks, and squeals as its momentum swept an avalanche of destruction across the field.

Metal tore from metal. Fire gushed into the sky in an enormous cloud of orange. Heat rushed past me in a rolling wave, singeing my skin and whipping my hair. The mirror, still in my lap, radiated warmth through my pants.

Kelly grabbed my arm and buried her face in my sleeve, screaming, "Nathan! They're dead! They're all dead!"

A man jumped past us and dashed toward the wreckage, then another limped by — the author we had met in the terminal building. I looked around and counted. Two, three, four … at least four other people sat or stood in horror while the first two hurried into the crash zone.

Still clutching the violin, I grabbed the mirror, rose, and staggered toward the burning wreckage. Kelly stumbled along beside me, her legs wobbly.

In the midst of crackling fires and sizzling metal, sirens wailed, drawing closer. The two men who charged ahead earlier just stood and surveyed the field of hopelessness. Burning body parts lay strewn in a swath of superheated fires. No one could save them now.

The author dropped to his knees. Clutching his thinning gray hair with both hands, he shouted into the rising vapors. "I knew this would happen! Why didn't I stop it?"

The first man joined us, short and stocky with a full beard and weary gray eyes. "I dreamed about it, too," he whispered to me. "Did you?"

I glanced at the mirror, now tucked under my arm, but I couldn't feel it. All sensation had drained away. My limbs, my body, even my face and hands were numb. Staring at the devastation, I could barely find strength to speak. "I saw it before it happened."

He scanned the other survivors. "I think we all did. The ones who lived, I mean."

I looked at each survivor— a young woman in seventies-style green pants standing petrified as she watched the fires burn, a middle-aged woman in a navy blue business suit weeping as she talked to Kelly, and a young couple sitting together in a sobbing huddle. "You're probably right."

He extended a hand. "Name's John, but my friends call me Jack."

I shook his hot, sweaty hand. "I'm Nathan."

"I suppose we should have said something about the nightmares. Maybe if all of us had spoken up, they might have listened."

"Maybe, but I doubt it. Don't blame yourself."

As fire engines roared close and a helicopter beat its blades overhead, I turned back to Kelly. She held the camera in her hands, the strap still around her neck as she snapped a picture of the crash scene. The flash lit up, though in the mid-afternoon sun it didn't seem as bright as usual.

When she lowered the camera, her voice matched her teary, anguished eyes. "One of the survivors asked me to take some pictures for her. I hope it's okay." She showed me a business card. "I have her address."

"I guess it won't hurt anything, but I don't know how you're going to get the pictures to her. She's dead in our world, and I'm not sure if we'll ever come back to Earth Yellow."

Kelly picked up the violin case, opened it, and nodded toward the saddlebag at her feet. "I found this near where we landed."

I laid the violin and bow in the case, closed the lid, and fastened the latches, then stuffed the case and mirror into the bag and picked it up. "Let's walk. The terminal's not far."

Staring at the airport buildings, I strode toward them, not wanting to look back as turmoil raged in my wake— blaring sirens, shouting rescue workers, and sizzling fires, a Danse Macabre performed on the strings of demonic violins. And I failed to prevent it.

Yet, the girl in red helped me save a few lives, including our own. The mystery surrounding her grew ever deeper. Since I had no answers, it probably wouldn't do any good to talk about her recent appearance, at least not yet.

Kelly's voice seeped into the flow of sounds. "Are you all right?"

"How could I be all right?" I winced. My words were too harsh. Heaving a deep sigh, I added, "I'm sorry."

Her cool fingers slid into my free hand. "It's not your fault."

I grasped them gratefully. "I know." But that was all I could say. Death loomed over my mind like a shadow— dark, empty, icy cold. And now I had to go to my parents' funeral.

After following an access road that led us to the front of the terminal building, we found the motorcycles where we had left them, leaning on their stands with the helmets still in place. Cars had parked in every lane, halting the flow of traffic. People milled around.

Their conversations buzzed, wordless in my ears. A few uniformed men and women hurried from place to place, some barking into walkie-talkies, but Simon was nowhere in sight.

I slipped my helmet on, attached the bag to the red motorcycle, and dug out the keys. "Still got your keys?"

"Right here." She displayed them in her hand.

"Then let's go."

She mounted the blue bike, her helmet already on and her dirty beige slacks and blue polo shirt rippling in the breeze.

I straddled the seat. "We'd better not travel together. Just stay close enough to keep me in sight."

"Why?"

"Word's going to get out that we survived. I said something about the engine to the gate clerk. If they think I had anything to do with the crash, they'll be on the lookout for two teenagers traveling together."

She nodded. "Got it."

I dug into my pocket, pulled out a wad of dollar bills, and pushed them into her hand. "For tolls."

With my grip tight on the handlebars, I started the motorcycle and weaved through the lanes of parked vehicles. When I approached the front, I reached a row of airport security cars. Apparently they had intentionally blocked the access road to halt the flow of traffic.

As I passed one of the cars, its siren squawked. When Kelly scooted by, the officer lowered his window and shouted over the motorcycles' rumble. "Stop! Pull over to the sidewalk!"

Kelly gave the engine a shot of gas and raced away. I roared after her, keeping watch in my rearview mirror.

The police car's blue lights flashed to life, and its siren howled as the officer gave chase.

When I caught up with Kelly, she shouted. "Ever done any dirt biking?"

"Yeah. Why?"

"Get ready."

When we came upon a merge lane where cars entered our road from an upcoming overpass, she slowed, spun a one-eighty, and headed into the entry curve in the wrong direction.

I swung around and tore after her. As cars blared their horns and darted out of the way, I checked my mirror and caught a glimpse of the patrol car skidding to a halt back on the main road.

Once we reached the left side of the four-lane highway, Kelly crossed the two oncoming lanes, hugged a guard rail that lined the median on the right, and rumbled across the overpass, still going in the wrong direction. Again, I followed. I dodged a car, a minibus, and a pickup truck before reaching the median and taking off after her.

She angled her bike through a narrow gap in the rail and kept going, this time in the same direction as the cars already speeding along. Keeping close behind, I looked back. No one followed.

After cruising far enough to get out of sight of the officer, Kelly pulled into a restaurant lot and parked behind the building. She cut her engine and leaned her head on the handlebars.

I hit the brakes hard and skidded to her side. "You okay?" I asked as I shut down my bike.

She lifted her head. "Just tired. You?"

"Same." I looked around the vacant lot. The restaurant was either closed or out of business.

A wailing police car screamed past, then another. I peeked around the corner. A third cruiser came by at a slower speed. An officer looked our way, scanning the front parking lot.

I pulled back. "We'd better cut through some side streets and get out of here."

I wheeled my motorcycle around and headed away from the main road. We pushed our bikes up a gravel embankment and over a set of railroad tracks. Once across, we ran down the other side and onto a residential street.

Now hidden from the highway by the railroad berm, I turned toward the airport. "If we head that way, we'll eventually get to Interstate eighty-eight. Since we were last seen heading north, they'll focus their search on that side of town."

She started her engine. "I'm right behind you."

"Remember. Not too close."

After meandering through the neighborhood, I came upon a ramp to the main highway and headed west, careful to stay just under the speed limit. In my rearview mirror, Kelly merged into the right lane and fell behind a little farther every few seconds.

As I zipped along, I kept an eye on her as she followed from about a half-mile back. Letting out a sigh, I shook my head. She was an unbelievable combination of female charm, sharp wits, and ice-water coolness. Most girls would've scrunched into a fetal curl and cried like a baby, but even locked inside a doomed jet already falling from the sky, she never lost her head. She even sang Amazing Grace. What an incredible girl!

Yet, ghosts haunted her, phantoms from the past.
They haunted me as well. Although I had no right to act
as her judge, doubts about her past plagued me. If I were
ever to want a relationship with her, could I exorcise the
phantoms?

I shook my head hard. Why was I ruminating about
this? I had just witnessed extreme carnage, a disaster that
killed hundreds and devastated the lives of many more.
And here I was dwelling on issues that were trivial by
comparison. I had to get back on track, refocus on finishing
this crazy journey. I had to stop Mictar and rescue the
Earth Blue versions of my parents.

Now that my brain had fought off the distractions,
I gave myself a nod of approval, though I knew I was lying
to myself. Even in the aftermath of disaster, I couldn't
shake the notion that Kelly was knocking on the door
of my heart. Before much longer I would have to decide
whether or not to let her in.

CHAPTER TWENTY-FIVE

I SET THE MOTORCYCLE'S kickstand, unzipped the saddle pack, and glanced around at the broken trees and scattered branches. No sign of Dr. Simon.

After Kelly parked her bike next to mine, she shuffled through the debris toward the tri-fold mirror. In the reflection, the Earth Blue scene had disappeared. Now it showed only the mangled forest surrounding us.

"You have to play the piece," Kelly said, the Quattro mirror under an arm and the camera strap still around her neck.

"I know. And it's cloudy. Let's hope the sun comes out in time." I pulled the violin case from the bag and fumbled with the clasps.

Kelly grasped my hand. "Nathan, you're trembling."

I looked at my shaking fingers. "I guess I am." Taking a deep breath, I tried to calm my nerves. In this state, I would never be able to play the Carmen Fantasy. I flipped up the latches and withdrew Mom's violin. Since I didn't remember much of the piece, the doorway to Earth Blue had to open in a hurry.

As I laid the bow over the strings, Kelly gave me a firm nod. "You can do this."

"I'm glad someone thinks so." I set my feet and watched myself in the tri-fold mirror. After starting with a short mid-range stroke, I ran my fingers across the neck and ended the series with a sweet high note. After another quick mid-range stroke, I played a second rapid run from the high to the low registers, then moved to a slower melody that lasted about fifteen seconds.

I paused and stared at the mirror. My own image gawked back at me, my shirt tail hanging out on one side and my dirty hair locked in a rigid windswept pose.

"I can't remember any more."

She clutched the camera tightly. "You *have* to remember. We don't have any choice."

"I know. I know." I took in a deep breath and began again, playing the same notes, but, after a long pause, I lowered the bow. "It's no use, I — "

"Nathan." She stared at the Quattro mirror, wide-eyed. "Look." As she turned it toward me, she smiled. "Help has arrived."

The reflection showed Mom dressed in gray sweats, standing in a home studio with her violin in playing position. Next to her stood a younger version of me, maybe two years my junior, also with a violin in hand as we both looked at sheet music on a stand. Mom spoke, but no sound came forth.

Kelly gave voice to the image. "Your mother says, 'Watch my fingers, Nathan.'"

My throat clamped shut. I couldn't reply. I shuffled close and readied my bow again, squinting at Mom's hands. After the first note, her fingers glided along the neck, then stopped as she spoke again.

Kelly whispered, "Now you try it."

I played the notes, this time with perfect precision.

Mom tucked her violin and clapped. Then, lifting her violin and bow, she played the next few measures. Her fingers seemed to caress her instrument as a gentle angel would pet a lamb. She paused and pointed her bow at the younger version of me.

This time, I didn't wait for a command. I played the notes flawlessly, copying Mom's tender touch.

The tri-fold mirror image slowly darkened.

Kelly held the mirror steady. "She says she's going to play the rest all the way through, so watch carefully."

I set my bow and leaned close. As she played the rapid-fire measures, sweat moistened my forehead. "It's so fast. I'll never be able to copy it just by watching."

"Yes, you can, Nathan. I believe in you!"

I looked at Kelly. "Did you say that, or did my mom?"

"I said it." Kelly bit her lip before continuing. "You're the best, Nathan. I've never met anyone like you. I know you can do this."

My mind drifted back to that day I stood with Mom, looking at her in wonder as she played this intricate piece with blinding speed and flawless beauty. As she leaned toward my reflected self and blew on his knuckles, the entire image seemed to envelop me, bringing her face so close that her fair skin and jet black hair loomed like a protective mother eagle.

Kelly gave life to Mom's words. "May the breath of God fill your soul with the melody of everlasting love."

Shivers ran up my arm, across my shoulders, and into my other hand. As Mom straightened and readied herself again, my fingers seemed charged with energy, begging to fly into action.

Francesca Shepherd played. Nathan Shepherd answered. Though her reflected instrument sang in silence, I channeled the sound to the same violin, feeling her energy and passion flow through my fingers as each note rang clear and true.

The celebration of musical zeal threaded rapid runs across the ebony fingerboard, and the reflection in the tri-fold mirror altered with the same fervor. Within seconds, the telescope room on Earth Blue took shape.

Kelly's voice seemed a distant echo. "It's working!"

Mom played the last measure with dazzling flair. I copied her movements and added a dip of my body and an accentuated vibrato as I pushed the bow through the final note.

The moment I finished, Mom bowed toward me. Tears welling, I bowed in return, barely able to restrain the spasms in my chest as I gazed at her gleaming eyes, her rose-petal cheeks, and her lovely smile.

She laid a hand on my shoulder and said, "Well played, my son, an aria of strings for our heavenly Father."

The touch brought an electrified jolt, shocking me back to reality. I turned to Kelly. "Did you say that?"

Tears streaming down her cheeks, she lowered the mirror and embraced me. "I couldn't say it," she whispered as she brushed her lips across my cheek. "You must have heard her yourself."

She pulled my wrist gently. "Come on. We can't wait for the sun. We'll have to use the camera."

After laying the violin in its case and packing it and the Quattro mirror in the saddlebag, I stood with her in front of the tri-fold. When Kelly raised the camera to her eye, a hint of brightening crossed the storm-ravaged field. The sun edged under the bank of clouds and aimed its beams directly at the mirror.

The rays bounced from the polished glass. The middle pane directed a beam straight out while the other two mirror panels angled the light, intersecting their reflections with the central radiant shaft.

At the point where the beams met, a vertical halo of brilliant colors formed, a six-foot-high, oval-shaped rainbow that pulsed at twice the frequency of a beating heart.

I grabbed the saddlebag and pulled Kelly's hand. "Jump for the colors."

We leaped together into the halo. The rainbow enveloped us in a wash of yellow, blue, and red, altering the grass at our feet into a blaze of hues, as if a frenzied artist had brushed every color from his palette across the littered field.

In the reflection, the telescope room expanded and swarmed over us. The familiar perimeter walls bent around our bodies, the tour entry door on one side and the elevator on the other. Soon, everything settled, and we were once again standing under the high-arching, reflective dome.

Kelly leaned close and whispered, "Looks like we're alone."

"You're not." The pert female voice came from under the computer desk. Daryl Blue emerged with the shotgun clutched in both hands.

Clara Blue followed, wincing as she straightened slowly. "Tight squeeze under there."

"We heard someone coming," Daryl said, "so we scooped up all our stuff, turned out the lights, and hid. We think it was Mictar, but we never saw him."

"I take it you delivered Francesca," Clara said.

"We did." I lowered the saddle pack to the floor. "She's in good hands."

Daryl gave me the shotgun, then reached into her pocket and transferred four shells to my pocket one by one. "Earth Red has sped up in comparison to Earth Blue, so you have to hurry."

"Let's send them home," Clara said. "I'll hang on to the other mirror for safekeeping."

Daryl sat at the desk and reached for the laptop's mouse pad. "Click your heels together, Kelly-kins, and remember to say your line."

Kelly picked up the saddle pack and looked at her feet. "You mean, 'There's no place like home'?"

"You got it."

"All right. Just for you." Kelly clicked her heels together. "There's no place like home."

"Perfect!" Daryl waved. "Have a good trip."

The room's lights flashed on. As before, the image in the mirror above seemed to descend and spread out, enveloping us in its grasp. Everything morphed into warped shapes and intermixing colors.

Seconds later, the scene cleared, revealing the telescope room once again with Clara and Daryl staring at us. If not for their different clothes and the lack of a dead man lying on the floor, it would have been impossible to tell that we had transported at all.

Clara Red ran and embraced me. "We have to hurry," she said. "According to the schedule on the computer, Interfinity is showing the telescope to a tour group in ten minutes."

Daryl Red typed madly on the laptop's keyboard. "I'm restoring the computer to how we found it." After a final tap, the mirror above transformed into a view of the morning sky, dark blue, with hints of orange filtering in from one side.

Kelly extended the saddle pack to me. "I'll trade you. I know how to shoot, and you know how to fight."

"Fair enough." I gave her the gun and the shells. "You'd better load it."

She slid the shells into the ammunition chamber with practiced hands. "Ready."

"I hear voices." Daryl nodded at the tour entry door. "Over there."

"Clara and Daryl first," I said as I pushed the elevator call button. "Kelly and I will follow."

Daryl pulled the camera strap over Kelly's head. "Let me lighten your load."

As soon as the door opened, Clara and Daryl squeezed in. The moment it closed and the elevator began its descent, I pushed the call button again.

When the car returned, Kelly and I stepped in. I held the saddle pack against my chest, while she hugged the shotgun close, the barrel aiming straight up.

I pressed the button for the bottom level. Across the way, the tour door opened. A tall man wearing a black business suit entered the telescope room. He stared at us, then the closing doors hid him from view.

"That was Dr. Gordon," I said. "He saw us."

She nodded. "That could mean trouble at the bottom floor."

"Could you tell if he had a wound on his cheek?"

"I don't think he did, but it's probably safer to assume he's not on our side."

When we joined Clara and Daryl, I led the way to the secured door and peeked through its window to the hallway. A heavyset woman stood with her back to us, vacuuming the carpet at the intersection to the exit corridor.

I stepped away from the door. "Clara, where's your car?"

"In the main parking lot out front. At least I hope it's still there."

"Kelly's Toyota is out in the woods, so we'll have to split up. They'll be looking for me, so while Kelly and I sneak out the back to her car, you and Daryl go out the front. Let's meet at the first gas station at the main highway, but if something happens, we'll be in touch by phone."

Clara nodded. "That sounds good."

I curled an arm around the saddlebag and pushed the door open. "Let's go."

Kelly and I jogged to the maid, cut around her to the right, and dashed for the exit. A shriek erupted behind us. We burst out the backdoor, still unbroken on Earth Red, and sprinted down the path that led into the woods. As soon as Kelly's car came into sight, she unlocked it with her key fob and tossed it to me. "You drive."

I caught the fob and flung open the driver's door while Kelly hopped into the passenger's side. I set the saddlebag on the rear seat and slid behind the steering wheel, inserting the key and cranking the engine in one motion.

Kelly pointed toward the back. "We've got company."

I looked in the rearview mirror. A handgun-wielding guard jogged toward us, heavy and slow. He stopped about fifty feet to the rear and pointed the gun. "Driver! Show me your hands!"

I whispered to Kelly, "I'll stall until you tell me he's in range, but don't shoot unless he shoots first."

I lowered the windows on both sides and raised my hands.

The guard made a wide circle toward Kelly's side of the car. "You in the passenger's seat," he yelled, "show me your hands! Now!"

She gave me a nod. "He's in range."

I grabbed the wheel and slammed the gas pedal down. The tires skidded in the wet grass. The guard fired. A bullet zipped through Kelly's window and whizzed past my nose.

Kelly pointed the gun out her window and fired back. In the wake of a deafening boom, she fell into my lap just as the tires finally caught hold. The car shot forward. I jerked the wheel to the right, narrowly avoiding a massive oak, then slid into a sharp turn to the left as I aimed toward the building's rear parking lot.

When the car straightened, Kelly pushed against the center console and slid back to her seat. She pumped the gun, racking the next shell.

I tried to look back at the guard. "Did you hit him?"

"Winged him. He won't follow us." She grabbed my arm. "Look out!"

Three guards stood at the edge of the parking lot about fifty yards away, aiming rifles with scopes. Kelly propped the shotgun on her window frame and fired again. The guards dove to the ground.

I swerved the car to the right. "We'll have to take a shortcut to the front of the building."

She pointed straight ahead. "You're heading for a creek!"

"I see a bridge."

"It's just a footbridge!"

"Not anymore." Loud gunfire erupted. Two bullets clanked against the car's frame. The steep-banked creek dug into the landscape a mere thirty yards away. The closer we got, the narrower the footbridge seemed — just skinny slats nailed over thin plywood.

Another bullet ripped into the trunk. I pressed the gas pedal to the floor, making the Camry roar ahead.

"We're too big!" Kelly shouted.

"Think thin!" After hitting a small incline just before the bridge, the tires leaped onto the slats and clattered ahead. The side mirrors slammed into the guardrails, folding them against the car. As wood splinters flew, the bridge sagged precariously. Seconds later, we flew off the end and surfed down an embankment that led to a covered walkway in front of the main entrance.

Kelly pointed. "More people!"

"Including Clara and Daryl." I pressed on the horn and pumped the brakes, trying to slow down without going into a full slide, but the wet, grassy slope provided barely any traction.

The crowd scattered. I jerked the wheel back and forth, avoiding a dog and a petrified old lady, until I finally spun the car and stopped on the concrete walk, leaving the rear door no more than three feet from Clara and Daryl.

"Get in!" I ordered as I straightened the side mirror. "No use taking two cars."

Clara threw open the door, and she and Daryl piled in, Daryl still clutching the camera. I slammed down the gas again, and, with at least a dozen people looking on, I jumped the curb, bounced into the parking lot, and zoomed away.

More rifle shots echoed behind us, but no bullets hit the car. With the shotgun barrel pointing at the floorboard, Kelly laid her head back. "I think I'm going to be sick."

I let out a long breath and relaxed my grip on the wheel. "When my stomach catches up with me, I'll pass around the barf bags."

Kelly gave my arm a light punch. "Where'd you learn to drive like that?"

"Boston. It's a nightmare place to drive."

Daryl leaned forward from the backseat. "Think they'll chase us?"

I glanced at the rearview mirror. "A Lincoln's following us. Gordon Red has one like it, but I don't know if Gordon Blue does."

"I don't trust either one," Kelly said. "We'll have to outrun him."

I pushed the gas again, but the engine responded with a clatter. "Uh-oh." As the Camry tried to climb a hill, it slowed and sputtered. "Better get the shotgun ready, Kelly. You might have to discourage another pursuer."

With the gun in hand, she leaned out the window and sat on the frame, her sneakers barely touching her seat. "I got him in my sights," she yelled.

"Is it Gordon?"

"Can't tell yet. He's staying pretty far back."

"To keep from getting shot." As the car's engine rattled louder, I tugged on Kelly's ankle. "I'm pulling over. I can't outrun him." I guided the chugging car to the side, stopped, and set the emergency brake. "Everyone stay here."

While Clara and Daryl stayed in the car, I stepped out onto the road. Kelly balanced on the window frame, her shotgun lying on the roof, though her finger stayed poised at the trigger.

As a warm breeze whipped our clothes, the Lincoln stopped about a hundred feet behind us. Dr. Gordon emerged and lifted his empty hands. "I surrender. I just ask that you listen to me. I have information that might change everything you think you know."

CHAPTER TWENTY-SIX

I WALKED TO THE rear of Kelly's car and leaned back against the trunk, trying not to show my nervousness. "Let me see the left side of your face."

"My face?" Dr. Gordon stopped and turned his cheek toward me. His skin was smooth. "I take it that my Earth Blue counterpart has some kind of mark there."

"He does." I nodded toward Kelly. "Come on over, but stay ready."

While Kelly climbed down from the car, Gordon walked the rest of the way and stopped in front of me, a scolding expression on his face. "I don't blame you for being cautious about my identity, but you have also thrown caution to the wind on more than one occasion."

"If you mean the highway chase, that was before I knew there were two of you."

"You were afraid," he said, pointing a finger at me. "I've been hearing reports about you. You've shown a lot of courage at times, but courage isn't something you can afford to switch on and off. Shooting at guards, racing down the highway like a madman, and refusing to hear me out at the school isn't going to cut it. If you want to rescue your parents, you'd better shake that yellow stripe off your back."

I scowled. "Wait a minute! I was—"

"A yellow stripe?" Kelly shouted as she stalked toward us, the shotgun still in hand. "Listen, jerk. Nathan dodged a murderer by diving into a river, searched for his parents through a bizarre maze in three worlds, rescued his Earth Yellow mom from a crazy shooter, stood up like a boss to a raging tornado, and boarded a doomed plane to try to rescue the passengers. Where do you get off questioning his courage?"

Gordon backed away a step and cleared his throat. "I see your point."

"And those guards shot at us first," Kelly yelled, her anger unabated.

"I understand your anger, and I hope you will accept my apology for my rash accusations." Dr. Gordon waved toward his Lincoln. "If you wish, I will drive you to the funeral site and explain what I can along the way." He popped the trunk with his key fob. "But I must ask you to deposit the shotgun in the back."

I looked at Kelly. "Should we trust him?"

"Either trust him or get to the funeral late." She shrugged. "I suppose so."

I gave Dr. Gordon a nod. "We'll come with you."

While I retrieved the violin and mirror from the Camry, Kelly snatched her sweatshirt from the backseat and lugged the shotgun toward the rear of the Lincoln, glaring at Dr. Gordon as she passed by.

Clara and Daryl got out of the Camry and slid into the Lincoln's spacious backseat along with Kelly. After depositing the violin in the trunk, I kept the mirror tucked at my side, seated myself up front, and introduced Dr. Gordon and Clara. After a terse and awkward exchange between them, Clara folded her hands in her lap and said nothing more.

Gordon started the engine and looked at me. "You still don't trust me, do you?"

I spiced my reply with a growl. "My Earth Blue father said I should, but I'm not so sure. My real father got killed because of trusting people like you, so I'm taking a big risk."

As Gordon drove, his tone stayed calm, mechanical. "When weighed against the alternatives, it is not such a big risk. Going with me gets you to the funeral on time as well as the vital information you've been seeking."

I pointed at the triple-infinity emblem on his jacket. "Let's start with your company, Interfinity. Tell me what you learned about the three worlds."

Daryl pulled forward on Gordon's headrest. "I already told them about how you heard the music from the other world before you played it in ours, so you can start from there."

"Very well." Dr. Gordon settled back in his seat. "When I discovered the existence of a world that parallels ours, I hoped to avert disasters and prevent loss of life. I wouldn't be able to prevent an earthquake, of course, but I could warn people and assist them in getting out of harm's way. Strangely, however, my Earth Blue counterpart had a profiteering mindset. This troubled me, because I had theorized that genetic duplicates would make identical decisions when presented with identical information.

"Bigger problems began when Mictar appeared. Long after the other Gordon and I created the twin observatories, we experimented with various cross-world transport scenarios. In one trial, after syncing with each other, we aimed our activation lights directly at the ceiling mirror to see what would happen if we hit the mirrors simultaneously. The beams made an intense splash of indescribable light. When it dispersed, a gaunt, white-haired man stood at the center of my observatory floor."

"Mictar, I assume," Daryl said.

"No. He called himself Patar, and he warned me that his brother, Mictar, had likely appeared at the same place in the other world." Gordon altered his voice to a snaky whisper. "Beware of my brother's schemes. He does not seek gold or silver, but discord and fear." Gordon shrugged. "Then he disappeared."

"And Mictar teamed up with Dr. Gordon Blue," I said.

"Correct. Mictar's powers made it impossible for me to fight him in the open, so I decided the only way to stop his plans was to play along. Mictar gave my Earth Blue counterpart and me the assignment of finding and killing you. That Gordon succeeded on Earth Blue, while I hoped to find you in order to protect you."

"What's so important about me?"

"This is where the matter becomes quite complex. Your father theorized that when we reached the point of moving from one world to the other, we began to create fractures. You might call them cosmic holes that alter the balance among the worlds. In other words, the three streams of parallel events began to run askew of one another, because interference from one world to the other could not be exactly duplicated due to the misalignment of time."

"You mean when someone travels to another world, his counterpart isn't doing the same thing anymore.

Both worlds get thrown off. They can't possibly stay in balance."

Gordon nodded. "Solomon and I learned that since the worlds no longer run in perfect parallel, the forces that separate them have weakened. When we began the project, we had three infinities that would never intersect, much like parallel lines that can never meet. Now, as they deviate from their linear path with relation to one another, they will likely experience random intersections that cause havoc."

"What would those intersections look like? I mean, if it happens, what would people notice?"

"On Earth Yellow, since it is behind us in time, I expect people would receive some kind of signal of future events, perhaps more soothsayers and other self-proclaimed prophets providing hints of things to come, but their fortune telling would actually come true, at least for a season. Eventually, the lines would shift so far away, future events would become unpredictable."

The Earth Yellow nightmare epidemic came to mind, as well as the crash survivors who had dreamed of the disaster before it happened. "What would happen here or on Earth Blue?"

"A bleeding over of physical events that is already happening. I believe we are experiencing weather conditions based on Earth Yellow's climate. Since Yellow is moving on the time stream far more quickly, our weather has wild swings. Only hours ago, it was probably early spring there, and we participated in their snowfall. Now it's approaching summer, and we are enjoying a much warmer afternoon, though that might not last long.

"This phenomenon prompted me to find out what you've been up to on Earth Yellow. I knew Simons Blue and Yellow had a longing to prevent some kind of disaster. It seems that the timing worked out perfectly for you to rescue the American Airlines flight."

"Not exactly. Besides Kelly and me, only six others survived."

"That's a significant number. Six new puncture wounds in the infrastructure. The resulting ripples could be enormous."

"But they stayed in their world. Why would there be wounds?"

"As I mentioned, a ripple effect. From now on, each survivor has no parallel activity in the other worlds, which will cause an increased deviation of Earth Yellow's timeline from parallel, and that will move us all closer to Interfinity, the final convergence of the lines."

"So, what can we do to fix the problem?"

"Repair the damage. You see, cosmic holes are like wounds. They might heal over time, but, since we're not sure, it would be better if we tried to repair them. Solomon studied the theories regarding dark matter, and he believed that your mother had a gift, a way to seal the holes if she could only get the opportunity to use it. But one of the Solomons and one of the Francescas were captured and another pair killed, so we must find a way to help the surviving ones escape."

"Do you know which Solomon and Francesca are alive, the Blue versions or the Red ones?"

"I suspect that the survivors are your Earth Blue parents, but I can't be sure."

I lowered my head. "That's my guess, too."

"In any case, that brings me back to your earlier question about your importance. Mictar desires to kill you, because he believes that you possess the same abilities that your mother has. He wants Interfinity to occur, and he wants to make sure you aren't around to stop it."

"So what is Mictar's motivation? What does he have to gain by bringing about Interfinity?"

"I have pondered that for some time. How could someone benefit from collapsing the cosmos?" Gordon shook his head. "No answer makes sense. Maybe the reason will come to light soon, but I think it will be a frightening one." He steered the car onto a cemetery entry road. "We will have to continue this conversation after the funeral, including more about the Quattro mirror. After that discussion, we will embark on our mission to rescue your parents."

I tucked the mirror under my arm. "The other Dr. Gordon might be here, so I'm keeping the mirror with me."

"As you should. I have people watching for him. I will tell them that he has a mark on his cheek." Dr. Gordon stopped the car behind a long line of others. About sixty yards ahead, a yellow tent canopy rippled in the breeze, sheltering the gravesites. Dozens of rows of tombstones lined the gently sloping grass between our stopping point and the tent, looking like morbid sentinels of stone in horizontal battle lines, each one reciting its occupant's name and age in etched letters.

I got out and opened the back door on Clara's side. While I helped her exit, Dr. Gordon opened the opposite door. He offered Kelly a hand, but she just glared at him as she got out on her own and marched around the car, her sweatshirt now covering her dirty polo. Daryl gave him a similar glare.

When we gathered on the cemetery lawn, I backed away. "I'll see you under the canopy."

As I turned to go, Kelly waved. "I'll get your violin."

I spun back. "I won't need it."

"We should bring everything with us, just in case."

"She's right," Dr. Gordon said as he pressed a button on his key fob. "Except for the shotgun." A muffled chime sounded. He pulled a phone from his pocket and waved. "Go on ahead. I will meet you there."

I jogged along the pavement toward the hearses while brushing off my dirty, smelly shirt. As I passed by the rows of tombstones, I tried to read the engravings but could catch only a couple of names — Phillips and Madison.

Just hours ago, the stone slabs would have meant nothing, mere decorations to be ignored, but now the terrified faces of the airline passengers gnawed at my mind. Who could tell? Any one of these stones might be marking the grave of one of those victims. Since this was a huge cemetery in the western Chicago suburbs, that wouldn't be a stretch.

As I continued, I passed a bearded man kneeling at a gravesite. He looked a lot like Jack, one of the survivors from the Earth Yellow plane crash, but that was impossible, of course. He held a crumpled hat against his lips as he bowed his head and stroked the marker's curved top, weeping. I sighed. Such a portrait of grief. This miserable man poured out his heart over a loved one, now an empty shell, gone forever.

At that moment I vowed never to ignore a tombstone again. Each one told a story of tragedy, at least to some poor soul left behind.

When I neared the hearses, a thin man in a black suit opened the trailing hearse's back door, revealing a coffin.

"Are you the funeral director?" I asked as I came to a stop. "I'm Nathan Shepherd."

"I am," he said in a calm, soothing voice. "We were quite concerned about you."

I gazed at my reflection on the coffin's polished black surface. Nausea twisted my stomach. A body lay within, either Mom or Dad. "The car quit working so I had to hitch a ride."

"I see. Did you try to fix the automobile yourself? Your clothes are quite disheveled."

"No." I smoothed out my shirt. "I had other problems."

The director shed his dark jacket and reached it toward me. "Please borrow this."

I allowed him to help me put it on. The sleeves fell past the heels of my hands, but the shoulders felt good — loose, but not too loose.

The director touched the coffin with a fingertip. "This is your mother. The other hearse carries your father." He signaled for the other men who were milling around near the graveside tent. "Your tutor selected these gentlemen from among your father's clients and your mother's orchestra friends. If you wish to renew your acquaintance with them, we can delay the proceedings further."

I scanned the faces of the approaching pallbearers. None resembled Dr. Gordon. "No. It's okay. Maybe I can talk to them afterward."

"Certainly." While two dark-suited men pulled the coffin out on a gurney, the director stationed the pallbearers around the coffin, setting me at the front and on Mom's left. "Your tutor designated this position," the director said, "closest to the heart of your mother."

I shuddered. The reality of the funeral sent a painful jolt through every nerve. My arms shook, and my knees weakened. Mom was inside that box, her dead body torn at the throat by a sadistic murderer.

I clutched the brass handle with my left hand and laid my trembling fingertips on the coffin's smooth lid. As if emanating from the polished surface, a tingle passed through my hand, the same hand Mom breathed on before every performance.

Mom's words flowed to mind as if blown there by the refreshing breeze, reciting the lovely phrases I had heard so many times.

When I breathe on your hand, I whisper a prayer that the breath of God will fill your soul with his music, the melody of everlasting love that guided our savior to the ultimate sacrifice. Because such love lasts forever, I know, my son, that we will be together through all eternity.

My heart raced. Tears dripped down my cheeks. Then, a warm grip rested on my shoulder. "Nathan, are you all right?"

I turned toward the familiar voice. Dr. Malenkov stood next to me, his expression sad. "You're here," I said.

"Yes, of course. I thought you saw me earlier."

"I was looking for someone else. Are you playing something for the funeral?"

He patted me on the back. "Yes, yes. It is a great honor, yet a tragic occasion."

"What piece did you choose?"

"The Vivaldi duet, an arrangement I created that allows me to play it as a solo. Your mother's part fades away at the end while yours finishes strong."

I swallowed through a tight catch in my throat. "That ... sounds great."

"You are welcome to join me. I can play your mother's part in the old arrangement."

"No. I don't think I could handle it."

"Very well. I will be on the other side of the coffin. I feel blessed that I was called to this task, yet heartbroken that my daughter left the earth before I did." He walked to his place and grasped a handle.

When the director gave a signal, we lifted the coffin and marched toward the burial site. As we approached, a woman standing under the canopy raised a violin and began playing Bach's "Jesu, Joy of Man's Desiring."

I sighed. This violinist was good, quite good, in fact. But she wasn't Mom. As the woman washed out a note that needed to be played with the precision of a musical surgeon, I cringed. Oh, how I longed to play with Mom. Just one more time. But it couldn't be. Never again.

I glanced at Nikolai. Tears streamed down the old man's cheeks, following deep lines traced there by years of loving care. He, too, probably wept for lost days — future days he had hoped to play with his favorite pupil as he awaited his own passing into eternity, as well as days in the past he once shared during peaceful bedtime songs and rousing morning lessons. This sad old man had more treasured memories, perhaps a greater loss than I. He had lost a daughter, once given to him as the result of a tragic murder, now taken away because of a devil's wicked hand.

I firmed my chin. This occasion, though solemn and tragic, deserved the best music possible. If Nikolai could do it, I could do it.

As we passed under the canopy, I scanned the audience, about twenty-five or thirty men and women clad in various shades of gray and black, sitting or standing among at least eighty metal chairs divided in half by an aisle down the center. Why so few? Hadn't Clara let all our orchestra friends know about the funeral? Or had the news about fast-moving blizzards scared them away? A graveyard wasn't exactly a place people wanted to go during a time of fear.

After setting Mom's coffin next to a huge display of flowers, I turned toward the array of chairs. Clara, Kelly, and Daryl sat in the second row, one row in front of Dr. Gordon.

I strode across the fifteen-or-so feet between the coffin and the front row and whispered, "Kelly. I need Mom's violin."

She lifted the case from her lap. "Right now?"

"When I get back with Dad's coffin."

I walked toward the second hearse with the other pallbearers. Dr. Gordon joined our group, but why? He hadn't mentioned doing that. I scanned his face, but since he walked to my left, I couldn't see if there was a cut on his left cheek. I then glanced back at the audience. His chair was empty.

As we closed in on the other hearse, I leaned toward him. "Dr. Gordon?"

"Yes, Nathan?" He kept his face forward, not allowing me to check his other side.

"You didn't say you were going to be a pallbearer."

"It was a last-minute decision. One of the other pallbearers fell ill." He turned and pointed at his left cheek, unmarred by a wound. "I sense that you need to see this to allay your fears."

I studied his face. He had to be Gordon Red, but something strange was going on. The sudden changes spelled trouble, but how could I investigate them? I just had to keep going through the funeral motions with both eyes open. Mictar lurked somewhere behind the scenes, and I had to find him.

CHAPTER TWENTY-SEVEN

T HE DIRECTOR ARRANGED us around Dad's coffin. With the head of the casket pointing toward the canopy, he guided me to the front handle on the left side. "Your tutor said you needed to be at your father's right hand. You were his stalwart helper and never failed in your efforts to come to his aid."

I grasped the handle and gazed at the coffin. My fingers were inches away from Dad's right shoulder. How many times had he touched my shoulder to give me comfort or encouragement? He lifted me more times than I could count. And now I had to lift him, only to lower him into the earth where he would rest in silence, never to encourage me again.

Walking quickly, we carried the coffin to the gravesite and placed it next to Mom's. As we set it down, one of the men bumped a partition behind the flowers. Covered with a white sheet, the partition shook, sending the sheet falling to the ground and exposing a mirror identical to the one in my room, complete with divider lines separating the individual squares. The reflection seemed normal, at least for the time being, showing only lush flowers and the seated audience.

As the other pallbearers filed to their seats, I glanced at the lower left-hand corner of the odd backdrop. A square was missing. Was this really the mirror from my room, or had someone transported it from Earth Blue?

Turning to the mourners, I found Clara in the second-row aisle seat. My mirror lay in her lap, angled toward me, allowing a view of the reflective surface. Across the aisle and three rows back sat a man with a familiar bearded face, the same man who was weeping at a gravesite moments ago. He straightened his crumpled fedora and clutched the brim against his chest.

I focused on his weary eyes. He really *was* Jack. How could he have come to Earth Red?

Nikolai, carrying his violin, stepped in front of the flowers and guided the bow across each string as he tuned his instrument. Kelly rose from her seat and brought my violin to the front. I took it and the bow and, trying not to move my lips, whispered, "Fill the empty spot," then nodded toward the mirrored partition.

She glanced that way, bobbed her head, and hustled back to Clara. As she walked, she did a double take at the bearded man. Apparently she recognized him, too.

Trying to ignore the distractions, I turned to Nikolai and bowed. "If you don't mind, sir, I reconsidered your offer. I will play my part if you will play my mother's."

The old man smiled. "Nathan Shepherd, I can think of no greater honor." He took my bow hand and blew on my knuckles. "Music is the breath of God," he said softly. "Let us tell of his love to these mourners and give them a reason to turn their mourning into joy."

While everyone else settled in their seats, I rolled my jacket sleeves up two turns and began tuning the violin, keeping an eye on Kelly as she sneaked around to the back of the mirrored partition. Kneeling and slowly reaching from behind, she set the square in the corner. It seemed to jump from her hands and lock in place as if pulled by a magnet.

A sudden gust rippled the top of the tent's canopy, a cold gust, much colder than normal for October. I shivered, thankful for the director's jacket. But what could it mean? Had Earth Yellow already moved into late autumn or early winter, and were its breezes invading the city?

As most of the onlookers tilted their heads upward, I focused on the mirror. Starting from the newly placed square, a wave of radiance crawled along the surface, brightening the reflection to razor-sharp clarity. When it reached the opposite corner, the strange light pulsed once and vanished.

Kelly stayed at the edge of the mirror, veiled by flowers and shivering as she drew her hands into her sweatshirt sleeves. When she looked at me, she pointed at the camera dangling from the strap around her neck. "It's the only light we have," she whispered.

Increasing the volume as I continued to tune the violin, I whispered back, "It'll have to do. I'm guessing Simon Blue put the mirror here, maybe as a way to rescue my Earth Blue parents, so we have to be ready to use it."

She nodded, then ducked low. I looked out at the tombstone-covered lawn. Snowflakes swirled through the breeze, already speckling the grass with patches of white.

The mourners reached for cloaks and sweaters, apparently prepared for unpredictable shifts in weather.

Nikolai set a hand on my shoulder and turned toward the audience. "We wish to honor our departed loved ones—I, my cherished daughter, and Nathan, his beloved parents— with the performance of a Vivaldi duet he and his mother played together many times. As we make these violins sing, do not be alarmed if you feel the spirit of Francesca Shepherd as she bids farewell to us all."

Raising Mom's treasured instrument to my chin, I shook off the chill and stepped to the elderly teacher's side. "I await your lead, Maestro."

Nikolai set bow on strings and, with a long vibrant stroke, played the beginning note of the duet.

I closed my eyes and answered with the familiar notes of my lightning-fast response. Then, opening my eyes a slit to watch the mirror, I played on, blending my music with the master's smooth, effortless tones. Soon, I would play solo. The last time I performed that part, Mom disappeared and I was left standing alone on stage, playing a solo that never ended. This time, I would watch all the players— Nikolai, Dr. Gordon, and anyone else who might spring a surprise.

As Nikolai backed away, I shifted to the center, angling my body enough to see the mirror. Every musical phrase massaged my mind, bringing back memories of Mom. The recollections soothed and stung at the same time, blessings that stabbed with the pain of love torn away before its season had ended.

Then, images of Dad mixed into the memories. As Mom wept and trembled, Dad laid a hand on her cheek, a tender caress that always seemed to calm her, no matter what troubles stirred her turmoil. He held her close, kissing and nuzzling as sweet words passed between them like the same silvery notes I played in their honor.

In mere seconds, Nikolai would play again, taking Mom's part at the point she had abandoned not long ago. As my solo built to a crescendo, her final words seemed to brush by my ears. *I will join you again when the composer commands me.*

A newcomer walked under the canopy and stood at the back of the seating area, a tall white-haired man. Was he Mictar? Patar? Dr. Gordon bent over and skulked along his row of seats, then headed toward the rear. He stood close to the gaunt man, and the two spoke quietly.

I glanced at Kelly, still hiding behind the flowers. She saw them, too. Could she tell them apart? Were they Gordon Red and Patar, or Gordon Blue and Mictar?

The mirror flashed. The reflection displayed bright, colorful shapes that quickly bled together to form a blurred figure, veiled by the floral decorations that separated the two coffins. Kelly crawled out and shoved the flowers out of the way, staying on her knees as she slid some to the side and knocked others over until the entire mirror came into view.

The image clarified. Mom stood with a violin, her bow at the ready position. On one side, a sheer curtain flapped in a gentle breeze, and on her other, a poster bed with a bare mattress sat on a carpeted floor.

Straining to keep my breathing in check, I swept through the final notes of my solo. As murmurs spread across the onlookers, Mom joined the duet from the other side of the mirror, answering the composer's call. The notes rang through like carillon bells, sharp and echoing, as lovely as any angel could hope to create. Nikolai, his eyes wide, lowered his violin and backed away another step.

As if guided by Mom's entrancing gaze, I walked slowly toward the mirror, my legs heavy. I focused on her eyes. Yes, they were looking right at me. And her lips moved, uttering a quiet whisper drowned by her thrumming melody.

Crouched at my feet, Kelly relayed Mom's words. "Take a picture of the mirror." Kelly leaped to her feet and aimed the camera at the mirror, backing away as she framed in the coffins at each side. When she reached the second row of seats, the camera flashed. Light spread out over me and my surroundings —the mirror, the coffins, and even Nikolai. A sizzling beam shot out and struck the lens, smashing it to pieces.

Kelly dropped the camera and shook her hands. "It's like fire!"

The mirror scene expanded. Our view of Mom's room widened, spreading out to show Dad standing nearby, shackles attached to his ankles and wrists, though the chains dragged freely. The floor where Mom stood pushed outward and blended into the cemetery grass as the two scenes merged into one. My parents' swelling room looked like a soap bubble with thick, rubbery walls, as clear as crystal.

Mom extended her hand and cried out, her voice finally penetrating the barrier. "Take my hand, Nathan! Pull us out of here!"

In the image, Dad held to Mom's arm. With chains dangling, he raised a hand. "Son! Now is the time! Rescue us!"

Dr. Gordon ran up the aisle, grabbed Kelly from behind, and pressed the edge of a knife blade against her throat. "Don't touch them, Nathan! If you bring them back, I'll slit her wide open!"

Several mourners jumped to their feet. With the blade already drawing a trickle of blood from Kelly's skin, most stood petrified. Daryl lunged, but Clara jerked her back. At the same time, Mictar walked to the front and stood behind Gordon.

As a gust blew snowflakes across my cheek and flapped the canopy's ceiling, I laid the violin down and watched for the slightest opportunity to lunge. Clara knew the drill. At any second, she would make a loud noise to distract Gordon. That would be my chance to attack.

Just as Clara rose from her seat, Jack stormed up the aisle, latched on to Gordon's wrist, and pulled the dagger away. As Gordon swung around to fight, the blade swiped against Kelly's shoulder and dug deeply into her sweatshirt. Jack wrestled Gordon to the grass, toppling chairs on the front row as they rolled to the side.

I lunged and grabbed Kelly's wrist, but Mictar wrapped an arm around her chest and pulled back. As we fought for control, blood dripped down her arm and over my fingers, but I ignored her wound and held on. I couldn't let him have her.

Three men from the audience rushed to help Jack subdue Gordon while two others leaped toward Mictar. He released Kelly and shot jagged streaks of blackness from his palms that slammed against the faces of the would-be rescuers. They collapsed and quivered on the ground, the blackness steaming like hot tar.

I pulled Kelly into my arms. The first three rescuers hauled Gordon upright. A trickle of sweat drew a purplish line down his cheek, exposing part of a bruise. Jack struggled to his feet. A bloody gash stretched across his forehead.

Mictar spread out his arms. Darkness coalesced in his palms as if ready to shoot black streams into the crowd. "Son of Solomon, heed my warning. If you take one step toward your mother, I will make these people suffer."

As cold gusts breezed through, everyone hushed. I pivoted toward the mirror. The image shifted forward another few inches and stopped. Mom and Dad, their bodies filling the screen, stretched out their arms.

A voice again punched through the barrier. "I'm sorry for leaving you alone on stage," Mom said. "We had to change places with the Blue Shepherds before it was too late. Since Mictar had killed them earlier, we used their bodies to make him think we were dead, too. Pull us home and we'll explain everything."

"No," Mictar hissed. "Do not bring that woman here."

His motives finally registered. Now that Mom was free of her bonds and armed with a violin, he was scared of her.

The mirror image slowly contracted. Mom and Dad slid backwards. They shrank with the reflection, their hands grasping empty air. A strong gust ripped the canopy away from the stakes and sent it flying across the cemetery. Biting wind squealed through the funeral party, and heavy snow cascaded from the skies.

Releasing Kelly, I leaped toward the reflective barrier, plunged my fists through, and grabbed Mom's hand while Dad and I locked wrists. I set my feet and pulled, but they moved only a few inches. With my feet slipping on the dampening grass, it was like dragging two anchored bodies through thick mud.

A scream made me glance back. Mictar held Kelly from behind and poised a hand over her eyes. "Cease your efforts, Shepherd, or she will die." Sparks of electricity arced from Mictar's hand, drilling pinpoint scorch marks on Kelly's forehead as more blood dripped from the ends of her fingers.

She cried out in a plaintive moan. "Rescue them, Nathan! I'm not worth it!"

"Silence!" Mictar roared.

Snow swirled between the mirror and me. My parents' hands and forearms were now on my side of the barrier, their faces close. The crystalline dividing wall magnified every line in their frantic expressions.

I whispered, "I need time to decide. Where's the girl in red when I need her most?"

Something popped. Blackness filled the sky and poured around me until I stood in a dark room. A glass window hovered within reach at each side, both of them the original size of the mirror at the funeral. The views showed the funeral scene, daylight from within providing the only illumination in my chamber.

In both windows, Mictar stood like a statue with Kelly in his grasp while the audience looked on. A copy of myself held to Mom and Dad through the shrunken mirror I had reached into to grab them, the scene frozen as if suspended in time.

I peered through the window to my left. Another copy of myself looked back at me — a reflection in the glass. As I stared, my eyes flashed. White beams poured forth and splashed against the glassy surface. My image in the mirror activated and jerked my parents through the barrier. They lurched into the funeral scene and sprawled over the ground. Mictar let out a raging scream. Fire sizzled under the hand he held over Kelly's eyes.

While Mom and Dad struggled to their feet, Mictar glowed with a shimmering light and vanished. Kelly collapsed in a heap, her limbs and torso limp.

As if in a slow-motion dream, my parents embraced my copy. Blood pooled under Kelly, and her body quivered fitfully, her scorched eye sockets staring straight up. After a few seconds, her death throes ceased, as did all other movement within the window.

In the other window, the funeral scene stayed frozen in the position I had I left it, my copy's hands still locked on my parents. I resisted the urge to stare at it. Animating that scene might result in even more tragedy.

I pivoted in a slow circle. What was this place? And how did I get here? Cupping my hands around my mouth, I called, "Can anyone hear me?"

My words echoed several times before fading to silence.

Footsteps sounded from the darkness, followed by a voice. "I can hear you." A tall man with white hair walked into the light and stopped, his hands folded over his waist.

I mouthed the man's name. *Patar.*

"The power you call Quattro awaits your decision," Patar said.

I blinked. "My decision?"

"You wanted time to decide. That request has been granted. You have the luxury of seeing the results of one of your options."

I looked through the window that had animated. A tear dangled from Mom's chin. Love flowed from her eyes along with pure joy at being reunited with me. Dad, too, seemed filled with joy, yet, with his jaw set like steel, he was ready to go to war.

In contrast, Kelly's black eye sockets looked like deep chasms — vacant, abandoned, forsaken. Her ravaged face reflected the sightless countenance of a terrified girl, wandering in futility, only to suffer and die in the midst of life's greatest search, lost forever.

Patar spoke again. "It is time to decide, son of Solomon. If you save your parents, your friend will suffer the fate you see before you."

I touched the glass. "What will happen to her if I don't save them?"

"Since there are multiple options, the results remain to be seen. You will learn the outcome only after you choose. But the moment I return you to the funeral, you must act."

"How much time do I have to decide?"

Patar crossed his arms. "Ample time, but I will not allow you to dawdle."

"Will you tell me what's going on?" I spread out my hands. "What is this place? What kind of beings are you and Mictar? And who is the girl in red I keep seeing?"

"This place and my species are not for you to know, but the girl in red is relevant to your circumstances. She is your supplicant, a Sancta who wields much power and has helped you thus far. Unfortunately, she is in danger, yet

370 | TIME ECHOES

out of your reach. As soon as I finish here, I will see if I can go to her aid. Therefore, the longer you tarry, the longer she suffers. If I am able, I will update you regarding her status at a later time."

I swallowed. "Okay. Send me back. I'm ready."

Patar vanished. I flew into the window that had not animated and found myself where I was before, my grip locked on my parents, Kelly in the clutches of Mictar, still alive, still struggling.

I released my grip and lunged at Kelly. With a whip of my neck, I bashed my forehead against Mictar's nose, sending him flying backwards. As he slid along the ground, dark blood gushed from both nostrils.

Pulling Kelly, I ran toward the mirror's contracting bubble, then released her and dove headfirst across the snow. My hands penetrated the reflection once again. In the other world, Dad dropped to his knees and grabbed my wrists. His lips moved, but his voice no longer broke through.

Kelly called from behind, her voice weak and shaking. "Pull, Son! Pull!"

I rose to my feet and pulled with all my might. A hand slapped over my eyes. Mictar spoke in a hideous, throaty voice. "Now, Solomon, you will watch your son die."

Painful needles of light shot into my eyes. Dad's fingers slipped away. I lurched backward, knocking Mictar's hand to the side. With a violent spin, I thrust an elbow into his stomach and kicked him in the groin.

He staggered back, his eyes pulsing like red beacons. Five men lunged toward him, but, when he lifted his hands, new streams of blackness shot from his palms.

Four of the men hesitated, but Jack leaped onto his back and pounded on both shoulders with his fists.

Carrying his stocky attacker, Mictar staggered toward the mirror. The image from the other world had become a flat reflection, showing Mom and Dad staring out, hand in hand, tears streaming down their cheeks. Mictar rushed into the mirror and disappeared with Jack in a splash of light.

At their entry point, a long crack etched the glass and branched out in all directions. The square in the bottom left corner popped off. Like crinkling cellophane, the rest of the mirror rippled, then crumbled and fell in sparkling shards that left the supporting wall standing bare.

I dropped to my knees and slapped the ground, raising a splash of slushy snow. I almost had them! Just another second, and I would have pulled them out of there!

Kelly laid a hand on my forearm, patting my sleeve as if searching for something. "Oh, Nathan, I'm so sorry."

I took her hand and held it against my cheek. As I shook, her blood-covered palm slid across my skin. "It's not your fault. It's mine. I had a chance to pull them out." I dared not mention that I could have sacrificed her life for their freedom.

Police sirens wailed in the distance, drawing my gaze to the onlookers. Several men escorted Dr. Gordon away, two in front, three in back, and two on each side.

I growled, "What did you do with Gordon Red?"

Gordon Blue sneered but said nothing.

Clara slid her arms under mine and helped me up, while Daryl hoisted Kelly to her feet. "We need to get both of you to a hospital," Clara said.

I brushed off my clothes. "I'm fine. Just Kelly. She's hurt pretty bad."

Staring into space, Kelly touched the wound on her shoulder. "I'll go, but we'd better find Gordon Red. He might need a hospital, too."

I waved a hand in front of Kelly's eyes. "Can you see okay? You look kind of dazed."

She shook her head. "Everything's foggy and dark."

I intertwined my fingers with hers, ignoring the streams of blood. "Let the police find Gordon. You're going to the hospital, and I'm not leaving your side."

CHAPTER TWENTY-EIGHT

CLARA STOOD ON Kelly's left as she sat propped up on the hospital bed. I stood on the right, pulled my sweatshirt hood back, and leaned over the metal side rail, holding a wrapped bouquet of long-stemmed pink roses. "I have something for you." I pushed the blossoms under Kelly's nose. "Like them?"

She took a long sniff, then folded her hands over her flowery hospital gown. The material draped her torso loosely, sagging at her right shoulder and exposing a wide bandage. "All I smell is the bacon in your cheeseburger. I'm so hungry I might just eat those flowers."

I reached the roses over to Clara, scrunched the top of the fast-food bag I had left on the serving table, and hid it behind my back. "What cheeseburger?"

Kelly stared into space, her eyes framed by dozens of black scorch marks. "What cheeseburger? The one that's shouting along with the fries in your bag." She cupped her hands around her mouth and deepened her voice. "Give me to Kelly! I must be eaten by Kelly!"

"So now you're hearing talking fries." I set the bag in front of her. "Can you read the label?"

She shook her head. "I think my vision's improving, though. I can recognize you and Clara, but you're both kind of ghostly."

"I'm so tired I feel kind of ghostly." I pushed the bag into my sweatshirt pocket. "But improved vision is a great sign."

"Indeed it is." Clara pulled up her trench-coat sleeves, unwound the green paper that held the rose stems together, and pushed them into a long-necked vase. "Your dinner will be here soon, a nice post-surgery helping of something soft and digestible."

Kelly rolled her eyes. "Baby food, right?"

"No," I said, grinning. "I saw the can. It's top-of-the-line dog food."

"Good. That beats mashed peas any day, but I'll be glad to trade you half of mine for half of yours."

"I wouldn't think of it. I'm too much of a gentleman to deprive you of even one morsel of such a treat."

"Oh, hush, you two," Clara said. "You're about as funny as a lanced boil."

Daryl popped into the room, a lively bounce in her step. As she lowered her hood, she shook out her thick red locks. "Brrr. It's cold out there this morning. Must be January or February on Yellow."

"Did you get the photos?" I asked.

"Right here." She tossed a packet onto the bed. "They salvaged some of the film, but the camera's a goner."

I grabbed the packet. "Did you already look at them?"

Glancing away, Daryl leaned against the bed. "What kind of girl do you think I am?"

Kelly snatched the packet from me. "Insatiably curious. Nosy. An incurable snoop."

Daryl turned back and smiled. "Yeah. That's all true. But I sneaked just one peek, and I couldn't figure out what I was looking at."

After opening the packet's top, Kelly slid the inner envelope onto her chest. "It's thin. Only a few pictures."

"Just four," Daryl said. "The rest of the roll was fried."

Kelly withdrew three photos from the envelope and lined them up across the sheet. "I thought you said there were four."

"I did." Daryl shrugged. "Sorry. I just glanced at them. My mistake."

Kelly pointed at the photo on her left. "I see four people, so that's the first one I took at the plane crash site. It should show the woman who asked me to take the shots, a husband and wife, and Jack in the background. Is that right?"

I leaned close. "Yeah, but it looks strange, like there's some kind of glow around them."

"Maybe that's the cosmic holes forming — the fractures Dr. Gordon talked about. Maybe all six of them came across to Earth Red."

"Maybe." I brushed a fingertip across Jack. It was a good thing he came. Who could tell what would've happened at the funeral without him?

Kelly pointed at the second photo. "This should be the one I took of the wreckage. You and that author should be in it."

"We are. We're standing near a pile of twisted metal and wires, and he has the same aura, but I don't." I picked up the last photo, a shot of the funeral scene — the mirror with Mom playing her violin within the reflection. Behind her, sheer drapes covering a window had blown outward, exposing the sill where two hands with long white fingers gripped the wood. Glowing red eyes looked toward us. Patar was preparing to make his entry, though how he transported me to that dark room remained a mystery that I had not yet told anyone about.

I showed the photo to Kelly. "Can you see that face and those hands on the sill? It looks like Patar."

"We'll have to get an enlargement so I can see it better." She settled back on her pillow and sighed. "Too many questions and not enough answers."

"Maybe Dr. Gordon will have some answers when he comes."

"He's in the waiting room," Daryl said, motioning toward the door with her thumb. "They wouldn't let more than three visitors come in, so he's waiting for one of us to leave."

Kelly, Clara, and I stared at Daryl.

She raised her hands, smiling as she backed away. "That's okay. I understand. You don't have to knock me over the head." She blew Kelly a kiss. "Thanks for the fun. I'm really just a supporting actress in this flick, but, hey, maybe there's an Oscar nomination in the wings, huh?"

"For an animated feature," Kelly said. "You're such a cartoon."

"Yep. Looney Tunes all the way." She winked. "Get better quick, girl. I'm ready for some more adventures."

When she left, I collected the photos, slid them back into the envelope, and pushed it into my sweatshirt's front pocket. "You know, I wouldn't mind if Daryl tags along. She's a huge help."

"I was thinking the same thing."

The clacking of shoes sounded from the hallway. Dr. Gordon strode in, his brow furrowed and his lips turned down as he glared at me. "Your actions on Earth Yellow were more far-reaching than I thought."

I took a step back. "Uh … okay. I'm glad to see you, too."

Gordon waved his hand. "I know. I know. Politeness demands a more genteel entry, but my head is still pounding from being knocked out and locked in my trunk, so I hoped to get right to business. We have pressing issues to discuss."

"Pressing issues?"

"Of course. Did you think the ramifications of your cosmic fabric perforations were over?"

"Well, no, I uh—"

"As I explained before, our worlds' timelines were parallel until we began crossing from one to another. Our presence in a foreign world caused slight changes that triggered an unpredictable domino effect. Maybe a driver slowed down to allow me to cross a street. Maybe he arrived home four seconds later than he would have and avoided a burglar who would have killed him. Later, this same man kills a woman who would have given birth to a research scientist who would have discovered a breakthrough cure for a disease."

"That's a lot of *would haves* you can't be sure of." I
crossed my arms over my chest. "But maybe our effects are
positive in the long run. Did you think of that?"

"Of course. That's been Dr. Simon's goal all along,
to create positive effects in the worlds that trail in time. But
I wanted to begin with small changes so we could track
the chain reactions. Dr. Simon had other plans. He couldn't
imagine how saving more than two hundred seventy lives
could possibly be a bad idea. And since Earth Yellow was
about to hurtle past the day of the airline crash, he didn't
bother to consult me. He worked very hard to get you to
the right place at the right time."

"I can't blame him for wanting to save lives."

"Agreed, but the ramifications are impossible to
guess. We cannot track the rescued passengers, and as you
know, one has even crossed over to our world, and we
have no idea where he is now. It seems that others have
crossed over as well. I have heard reports about long-lost
plane crash victims appearing at their former homes. Who
can tell how either world will be affected?"

I pushed my hands into my sweatshirt pockets. "So
maybe Francesca and Solomon won't get married on Earth
Yellow."

Kelly patted my elbow. "Don't worry about that.
Dr. Malenkov and Gunther will make sure they get
together."

"As soon as you are able," Dr. Gordon said, "I
would like to meet with both of you again to work on
these matters. Obviously your most pressing concern is
finding your parents. Earlier, before the funeral, Simon
Blue helped them escape from the observatory. Since he
no longer had access to the telescope room, he took them

to Nathan Blue's bedroom so they could use that mirror to transport. But it was missing a section, so we set up the Earth Red mirror at the funeral so you could get them out from our side. After that failure, Simon conducted a new search through the Earth Blue house for the missing section. While he was searching, he heard a loud pop. When he hurried to the bedroom, your parents were gone."

"Gone?"

Dr. Gordon nodded. "The Earth Blue mirror is intact, so we will get the final piece and see if they can be traced. According to Daryl Red, Clara and Daryl Blue have it."

"They do, but I noticed that one of the squares of the Earth Red mirror dropped before the rest of it crumbled. With all that was going on, I forgot to look for it."

"Interesting." Dr. Gordon stroked his chin. "I'll ask Simon Blue about that. He had an agent in attendance at the funeral. Maybe he picked it up."

I let my head droop. It was so strange. I wanted to pump my fists and celebrate that my parents were still alive, but in some ways, I felt worse than ever. They were in trouble, and I wouldn't be able to rest until I brought them home.

Dr. Gordon walked to the door and opened it. "The two surviving Simons are working together, and I'll join the search very soon. In the meantime" — he spread two fingers at Kelly and me — "you two need to rest and get well. You make quite a dynamic duo."

Kelly pulled my hand from my pocket and held it tight. "We do, but Nathan is the real hero."

"You're both heroes." A hint of a grin cracked Dr. Gordon's stoic face. "But leave the shotgun at home. The world's not ready for the rebirth of Annie Oakley."

"One more thing," I said, raising a finger. "Do you know anything about supplicants? Something called a Sancta, maybe?"

He pressed his lips together and shook his head. "No. Why?"

"Just something I heard. If it comes up again, I'll let you know."

"Good enough." He walked out and closed the door behind him.

Clara tied her trench coat's belt. "I must catch Dr. Gordon. I need to consult with him about lodging here in Chicago and transportation back to Iowa. When I return, Nathan and I will have to leave for the night." She raised her eyebrows. "Is that a suitable plan?"

"Sure, Clara," I said. "Thanks for everything."

Kelly grasped her hand. "You're the best."

"I am very impressed with you, young lady." Clara's eyes glistened. "Very much impressed."

"Thank you. That means a lot to me." When Clara left, Kelly felt for my hand and clutched it to her chest. She took a deep breath and smiled. "I really like her."

"Yeah. Me, too." As her hands enveloped mine, her fingers trembled. "Are you cold?" I asked.

Her faraway eyes each shed a tear. "No, just scared."

I leaned closer and lowered my voice. "Scared of what?"

"Lots of things." She slowly tightened her grip on my hand. "What if all of creation collapses? What if I never get my eyesight back? What if we can't find your parents? What if —"

"Shhhh." When her hands settled and her eyes turned toward me, I continued in a hushed tone. "Those are just *what ifs*. Everything's going to be all right."

A tremor ran across her lips. "But if your parents die, it'll be my fault."

"Your fault? Why?"

The tremor spread from her lips to her cheeks and echoed in her hands until her entire body shook. Her voice broke into a plaintive call. "Because you could have saved them, but you saved me instead."

"Of course I saved you." I set a hand on her cheek. As if calmed by my touch, her tremors faded. "Saving your life was more important than getting them back."

As her brow arched, her voice pitched higher as well. "But why? You've been trying to rescue your parents ever since I met you."

I drew my head back. "You mean … you don't know?"

"No. That's why I'm asking."

I pulled my hands away and set them on the bedrail. "I can't tell you."

"Why not?"

"You said not to use that word."

"What word?" Even as she asked her question, she drew in a halting breath. Her wounded eyes misted. "Do you mean …"

"Yes," I said softly.

New tremors raced across her hands as she reached out for mine, her eyes wide and searching. "Go ahead. Say it. Say it right now."

As our four hands intertwined in a soft embrace, I whispered, "I saved you, Kelly Clark, because I love you."

Again the tremors faded. Tears streamed down her cheeks. After suppressing a sob, she looked at me with her glassy eyes. "But why would you love someone like me? I'm just a — "

"A girl who's searching." Bending closer, I raised our clasped hands and breathed on her knuckles. "Love is the true breath of God. And I'll do everything I can to show his love to you so you'll find what you're searching for."

As she looked at her hand, tears dripped to her knuckles. "But I don't know what I'm searching for."

"Maybe I do, at least a couple of things. We'll search for them together." A vibrant song rang through the halls, drawing closer. I released her hands and smiled. "Sounds like you have a visitor."

The door swung open, revealing Tony. His eyes bulged, as usual, and he carried a pizza box high on his palm. Singing something lively in an odd mix of Italian and English, he strode to the bed and laid the box on Kelly's stomach. "I heard you were hankering for some real food, so ..." With a dramatic turn of his hand, he opened the box, revealing a large pizza with extra cheese and pepperoni. "Bon appétit!"

Kelly smiled. "I smell pepperoni. It's my favorite."

"It is?" When he looked at the pizza, he slapped his forehead. "I can't believe they forgot the liver and anchovies!"

"Daddy," Kelly said as new tears traced to her chin, "you're my hero!"

His own eyes tearing up, Tony shifted from foot to foot, and his voice tracked up a notch. "A hero? Because I brought you pizza?"

Kelly shook her head. "Because you love me. If you hadn't taught me to be tough, I never would have survived."

"Yeah ... well, I knew all along that you needed to learn ..." His face reddening, he cleared his throat. "What I mean to say is ..."

I turned my head but watched out of the corner of my eye.

Tony looked at the floor briefly, then gazed at her, tears streaming. "What I mean to say is ... I'm glad you're my daughter."

Kelly spread out her arms. Tony pulled her into an embrace. As they wept together, I backed away from the bed and eased toward the door without a sound.

Kelly opened her eyes and peered at me over her father's shoulder, blinking through a shower of tears. The joy in her expression said it all. This embrace was one of the treasures she had been searching for.

I smiled, formed an "I love you" sign with my fingers, hoping she could see it, and left the room.

As I walked down the hall toward the waiting area, I withdrew the photo envelope from my pocket and slid out the three photos, but something was still inside. A fourth photo had adhered to the envelope. Daryl was right about the number after all. Kelly's poor eyesight just didn't catch it.

I pulled the fourth picture out. This had to be the one Kelly took while we were aboard the plane, but the flash unit hadn't been turned on. I had forgotten all about it.

In the photo, Mictar appeared to be walking through a vast chamber, dark except for a shaft of light cast on him from above. Over his shoulder, he carried a limp girl — a girl dressed in red.

Stifling a gasp, I drew the photo close. Mictar's ponytail was in view, proving his identity. Patar had said my supplicant was in danger and out of my reach, but would he be able to help her? And now that she was either dead or being held captive, she might not be able to help us anymore.

I slid the photos back in place. Regardless of what Patar said, I had to find a way to help this Sancta, my supplicant, and, in many ways, my newfound guardian angel.